I0616046

Gwendoline
Goes to School

Gwendoline
Goes to School

by Gwencoline

Gwendoline is a fictional character.
That is:
She is as real as you or I.
She is a Story
Such as those we tell ourselves
And those stories are
What we are.

TWIN RIVERS
PRODUCTIONS

This is a work of fiction. Names, characters, places, institutions, and incidents either are products of the author's imagination or are used fictitiously. Any resemblance to actual persons, living or dead, events, or locales, is entirely coincidental.

Copyright © 2021 by Gilbert Reid

All rights reserved. No part of this book may be reproduced in any form or by any electronic or mechanical means, including information storage and retrieval systems, without permission in writing from the publisher, except by reviewers, who may quote brief passages in a review.

Issued in print and electronic formats
ISBN 978-1-990255-04-5: *Gwendoline Goes to School:* Paperback
ISBN 978-1-990255-03-8: *Gwendoline Goes to School:* EPUB
ISBN 978-1-7771580-1-9: *Gwendoline Goes to School:* Kindle
ISBN 978-1-990255-02-1: *Gwendoline Goes to School:* Amazon paperback

Cover and text design by Counterpunch Inc./Linda Gustafson
Illustrations by Niki9door

Published by
Twin Rivers Productions
20 Bloor Street East
PO Box 75070
Toronto, Ontario, M4W 3T3

To receive a free book or novella, sign up at:
https://gilbertreid.com

CONTENTS

CAST OF CHARACTERS   vii

PROLOGUE – STEAMY ENGLAND   1

CHAPTER 1 – CRIMES & MISDEMEANORS   9

CHAPTER 2 – ETERNAL CITY   21

CHAPTER 3 – THE SEA   45

CHAPTER 4 – CHAINS   53

CHAPTER 5 – DANGEROUS GAMES   65

CHAPTER 6 – COSMOLOGIES   95

CHAPTER 7 – SUPERGIRL SLEEK   117

CHAPTER 8 – OBJECT OF DESIRE   125

CHAPTER 9 – FEAR   137

CHAPTER 10 – DISPLAYED   145

CHAPTER 11 – MISTRESS NICOLE   167

CHAPTER 12 – PERFORMANCE ART   241

CHAPTER 13 – A MAID'S TALE   265

CHAPTER 14 – OWL   303

CHAPTER 15 – HOLY WAR   393

CHAPTER 16 – TWILIGHT   417

CHAPTER 17 – BETRAYAL   425

CAST OF CHARACTERS

Agnes Sinclair – French journalist
Alcide Bianchi– James Hewett Spencer's chauffeur in Italy.
Alfredo – restaurant owner in Rome
Allison Hughes – head of Jame's office in New York
Amadou – orphaned African child, brother of Awa
André de Valle – French intelligence officer
Antonia Faye – African nurse
Awa – orphaned African child, sister of Amadou
Claudia Clermont – Gwendoline's grandmother
Cynthia Wilson-Smyth – English lady
Professor Ho Chan Lee – famous mathematician
Giuseppe Esposito – concierge in a Rome building.
Gwendoline Clermont– genius mathematician and hacker
Karen Spellman – seductive American DEA agent
Kate Chastain-Pembroke – Epidemiologist, Gwendoline's friend
Jack – British intelligence officer
James Hewett Spencer – British millionaire, venture capitalist
Jean Marseille – French general
Jo Delyle – Parisian, famous black choreographer, dancer, artist
Justine d'Artois – MIT student, daughter of Nicole d'Artois
Linda Roberts – Gwendoline's landlady in Cambridge, England
Mansour Niang – Senegalese intelligence officer

Maria Esposito – concierge in a Rome building

Marlene Richter – German artist, Jo Delyle's partner

Martine Aubin – French actress and film star

Martin Stern – journalist, murdered by Sergei Platonov

Nicole d'Artois – courtesan, owner of La Petite Boutique Rouge

Omar Sarr – A runner, fastest boy in the village

Philip d'Este – famous French-Italian film director

Professor Ralph Higgins – English mathematician

Rufus Wilson-Smyth – son of Cynthia Wilson-Smyth

Seydou Issa – young African man, friend of Omar Sarr

Stephen Clermont – Gwendoline's grandfather

Sergei Platonov – ruthless Russian drug and arms dealer

Stephen Clermont – Gwendoline's grandfather

Three months ago, my cellphone rang.

The voice mail was off.

I was alone. It was midnight in Manhattan. I was in Grandmother Claudia's penthouse on Central Park South.

The screen displayed a Moscow number. James Hewitt Spencer, my ex-lover, often worked in Moscow.

Two years before, while I was away, lecturing in Cambridge, England, James emptied our flat in Paris of all his belongings. He disappeared, leaving behind not a trace he had ever existed – except one.

A handwritten note was propped up on the kitchen table. He loved me too much, it said; he could not stay with me, it said; he was incapable of love, it said; his love for me would destroy him, it said. His words punched me in the gut. They left me devastated; I was an empty wreck.

So, three months ago, that midnight, in Manhattan: I let the phone ring – and ring, and ring, and ring.

Then, taking a deep breath, I picked it up. "Hello."

There was silence, just silence – the frightening, crackling silence of deep interstellar space.

Then, there was a click.

The line went dead.

≈

Now, three months after that mysterious call from Moscow, I was here – comfortably installed in three second-floor rooms in a cottage in a tiny village, just outside Cambridge, England.

It was eight o'clock in the morning. My hair was soaked from my morning shower, and, except for a skimpy white towel wrapped around my waist, I was naked, perched on a swivel chair in front my computer, fidgeting, and fingering the thick, warm handle of a stout brown coffee mug.

I lifted the mug, took a sip, sighed, looked away from the screen, and stared dreamily out the window.

My rooms were in a sixteenth-century Tudor cottage, just under the genuine, recently restored thatched roof.

Whenever it rained, the thick thatch murmured – a hushed, feathery, whispering sound – a sweet lullaby, just for me. I was delighted, living in a delicious time warp. The cottage dated, my landlady Lucinda Roberts told me, from when Shakespeare was writing *Hamlet,* around 1600. Ancient, mahogany-stained roof-beams supported the white plaster ceilings. Faded Persian carpets covered the scruffy, uneven wooden floors. It was like it had been my home forever. I loved the place!

I glanced at the morning emails. One was from my former Boston housemate, brilliant, adorable Kate. She was in West Africa, working in a hospital laboratory in Dakar, Senegal, where she was studying, at dangerously close range, the spread of a fearful new outbreak of the Ebola virus which was ravaging some of the countries inland from Senegal. The virus, she said, might be mutating, and quickly. Rapid mutation could make it much more dangerous – more mobile, more contagious, and even more deadly. She asked if I could send her any updates on the epidemiological model – the math of how diseases spread – that I was developing.

Yes, I could. I had some new, possibly useful tricks that could help predict paths and vectors of the virus, and how best to fight it.

I had just begun writing a reply to Kate, when a little "ping" told me another email had arrived.

I swallowed a swig of instant coffee – I love true espresso, but early in the morning, I am lazy and need a quick caffeine fix.

The email was an invitation to an "International Conference on Mathematics, Information Technology, Artificial Intelligence, and Criminology."

The site of the conference was Rome.

Rome ...!

I hadn't been to Rome since ... since James ...

Rome – the name stirred up a trauma I had buried and hidden away under a thick layer of emotional scar tissue.

I took a deep breath.

Rome – what should I do?

Damn it!

I stood up and stretched. Letting the towel drop away, I leaned on the desk. I glanced down at my hands, at my palms, at my wrists. The veins were pale blue, gently pulsating, visible under the chalk-white, vampire-cool skin. Once, when I was a teenager, I'd tried to hang myself. The knot unraveled. I crashed to the ground, bruised my knees, and looked ridiculous. When I was a teenager, I cut myself with a razor. The pain and fear were delicious. Flirting with death, with oblivion, was inebriating. The visible scars had faded – but the inner scars?

Rome!

My heart beat extra fast, my temples throbbed.

I pushed myself away from the desk, ran my fingers through my hair. Drops of water streamed down my face. Grrrh! I growled. I bit my knuckles. I paced around the room. I stared at the faded ancient carpets. Rome? No! I can't! I can't go to Rome!

I kicked the innocent threadbare old carpet, and stubbed my toe. Ouch!

What a klutz!

James would have laughed.

James ...

And so – damn it! – it all surged up, all the memories: his smile, his laughter, the touch of his hands, the caress of his lips, the sound of his voice, the irony, the mockery, the perverse games, the mystery, dallying with the psychological abyss, flirting with Dionysius – and with little whiffs of Nietzsche and nihilism – and the endless fun, every day an unpredictable delight.

I went to the ancient half-open window, a Tudor relic, small panes of distorting, dimpled glass, framed with lead. The morning heat glared off the poplars at the far side of the village green – which is really just a big empty field of scruffy, patchy grass. Two teenage girls, one black, one white, both with ultra-long legs, and both dressed in white shorts and T-shirts, were already out, in the steamy air, throwing and kicking a soccer ball back and forth.

The faint thwack of the ball and the murmur of the girls' voices came from afar. The ball moved in slow motion, drifting lazily through the bright, hazy air. Everything was muted, sleepy, distant – unreal.

Rome – dare I return to Rome?

Rome was the city of my initiation to the mysteries of perversity and uninhibited passion. Rome was where I had been deliriously happy and utterly irresponsible. Rome was the Eternal City, the city of those mythical twins, Romulus and Remus, raised in the wilderness by a she-wolf, it was the city of Julius Caesar and Marc Antony, the city of popes and prostitutes, of sin and degradation, of transcendence and exaltation, of sexual depths and mystical heights; it was the city of the sweet life, *la dolce vita*, the city of long, languorous summer nights and torrid summer afternoons. Rome was a familiar ghost – a whole gallery of ghosts, with its layers of ruins and archeological relics, with its thousands and thousands of lives lived, and of deaths, and with its infinite, piled up memories and stories. Rome was intimate too, a voluptuous, lazy lover, perfect for siestas, sleepily curled around the sluggish, muddy Tiber that wound its way slowly from the mountains to the sea. And Rome was a gateway to a pagan paradise, so close to the Mediterranean beaches, only 40 minutes in a fast car along the highway or dusty twisting back roads down shadowy valleys, only 40 minutes to sagebrush and dunes and nudist beaches and the naked blue, blue sky. Rome was a caress. In summer, just at dusk, the perfumed breeze arrives from the sea, smelling of pine and cedar and wheat fields and ozone; it touches the skin, it freshens the spirit. Rome was where I discovered aspects of myself I hadn't even dreamed of, where I got into as much mischief as James and I could devise. Rome was where I gazed into the heart of darkness, into my nihilism, the emptiness within, and into the dangers of true evil, into my own dark side. But with that came joy, and liberation, true freedom, as I discovered who and what I am. Rome was where I fell in love, truly in love – Rome!

Damn it!

The sun glared down on the village green.

The scorching English breeze wafted against my skin.

Why awaken old memories, old wounds?

Ruins!

The two girls were livelier now. They moved faster, kicking the ball, throwing it. Their laughter was a whiff of coolness, of life – voices from a great distance, from another world.

It was blazing hot and getting hotter. England was becoming

a semi-tropical country. Dazzling reflections of white sunlight blasted off everything, even the blades of grass.

I thought of Rome and of my past self. The "me" of two years ago was a stranger – vaguely familiar, but alien. I was not the person I was two years ago.

But maybe – just maybe – I was waiting for myself back there, in Rome, in the past.

Maybe the Gwendoline-of-Times-Past, the old-young, fresh Gwendoline, always ready for adventure, would smile and open her arms, say, "Oh, Gwendoline, at last! You are back!"

And she would welcome me home.

I went to the computer and sat down. Rome? I reread the invitation. I mulled. I squirmed. I muttered. I growled like a panther. I straightened my shoulders. Grrrh!

I took a careful sip of coffee from the big mug Lucinda had given me. My landlady is a famous archeologist, often on TV. She explores ancient underwater shipwrecks in the Mediterranean. By now, the coffee was cold, slightly bitter. I liked it that way.

My fingers flew over the keyboard.

The white muslin curtain drifted in, catching the slightest of breezes. It touched my shoulder, tickled my skin, awakening slumbering sensations – stirring up a flock of unruly desires. The girls' shouts and laughter came with the touch of the air – their voices, too, were a beckoning call.

Life, these sirens sang, *don't forget life.*

Don't forget to live.

I glanced out the window. The two girls seemed to belong to another world. Did they have perverse fantasies? They surely did. I suspect everyone does. And if so, what were their fantasies? Had they lived them? Had they acted them out? Were they virgins? Were they innocent, in their bodies, in their minds? And what, after all, is innocence? Is anyone fully innocent?

Surely, in the strict sense, no one is a virgin, not really. Our minds consist of desires, are born with desires. And as we go through our lives, so many of our desires, our wild possibilities, are buried, denied, forgotten, and lost – forever. We can so easily forget who we really are, who we really were.

≈

A few hours after accepting the invitation, I received a note from James' assistant Allison Hughes in New York. She said that she had heard that I was going to the conference in Rome.

This, I thought, was a suspicious coincidence. Just who had decided to send me the invitation to Rome, and why?

Allison said that she would like me, if I agreed, to return to the apartment near the Tiber. James Hewitt Spencer, she said, wanted to see me.

I stared at the computer screen.

What? How dare he presume that I would want to see him? How dare he presume I would even agree to see him? What an arrogant asshole! What an idiot! How could such a brilliant man be so obtuse?

I got up and walked around the room.

I went to the window and looked out.

The day was a golden blaze of sunlight.

The two girls had disappeared. The village green was empty, desolate, dry, baking, by now, in the pitiless sunlight.

I glanced at the computer screen. I was to go to the Rome apartment, Allison said, and treat it as if it were my own; James would turn up. She didn't know quite when the man would turn up, but he would turn up. So like James! So cloak-and-dagger!

Damn it! How dare he? I rubbed my forehead. I was hurt. I was tempted. I was amused. The man was an idiot. He had the emotional subtlety of a two-year-old. I was terrified. Even his glance would hurt me. And I was afraid of me, of Gwendoline! Gwen-doline might do something foolish, something terrible, something she'd regret. A gamble was in the offing, a risk. Was I brave enough to leap?

"Maybe, dear Allison," I replied, "Maybe."

CHAPTER 1 – CRIMES & MISDEMEANORS

"Thank you, Karen! That is an extremely interesting question." I gazed at DEA agent Karen Spellman.

Sitting in the front row, with her legs crossed, with dark stockings and high heels emphasizing her marvelous legs, and with her skirt hitched high, Agent Karen Spellman from the United States Drug Enforcement Agency was pretty – No, she was beautiful. She had the most intense blue eyes, and those eyes, these last few days, had been focused, more often than not, on me.

I cleared my throat. "Yes, criminal and terrorist networks share many characteristics with plagues, diseases, and pandemics. The way these networks spread is also, in some ways, similar. So, you can apply the same models, types of data, and investigative techniques to all three – plagues and terrorist and criminal networks. There is even some overlap with the way traffic jams form. You can use Artificial Intelligence to search for patterns, to locate weak points, nodal points, and contagion patterns, so-called *super-spreaders* who transmit contagions or behaviours to many others, and to locate vulnerabilities to infection, and to predict what the criminals, terrorists, or deadly bugs might do next."

I had been staring straight at Karen and smiling, somewhat hypnotized by her bright blue gaze, blond hair, wonderfully eager smile, and honey-gold skin.

I glanced around at the rest of the audience. I was standing on a stage, at a lectern, in front of about three hundred people – security experts, police, mathematicians, scientists, sociologists, historians, academics, and intelligence people – spies

The "Rome International Conference on Information Technology, Artificial Intelligence, and Criminology" was taking place in a big modern convention center hotel just outside Rome. I knew some of the people, but not all.

I had decided that I must be careful about how I presented myself. I was a "personality" – a minor "personality" – but, still, I had a public persona, or several public personas, all rather controversial, and I had to control how I managed them. It was a juggling act.

Professionally, I had won two of the major mathematics fellowships and was known as a quirky – and, frankly, brilliant – pioneer in many aspects of math and applied math.

But, in the tabloids and the quality art press, I was also known as a fetishist, performance artist, and sexual object – and sexual subject. So, many of my colleagues at the conference had seen me online naked, playing soccer, or naked in chains or a skintight fetish catsuit, or on my knees offering myself, naked, to my lover, in classic profile and black-and-white, performing fellatio. I was on the Internet, in stills and videos, in garish color and stark black-and-white, in all sorts of poses, naked and dressed.

And, also, many of them had also seen me with my friend and lover, French film star, Martine Aubin, in photoshoots in *Vogue Italia* or other fashion magazines, and fashion and fan sites, where we were sometimes caught in restaurants or the street, kissing, or our arms wrapped around each other.

To contain all these contradictory images, I had dressed, for the conference, in a conservative but fashionable way, a charcoal Armani suit, with a white silk T-shirt, a short – but not too short

– pleated skirt, sheer black stockings, and flat-heeled black patent shoes.

My getup had to be smart: after all, I was a shameless libertine and minor fashion icon. Above all, I was Martine Aubin's eye candy and playmate. So, without being a total hypocrite, I couldn't deny the image and slouch around in a sweat suit or ragged washed-out jeans with holes torn in the thighs and shins – though I was tempted.

After an initial bit of curiosity, my other life – as art house porno star and Martine's sex partner – faded into the background. I was just a human being, a mathematician, a nerd, a geek among nerds and geeks and spies – appreciated for my hacking skills, in-depth snooping abilities, and for the math.

I sat in on seminars on "Drug Trafficking and terrorism: overlapping networks," and I chaired a round table on "statistical analysis of religious radicalization trajectories: How normal boys and girls turn into merciless jihadist killers."

And here I was, up on stage, giving the opening paper in one of the plenary sessions on how to trace terrorist and criminal and kidnapping networks using mathematical and statistical techniques.

I gave a few examples of how superimposing the various logistical, family, tribal, and financial networks and using Artificial Intelligence to sniff out connections – could lead to precisely targeted investigations with results that were sometimes stunning. I livened up the presentation with anecdotes and slides and maps and graphs which showed – and compared – all the various types of interrelated criminal and terrorist networks and how they locked into each other and overlapped at certain crucial points.

In one example, from three months ago, working with some people at the DEA and the UN Drug Agency, I had predicted which trucks would be carrying what drugs, when, and on what roads. The investigators invited me to be on the spot for the arrests. One of my predictions was about to be tested. It was a rainy, misty, chilly night, in a mountain pass, on the Austrian-Slovenian border. I was standing, just off the road, next to a police car, my collar turned up, and my nose running. I watched the police approach the trucks. And, in fact, the drug shipment was there, exactly as predicted. It was dramatic. There was even a brief shoot-out. I filmed it. It was spectacular.

Interpol and the UN had also insisted I learn to shoot. I practiced, and, it turned out I was good at it, even excellent, but I didn't tell my audience about my new skill set. "Best that you surprise people, if that moment were ever to come," said my instructor, "Keep your martial skills and shooting skills under wraps, as it were."

I gave another example: working with Interpol and the Turkish police, we'd been able to predict and then pinpoint which bank employees had to be corrupt to enable a Turkish-Iraqi criminal network that was involved in people smuggling and drug smuggling to transfer funds. Again, I was there when the arrests were made, in a bank in Istanbul. I pretended to be a client, and I stood back and watched when the police took the man down. For me, it was fun – very instructive – and it was weird stuff for a mathematician to be doing.

At the end of my talk, I was surprised – and humbled – by the applause, it was enthusiastic, and it lasted.

That was when Karen Spellman asked if the spread of organized crime was like the spread of a disease or plague.

"That's a very good question, Karen." I gazed at her – her long legs, bright eyes, tanned skin, tempting lips, blond hair – forcing myself not to blink and gave a long, technical answer.

Somebody else – a German, Karl Biermann – asked whether I thought abstract models like these, and Artificial Intelligence could replace human intelligence. Maybe robots and drones and computers could do the whole job.

"There's a real debate about this, Karl. But, I don't think so, no, definitely not, not now. Math is a tool, as are robots and drones, and even, especially, Artificial Intelligence. And they can help a lot.

"But investigators – and you know this much better than I – need human intelligence, on-the-ground information, people who are streetwise and street-savvy, people who speak the languages and dialects, people who know the terrain, who know the theology or ideology, who know the tribal and familial and religious and business affiliations. Investigators need intangible and often unmeasurable skills such as intuition, and a sense of history and psychology. The more detailed and closer to the ground, the more 'granular' our information is, the better it is. Artificial Intelligence can only work with the data it is provided with, and the collectors of that data, in rapidly changing situations, are often, crucially, human beings. So what is going on down in the local market, in the café, in the alleyways, or out on some farm, is essential. Big contagions, of criminality, of terrorism, or of disease, often start with very small events – some animal handled by a customer or vendor in a wet market, somebody sneezing in a bar or cafe, some chance meeting in a temple or mosque or prison, some individual sojourning in a city, and meeting the wrong person."

≈

After the talk, I had lunch with Karen. Not only was she luscious, but she was also known, rightly, as one of the sharpest minds in the DEA.

She had visited my website. She had browsed the section with the photographs of me naked or bound or wearing chains that

I had put on the site to avoid being a "victim" and to pre-empt others from exploiting the images. I framed it and turned it into *my* choice: if people saw me naked or having sex – a blowjob, an orgasm, masturbation, or just straight, old-fashioned missionary acrobatics – okay, so what! Here are the images. Gaze away, guys and girls, ogle all you want!

Karen mentioned my sexual exploits with a smile. She told me she was jealous. It seemed I could strip off in public and even be seen having sex – the infamous blowjob shot, and all the others – with impunity.

She particularly liked the naked soccer game on the beach. "I'd ask you what it was like, but perhaps another time," she said, putting her hand, delicate and smooth, tanned and warm, on my hand, and pressing slightly.

"Certainly, another time," I said. Karen truly was a ravishing blonde, tanned, squeaky clean, all soap and shampoo, the all-American perfect girl next door, but with a formidable intelligence, deep knowledge, and quick wit. I should consult Martine about permission for a possible dalliance.

But no, essentially, I am monogamous, one man and one woman at a time, that is my doctrine and my taste. For myself, I do not like promiscuity. Strangely for such an exhibitionist, I'm a very private person, and even shy. I am like Martine in that aspect.

Karen slowly withdrew her hand, but kept the friendly twinkle in her eyes. At that point, we were joined by several people from the FBI as well as some Italian colleagues, and the conversation turned to more serious matters.

The young mathematically talented Carabinieri lieutenant whom I'd often seen at Alfredo's restaurant in the old days in Rome and his colonel turned up and joined us for coffee.

"Signorina Gwendoline," the colonel said, and kissed me on both cheeks.

"Signorina," said the lieutenant, and he shook hands, rather formally, I thought. He was a handsome young man. I'm pretty sure he found me scary. Mirrors are scary, and other people's scandalous behavior can be like a mirror, particularly if their behavior reflects part of our secret desires. I was a symbol of depravity, and at some level, the lieutenant, like most men and women, undoubtedly had his own depraved imaginings. I liked the young lieutenant. I think he had had a smidgen of a crush on me ever since he'd seen me that night in Rome hooded and masked, and in a skintight catsuit, being led on a leash by James. If I were him, I'd have found it interesting too. Probably I'd have had a crush on me. What would it be like to be with a woman who would do such things? What would it be like to possess a woman who would permit you such liberties as displaying her virtually naked, and leading her on a leash?

I gave the colonel and the lieutenant my best smile. It was like seeing old friends. It brought back all the pleasant associations of those Roman nights: Long talks at Alfredo's restaurant, strolls down the narrow lamplit cobblestoned streets and alleyways, coffee and croissants, casual encounters talking to strangers, and lingering in any number of little bars and cafés.

The lieutenant – his name was Giuseppe – was eager to talk about my presentation. He knew a great deal about mathematical models, forensics, and criminology, so we had fun – two young geeks chattering away, with a little bit of flirtation, the mildly electric erotic undertow of shared ideas and shared youth, flowing between us, which was not unpleasant.

While Karen talked with one of the other Americans, a black, very handsome and athletic-looking FBI agent, the lieutenant's colonel, a good-looking, rugged man who was in his 30s maybe, sat there, occasionally making pertinent very savvy technical comments, following the conversation between the lieutenant and me, and gazing at the two of us as if he were a favorite uncle overseeing a discussion between a precocious niece and nephew.

∞

During the four busy days of the conference, I hardly had time to think. But then the conference ended. People were gathering in the atrium of the hotel; taxis were speeding away; people were heading to the airport.

Karl Biermann, who worked with Interpol, gave me his card. He was a dark-haired, dark-eyed German from Hamburg, and he was sharp, and handsome, with tousled hair and crinkly smile lines around his eyes. He had asked some very probing questions. I'd had fun answering them. It was like we were playing ping pong. We bounced ideas back and forth. He knew a great deal about Russian and Georgian crime syndicates – so I learned a lot, arguing with him.

"Thank you," I said. I gave him my card. I intended to keep in touch with everybody: I'd looked up all their twitter accounts and all their homepages, when they had one; some of them, being in intelligence or special police units, kept a very low profile and left little or no trace online, from those I usually got a scribble note with confidential contact numbers. I intended to expand my "Rolodex" database as fast as I could.

I confess. I was ambitious. I was an academic, of course, but my interests swept me into other fields; I had become a contact for law enforcement agencies and, discreetly, for some intelligence-gathering agencies – American, British, French, and German. I'd also done a quick series of contract jobs for the World Health Organization: it was to help develop a math-based app to quickly calculate contagion rates for certain diseases, particularly those that originate with or hitch a ride on insects or animals or birds; this work I had done with my friend Kate, brainstorming on WhatsApp and through texts and emails. My hacking skills had soared and seemed almost magical; these were useful for my friends in intelligence. Math is good training for hacking and decrypting; it's also a lot like learning a new language, and I'd had lots of practice at that with French and Italian – and some Spanish and German.

But it was more than ambition. I was fascinated by the people and the problems. The ideas that came from outside academe were stimulating. They fire me up, just like conversations with Kate, Martine, or Philip, or, above all, with James. James, aside from being conveniently perverse and imaginative, dancing always close to the abyss of abjection, the loss of self, the dissolving of frontiers, limits, and barriers, and Dionysian-Nietzschean abandon, was also extraordinarily intelligent and curious about everything. And he knew how to listen, a quality rare in rich and powerful men.

As I stood there, saying goodbye, I heard thunder. Glancing towards the plate glass doors, I saw that the day had darkened. It looked like rain.

"Are you going to the airport? We could share a cab." Karen Spellman was a temptation, radiating health, wholesomeness, and friendliness, like Martine.

The way Karen had squeezed my hand at lunch echoed in my mind. My imagination flared up, inventing a hotel bedroom, a villa by the sea, and Karen's blond, sunny body, blue eyes, soft lips – all mine, all at my mercy.

I'm afraid my libido was at that moment – at the end of the conference – without bounds, irritated, aroused, but without, for the moment, any object in mind.

Martine was in Paris, shooting a high-budget feature – and would be unavailable for two more weeks. I felt I could easily become a true libertine, a classic fallen woman. No, I exaggerate. As I said, I am quite conservative, one man, one woman – or maybe two – women, I mean, at a time.

"No, unfortunately, I have business in Rome." I smiled. "I'll be staying tonight, maybe tomorrow too."

"Goodbye, then." Karen flashed an extra bright smile, with just a hint of sadness.

"Yes, goodbye," I said, "But I have your card. Let's stay in touch. I do hope we meet again."

"Me too," she said. She kissed me on both cheeks. Her perfume was sweet as a sea breeze, tangy; her lips were smooth, soft, and extra-sensitive. Yummy! I suppressed a sigh.

As she walked away, trailing her little suitcase on its rollers, her head was turned, and we kept looking at each other. We exchanged a final wave. It was almost as if we were already lovers. Even outside, hailing the taxi, she kept casting through the glass doors that symptomatic amorous sideways glance of regret. I blew her a kiss; she returned it, stepped into the taxi, and disappeared.

"Goodbye! Goodbye!" I waved people off. I kissed people on the cheeks. I shook hands. I wrapped my arms around people. I laughed at parting jokes. I winked. I smiled. In the last moments, as so often happens at such events, I collected dozens more business cards and email addresses.

Then, suddenly, I was alone.

There is something desolate about the end of a conference. All the human activity suddenly ceases; all the passionate debates are over; all the warmth disappears; all the glad-handing ends; all the friends and colleagues are suddenly gone.

I sat down in a gilded, faux-Louis XV chair in a corner of the lobby. It was a vast space, with squared off white marble columns, and white marble floors that stretched off into the far distance, reflecting the cold light of the huge gilt chandeliers.

What next? I could go back to my room and mope or work or lie on the bed and think deep melancholy thoughts. I could go to the bar and have a martini and steel myself for a boring evening. Or I could go to Rome and do some shopping or sightseeing.

I was dressed in a broad-shouldered black-and-white fine chequered tweed jacket, a cream-coloured silk blouse, and black tightly tapered slacks and flat-heeled shoes.

I was tempted to go to the bar, drink a dry martini and perhaps find somebody interesting to spend some time with – a chat, a drink, a meal, and who knows ...?

Part of me wanted to do something utterly depraved. I don't know why, but hotels often have that effect on me. They seem to be hygienic neutral spaces, anonymous spaces, where anything can happen, designed for casual encounters, suspended outside the discipline and constraints of everyday life.

But of course, hotels, nowadays, are anything but anonymous spaces. Everything is clocked, monitored, photographed, videoed, timed, and controlled. Security, however discreet, is everywhere.

I hesitated. What to do? I was nervous, and undecided. I hate indecision.

I glanced at my phone. There was a text from Kate, in Africa, where she was busy fighting that new outbreak of Ebola. I had told Kate and Martine about James' request that I go to his flat in Rome and wait for him there.

Kate didn't mince words. "Darling, you must go and see what the man has to say! James, after all, is, aside from his utterly shameless cowardice, an absolute jewel! I wish you good luck! *Bonne Chance! Buona Fortuna!* And, darling, I want all the juicy details!"

There was a text from Martine on her film set in Paris, written in her boldly colloquial English. "Okay, kid, get off your fucking lazy ass and face the man. I want him back. I miss the old days when we four were pals! Philip misses the old days too! If it doesn't work with James, you are still mine!!! If it does work, you are still mine! Do you promise me??? In two weeks, I will be free and could use some TLC and even provide some too. Love!!!! I hug you from the bottom of my heart!"

I was truly spoilt as far as girlfriends went. I texted back. "I'm thinking. I'm sitting here in the hotel lobby thinking. I am thinking and thinking, deep and hard."

I walked up and down; I sat down, suspended in limbo, sitting there in the lobby, as if waiting, awkwardly, for someone who would never come.

Finally, I went back to my room, showered, changed into jeans, a T-shirt, and sandals, packed my bags, but left them in the room, which I had booked for another three nights – just in case.

Then, carrying a tiny over-the-shoulder overnight bag with a minimum of vital supplies, I went downstairs and got into the first taxi that appeared under the awning.

CHAPTER 2 – ETERNAL CITY

"So, where are we going, Signorina?" The taxi driver – who had a full white handlebar mustache and a full head of white-and-black, combed-back hair – glanced at me in the rear-view mirror. I was still "Signorina" – Miss! That was rather nice. More than two years had passed since I'd been in Rome, but I was still, at least for this gentleman, the fresh-faced, chalk-skinned, nocturnal, pallid, virginal vampire – naïve and hungry for blood – that I was that day long ago near Boston when Kate first left for Paris, and I first met James. I glanced at my iPhone.

Kate had just sent another text: "Go for it! Nothing ventured, nothing gained, darling!"

And Martine: "I won't be jealous as long as you don't leave me. So, do it! Give him a chance. I will punish you if you don't."

"Campo de' Fiori," I said, thinking – now I've done it.

"Campo de' Fiori," the driver repeated. He stared at me with his grandfatherly eyes, then adjusted his rear-view mirror to watch the street and not me, and we were off.

The sky got darker. Big splashes of rain hit the windshield, streaked the glass. What would I find when I got to my old "home," that big strange ghostly old building close to Campo de' Fiori?

We spread down long avenues, we sped over a big bridge, we sped along tree-lined streets, and, suddenly, or so it seemed to me, we were in the center of Old Rome, what the Italians call "the Historic Center" of the city, "*il Centro Storico*." The rain came down hard. Luckily, I had an umbrella.

≈

I asked the driver to stop on a small street leading to the Campo, about three blocks away from "my" building.

"Grazie, Signorina." The driver smiled into the rear-view mirror and thanked me for the tip.

I stepped out of the taxi, opened the umbrella, and adjusted the shoulder strap of the overnight bag, hooking it around my neck so no motorbike purse snatcher would be tempted by a quick "snatch." He'd have to strangle me or break my neck to get it. That would be spectacular, me being dragged over the cobblestones by a motorbike. Just the thought of it roused my blood and made me furious. I'd once seen a Japanese girl dragged that way. She fought like a tiger, refusing to let go of her purse, and finally, the thieves gave up, and sped away, leaving her, bloodied and shaken, but in one piece and still – triumphantly – clutching her purse. I told myself that if I were attacked, I would leap up and scratch the guy's eyes out. Vengeance would be mine!

The taxi sped away, splashing through the silver-gray puddles that reflected the low, silver-gray sky. I stood on the narrow cobblestoned street, hesitating. I realized I wanted to walk in the rain, to breathe the wet Roman air, to see and feel and smell and touch the old neighborhood.

Above all, I wanted at any moment to be able to change my mind, to be able to turn back, run away, duck into a bar, or a restaurant, crouch in a toilet. I wanted to be able to hide. Then, having retreated, having heeded my wiser, more cautious self, I would head back to the hotel, have another shower – a cold shower this time – a strong drink, and dine alone – or find some company and console myself with conversation – or debauchery. And the next day I would fly to London.

The rain was heavier, a torrent. It splashed up my legs; my sandals were soaked; the umbrella was useless. I was drenched; I was not equipped for real rain.

To hell with it! Muss and fuss! What a wuss! What a perfect idiot you are, Gwendoline! So, my feet and legs will get soaked! So, I will get soaked!

So what?

Who cares?

I was tempted to take off my sandals, fold up the umbrella, and walk barefoot – and just let the rain stream down and wash over me.

Yes, that's the idea, Gwendoline! Be bold! Take off all your clothes, every stitch! Go barefoot and naked. Bathe in the rain! Dance, cavort, and turn cartwheels! Display yourself as a Dionysian Fury! Make a spectacle of yourself! Get yourself arrested!

The spirit of Rome had infected me.

Pagan!

Dionysian!

Danger!

Delightful scenario: I would end up in a jail cell full of interesting scantily clad women of the night; then, that mysterious, romantic stranger, James Hewitt Spencer, would come – looking disgusted yet amorous and very, very concerned – and bail me out. It was a pleasant fantasy. I let it drift away. The rain poured down. Just next to me, rivers of water, thick ribbons of quicksilver, swirled, twisted, and raced along the gutter.

The silver-gray air projected a dark sheen over everything. All around me, ancient buildings loomed up – alien, dark, gloomy, and ominous. The city was a stranger. It had aged; it had been silvered over; some witch's or shaman's magic spell had transformed my vibrant sunny paradise into an ancient black-and-white photograph. Or was it me? Had my world that, without James, become lifeless and monochromatic?

Okay – let's swim in the rain!

I folded up the umbrella and slipped it into its case.

I turned my face up to the sky.

I let it come – rain, rain, oh beautiful warm rain!

Okay, let's go, Gwendoline!

I headed down the street. Rain streamed over me as I walked into Campo de' Fiori and walked across the square. The outdoor market – which is open only in the morning and early afternoon – had long since closed; all the wooden and canvas stalls had been folded up and carted away. Along the edge of the Campo, the wine bars were open, with people crowded inside, sheltering from the rain. I could imagine it, smell it, and feel it, the intimacy, steamy, damp and acrid, with the taste and odor of wine and wet hair and wet clothes, the bodies pressed close together, the babble of conversation; it was a physical memory, a sensation like a familiar caress. Oh, how I'd like to be part of one of those crowds, immersed in the human smell and warmth and humidity, meeting with old friends, with neighbors, drinking, gossiping, and sampling the cheese. It was the cozy, familiar neighborhood world – a squeezed-together myriad of picturesque characters, reputable and disreputable, famous and infamous, rich and poor, and of intense friendships and passionate affairs – all the glory of an ancient city – and all the comfort of the small, familiar, neighborhood, an intimate world of people who had always lived here and who would die here.

I gazed up at the statue of Giordano Bruno, the philosopher, glistening wet, lonely and sad, high on his pedestal, gloomy in his heavy metal hood and cape and cloak.

The Church had burned him alive for heresy, right here, on

this spot, just when Shakespeare was writing *Twelfth Night* and *Hamlet*, just about the time when, in England, thatchers and carpenters were putting together the cottage where I lived.

Bruno had been a true outsider. He'd argued that the universe itself was divine; that our world was only one of an infinity of worlds; that the stars were distant suns; that the universe was quite possibly infinite; that Jesus was not the son of God; that Mary was quite possibly not a virgin. Of course, none of this was acceptable.

So, the Church, in its wisdom, muzzled him, locked his jaw with an iron clamp, and pierced his palate and tongue with iron spikes, so his "evil tongue" could not speak. They were not taking any chances. They tied him to a stake, right here, and set him alight. Even his screams were condemned to silence.

Just behind Giordano Bruno, some teenage kids, girls and boys, about eleven or twelve years old, just on the cusp of adolescence, in shorts and T-shirts, were playing and prancing in circles beside the small drinking metal fountain, what the Romans call *un Nasone*, a Big Nose. It was round, stubby, and gray, and looked like a miniature metal silo with a thin, curved waterspout – the nose – sticking out. The kids were goofing around, laughing, shouting, splashing each other; they were soaked, their clothes semitransparent.

A gray, weathered, wooden two-wheeled cart, with some crates of vegetables – glossy apples, oranges, pears, bright in the gloomy light – sat there, its long timber shafts resting on the cobblestones, waiting to be taken away.

Just as I stopped to look at the cart, a brightly lit, brightly colored miniature municipal bus splashed into the square, stopped, picked up two ladies sheltering under their umbrellas, and splashed off, carrying its little cargo of dry, brightly lit people, sitting primly erect, like manikins, behind little square windows, its headlights turning the gray, rain-filled air into bright silver ribbons.

A few brave or stubborn characters, mostly tourists, were sitting outside, huddled at café tables on tiny terraces, and just barely sheltered under the café awnings. The rain thundered, pouring down all around them, gushing from the canvas awnings, and rushing, gurgling, in thick silver streams along the stone gutters.

Blinking against the rain streaming like a Niagara over my face, I was swept into the past. I stopped and stared. There, in front of me, was the café where I used to sit and work, early in the morning. It was a tiny narrow place, a hole-in-the-wall, and the terrace was just a few tables arranged on the cobblestones and protected from sun and rain by a narrow extendable black-and-white canvas awning.

Mornings and afternoons, I sat there, sheltered from the sun, nursing a latte or a double espresso, and writing or reading, while just a few feet away the fruit and vegetable and fishmongers shouted and touted their wares – oranges, tomatoes, melons, eggplant, squid, octopus, sea bass, mussels, sole.

One of the waiters, Marco, who was standing under the awning, recognized me and waved. "What are you doing, Signorina Gwendoline? You're getting all wet!"

I wiped my eyes. "I love the rain, Marco!" I shouted in Italian. "It's so warm, it's so strong, and it's beautiful!"

"You are crazy, Signorina!" He smiled his big little-boy smile. "I haven't seen you for a couple of days, Signorina," he shouted, "Where have you been? We've missed you."

"Traveling, Marco, I've been traveling!"

"Come and see us, then! Tomorrow the sun will shine! Ciaò!" he waved and headed back into the bar.

"Ciaò, Marco!" I waved.

The few tourists sitting huddled under the awning stared at me and grinned. One of them pointed, laughing. "Look at that one! A real Roman!" he shouted, in English. I was clearly one of the local Roman eccentrics – the crazy girl without an umbrella who runs around in the rain – part of the circus of Campo de' Fiori.

It was comforting and humbling – Marco talked to me like a friend, who'd only been away a day or two; for him, it was as if I had never been gone; he hadn't noticed that I had been away for more than two years. I was part of the landscape, but I could easily disappear. By now, of course, I was totally soaked. The tourists were watching me. A tanned older woman with a silver crew cut, and big, white-framed glasses, took a photograph.

Like the good local performer that I was, I bowed low – a true clown – to the laughing tourists. Then I turned away. I left Campo de' Fiori, walked along several narrow, winding cobblestoned streets, and finally entered the small crooked side street that led to "our" building.

At the end of the street, right at the corner, was one of my other favorite cafés. It was open. Paolo, the waiter, was standing in the doorway. I stopped and smiled.

"Signorina Gwendoline! How are you! Oh, you are all wet, but you look marvelous! It looks like you have just stepped out of a shower! Where have you been? I haven't seen you these last few days. Ah, yes, but you have been away – Maria told me!"

"Ciaò, Paolo!" I slipped in under the awing and thought, Yes, I could use an espresso, maybe even a croissant, or *cornetto*, as a pick-me-up, even if it is late in the day.

My Italian was, by now, fluent. Martine, who spoke English, French, and Italian – her father was French, her mother was Italian – was an excellent teacher, and cruel taskmaster. She would switch from one language to another sometimes without even seeming to notice, which was charming but disorienting – and particularly annoying for an Italian neophyte like me. I was determined to overcome my handicap. I read Italian and French newspapers online and even picked up *Le Monde* and *La Repubblica* at the newsvendors when I was in Paris, so I'd expand my vocabulary.

When Martine slid from one language to the other, I'd get exasperated and growl, "Don't do that!"

"It's good for you, darling," she'd whisper, and tickle my ear with her lips, "It keeps your mind flexible and on its toes."

Martine was like Kate: affectionate, opinionated, and the master, except when I revolted, then she, like Kate, suddenly turned submissive – and, in her submissiveness, Martine, like Kate, would clown around, my own glamorous famous little jester and servant, mutinous, and a bit boyish, just like me.

There was something mirror-like in our relationship, and in these role reversals; it was as if we were twins, or one soul distributed between two bodies.

I stood at the bar – dripping wet and making a mess which nobody seemed to mind – and sipped the espresso and took my time enjoying the fresh warm cornetto, while Paolo – who now realized how long I'd been away – reported on the latest news. There was a new waitress at Alfredo's, and she was charming and flirtatious if somewhat cross-eyed, which only added to her appeal. I'd like her. Alfredo had added four additional tables outside, at the far end of the piazza, after finally winning permission from the city authorities. The old junk man who went by with his wooden cart every week or so – calling out for people's leftovers and throwaways – had had a heart attack and had been in hospital for two weeks but had recovered – thankfully – and was back wheeling his cart, pushing or pulling it, from street to street, and shouting out his jolly-sad little refrain. The overweight one-eyed jeweler in via Giubbonari who wore those colorful yellow-and-red vests, and those wide, canary-blue, button-on braces to keep his trousers up, and who had that little, pointed, salt-and-pepper beard, had closed his shop, and retired to a farm near Orvieto; his shop was now a miniature swimsuit emporium run by a skinny tanned blond lady from Naples who was terribly fashionable and had a sharp tongue but a heart of gold. And, then, most important: Maria, the porter's wife in "your" building, had had a bad flu last month, but now she was better. "She will be so happy to see you, Signorina Gwendoline. She always says how she misses you!"

Suddenly, I felt I was truly back in Rome. In a strange way, I was home, well, it was one home – home for a part of me. I tried to pay for the coffee and cornetto, but Paolo and the owner – Simona, a very good-looking, sharp-featured woman from Tuscany who rarely said a word – insisted that it was "on the house." "You are family, Signorina Gwendoline, true family!" she said and kissed me on both cheeks and held me, soaking wet as I was, for a long minute, gazing into my eyes, then smiled a glorious smile, and let me go.

I thanked Paolo and Simona and stepped out into the rain, which was thundering down. I walked along the narrow street and came to the entry to the building. I stood there for a minute – scared and doubtful. The big gate was open; the dark interior beckoned.

"Okay!" I squared my shoulders. The rain bounced off the cobblestones, splashed up on my legs and jeans. The T-shirt was transparent; the jeans were a sponge. I was utterly soaked.

I entered the gate. Out of the downpour, the sudden sensation of hush, of silence, was shocking. I was dazed. It was as if I had stepped from one world into another. Just a few feet away, the rain poured down, a thick curtain, but I was sheltered, in a spookily quiet zone. I shivered, sending off a cascade of spray. The keys were in the porter's lodge, so Allison had told me. I knocked on the porter's door. It opened. Maria stood there; her mouth open in shock; her hand shot to her mouth. "Oh, you are all wet, Signorina Gwendoline!"

"Yes, I am, Maria. I've been dancing in the rain."

She seized me and hugged me – getting soaked in the process.

"You are crazy, Signorina!" She stood back. "But even wet, you look so elegant!"

"Like a wet dog," I said, "And Maria, you look beautiful, more beautiful every time I see you."

"That is not true!" Maria laughed. "Signorina Allison emailed me that you might come. It's been empty since you left, Signorina Gwendoline. The Professor has not been back. I have had the cleaners in every week. And Giuseppe has seen to repairs. Everything should be working perfectly. I have put food in the refrigerator and several bottles of wine – that dry white wine you like so much, the Chablis. I was hoping you would come. Do you want me to come up and show you where everything is?"

"No, I see you're cooking."

"Yes, I am. Here, try a sample. I'm experimenting. It is a new recipe, a bit spicy."

She led me into her lodge – cozy and warm and perfumed with the beautiful smell of cooking – and insisted I try a few large spoonfuls of soup, tomato, and celery, and red peppers, and aubergines. I drank and breathed it in.

"It is delicious," I licked my lips, "Yummy! It has exactly the right degree of spices, a wonderful mixture."

"Oh, your Italian is marvelous," Maria said.

"I've been working on it."

"I imagine it is with your friend, the actress, Signorina Martine?" Maria gave me a sly smile of complicity. She read the tabloids – and followed the Internet – and my friendship with the famous Martine Aubin was no secret.

"Yes, Martine's an excellent teacher." I tried another big spoonful of the soup.

"I will put some soup aside for you. And when you have time, Signorina Gwendoline, we can have a good gossip. I'll bring you up to date on all the latest," she said, beaming.

"I'd love that," I said. I kissed her on both cheeks – and she hugged me. When she let me go, I saw there were tears in her eyes.

"What's wrong, Maria?"

"Oh, Signorina Gwendoline, you are so young and so beautiful. It just makes me think about life, about the possibilities gone by. Life is so quick, so fleeting, so strange ..."

"Yes," I said, life is strange, isn't it, Maria."

"It is, Signorina, it is."

"We will talk about it when we sit down together."

"Oh, that will be grand, Signorina!"

"Till later, Maria. And, Maria, as I said, you are more beautiful than ever! Giuseppe is a very, very lucky man."

"Oh!" Maria looked down, embarrassed like a little girl, and then she looked up. Her eyes were wet. "Till later, Signorina Gwendoline."

I took the creaky little cage of an elevator up to the flat. Maria was in her sixties, and a very beautiful woman. As a girl and young woman, she must have been stunning. I wondered about her life – and thought I must ask more questions and be more empathetic and attentive the next time I saw her. There must be reasons for her tears, and I did not know what they were.

I got out of the elevator and stood for a moment on the vast landing, with its alcoves and stone busts. I remembered the night I was dressed in a latex catsuit and hood and how I stripped James stark naked right here, on the big drafty landing, under the disapproving stony eyes of the long-dead ancestors and philosophers. James laughed, but it was hilarious how nervous he became when we heard the elevator door open and shut downstairs, and the elevator began to creak its way upwards. The "Professor" was in danger of being revealed in all his naked splendor.

There it was – the door to the flat. A giant darkly varnished oak door, at least eight feet tall, with huge creaky handles and elaborate brass fittings that seemed designed for a population of giants.

It suddenly occurred to me that I had walked through the streets, come to the building, picked up the keys, and was now standing here on the threshold of the flat, without ever really deciding that I was going to do this; and without thinking through the consequences.

But now I was here.

I took a deep breath, inserted the key, turned it, and opened the door. I entered the apartment. My shoes squelched. I was suddenly aware, in the still quietness and utter silence, of how soaked I was. Rivulets of water streamed off me. A puddle formed at my feet. I switched on the lights and closed the door.

The entry hall looked like nothing had been touched – it smelt all polished and clean, but it felt like a tomb, like it had been sealed off, and without life, for a long time.

I put down my umbrella and shoulder bag. I took off my T-soaked shirt and my squishy sandals; I unzipped and slid out of my jeans, which were dripping wet, as if I had been swimming underwater. Even my panties were soaked.

I shook myself like a wet dog and went to "my" bedroom where I found, yes, luckily, a bathrobe of mine, hanging in the bathroom, and in the wardrobe in the bedroom, panties, two pairs of jeans and some T-shirts. I dried myself with one of the fluffy towels – conveniently warm from the stainless-steel towel-warming rack – and I pulled on the jeans and T-shirt. It felt good to be dry again.

I walked barefoot into the living room and to the terrace

doors; I opened the doors wide, letting in the smell of the rain, of the plants on the terrace, and of the gloomy Roman dusk.

I stood for a minute, my arms crossed on my chest, looking at the lowering steel-dark clouds. Thick slanting waves of rain swept across the terrace in the dying, leaden light.

I walked around the flat, opening windows. The smells of the rain and the city – the smells of life – flooded into the rooms.

I looked around. Yes, it was a magical place.

I opened a drawer – the handcuffs, the cords, the whips, the blindfolds, and masks were all there, neatly displayed and labeled, in their little boxes.

James was super-organized. He had a system for almost everything. I opened the built-in wardrobe: the various catsuits and corsets and skimpy dresses, latex, leather, and spandex, all there, hanging neatly, waiting for the next performance.

Hmm!

I slid the drawers shut, and I closed the wardrobe. I felt a little tingling sensation in my belly and thighs – for a second, just a second, there was a catch in my breath. The dark side was waking up; the shadow side was surging into the light.

I bit my lip. "Okay, Doctor Frau Herr Professor Gwendoline Clermont, sober up!"

I decided, since I was in the place, I might as well act as if I really was in the place. It made no sense to wander around from room to room like an unanchored and disembodied ghost.

I opened my iPad and tried to connect through the high-security Wi-Fi. Yes, it still worked, and the password was the password I had used before. Of course, the bills would have been paid – this was a stage set, kept alive by James. It was ready to spring into action at any moment. All it needed was a cast, the actor and actress who would step out of the shadows and begin their dance.

I set the iPad down on the divan, and I walked around. I went to the terrace doors and looked out. The rain streamed down, a silver curtain, slashing down sideways, at a steep angle, slashing at the plants, the stone urns, the stone seats, the balustrade.

I went to the fridge, took out the bottle of Chablis. I considered it for a moment, and then I uncorked it and poured myself a glass. I inspected everything in the fridge. The cheese was fresh, put there – with a little note from Maria – this morning. The bread, a French baguette, placed neatly on the cutting board, was fresh. I made myself a sandwich of prosciutto and brie.

I sat down on the divan in front of the fireplace – no fire, of course – and I began to read some papers on the iPad. I listened to the rain. I was alone in the world, cast up on a desert island. The apartment felt vast and empty, and – though it was a warm night – the air seemed cold.

I got up and turned on the gas fireplace. The flames sprang up, warm and friendly. I poured myself another glass of wine. I got a shawl out of one of the cupboards and put it around my shoulders. Outside, the rain beat down, unceasing. The light had darkened, faded into night.

Yes, I was comfortable in this vast apartment; I was too comfortable; it was as if I had never left; it was unreal. I was unreal. I felt myself fading away. I stared at the fire, so cozy, so perfect!

"I shouldn't be here. I am a fool," I whispered, "I am a fool, most definitely a fool. I haven't even been thinking about why I am here. I have been avoiding thinking about why I am here – it's the temptation of the void, of my dark desires, the violence, the unknown, nihilistic forces that ... James ... No, I can't allow myself to think about why I am here. I should get up, right now, and leave. I must get out of here – now!"

I put down the iPad, and I stood up. I had set my sandals out in front of the fire – perhaps they were dry by now. I would go. I would go back to the hotel, have a big steak dinner, a full bottle of wine – and I would go to bed. And I would catch a flight to-morrow – back to London, back to Cambridge. I would bury my-self in work.

The doorbell rang.

My mind veered 180 degrees. It might be Maria with some of that warm and spicy soup. We could have that gossip she prom-ised – it would make me feel better, it would make me feel real. Maybe, then, I could stay the night and leave in the morning.

"I'm coming," I shouted. I walked over and opened the door.

He was standing there.

"You're soaking wet," I said. I swallowed. Blood drained from my face. My heart flip-flopped.

"Yes." He stood there, water dripping.

"Come in."

"Gwendoline ..." He didn't move.

"Shush! Not a word. Come in."

"Gwendoline ..."

"Shush, you idiot. Come in!"

He hesitated; then, he entered. I shut the door behind him. His suit, Hugo Boss or Armani or something – something very classy and dark and expensive, was utterly soaked; rivulets ran from his hair; his shoes made a squishing sound. His briefcase drooped and dripped silver drops. His eyes were bright, feverish. His cheeks seemed thinner, hollow, as if he had lost weight. There was a vague suggestion of five o'clock shadow.

"Well," I said, trying to sound exasperated. I could – I should – throw a scene; I should show him how much he had hurt me. I should thrust my pain and his guilt onto his shoulders. Inwardly, I raged. I should cry and shout and pound on his chest and per-haps pick up something expensive and smash it over his head.

But ...

But, suddenly, I was engulfed in a flame of desire and

emptiness, I ached for him. It was a dangerous, knife-edge situation: I didn't know why he asked me here; perhaps he wanted to bury our relationship, turn us into friends; I could manage that, however painful it might be, but it was not what I wanted.

And, maybe, on second thought, I could not manage friendship. Desire and aching nostalgia would drive all thoughts, all possibilities, of friendship away. Seeing him, and not touching him, would tear me apart. I would be angry and hysterical and crazy, and I would not be able to hold it in. I would mourn like a wild beast, tear my hair, and gnash my teeth and howl at the moon. I would strip myself naked and cover myself in sackcloth and ashes. I knew now how much I wanted him. I wanted him as a lover. I wanted him as my master; I wanted him as my slave. Everything boiled up – he was danger, he was the dark side, he was nihilism, even his business was full of mysterious secrets, and dangers, and underground terrors, even his physique, dark, strong, tight, muscular, spoke of danger – perhaps, even, of death. And ... And maybe all he wanted to do was to liquidate our affair, to get rid of me. Well, we would see. Be bold, Gwendoline, be bold.

"Take off your clothes," I said. "All of them. No, on second thought, James, I'll take them off for you."

He opened his mouth.

"Don't say a word," I said; I put my finger up and pressed it to his lips.

He walked into the room and then stood still, like a statue, waiting for me. I came to him. The shawl was still over my shoulders. I let it drop.

I began to undress him, putting on a very serious short-sighted expression. I concentrated on the details of the clothes, on the jacket, the buttons, the belt, the zippers, pulling and lifting things off, carefully, gently, not looking at the man, not touching him; it was as if I were undressing a manikin. I'm a nurse,

I thought, it is the Western Front in the First World War. He is someone I don't know, someone just come in from the battlefield; he is someone soaked in mud and water and whose horrible, ugly, suppurating wounds I must dress. He is a stranger. Treat him like a stranger. He is not human; treat him like a robot. Treat him as if he were already dead. Control yourself, I repeated silently, over and over, control yourself – you are cool, Gwendoline, you are masterful, you are logical, you are so ultra-cool, you are the master! You are not going to beg or cry or scream or beat him on the chest or scratch his eyes out.

The body – as I unveiled it – was what I remembered: the tight, smooth muscles, the tan, the scar from the bullet in Moscow, the tense, flat belly. And the face, when I dared look at it, was unbearably handsome, even more so now that it seemed more rugged, haggard, even haunted; and then too, there were the eyes, the penetrating dangerous eyes, and the mouth that could smile so easily.

I pulled down his underpants and threw everything in a heap.

"Now," I said, "talk." I put my hands flat on his chest and looked into his eyes. Then, before he could speak, I said, "You are a coward."

"Gwen ..."

"Shush! Don't say a word!" I put my hand over his mouth.

He nodded.

I took my hand away from his mouth and I gave him the look, the old mutinous look from under the eyebrows that Kate and Martine said they adored. Dark fire, they called it. I took a deep breath. "Okay, Master, it is time. Are you going to undress me?"

He smiled. "Yes."

"Good. I've been wearing clothes for too long. I haven't been naked, not really naked, not for a long time. Also, I have wanted to feel your hands on me; I have waited too long."

He lifted off my T-shirt and folded it carefully over the back of a chair. He opened the buckle of my belt, and I worked the jeans down to my ankles. He slid my panties down to my ankles, and I stepped out of the jeans and the panties.

He knelt in front of me and began to kiss my tummy. I stroked his hair.

"You've been a naughty boy James," I said, looking down at him, "very naughty." My voice was throaty; it threatened to break. My eyes were glossy and might overflow. What was I doing? Into what abyss was I tossing myself? I should have stayed at the hotel, convinced that sunny lusty DEA agent, Karen Spellman, to stay the night and ...

He kissed and licked me. His body was still wet, glowing in the lamplight. His hands closed on my backside, kneading and caressing, then he clasped my waist, pulling me into him.

I swallowed. "Does that shower on the terrace still work?"

Still on his knees, he looked up at me.

"Probably," he said.

"Let's go, then."

I was taking a risk – shamelessly throwing myself at him, laying myself wide open to catastrophic rejection. I buried all my fears deep inside. I was not going to let my doubts show. Love and lust can die so easily. If you are too timid, too shy, too unbending, you can in a moment toss away a whole lifetime. I steeled myself. If I displayed total self-confidence, no recriminations, no pleading, no tears, no scratching his eyes out, no throwing crockery, no hitting him over the head with a frying pan, all of which I would dearly love to do, then perhaps, without too much difficulty, we would be back where we were before.

Where we were before was dangerous, of course, a spiraling darkening threatening abyss, but ...

We chastely soaped in the shower. I covered him in suds. I

kissed him. It was a chaste little peck. He kissed back, a chaste little peck. I soaped his hair. He was blind with suds.

I kissed him, and he blindly returned the kiss, a little closer now.

He had a splendid erection. I thought, well, that was simple! That was an easy equation to solve! No need to be a math prodigy to do that! Is it a good sign, or is it just animal lust for the female, any female? Maybe I think too much!

As for me, I was wet – I was ready, I was itching for him to take me in his arms, possess me, and break me into scintillating little bits, tiny scattered sequins of desire, little explosions of sensuality, cartwheels of ecstatic abandon, pinpoints of light, and sprinkle them everywhere and nowhere.

Let's go slow! Slowly, slowly, I told myself.

We made love right there and then, in the shower, chastely, carefully, cautiously, and then we made love on the mattress, on the terrace, beyond the awning, lying naked in the warm, pounding rain, then, almost exhausted, we wandered hand in hand – strangely chastened – into the bedroom.

Circling around him, kneeling before him, I toweled him down, being very attentive to all the details.

"Now, Master, lie down, on your back, on the bed."

He did.

I climbed on top of him and sat astride his midriff. I bent forward and kissed him. He kissed me back. I raised myself up, seized his cock, once again splendidly erect, and guided him into me. I bent forward again, kissed him on the ear, and nibbled at his earlobe.

"I've been so hungry," I said.

"I've been starving," he said

"For you."

"For you."

He seized me and in one quick movement flipped us over, so

I was under him; it was so quick, so gentle, so deft and so violent that, before I knew what was happening, I was offered up, vulnerable, breathless with surprise, pinned under him, splayed out, wrists locked down. He plunged deeper into me, deeper, and deeper, back and forth, a flaming sword searing through my hungry, liquid, parted flesh.

He kissed my mouth, hard, to stifle my cries; he kissed my breasts; he licked and bit my nipples, gently, gently, twisting, teasing; he lifted me up, held me close against him, locked me to his body; I wrapped my arms around him, and clasped him to me; I kissed him, and I whispered, "Yes, yes, yes, yes!" His hands and lips seemed to be everywhere, and then ...

"Oh, oh, oh, oh!" I couldn't keep it back; I couldn't stifle it, couldn't fight it.

"Oh, oh, oh, oh!"

"Oh, oh, oh, oh!"

And then ...

... then we were back out on the terrace, scampering naked under the rain; then we were laughing, grasping each other, kissing each other, slippery with falling water, slick and silver and ghost-like in the dim reflections of the Roman night; then we were down on the terrace pavement on the thin deckchair mattress; his kisses and his caresses were everywhere.

Then I slipped away, leaped to my feet.

I was up and running. "Catch me, catch me if you can!"

He was just behind me, swerving, leaping, his hands reaching out. "Oh, yes, I can catch you, I'll catch you! I've caught you!"

When he caught me, our bodies, slippery wet and gleaming like silver, were in an instant once again locked together as one. The rain filled my eyes and blinded me; he was in me, stroking me, he was enormous inside me, and he was outside me, pressed against me. I cried out, "Yes, yes, yes!" Again, approaching orgasm, I felt myself teetering on the edge; then I came, and in the very same instant, he came, shuddering, seizing me, clinging to me, and he kissed me so deep, so quick, he buried my cries, buried my screams.

He held me. I was shaking, shaking, as it continued, and seemed to continue, wave after wave.

His mouth sealed my mouth; I could not even cry out.

The waves subsided; the aftershocks faded.

We lay there, in the wet warmth of the night, tangled together, me sprawled on him, soaked, running with rivulets of water, the warm rain pounding down on us. Finally, I roused myself, stood up, and looked down.

My man – for this moment, for this little bit of time seized as an instant from eternity, my man! I took a deep breath. The instant was unique, to be remembered – forever.

He lay there, eyes closed, the rain pounding down, bouncing on his chest, gilding his face, running in his hair.

I crouched and lowered myself onto his midriff. I kissed him and lay down, with my body curled against his body – his body, my shelter, my refuge, so muscular, so strong, so smooth. I felt the curves of my own body had been designed for all eternity to fit precisely into his.

His arms enclosed me. His hand was in my hair, caressing each soaked strand, his hand was on the curve of my buttocks, slapping gently, shaping, molding, reinventing each curve and slope; his hand was creeping up my spine, rousing each electric pressure point, causing waves of pleasure to ripple outwards. Oh, oh, oh, the pleasure one body can give to another!

I wondered at it.

Finally, we got up on our hands and knees, in the pouring rain, and doggy style, on hands and knees, we just laughed, we laughed and laughed. Then we got to our feet, and, holding hands, we walked into shelter, under the awning.

Suddenly the sound was different; it was stillness, with the hollow, echoing hammering of the rain bouncing on the awning, running off its edges. The air in here, sheltered, was strangely quiet, warm and intimate, humid, smelling of hemp and canvas, while, just an arm's length beyond us, the rain poured down. The night was pitch-black. He put his hands on my shoulders – Oh, I adored the feeling – and he said, "Maybe a shower and a drink?"

"Yes, Master," I licked my lips. "That sounds excellent."

≈

So, we had our drinks – Black Label with ice cubes – in plastic cups just to be safe, in the large walk-in shower with the white ceramic walls, heated towel racks just outside the glass partition, two shower heads and several little hoses for special intimate work and ablutions, if you wanted to spray yourself from all the various possible directions.

I carefully soaped my man all over.

Bright white suds everywhere, dribbling down his lean, tanned body, streaming down his chest hair.

He was resigned and very patient during this process, giving me a bemused look, touching my face, lifting my chin, so I was forced to gaze into his eyes.

I got down on my knees and examined him in close-up. "Testicles are such sweet, ridiculous things." I soaped them carefully, weighing them judiciously, considering them, as a pair, like twins, and then individually, each on its own.

So, there I was, crouched thus, in front of him, my master, my totem, my god, my religion. "And this creature," I took his cock in my hand, "He is the serpent in the garden." I soaped and caressed it. "Nice fellow," I said, "He's very obedient. I beckon, and he comes."

James stroked my hair. "Yes, he is your obedient servant."

I stood up.

"I see the Bermuda Triangle has returned," James said, "in full and eternal glory."

"Yes."

"It is as beautiful as before."

"Truly geometric, Martine says."

"She is a marvelous navigator and geometer, your friend, Martine Aubin," he said, "And a young woman of exquisite good taste since I see by the papers and tabloids, she has chosen you – and you have chosen her."

"Indeed, Master, that is so."

He knelt and kissed the Bermuda Triangle; he shampooed it; he rinsed it with one of the little shower hoses; the hot water tickled and aroused me, and was very, very stimulating; he kissed my labia and licked them. I sighed and leaned back against the steamy ceramic wall and closed my eyes. His tongue explored me, and entered me, and caressed the clitoris with famished liquid strokes, sideways and circular, every which way; I drifted upward in a sort of ecstasy of abandonment, my fingers grasping his hair, my back against the warm streaming wet ceramic wall. I was no longer me, I was everywhere and nowhere, and I was reduced to a tiny vibrating rippling trembling part of my body. "Oh, oh, oh, James, oh, oh, oh," I cried out, my fingers plunging into his hair.

Whew, the crescendo rose!

Whew, it peaked!

Whew, it slowly subsided, gentle waves and aftershocks.

≈

Lazily we toweled each other.

We crawled to bed and turned out all the lights.

The storm had turned violent; thunder battered the walls; lightning, flashing through the wooden shutters and muslin curtains, flared in the room. Rain slashed and battered the windows.

"I must ask forgiveness," James said, "for leaving the way I did, without a word. It was cowardly, as you said, cowardly."

"Oh, Master, I think the master does not need to ask forgiveness from his servant."

"Oh, but he does."

"And the servant, then, must ask forgiveness of her master. She said evil, ill-considered, quick, angry words, she thought angry, cruel thoughts ... She wanted to tear his eyeballs out and pound his flesh into little smithereens and cut the smithereens into tiny little itsy-bitsy cubes and roast the little tiny cubes and throw them into a boiling pot of stew, a witch's brew and cauldron of fury, steam rising, and cast evil spells. She wanted to cackle over the steaming broth like an insane wild shrew. She cursed the very name of her master."

"She was right to do so," he said.

"No, not really." I closed his mouth with a kiss.

We slept.

CHAPTER 3 – THE SEA

I woke to sunlight. The sheets had been tossed aside, and we were lying naked and uncovered in the burgeoning morning light.

James lay on this side; he was already awake, gazing at me in a dreamy sort of way; seeing I was awake, he began to stroke my belly and then my breasts and hips; he kissed me, and I kissed him back gently; the sunlight shone through the shutters, beams of soft smoky-blue-gold sleepily entered the room.

I kissed him, and I crawled onto him and without a word, I lifted myself up so that he could enter me.

As I rose up and lowered myself down, I guided him, slowly, slowly, so he entered me delicately, a gentle stroke at a time, prolonging the pleasure – and the agony.

Then he was deep inside me.

I rode him.

I wanted to shout out, "Giddy Up Little Pony!"

But I didn't.

For some reason, as the excitement rose, I wanted to laugh, to scream with laughter like an idiot and then, suddenly, without warning I came – an orgasm without warning, an orgasm out of the blue.

I screamed.

He insisted – cruel master, cruel slave – on keeping me in a state of excitement for a long time, riding up and down, trembling and sweating with pleasure; he didn't come, but he made me come, over and over; and he took me close to orgasm, over and over.

"Oh, cruel man," I murmured.

He kissed me. "My goddess and my princess," he whispered.

"Master," I stroked him and kissed him.

Finally, we got up, showered, and fought over who would prepare breakfast. I won. So, I made breakfast.

We ate on the terrace, under the awning. The day was bright and warm and fresh; the air clean and glittering, swept of all its impurities by last night's storm and rain.

Over breakfast, we discussed our future – our near future. I wondered: Now, do I want to explore the depths and heights, do I want to live dangerously – or not? Do I want to go, or do I want to stay? If I stayed, was I surrendering my liberty? If I stayed, was I proving that I was truly a miserable passive object, a stupid infatuated young woman; that he merely had to crook his little finger and beckon and I would come? Did I care if I was a stupid little masochist? Did I really care? And if he did despise me, did I really care? The answer was clear.

"I can stay for a week," I said, "maybe two."

"Wonderful! I'll stay for a week too, or two weeks, or longer, Gwen, if you want me."

"What do you think, Master? I want you. I think that is quite clear. And besides, this is your flat we are sitting in, and your terrace. I am here for you. If it weren't for you, I'd be gone already, to London and Cambridge."

We decided that in the late afternoon when the sun would be less hot and lower in the sky, we would go to the beach.

I rummaged among the clothes I had left here from two years before. I chose G-string panties, spandex short shorts, a T-shirt, a baseball cap, and big dark glasses with a thick white frame, and plastic flip-flops.

After lunch, we set off in a rented car, again a Porsche convertible. Soon we were outside Rome and close to the sea. We drove along the old seaside road until we came to the nudist beach.

We parked on the edge of the road, where there were only a few cars. One was very striking – an antique red Mercedes roadster.

"Do you wish to disrobe, Princess? Or wear a swimsuit?"

"A swimsuit for the moment, Master," I said. I slipped out of my shorts, panties, and T-shirt. But I kept the glasses and the baseball cap. I took the swimsuit – a tiny black string bikini – out of his shoulder bag and, standing on the sun-baked asphalt, I slowly, thoughtfully, put it on.

I wiggled and tugged at the strings. It felt strange to be dressed, even in this flimsy little thing. I was tempted to pull it off. Wearing anything seemed a violation of this place – everything was so elemental, naked, and natural – the sun, the sand, the scrub, the sea – the world was telling me that the body should be elemental, naked, and natural too.

James' eyes crinkled in a grin. He saw right through me. He perfectly understood the contorted little waltz of temptations and ratiocinations churning around in my mind: The idea of being naked and under his gaze, here on the side of this shimmering dusty old seaside road, where I might be seen by any passers-by, thrilled me with a nostalgic edge of naughty and illicit adventure, a dizzy pretense of being a wild thing, of being an elemental nymph, sexual and free, a purely natural creature, a tantalizing echo of times and adventures past, and times now – perhaps – to be regained. But I thought, for just a moment, that I would resist. I would be a modest, shy, and retiring Gwendoline, for the moment, such was my thought.

James favored me with a light, cool kiss on the lips. "Wild

child," he whispered. I blinked at him, dazzled by the light. He looked perfect, strikingly handsome, like an advertisement in GQ. His black shorts and black T-shirt formed a perfect ensemble, indeed worthy of the *Gentlemen's Quarterly*, with the sober dark glasses, and black leather sandals. He folded my shorts, and panties, and T-shirt and put them carefully into his shoulder bag.

I took his hand.

It seemed so natural, as if no time had passed at all.

We left the road and walked into the dunes.

The sand underneath the thin hot crusty surface was cool and damp and dark from the storm the night before. Only the surface crust was warm and crisp and pale from the sunlight of today.

We climbed to the crest of the highest dune. Suddenly, in front of us, the beach stretched off to the left and right, vast and almost empty. The sky glowed, a pale, uncertain blue, quiet, immense, and still, as if in suspense, as if waiting for something – anything – to happen. The vastness muted all the sounds, reduced the few humans and the little hot dog stand to tiny shadows.

We slid down the dune and walked across the beach to the edge of the water. We dropped our things on the sand. James took off his sandals, and I lifted off my flip-flops. We waded in. When we were fifty feet out in the sea, we looked back at the beach.

The wood-and-bamboo hot dog stand was open for business; its brightly colored flags fluttering gently, the tall, thin flagpoles leaning crooked, sideways. There were a few families, each with its little establishment of coolers and deckchairs placed right at the water's edge.

Some naked kids were building castles in the sand, using the dark wet sand at the water's edge. Next to them, a woman wearing large dark glasses, a baseball cap, and nothing else, probably their mother, was lying on a deckchair reading a very thick book.

Another woman, blond and deeply tanned, was lying isolated

and far away from everyone, near the dunes. She was naked and alone and without any visible possessions, no towel, no purse, no swimsuit or clothes. I wondered about her; such solitude and nudity were enticing, just her body and the vast landscape. Who was she? Behind her, up in the dunes, the long stalks of pale, rustling grass glinted gently, like stalks of straw in the sunlight.

Not far from us, two women were sitting on towels, right at the edge of the water, knees up, elbows on their knees, gazing out to sea. The older, with short gray hair, was naked; the younger was wearing a turquoise bikini-bottom. The older woman noticed us and waved – at James.

"Ah," he said, "I know them."

We waded out of the water, picked up our things, and walked over to the two women and sat down. They were in the film business – and had worked with some famous directors and actors – so we talked about movies and television serials. We shared our bottle of wine.

I took off my bikini, folded it carefully on my towel, and waded, naked, into the water and then swam. James joined me. "I like them," I said. James nodded. "Yes, they are nice, charming, highly intelligent and cultured, but relaxing company. One of them was famous, once upon a time." He kissed me, and we swam for a long distance, far out into the blue, and then along the coast.

Finally, we swam back, climbed dripping out of the water, and sat down with the two women. They had sandwiches and another bottle of wine and a bottle of mineral water. It was like a country feast, like family. We talked lazily. The sun slowly lowered towards the west; the day eased its way to a close; the light became more delicate; the shadows stretched out, longer and longer, until they began to fade and disappear. It was dusk.

The two women left. James and I lingered. We swam in the dusk, in the pale dusty golden light. I stayed naked. The direct sensation of the elements, the sun, the sand, the sea, at one with my body, kept me in a sort of excited, ecstatic mood. Silly, I know, but somehow this simple nudity seemed to me to be metaphysical, some sort of philosophic statement, like a return to the origin of the world, despoiled of everything, naked with the elements. Please don't ask me what I mean by that. I haven't the slightest idea.

The naked blonde – who had been lying there all alone – got up and walked up towards the dunes and the seaside road just as she had been on the beach – naked, no purse, no clothes, no towel. We were heading up to the road, too, just behind her.

She was a handsome woman, with a trim, muscular body. I felt an itchy desire to know her, to know all about her. I now saw that she had a thin chain around her waist and attached to the chain a tiny wallet and a bunch of keys.

She got to her car – it was the red antique Mercedes roadster we had noticed earlier. She opened the trunk, got some clothes out, and began to dress – a flesh-colored tank top, flesh-colored short shorts, and leather sandals – the bare minimum. Our shared nudity, I felt, had been an unspoken bond. I had the satisfaction of not wearing any clothes too – as James and I walked hand in hand up to the Porsche.

The blonde, who had ignored us till this point, suddenly turned and waved at me, and blew a kiss. I waved back, blew her a kiss, and gave her my best smile – which she returned, dazzling, just for a second, and then she turned and opened the car door.

She got into her car and drove off, leaving James and me alone, beside the road, in the sudden immense stillness, listening to the gentle roll of the surf and the cicadas in the bushes and scrub. The sand and asphalt still radiated heat. The first stars had come out. James took my face in his hands and kissed me. "Little Goddess," he said, "Wild child."

∞

Ah, Rome, Rome ...

It was easy, all too easy. I smiled. I laughed. I played the clown. And I steeled myself for the catastrophe – rejection and abandonment – which surely would come.

We were soon back into the rhythm of Roman life.

Evenings, we ate mostly at Alfredo's on the small piazza just down the street. Early in the morning, I often went alone to Campo de' Fiori to buy tomatoes and arugula and cucumbers and red and green peppers. I made a great fuss of making salads for lunch – Greek salad, Arugula salad, Tuna salad, Cobb salad, Pesto and Chicken salad. Usually, we ate lunch while working at our computers, just talking now and again, out on the terrace or in the living room by the fire, depending on the weather and our moods.

James went to meetings. He consulted with Allison in New York. He made phone calls, pacing up and down on the terrace. He had a project in West Africa, and to get it off the ground, he was continually liaising with the Italian Foreign Ministry and with several of the Embassies, including the French Embassy in Piazza Farnese and the American Embassy on via Veneto.

I was worried about some of his projects. I knew that criminal networks were operating in the same area. One of his projects in the Czech Republic was particularly disturbing. I suspected some Russian and Georgian gangs – powerful arms dealers, people smugglers, and drug lords – had their eyes on the company that James wanted to acquire. That could be very, very dangerous. Those people would stop at nothing. And some of the company's products almost certainly had military uses – this would make the stakes even higher, and the "players" even more ruthless.

I worried about Kate too: In Africa, Islamist jihadists and the mutating plague were both getting too close to where Kate was working, in a vulnerable landlocked country not far from Senegal.

James and I continued to play our little games. He exhibited me as his captive and lover, his trophy, and I took pleasure in it.

One night, James suggested I wear a very tiny miniskirt and a black fine net semitransparent tank top on one of our evening outings to the wine bar on the Campo. People did notice. And the waiters, who knew me and usually saw me in T-shirt and jeans, were particularly gallant and attentive. And one evening, at Alfredo's, I wore a semitransparent latex dress which did draw quite a bit of attention and quite a few compliments from Alfredo and the waiters. Two people asked for my autograph. They'd seen me in *Vogue Italia* in a photo spread with Martine Aubin.

CHAPTER 4 – CHAINS

"I'm antsy," I whined to James. It was a bright hot and steamy Roman morning.

"Antsy?"

"I have to finish this damned bloody really annoying paper for *The Mathematical & Philosophical Review* by three o'clock, and I just can't concentrate."

"Oh, I see." He rubbed his chin, narrowed his eyes, and examined me, looking me up and down – once – then twice; a merciless examination.

I was standing slouched, pouting, in the doorway to his office and wearing, as today's costume, a pair of James' black-and-gold striped shorts – sagging down over my hips and much too big for me – and an old ragged, paint-splattered black T-shirt that belonged to my Boston days doing house repairs.

I came into his room and paced up and down, barefoot, biting my fingernails. I was sizzling like a cat on a hot tin roof and in a foul, frustrated mood: I have discovered that the mind sometimes slows down and freezes, and feels like a barrel of cement, or, at best, a tub of thick sticky glue; and sometimes, just to confuse things, it goes too damned fast, spurts off, and travels in too many directions, all at once, scattered all over the place; right then, that particular sultry sweaty morning, it seemed to be doing both, at the same time – useless gluey immobile non-thoughts, and too many half-thoughts squirting off hopelessly all over the place.

"Well, then," James rubbed his chin and narrowed his eyes and adopted his most thoughtful, philosophic expression, "I think I may perhaps have a solution."

"Oh?" I stopped and stared at him, steaming in my own sweat, exasperated, my arms akimbo, about to jump out of my own skin. "And, what, dear, divine Master, might that be?"

"Take off your clothes."

"Everything?"

"Yes, nakedness is essential."

"Okay – but not sufficient, perhaps."

"No, not sufficient for our purposes: I propose, with your permission of course, that I chain you, naked, to your steel chair and desk, and to your computer which I shall also chain to the steel desk. You will not be released until you finish the paper."

I thought for a moment, did one more pace up and down the length of the room, gnawing at my knuckles. "Okay," I said. "That sounds perfect, Master. Just let me pee first."

I peed and slipped out of the boxer shorts and T-shirt, and James set to work, transforming me into a shackled prisoner. He clipped my neck into a high stiff black leather-and-steel collar; he attached the collar to a chain which he linked tightly to the chair and the desk. He used ankle chains and manacles and a tight, chained, and corset-like leather waist belt – to tie me to the chair; among other things, it pushed my breasts up ... oh, oh, oh!

My wrists he loosely chained to the desk – so I could type and flip the mouse around – and even reach my iPhone. But I couldn't touch my mouth or face.

Using the anti-theft cable, he chained my computer to the desk. He stood back and contemplated his work. "Comfy?"

"Yes, Master, I'm comfy." I was truly helpless; no way to escape; a trickle of sweat tickled its way down my spine; sweat was beading under the tight collar. My thighs were antsy, glowing, coated in sweat. I wanted to rub them together. But I couldn't shift my legs very much.

My master went off to brew me some strong espresso and came back with a steaming cup of coffee, and he fed me a square of dark chocolate.

"Drink your coffee," he said, "Finish it up." He held the cup to my lips. I drank. Glug, glug, glug.

"You are very kind, Master."

"I am indeed kind."

"You think of everything."

"Yes, well, speaking of which, I had an idea while the coffee was brewing: Would you like a ball gag? You won't be able to babble or talk. Your mouth does run away with itself sometimes. Not having it available to distract you will help you concentrate."

"Hmm," I thought. Would it help me concentrate? It would probably keep me in a state of exalted excitement, a tizzy of frustrated desire. Just think – a whiff of mouth-filled, fully fulfilled fellatio, a symbolic return to the maternal breast, a jaw-breaking rigidity, mute servitude! Was that concentration? I half-closed my eyes, picturing it. "Yes, okay, Master. A ball gag does seem advisable. That's a very good idea, Master."

My master went off to the bondage armory and quickly came back; he held up the gag, a complicated looking black-and-red gizmo. I nodded, and he knelt next to me. He carefully fitted the ball gag harness and clasped it around my head. Then, in one swift movement, he shoved the ball itself – and it was hard red rubber and very large – into my mouth. I tried to protest.

"Gmmphhh!"

"Exactly," said James, smiling. "Gmmphhh."

"Gmmphhh!" I tried to wiggle. Saliva filled my mouth; I drooled. I was a pony being fitted with an oversized bit. It filled my mouth, forcing my jaw wide open; saliva bubbled and dripped. The four straps went around my head and up over my head and under my chin. There was no way I could break free; the ball gag was firmly fitted and locked. My hands, securely chained to the desk and to the corset-belt, couldn't reach it. My destiny was sealed.

"Happy?"

"Gmmphhh!"

"Good." My master pinched my left nipple, kissed me on the forehead, and left the room. I was alone in the steamy summer light that streamed into the room.

Naked and bound and gagged, it was perhaps odd, but I felt entirely calm, aroused, and yet serene.

"All right, now." I took a deep breath.

I concentrated and wrote as fast and furiously as I could. As I wrote, the thoughts came. I scribbled down equations and plugged them into the programs on the computer. The hot day got hotter. Sweat beaded my body, dripped from my breasts, and streamed down my belly. A ticklish electric tingling sensation sparkled at every pore. Nothing broke my concentration. From time to time, my master looked in to check that I was okay; that didn't break my concentration either.

By 2:45, the article was ready. I read it through, doing the proof-reading quite quickly, but finding nothing wrong, except two typos and one spelling mistake.

"Time is up," James looked around the door, "are you done?"

"Gmmphhh!" I nodded.

"Do you want to be released?"

"Gmmphhh!" I shook my head back and forth: No.

"Text me when you want your freedom." He caressed my sweaty, sticky hair and tickled both my wet, sweat-dripping nipples, and slid his hands over my breasts, slick now with sweaty excitement and with warm drool, which was dripping from my chin.

"Gmmphhh!" I nodded: Yes.

"Good girl," he said, and pinched a nipple.

"Gmmphhh!" Which meant "ouch," a sensuous drawn-out appreciative "ouch," since he had pinched and twisted, gently, cruelly, prolonging the sweet pain, gifting me with a miniature, twirling, rising, spiraling surge of excitement.

I sent the article with a covering letter to the editorial board of *The Mathematical & Philosophical Review*. I felt a naughty childish ticklish thrill picturing myself corresponding, naked, gagged, and bound, with some of the most important mathematical and scientific minds in England, France, the United States, Japan, and Russia. If only they could see me!

The way the ball gag filled my mouth to overflowing, forcing it wide open, gave me a shivery voluptuous orgasmic sensation; now, finally, I understood why dogs get so excited by balls. They are all perverts! Loyal, loving Fido! Who knew?

While I sat there, still working but letting a few reveries and visions of delicious comic naked Gwendoline humiliation slither through the cracks in the calculations and sober scientific prose, an email arrived saying that Professors Higgins, Davies, and Weinberg would like to see me in Cambridge – and asking if I could chair two seminars next week. I quickly typed out: "Yes, I'd be delighted!" And I sent off the message.

The King's College fellowship that I had been awarded last spring meant that I was supposed to spend some time in Cambridge, but it didn't mean I had to live there. They knew I was spending most of my time in Rome and Paris. But I had my three rooms in Lucinda Roberts's Tudor cottage, so I had my own cozy place to stay when I was teaching in Cambridge.

As I was answering these emails, the overflowing saliva was getting even more sexy, dribbling on my breasts and down under the tight, waist-constricting corset onto my belly. I was feeling more and more frisky, and the friskiness, combined with the constraints which forbid all physical expression of friskiness, was excruciatingly stimulating. Obstacles, as Shakespeare well knew, like all the other the masters of romantic comedy, are the spice of romance.

The tension was soaring; I was eager to be released and wrestle with James, but I would only insist on a wrestling match if my master had time to wrestle – we were scrupulously respectful of each other's work schedules. If he didn't have time to wrestle, then I might just have to ... Well, a warm bubble bath rose in my mind, and the thought, too, of a soapy, oily self-stimulation, fragrant oils, self-applied, and pleasant onanistic imaginings – featuring some of my favorite people – Martine, Kate, James, perhaps Karen Spellman – perhaps under the terrace shower, and also ...

Just as I was indulging in these idle and lascivious reflections – and thinking of the dildos and other do-it-yourself sex toys, James had thoughtfully packed in the supply-and-gadget drawer – the doorbell rang.

The doorbell!!!

Oh! No!

James came striding through the room on his way to open the door. He winked at me.

"Gmmphhh!" I struggled.

"Don't worry, Gwendoline. I'm sure whoever it is will be delighted to see the great mathematician in her present unadorned state, just as the Great Creator and Intelligent Designer of the Universe framed her for all to see in all eternity. By the way, have you ever wondered why the Intelligent Designer didn't design clothes and shoes? He left us in a pretty defenseless state, when you think about it. Why did He neglect T-shirts and flip-flops, hammers, nails, and AK-47s, I wonder?"

"Gmmphhh! Gmmphhh!" Which, roughly translated, meant, "Don't you dare let anybody see me!"

"Perhaps it's Professor Higgins, or Doctor ..."

"Gmmphhh! Gmmphhh!" I wiggled, rattling my chains, my eyes flaring, drool dripping from my ball gag-stretched lips, drops dripping, flying, and coating my chin – silver drops flying every which way.

"I believe the French Ambassador, Henri Martinet, said he might drop by, charming fellow."

I squirmed. "Gmmphhh! Gmmphhh!"

Another wink and then James was gone into the front hall, and I was left chained and gagged, stewing in the delicious juices of sweat-soaked, saliva-varnished, nipples-erect-and-engorged nudity, fearful, and trembling with exquisitely anticipated utterly ridiculous humiliation; the sweltering heat of the Roman afternoon which had soared to extreme sultriness, simulated, in the sweetest, most liquid way possible, all my nerve endings.

"Ah, Maria!" James' voice sounded delighted.

"*Buona sera, Professore*, I brought this for Signorina Gwendoline." Maria's voice echoed; I could see her in my mind, dear, dear Maria, probably wearing that nice loose blue-and-white flowered dress she favored on hot days, standing on the big gloomy landing. "It's pasta sauce. I just made it. And some chilled vichyssoise. I know the Signorina likes it!"

"It looks and smells wonderful, Maria. Signorina Gwen is all tied up right now, working on a strict deadline, Maria, but I'll put this in the refrigerator, and I'll tell her you brought it. I'm sure she'll be down to see you later this afternoon."

Maria had seen me in several of my more outrageous costumes, and she had seen photographs of Martine and me online and in the tabloids, and of me naked, and having sex, certainly. But maybe seeing me, in the flesh, naked, chained to my desk and computer, and dribbling saliva, just maybe that would be too much. My illustrious tabloid image might emerge from such a traumatic experience a trifle tarnished. On the other hand, it would certainly add to my renown in the neighborhood, for Maria, bless her heart, was like a super-efficient Roman press agency; anything you told her ...

I heard the door close.

James appeared and held up the treasures as he detoured through my room on the way to the kitchen. "I'll stow this away," he said, and "If you wish to be released, Gwen, I am free for the next two hours, and I am all yours."

"Gmmphhh! Gmmphhh!" I nodded. I was excited, a frothy sweating filly eager to trot, gambol, cavort, gallop wildly in the wind, and ride my master and be ridden by him.

During the next delicious few minutes, I remained bound and gagged. James kissed my breasts and my belly, stroked my flanks, and – as I began to groan and twist in my metal prison – he slowly undid my chains, but he left the collar and gag.

I stood up and stretched.

"Just a minute." James went to the drawer and lifted out a coiled leather and metal leash and came back and hooked it to the collar.

"Gmmphhh?" What was he going to do to me now? With my hands free, I could, of course, have removed the collar. But I trusted my master. And I was curious. And being mute was in its own delicious, devious way, quite exciting.

James led me, still collared and gagged, on a leash, out onto the terrace, and walked me around in the sunshine, the blazing heat, and the hot breeze; the air had turned dry; this was very pleasant and liberating. It evaporated the sweat and the drool, and the evaporation was itself a tickly, sensuous experience – vividly painting each tiny shift in the air, each hint of a breeze, onto my flesh.

James hooked the leash to the doorway and then stood back and considered his work. Then he came forward and caressed me and touched me and knelt before me and kissed and licked the Heart of Darkness, the Bermuda Triangle, and I squirmed and wanted to kiss him.

I clutched my fingers in his hair and protested at the excessive amount of one-way pleasure he was conferring on me. "Gmmphhh. Gmmphhh!"

He brought me to the very edge of climax, and then back, and then again, he drove me to the very tipping edge, and then pulled me back again, into a cartwheeling limbo of nerve endings exploding in fireworks. I clutched his hair, desperate for relief, tottering in painful ecstasy. Again, he took me to the very edge, and then, slowly, slowly, backed me off from the cliff. My nerves were by this time like a violin string, vibrant, humming hysterically to every tiny touch of his tongue and hands.

Only then, with me near hysterical with desire, did my master finally consent to unbuckle and lift off the gag, and take off the collar, and finally, I could kiss him – and I did, fiercely, hungrily, leaning my body into his. "Oh, let's do this, let's do this!"

Then, with great and formal gallantry, he asked me if I would please do him the favor of undressing him, but slowly, very slowly, and, where possible, with my teeth.

"Slowly, Master?"

"Slowly."

"With my teeth, Master?"

"With your teeth."

I growled, baring my teeth. I was sweating, trembling, eager for instant satisfaction, instant climax, but I was also a tiger, a panther, wild, naked, unabashed, wordless.

"Perhaps you could make animal noises, no human talk while you do it. You are no longer human."

"Really, Master?"

"Wolf or pig, for example."

"Hmm." Oink, oink or growl, growl?" I gave him the look, from under my dark, dark eyebrows.

"Yes. Either."

"Grrhh." Yes, I would growl. I would snarl. Being a wolf suited my mood. Perhaps, later, on some other delightful occasion, I could recite oink, oink, wallow, wallow, and snort, snort, and play the frisky muddy sow. Come to think of that, a muddy oink-oink wallow sounded splendid, but, for now, I was an aroused she-wolf or werewolf, a randy panther, a growling leopard.

"I'll make it easy, tiger." He unbuttoned his shirt and unbuckled his belt. He was barefoot; so, there were no socks or shoes.

He stood there while I knelt and crouched before him and opened his shirt with my teeth and pulled it off one shoulder, and then off the other and then down his arms, until it fell away. I triumphed and licked my lips.

"Grrhh."

"Grrhh."

"Next, the trousers."

And, finally, his underpants, those splendid black-and-gold striped boxer shorts, of which he had many pairs, and which I delighted in stealing and wearing, though they sagged down around my knees and I had to hitch them up all the time and pin them with an oversized safety pin. This part was fun – down from his hips, down his thighs, past the knees – me all the time on my knees on the nice rubber mat – and then working it down to his ankles, me foaming at the mouth, and me by this time on all fours, "Grrhh, Grrhh," worrying the boxer shorts like a dog worrying a bone.

"Grrhh."

"Grrhh." I shook the shorts. "Grrhh!"

I looked up: there he was, my master, naked, standing in the cool, vibrant shadow of the awning – the cicadas strumming their rasping polyphonic hymn all around us.

I took the boxer shorts from my mouth and placed them carefully on a deckchair, and I knelt on my knees before my master and licked him carefully and caressed him hungrily until his sword was smooth and oiled and shiny and could enter me as easily as if he were a part of me.

I stood up. He held me, lifted me up, kissed me, and entered me; we merged into one and into the cicadas and the vibrant endless heat of a Roman summer.

James canceled his four o'clock appointment.

And I canceled my conference call.

The rest of the day, and that night, was heaven, or paradise, and it went on, and on, and on.

CHAPTER 5 – DANGEROUS GAMES

A few days later, with my slim computer, and a few notes, and my smallest wheeled suitcase, I set off for Cambridge.

James wanted to accompany me to the airport, but he had a lot of work to do – and many important looming deadlines – so I insisted that he not waste his time. "I'm a big girl, Master. I am perfectly capable of taking care of myself and traveling alone – even to the airport."

He called a taxi and came down to the street and kissed me and held me and handed me into the taxi. Maria was standing there too, and she waved as if, perhaps, I was disappearing forever, never to return.

I looked back – the two of them were standing side by side, framed by the big dark double gate of the palazzo; it was as if I were leaving my family; they looked like two parents, mummy and daddy, standing side by side, watching their wayward daughter head off towards some unpredictable, perilous adventure in a distant foreign land.

I waved and wiped my eyes. The taxi zipped around the corner. They were gone. I sniffled and blew my nose. Then I blew it again and wiped at my eyes. Sniffle, sniffle. There was a lump in my throat; I wanted to sob. I was annoyed with myself. I really can be childish!

My ticket was waiting at the airport. I sat in the lounge and read some papers on mathematics and flipped through the Italian and British papers and *The International New York Times.*

An item in *The Financial Times* caught my eye: The Czech chemical start-up James was interested in purchasing had become the object, apparently, of several additional mysterious and murky takeover bids. "Rumors of Russian Mafia involvement," the story said, "Perhaps related to the assassination of Doctor Martin Stern in Prague two months ago." That was exactly what I feared. James was heading straight into dangerous waters.

James did seem invulnerable, so strong, so sure, so savvy and competent. But there are some very dangerous people in the world – dangerous even for a tough guy like James.

James had asked me to find out about the company, to snoop around, using my hacker, mathematical, and encryption talents, and exploiting some of my police and intelligence connections; to see if there was anything fishy. I already knew there was something fishy.

There was no proof, not yet, but there were more than a few hints. Some of the research the Czech company was carrying out might have military and terrorist applications. It was rumored that a Russian-Georgian Mafia gang headed by a renegade Russian special forces officer, Sergei Platonov, was interested in the patents the company controlled. Platonov, it was said, sold military equipment and information to some of the deadliest terrorist organizations in the world. Martin Stern – a financial journalist and expert on the sector – had written an article criticizing the authorities for not looking into the attempted takeover; two weeks after it was published, he was shot dead in the garage of his Prague townhouse.

From the airport, I sent James an encrypted email: "I think

there are some red flags on your new girlfriend. Proceed cautiously, Master. There are sharks in the neighborhood."

I'd just sent the email when a text arrived from Kate: "The Ebola-type plague is spreading fast and seems to be mutating more quickly than anticipated. It may now be spreading through the air.

"Oh, and, Gwen, the Director General – who was just here from Geneva for two days – told me to tell you, Gwen, that your epidemiological computer program has been invaluable. As somebody who is here on the ground, I totally agree with him. Your statistical model has linked the detailed, granular, real-time situation to the ongoing big picture in a way nobody before was able to so quickly. It's helping us predict the spread of the disease and allows us to apply AI to a rapidly evolving situation. That work we did is paying off!

"So you see, darling Gwen, you are a genius as well as a uniquely delicious perv! Now, it is official!

"Also, just to make things more interesting: jihadist rebels are advancing on a collision course with the spreading plague, which will undoubtedly complicate our work.

"Meanwhile, you, my love, are going to Cambridge. Drink a pint of bitter for me! And love to James – and to that beautiful minx (I am truly jealous) Martine Aubin! Yours forever, Kate."

One from Martine: "Going to Cambridge? How long will you be there? I'm filming this week. But Philip says I will have four days off next week. I could hop over – if you'd like – and if delicious, wonderful James allows his princess to receive a visitor, that is! Let me know! Love, hugs, kisses! Your servant and mistress and lover and friend, Martine A"

As far as friends and lovers go, I am truly blessed; I would pray if I were a believer in prayer. But, silently, just in case, while sitting in the plane, I sent out a little whispered message of thankfulness: "To Whom It May Concern – thank you for all the blessings that have been showered upon me and for all the wonderful friends I have and for my grandmother Claudia who has always stood behind me."

My flight landed at Heathrow. I went into London for the afternoon – and bought some books at Foyles and at the London Review Bookshop – and walked around Charing Cross Road, Leicester Square, and Covent Garden; then I took a late afternoon train from London Kings Cross to Cambridge.

I had a window seat, and after we left Kings Cross, the landscape slid past, brick houses, row upon row of brick houses, then, later, in the country, fields and a row of trees that suddenly rose up, and flashed by in a fluttering blur of green and yellow, and then, with a painterly swish, the trees whipped by and fell below and behind us, and, equally suddenly, a broad river, flat and sliver in the late afternoon light, appeared and drifted by at an angle, its rippling metal-like expanse slowly turning, twisting away from us, and the onrush of the train changed its music, leaving the constant solid rhythm and suddenly acquiring a hollow, drumming, thudding echo as it raced over a rusty steel bridge, a visual whish of streaking girders and cross-braces, zipping past the windows, and the silver river was gone in a flash of steel beams, and then a blur of onrushing trees, and as we rose up high above the woods, and the woods swept down, the trees shrank, plunging below us, falling behind, magically transformed into distant miniature trees, far below, toy trees in a toy wood, all of them leaning towards us, in yearning; then, as we rounded a bend, the trees disappeared, whipped away into oblivion, a farm rushed up, coming close, a quick flash of fences and thickets and fields, with a herd of black-and-white Holstein cows, not far away, munching on the grass; one cow raised her head to look at us, and then in an instant she was gone; we rushed past a siding, and then a country road, with a line of cars, pointed towards us and foreshortened, waiting on the black tar road, its surface shining in the sunlight like polished mica; then we were again in the country; I turned away from the window and looked down at my book.

≈

As I concentrated on my book, I noticed – from a quick furtive glance – that the woman opposite me – the only other person in the compartment – was staring at me. She was gaunt with a long thin nose, and a touch too much rouge on her cheeks and she was wearing a tweed jacket of the old-fashioned kind some English women seem to favor, as if they lived on a country estate and went fox hunting on a horse from dawn to dusk seven days a week. But it was an expensive tweed jacket, I could see that. Perhaps from Norton and Son, or one of the other elite tailors that cater to the English gentry. She was pretty, but her prettiness I felt had with the passage of time gone a bit bony and thin and bitter – her lips were finely drawn and thin, but nervous and creased and chapped; she was not happy in her body; nor, I thought, with her life. I glanced up from my book. She saw me looking at her, and she spoke.

"You're the brazen hussy," she said, "the famous one."

Oh, dear, I thought. I gazed at her steadily and smiled. "Why, yes, I suppose I am – the brazen hussy, I mean."

"Why do they let such trash on the train?"

"I don't know: why *do* they let such trash on the train?"

"Oh, you're a whiplash too, then," she said.

"A whiplash?"

"A clever one, shameless, quick, good at repartee."

"I don't know about that. I'm not at all sure I'm good at repartee." I held my gaze steady. "I like that jacket. It looks as if it were made especially for you. Is it Norton and Son, or Jasper Littman?"

I know, I know! How could I know such a thing? Well, hanging around *Vogue* and Martine – a fanatic who had an encyclopedic knowledge of costumes and design and art direction – and my grandmother's tutoring in the finer points of snobbism and sartorial distinction – that education was finally turning out to be useful. The thin-nosed woman looked down at her jacket, smoothed the lapel. "Why would you care about my jacket?" she said.

"I like the color and the cut, and I think Norton and Son make very fine jackets. I'm rather jealous, actually."

"My name is Cynthia Wilson-Smyth," she said.

"I'm Gwendoline," I said, "and I am pleased to meet you."

"Why do you those terrible things?"

"I don't know. Are they so terrible?"

"You're not a good influence."

"Why?"

"Well, children, young girls, and men – men might expect such behavior from women. It's dangerous."

"Well, Cynthia Wilson-Smyth, it is my opinion that people have to grow up; they have to learn to distinguish between fantasy and reality. We are playing. People should learn – I think – to play more. Then people will be less afraid. It is mostly hatred and fear that make people do terrible things, not desire. Rape isn't desire or love – It is fear and hate, the equivalent of shooting somebody. As for fantasy, people have different tastes. Nobody is obliged to follow anybody else. Sorry! Excuse me, Cynthia. I'm giving a lecture. I talk too much! I really should shut up."

Her eyes were wet.

"What's wrong, Cynthia?" I moved to her side of the compartment and put my hand on her arm. I expected her to jerk it away. She didn't. She let my hand rest there. "What's wrong? Did I say something to hurt you?"

"My son ..."

"Your son ...?"

"He has a crush on you."

"What?" I thought: Oh, no! Oh, oh, oh, dear. How did ... I mean, how did that happen? I mean ... Well, Gwendoline, don't be an ass! Of course, you know how it happened. People fall in love with icons all the time. Hundreds of people, I'm sure, are in love with Martine, maybe thousands or tens of thousands! And in the pages of some newspapers, online, and in the tabloids, I was an icon, a tiny little icon, but an icon, and an icon of perversity; and I was associated with Martine, who had over eight hundred thousand followers on social sites. Magic does tend to rub off. And around an icon, all sorts of ideas crystallize – ideas of wonderful romance and a wonderful life, of marvelous sex and total love and total acceptance. I pressed Cynthia's wrist. Outside the window, a small village whirled past, a blur of suburban houses, a commuting village, and then a blur of trees, and then, once again, open fields.

"I'm sorry," I said.

She sniffled. She looked down at my hand as if she had only just now noticed that it was resting on her wrist. Again, I thought she would push it away. She looked up at me and blinked. Her pale blue eyes were bleak and naked; she was defenseless, and beautiful in her sudden nakedness.

She left my hand where it was. She put her hand on it. "Perhaps you can help," she said; it was almost a whisper, as if she were talking to herself and not to me.

"Help? How?"

"Are you staying in Cambridge?"

"Yes, for a week, probably two."

"Oh, that's right, isn't it? You are a famous mathematician – a sort of prodigy."

"Well ..." I gave her my modest shrug, my mutinous submissive from-under-the-eyebrows naughty-little-boy glance.

She held my gaze. "If you were to meet my son. I could say, I know you. We could meet. I think it might dispel his illusions."

I smiled. "You mean, if he sees me, if he sees this slut, this hussy, he'll skedaddle, screaming." I squeezed her hand. "I'm joking, but I see your point. You want to give your son a reality check."

"Yes, as you say, a reality check. If you agree, we could have tea, the three of us."

I thought about it. This was an experiment that could easily go terribly wrong; on the other hand, it might be interesting, and it might help the lady with her problem and her son with his unhealthy obsession. Hmm!

I patted her hand. "I have no objection, Cynthia, but we must think about this very carefully." I paused. "Let's say we present me as a good friend of yours. You never told him about me, but we met at some event at, say, Pembroke College, in Cambridge. That should take the wind out of his sails. I mean, if someone's mother approves, then there's no transgression, no secret, no rebellion – and that would make the obsession totally uninteresting, I should think."

She gave me an appraising look. "You are not stupid, are you?"

"Oh, I can be supremely stupid on occasion," I said, "Quite often a total idiot in fact."

She gazed at me as if she wanted to bore into the very center of my soul.

In the end, I gave Cynthia my cell phone number and my email address, and we agreed that we would try to set this up and make it seem a coincidence that we met. Her poor son, I thought. What are we doing?

And so just as this plot was hatched, the train rolled into

Cambridge station. I really am a devil, I murmured to myself, as I said goodbye to Cynthia Wilson-Smyth.

≈

Professor Higgins – who was back in Cambridge after teaching in Japan for a year and whom I had not yet met in person – was waiting for me at the station. This was quite an honor. Maybe it was because I was supposed to be such a brilliant mathematician – and, in fact, he had read a lot of my work, and commented on it, in a very generous way.

But I rather think it was due to my notoriety as the shameless girlfriend of that libertine millionaire venture capitalist, James Hewitt Spencer, and as the girlfriend too, of the French star Martine Aubin. I was a sort of model of scandal, and so, naturally, an object of curiosity; even austere professors of mathematics can succumb to the stardust appeal of money, fame, sex, and perverse infamy.

"At last we meet, Doctor Clermont," he said, and reached out his hand. I took it. The Professor had pale, clear skin, long thick black hair brushed straight back from his forehead, and a thin straight nose on which perched steel-rimmed glasses, a decidedly pointed chin, and a rather large mouth with thin lips which gave him an appropriately handsome and delicately nervous scholarly air, with the merest suggestion that, put to the test and under stress, he might be a fastidious over-excitable fussbudget. He was what was once known as a "TV Don," a celebrity professor who talked on British television about problems of philosophy and science and even mathematics. If there was a panel on anything of that kind, he was invited to be on it. To counteract his fame, or give it a quirky, old-fashioned flavor, he cultivated, I think self-consciously and tactically, a dandyish air of the absent-minded professor – tweed

73

jacket, shirt with off-color tie, tan corduroy trousers, and scuffed brown oxfords.

"I am delighted, Professor Higgins," I said, as we continued to shake hands. His handshake was strong, warm, and dry; it rather belied his cultivated air of feline delicacy.

"May I call you Gwendoline?

"Of course, you may."

"Call me Ralph. Please."

"Yes, of course – ah, Ralph."

We got into his car. It was an old and rather battered, mud-splashed, gold-colored Mini Cooper with a noisy engine. We set off with a spurt of gravel and drove into Cambridge and through the town. I took a deep breath. It was nice to be back.

≈

The whole idea of Cambridge had intrigued me from the first time I read about it in my grandmother's library. It was a seed-bed of genius: Isaac Newton had taught in Cambridge and had formulated the laws of gravity and of motion, changing our whole concept of the universe and of our place in it. The Austrian philosopher Wittgenstein had slouched in his rooms in a deckchair and emitted puzzling aphorisms, turning philosophy upside down. And the philosopher Bertrand Russell had tried to prove that mathematics is a branch of logic, and that both are deductive structures; that is, they are purely logical games, that don't require any empirical or factual input. And then there was the economist John Maynard Keynes, who had revolutionized economic theory and policy and who had worked on probability as well as mathematics. He was an aesthete, gay, with an insatiable appetite for young men – he totted up his encounters in his diary – and he married a free-spirited and very bohemian Russian ballerina, Lydia Lopokova, made a great deal of money on the markets, contributed to the arts, and, with his financial wizardry, he had helped Britain finance and win two world wars.

And it was in Cambridge that James Watson and Francis Crick, helped by the work of Maurice Wilkins and the brilliant Rosalind Franklin, discovered the structure of DNA, totally transforming our idea of how life is designed, and laying the basis for a revolution in crime detection, in medicine, and in the history of our species and all other living beings on the planet. It was in Cambridge that brilliant, tragic Alan Turing studied. He laid the groundwork for computers and computer sciences, and Artificial Intelligence, and invented a machine – a sort of pioneering general-purpose computer – that could decipher Nazi codes during the Second World War. I would not be me, and I could not do what I do, if it were not for his work!

It was a thrill to be in the same landscape as all those great minds. Who knew – maybe some of the genius would rub off?

≈

Professor Higgins left me off at Lucinda Robert's Tudor cottage; he suggested that we might meet later with some other mathematicians and go out to dine. He knew of an interesting pub not far away, he said, that I might enjoy.

I said that would be great.

Lucinda – or Lucy – my landlady, was an archeologist and author of books on ancient mythology and literature and on oriental and ancient mysticism – and, as I may have mentioned, she was also a famous explorer of ancient underwater shipwrecks; TV documentaries on her work had made her name a household word around the world.

I was delighted to discover that she was back in Cambridge. I was worried that she might already have left for Greece on one of her underwater archeological expeditions.

Lucy was in the kitchen, toasting some scones. "Well, here is the prodigal," she said, washing her hands and giving me a big welcoming smile, "I've made sure everything is in order in your rooms, my dear. How are you? This old house seems very quiet and a bit lonely without you! I've made a good pot of tea. Or would you like some sherry?"

"Tea," I said, and I grabbed her and hugged her, and kissed her on both cheeks.

"Oh, darling, what did I do to deserve that?"

"I just felt like it – you are so adorable and understanding and wise," I said, feeling a sudden rush of sympathy and gratitude. She put up with me only appearing at intervals, and being absent almost all the time, and I think she had rented the rooms to me more for the company than for the money. And here I had betrayed her by being away virtually all the time.

Lucinda was a slender, handsome woman in her sixties with a lean, muscular body, and who kept her white hair cut short pixie-style and who favored pressed blue jeans and crisp blue men's shirts open at the neck; she had sparkly blue eyes, plentiful smile wrinkles, and a rugged golden tan that came in part from her trips to the Mediterranean – where she grubbed around in the ruins of ancient cities; and scuba dove down to ancient underwater Roman, Greek, and Phoenician shipwrecks. She was, among other things, an expert on ancient shipping, a master of Latin and Ancient Greek, and an authority on the Mother Goddess, that mythical creature from our deep distant pre-historic past. And, in part, the tan came from her garden, behind the cottage, where she puttered among the flowers and often sat in a deckchair, in a skimpy bikini, and read the papers or scanned her iPad while consuming big mugs of very dark English Breakfast tea spiced with honey.

"Have you got time for a chat?"

"Quick shower first, then chat," I said, "If that's okay?"

I had a quick shower, sent a text to James saying I had arrived safely, and then, barefoot and dressed in shorts and a T-shirt, I sat with Lucy under the trellis in the garden. I told her about Rome, about Martine and James and Kate, and she told me about recent events in Cambridge, who was in, who was out, who was sleeping with whom, and about the recent drift of British politics, as well as about the latest fascinating shipwreck she intended to explore: A heavily-laden Phoenician merchant galley that sank near Malta about 2700 years ago and which was resting on the bottom about one hundred and fifty feet down.

I went back to my rooms and looked over the notes for my lecture and for the roundtable and seminars. I decided I had better dress with scholarly but casual sobriety: black flat-heeled sandals, black jeans, and a black T-shirt, and a light linen burgundy jacket, with as a dandyish touch, a black silk handkerchief spouting out of the front breast pocket.

I looked in the mirror. "You, my dear, are the famous shameless hussy who is somehow allowed on trains."

I decided I had better in some small way recognize my role as shameless hussy: after all, I was known as a shameless hussy all over the whole bloody world; denial would be ridiculous and evasive and in bad taste.

I put on the Marquis de Sade choker – not the collar – but a slender black velvet choker James had given me at Nicole's the night we met Martine and Philip. Like the collar, it had a red-and-black cameo profile of the Marquis with the letters S/M in black Gothic script. I stared into the mirror. It looked rather nice.

So, they will see that I am not in denial. I am what I am: I am the brazen hussy; I am Jezebel, a worshipper of strange, ancient gods, and a practitioner of dangerous deviant rites. I added a low-slung silver chain necklace, which hung over my black T-shit, and under the unbuttoned jacket, which had a large oval yellow-and-black smiley face as its only ornament.

Professor Higgins came by and picked me up.

"Oh, charming, most charming," he said when he saw me.

"Thank you," I said.

"You don't disappoint, do you?" He opened the car door.

"Well, I try not to, Ralph," I said, as I slid into the car and he closed the door with a solid and gallant chunk sound.

The pub was a rustic, chic, snobbish place – the Tickell Arms in a little village called Whittlesford. It was a sultry English evening, so we sat outside on the terrace. "Well, this looks fine, then," said Professor Higgins, or, as I had to remind myself, "Ralph."

We were four young mathematicians, Professor Higgins, and me. One of the youngster mathematicians was a woman. She had a thin pale face, a very attractive case of overbite, thin pale lips that she had painted scarlet, watery gray eyes, and fine auburn hair brushed back from her high, earnest forehead. Her mouth was slightly open, and her pale gray eyes blinked at me as if I were an unknown species, an exotic and dangerous freak. In fact, they were all looking at me in a rather intense and occasionally sneaky and askance way, as if I had just been washed up on the beach and might bite or sting them with a poisoned dart or tentacle and infect them with a dreadful disease called "depravity." Even my glance, like that of the Medusa, might prove deadly. I decided I had better reassure them – I don't bite.

I smiled and took a dainty sip of wine. Professor Higgins toyed with his knife and fork and then asked me a question about my work. I answered and went into considerable technical detail. Suddenly, they all relaxed, and the conversation became interesting – all about mathematics and about statistics and the scientific method. I forgot who I was and what I was, and we just had fun batting ideas back and forth.

The next three days were excellent. I led some seminars. Professor Higgins sat in on two of them. I think I performed rather well. The Professor was lavish in his praise, and several of the graduate students asked if I could supervise their theses, and they all said that they wanted me to do more seminars, perhaps next month, if I was free. I said I'd be delighted, though it would mean more time away from James, unless he came to join me in Cambridge, but I didn't want to inflict that on him He had a very heavy workload, and, besides, I'd be working most of the time.

Each evening or night, however late I got back to the cottage, Lucinda was always up, reading or writing, and we usually had a nightcap and discussed the day's events – sometimes in the kitchen, sometimes out in the garden listening to the crickets.

Cynthia Wilson-Smyth and I managed to carry out our little plot. We ambushed her son in a tea shop. The boy turned out to be a pale gawky young lad of about seventeen with a straggly reddish beard and long hair. The tea shop where the evil deed took place was just off King's Parade, the spectacular, old, college-lined street in the center of Cambridge. It was there, on King's Parade, stepping off the curb to cross the street, that Francis Crick, according to one account, first "saw" the vision of DNA as an entangled double helix. I loved these associations of specific places, even curbstones, and pedestrian crossings and stoplights, with historic break-throughs and scientific and philosophic discoveries.

For the ambush, I had prepared by dressing exactly as I had been dressed for the first night's outing at the pub, except for the Marquis de Sade choker. With regret, I had left that treasure in its little box back in the cottage. But I did keep the big round smiley face, dangling above my black T-shirt.

I entered the tea shop and pretended to be surprised. "Hello, Cynthia! What an amazing surprise. How serendipitous. How kind the fates are! Oh, it has been too long." I sat down, and began: "Did I tell you about the new pair of shoes I bought when I was in Paris? Oh, they are divine! And the earrings I found when I was in Milan." I finally glanced at the boy. "Oh, this is your son. How absolutely divine to meet you at long last! What is his name again?" I turned to her, and again treated him as if he were not there.

"Rufus."

"Oh, Rufus – how delightful!" I gave the poor lad the limpest of handshakes and the briefest and snottiest and most dismissive of glances, and then I plunged into an endless litany about shopping – about earrings, purses, necklaces, shoes, and scarfs – making myself as loud-mouthed and as boring and objectionable and superficially snobbish and inane as possible. I was amazed that I had all this nonsense in me, a mountain of rubbish. Seething just below the surface were all the ingredients of a total bubblehead; I just had to turn on the tap, and it all came out in a virtual stream of consciousness, automatically, and unstoppable. It was horrifying. I went on and on. I could see poor Rufus staring at me, and wilting. He looked away. I could see, I think, a single tear dribbling down his pale sallow cheek and getting lost in his straggly dirty red beard.

I moved in for the kill, launching into a long gossip about the Royal Family, about which Royal Babies were on the way, about how the young "Royals" were turning out, about what color the baby rooms were painted, and how the Duchess looked, and what nice dresses she chose when she was "preggers," and you know "in the family way" – wink, wink – and I added an admiring rhapsody on the Queen's taste in hats, mentioning at least ten models – how I knew all this and where it was stored away I have no idea – so on, and on, and on.

Even Cynthia could hardly get a word in sideways and looked utterly appalled. It was dreadful. I began to hate myself. Who is this horrible woman? But I was on a roll.

I went on to praise fox hunting – which Cynthia had told me her son despised – and how it should be brought back, and made compulsory – like military service – and I said in an overbearing horsey voice, "It makes men out of boys and women out of girls, eh, young man!" I whammed Rufus in the ribs with my elbow and accompanied the poke with a big sloppy, almost lascivious wink. It was the only time I paid any attention to him.

Shortly after that, Rufus said he was late for a class and that he'd better be on his way. He kissed his mother on the cheeks and then shook hands with me – again, I gave him the limpest most dismissive recognition, and he was gone.

"Rufus?" I said.

"His father's idea," Cynthia said; she took a dainty sip of tea; she was smiling.

"Well?" I lifted my cup to my lips; the tea had grown cold; I had been talking so much and so fast that I had not bothered to take a single sip.

"I think it worked," Cynthia said.

"Good. Now I want to eat a chocolate brownie."

"Yes, I rather think I could use one too." She gazed at me for a moment. "You make a fine idiot," she said.

"Thank you, Cynthia! Never in my whole life have I received such high praise."

I felt very sorry for Rufus and thought that, were I a really good girl, I should email him an apology with attached some pornographic pictures of myself. But that would rather undermine the point of the exercise, wouldn't it?

≈

Martine managed to fly over for two days and two nights, and I showed her Cambridge and, luckily – Praise the gods! – She and Lucinda immediately hit it off. We had dinner, the three of us, out in the garden of the cottage, and discussed the Ancient World, and the Mediterranean – all three of us loved the Middle Sea in different ways, but we all did love it – and then Martine and I retired, with Lucinda's blessing, to my rooms and there was an interesting amorous session on the rug and then in my bed. Martine was very delicate, and she was the active, dominant lover – "I have come to conquer you," she said – and I, on that occasion, was the one who allowed herself to be loved – though I was not entirely passive, and at the very end I counter-attacked and forced Martine down and pleasured her the best way I knew how.

Both mornings, Lucinda prepared a marvelous breakfast which we ate, all three of us, in the garden. It was a relaxed, easy ritual and seemed timeless, there under the dappled sunlight, drinking coffee and tea, reading the newspapers, the *London Review of Books* and *The Times Literary Supplement*, and fiddling with our iPads, and eating eggs and bacon and toast and marmalade. It was, I think, a certain kind of pagan English paradise.

"It reminds me of what I think life in the Bloomsbury Group must have been like," said Martine.

"Yes," said Lucinda, "I have a nostalgia for that time too – though, of course, it was over many decades before any of us, even I, or even our parents, were even conceived."

Martine left, and the two weeks were almost over. I was giving my second last seminar in a room we had borrowed in Pembroke College. I was having fun. I was striding around the room, talking, asking questions, listening. I loved teaching. And I loved the students – they were eager, savvy, and sophisticated, and not at all blasé or know-it-all, and they were tremendously bright! Every time I debated with them or lectured or quizzed them, I learned as much as I taught.

Then – just as I was putting the finishing touches to a complicated type of equation on the blackboard – there was a knock on the door, and two policemen appeared at the back of the seminar room.

Doctor Renzi, the resident mathematician, who came into the room with them, asked if I had long to go. I said we were almost finished. I wondered what I was being arrested for. The policemen looked very stern and serious – they crossed their arms and just stared at me. Or, worse, had something happened to Kate or James or Martine or my grandmother?

I finished the seminar. As they filed out, the students all shook my hand. Two of the girls kissed me on the cheek. The police said, "Would you please follow us?" It was not really a question.

"May I pick up my things?" I asked.

"Yes, of course, but you must be quick about it."

My laptop was with me, but I needed a few other things. I wondered if they allowed you to take a toothbrush into prison. Two unmarked cars – I was sure they were police – were waiting outside Lucinda's Tudor cottage.

Had my super cool hacking adventures caught up with me?

Would I disappear never to be seen again?

Lucinda looked concerned. "They arrived half an hour ago. Do you think you are in trouble?"

"I don't know."

"I offered them some tea. They accepted. They seem quite friendly, but absolutely serious. They didn't want to come in, but they stood outside. One is in the garden, and one is out back."

"Surrounded?"

"Yes, we're surrounded."

"No escape routes?"

"No escape routes." She smiled, but it was a wary smile; she put her hand on my arm.

"Well, then, I guess they've got me! They told me they want me to collect my computers and papers and come with them."

"Well, I suppose you'd best do that. I'll keep your room just as it is."

"For when I get out of prison?"

"However long it takes, dear."

"Britain doesn't have the death penalty, does it?"

"No, dear, it doesn't."

"Good."

"Surely it's not that bad."

"Will you give my excuses to Professor Higgins? I was supposed to meet him at the Tickell Arms in Whittlesford tonight. And tell him that I might not be able to do the last seminar."

"Absolutely, I'll send a note and ring him up just to make sure."

The police had told me not to bother changing; so, I remained as I was – in black jeans and a white blouse and a light black linen jacket. We drove to the old Duxford Airbase, which surprised me. Duxford sits out in the middle of the flatlands of East Anglia a few kilometers from Whittlesford, and it was used during the Second World War as an airbase, during the Battle of Britain and afterward.

I asked the very well-dressed man who was sitting beside me what it was about.

"You'll find out," he said. He gave me a smile; I couldn't tell if it was friendly or hostile. "Don't communicate with anybody," they had said. "Okay," I had said. I had been tempted to text James when gathering my things, but I decided I would be a good girl and not do it.

At Duxford, we drove straight out onto the runway. There was a vintage 1940s gray-metal Lancaster bomber not too far away at one side of the tarmac. In front of us, a helicopter was waiting, the rotors already turning.

"Good luck, lass," one of the cops said. "Thank you," I said, "And you too!" I got out of the car, and, carrying my small overnight case, I was escorted to the helicopter by two constables. I wondered if they thought I was going to run away. A light breeze was blowing across the runway, and the striped windsocks were billowing out almost horizontally, and the daylight reflecting from the fens and the low farmland was immense and shimmering white. Behind the Lancaster, I noticed a 1940s Hawker Typhoon, out on the runway, a small group of people looking up at it. A man using a cane was pointing out its features, obviously a guide. If I survive this, I thought, I'm going to come back and do the tour of Duxford and its aviation museum.

"A pleasure to meet you, Doctor Clermont," said a handsome man standing beside the helicopter. He was wearing a dark pinstripe suit. His shoes were highly polished, his hair combed back, his face deeply tanned. He reached out his hand and shook mine. He didn't give his name. We climbed in. I sat down, and, as I began to buckle myself in, the helicopter lifted off. I didn't think I was important enough – as a perv and fashion and porno icon – or even as a subversive hacker – to be treated this way if I was being arrested.

"You'd better have a look at this," said the man in the dark suit. He handed me an iPad sort of tablet. "Thank you," I said, deciding to pretend I knew what was going on. I read: "MI-6 asset A-412 kidnapped at gunpoint 07:53 hours on Tsar Simeon Street in Sofia Bulgaria. Satellite coverage inadequate. Kidnap vehicle lost at 08:13 hours. Kidnap vehicle found, burnt out, at 10:11 hours in the town of Tran. I looked up at the unnamed man in the dark suit. I raised an eyebrow.

"Call me Jack," he shouted over the noise.

"Call me Gwen," I replied, "if you wish to, that is."

"Well, Gwen, you see our problem."

"Yes, needle in a haystack. You want to know where your man

disappeared to. Who took him? Why? Where might they take him? Is he alive? How to find him. How to rescue him."

"Yes. That's what we want to know." Jack looked grim. "In fact, that's what we absolutely need to know."

"I presume he is a very important person – or asset."

"Extremely."

"Hmm. So, you think I can ... do what exactly?"

"Doctor Clermont, you have a reputation ..."

"I sure do ..."

"No, I mean your *other* reputation." He smiled. "You have a reputation as a bit of a magician in mathematics, in the study of networks and connections, and for clever deductions – finding needles in haystacks, deciphering criminal and terrorist networks, that sort of thing."

"Ah. Well ..."

"We need a fresh set of eyes; we want you to try your magic."

"I'm not sure I ..."

"You will know all we know, and you will have access to our best people, all our resources."

"I'm flattered and honored."

"Scroll to the next pages. That will give you some background."

We landed on the roof of a building that was not far from central London. I could see Big Ben, Saint Paul's Cathedral, the Needle, and the big Ferris-Wheel on the South Bank.

The rotors were still turning when we got out. Bending down, ducking from the downdraft of the blades, Jack and I ran towards a stairwell. I glanced back. There was a cloud over the west end of London, and rain slanting down, a veil of steel-gray, but the wind was warm – a beautiful changeable English summer day. We clattered down the steel steps of a staircase.

It was quite a shift, I suddenly began to realize, from strutting around a lecture hall or a seminar hall and talking to students about chaos theory and probability, and from lounging around with Lucy and Martine and reading the *London Review of Books*. And it was certainly a change from being chained to my computer, gagged and naked, sweating in the sweltering Roman afternoon. But I do like change. Variety, they say, is the spice of life. I hoped I would measure up to this new test and make James and Martine and Kate and Claudia and Professor Higgins proud of me. Of course, most of them would never hear about this. Suddenly we were in a blank white cement corridor and then in a rather unadorned office. Just a table several chairs, a steel bookshelf filled with books – various Jane's publications on weaponry, various strategic studies, books of military history, and tactics.

"We'd like you to sign this."

It was a confidential form. I scanned it quickly. I was not to divulge to anyone anything about what was about to happen. And I was not to divulge that I had promised not to divulge anything nor even the fact that anything at all whatsoever had happened. I looked up, "What about James?"

"Don't worry about James. I'll talk to you later about James," said Jack; he gave me a smile meant to be reassuring.

I signed.

We went down the corridor, down several more flights of stairs, and, via an elevator, we went down still further; finally, we were underground I figured, though it was hard to tell; we walked down another corridor, and we entered what they call in the movies "a situation room." There were computer screens everywhere, and banks of monitors, with what looked like satellite or drone feeds, and news channels from various networks, in a slew of languages.

A young blonde – she introduced herself as Ashley – laid out the events, and what they knew and what they didn't know. "So that's the situation. What do you think?"

The next few hours were a whirlwind of information and analysis, and ideas. Tension was high. Here I was, in the middle of it all. We combined all the factors and networks and information they had accumulated plus a few random bits and pieces that I had picked up, and I was able to apply my systems analysis, which meant superimposing all the different kinds of information on a single grid and map and timeline.

"Okay, as you said, the most probable group responsible is East European Jihad, EEJ," I said, "and they do subcontract their dirty work to the local Trans-Balkan Drug Lord Syndicate or TBDLS So this possibly a contract job, since East European Jihad – EEJ – is assumed to be pretty thin on the ground in this area."

"Yes," said Ashley. "Can you combine the various levels?"

"Yes. See – here." I pointed. "If we superimpose these three networks ... the EEJ, and the TBDLS, and the local Sofia-Slivnitza Gang, which controls the neighborhood where he was snatched, then we get these crucial nodal points where exchanges and deals might be made."

Several of the officers glanced at each other.

I figured that meant I was to continue. "Okay, it's probable that if EEJ is subcontracting the work to TBDLS, and TBDLS has many links, through the Sofia-Slivnitza Gang to the New Revolutionary Party or NRP. So NRP might have participated in the actual operation. I would guess they did. The NRP have at least half a dozen safe houses."

"Ah, ah," said Jack, "And if you look at traffic patterns at that time of day, see this diagram, here," he brought it up "the best way to get your man out of town would be this route, or this route."

We all looked at how the various maps intersected when superimposed on the large computer screen.

"That's right," I said, "There is also a large sewer in the sewer network that runs from here to here." I pointed to the map. "People could be moved via the sewers if the water level is not too high; given there's been a drought these last five months, the water level should not be too high."

They superimposed more of the maps, and we isolated the most probable safe houses, and bases of the NRP. "So, the probabilities are that he is either here, or here, or here."

"Can we narrow that down a bit?"

Detailed satellite maps were rolled out. Jack glanced at them and turned to some experts. "Any unusual activity anywhere?"

"Here, and here," one of the grizzled experts said, "and there."

"Get eyes on that," Jack said.

While we were talking, people on the ground were moving into position to observe – get real-time eyes on – the three possible – likely – places we had identified.

"You said you wanted to talk to me about James."

"Yes. Come over here." Jack took me into a side office.

"Okay." I gulped; I thought – I'm going to find out that James is an enemy agent, and ...

Jack narrowed his eyes, smiled a sly smile. "He's one of ours."

"Really?"

"Yes."

"Oh, boy."

"He is privy to what is happening right now. But it is best you and he not talk about any of this except in the most secure of environments. And no environments are secure. We can arrange to have your Paris and Rome flats swept periodically to check for bugs, cameras, that sort of thing, and we could put in our own surveillance equipment."

"You'd better discuss that with James. Then he and I can decide."

"Splendid idea – equal in all things, are we not?"

"Indeed, we are." I gave him my best smile.

Somebody brought me a ham and cheese sandwich and a fresh mug of strong tea. I ate the sandwich and sat watching them prepare the operation. It occurred to me that something was wrong – just a hunch. "I think maybe it is objective two," I said. "Not one or three."

"Really – why?"

"It's a hunch, but I think the hunch is based on a thought. Something I noticed but didn't notice I had noticed. Let me think, just a second."

"There's no time."

"Ah, give me just a second!" I flipped through reams of tables indicating activity in the zone. Electrical bills, road work, cellphone activity, car rentals, car thefts, Google searches, house, or flat renovations of any kind. "I've got it, the surge in electric use, and the fact that this house was hooked up three weeks ago. That was just when ... Yes, that's it. I'll bet that's it!"

So, the objective was changed at the last minute.

The raid went in like clockwork. The agent was found, and in the shoot-out, he survived, not even scratched. Six jihadists were killed, and two drug dealers from the local gang. Three members of the Jihadists for the Creation of the New Eternal End of the World Caliphate were captured alive. A mass of information was captured on hard drives, computers, and smartphones.

Whew!

I felt the adrenaline. It was addictive, exciting, almost as exciting as making love, or being tied, bound and gagged, by the man I loved, to a steel chair.

"You are a strange creature." Jack was sitting back in his chair. We were in his office, eating croissants, donuts, and drinking coffee.

"I suppose that is what passes for understatement."

"Yes, perhaps it does. Your games, the games you play with James and with Martine Aubin and ... and so on ..."

"Yes?" I thought, Oh, oh! Now they're going to tell me I have to stop; that behaving like that I would be a security risk. But I was addicted; it was part of me; I liked what I was – I liked what I did and what was done to me – and I didn't know if I could give up that part of my personality.

"It's a good cover," he said, "you are a public person, rather scandalous, it's a useful distraction."

"Ah," I said.

"Yes, your hijinks are both useful and amusing." He leaned forward and dipped his croissant into his coffee.

"How can you do that? Ugh!" I displayed my best grimace of disgust. I found it ruined both the coffee and the croissant.

He smiled. "And how can you do what you do?"

"Good question," I said.

As it turned out, I was back in Cambridge the next afternoon, just in time to give my seminar on the history of probability theory.

Lucinda was busy in the kitchen, preparing scones and late afternoon tea, "Well, my darling, what was that all about?"

"Oh, there was a little problem with a traffic computer program in London, and they thought I could solve it." I had been given my detailed cover story, so I just repeated the executive summary. Lucinda raised an eyebrow and smiled a knowing smile and handed me my tea. I was certain she knew it was not a computer glitch that had sent policemen to interrupt my seminar at Pembroke. I later discovered that, as an expert linguist, with lots of contacts in the Mediterranean and the Middle East, Lucinda had several times been used as a "resource" by MI-6; so she was savvy and perfectly aware of the workings of that particular underworld, the demi-monde of intelligence gathering and special ops.

We went out into the garden. It was a glorious golden perfect English summer afternoon. We discussed ancient mythologies and religions and how they had morphed to become the main monotheistic religions of today – Judaism, Christianity, and Islam. She told me about the Phoenician god Baal and how he was a sort of cousin to Yahweh, perhaps even a prototype for the Hebrew God, and why Jezebel, the Phoenician princess who married Ahab, the King of Israel, was so objectionable to the prophet Elijah who had her put to death – he particularly disliked her wearing makeup and dressing up in finery to meet her end – and so he arranged for her body to be eaten by pigs, which was not very gallant of him. I concluded that I rather liked Jezebel. The next day I took an evening flight to Rome.

≈

It was twilight when the plane landed, and James was at Leonardo da Vinci airport, which is right by the sea, and close to all those lusciously tempting Roman beaches.

"You had a busy time." James smiled, the tanned crinkle lines around his eyes, lighting up his face.

"Rather," I leaned upon tiptoes and kissed him, and I made the kiss last – and last. "Yummy!"

"In the mood for dinner on the beach – or straight to bed?"

"Hmm! Both prospects are delicious." I kissed him again. "But, let's do dinner on the beach."

We drove along the coast to Fregene, the tiny beach-side resort town, and then to the "Fishermen's Village" – *Il Villagio dei Pescatori* – at the northern end of the village. We stopped at one of our favorite restaurants. A fire was burning on the grill, and the delicious smell of wood smoke drifted in the warm air.

We went out onto the terrace, and we sat down, and the owner came to greet us as if we were old friends, which in a way we were, and we were quickly served a delicious meal: Mussels with beans and pasta and grilled sole and a delicious dry white wine. "You look like a wild and barely tamed animal, my beauty," James said.

"I do? And you look like perfectly groomed, perfectly wonderful Mr. Perfect."

We began to talk about politics, the latest changes in the US, in the UK, and in France and Italy. We understood each other with a glance and a smile or just a quivering of the lips; we argued over things, in detail, plunging into the depths. I tried to read all the papers and magazines and sites I could. I wanted to be well-armed for these delicious little skirmishes. James tended to be a bit more cynical and worldly-wise; I was bumptious and inclined to see hope and promise everywhere. In my books, good intentions counted for a lot, even if people's actions ended in catastrophe.

The drive back with the top down and the moon keeping us company was a beautifully sensuous way to return to Italy: the wind was in my hair, and I leaned against James and part of me wished that time would stop and that we could forever be like this – drifting together through the warm wind, tired, sated, affectionate, comfortable with each other, and in deeply love.

CHAPTER 6 – COSMOLOGIES

Three days later, I was sitting on the divan, relaxing, drinking a chilled glass of Chablis, and glancing through a big book on the history of astronomy.

I was, as usual, when at home, topless, wearing nothing but skimpy ragged shorts. James liked me in scanty rags. He loved the androgynous waif-tossed-up-on-a-savage-shore look – Viola in *Twelfth Night* – and, frankly, so did I. In this regard, I easily acquiesced to his every whim.

In fact, when I was in skimpy mini-shorts and nothing else, I had a sort of embodied fantasy, a Peter Pan corporeal feeling, a physical sensation that was more than just an idle fantasy: I was a boy-girl castaway on a desert island, and there, James, threatening and adorable, got up in a pirate outfit and stepping ashore from his pirate ship, was my jailor and my savior, my lover and my master, all in one.

Even when I was concentrating on work, these half-conscious images tickled my fancy and stirred an undercurrent of tingling excitement, which, weirdly enough, gave energy to my purely intellectual pursuits.

Just when I had plunged into the history of astronomy in the Islamic World, James came into the room carrying a glass of chilled wine. He was barefoot and just wearing ragged shorts.

"We look like twins," I said, glancing up, and thinking, for the millionth time, what a bloody marvelous handsome man he was. And to think that it was pure chance that we met!

"We *are* twins. Our souls are one," he said, his eyes crinkling. He knelt next to me and caressed my hair, which had grown longer; he touched the back of my neck, making the little strands and filaments of hair stand on end. Electricity raced down my spine, giving me goosebumps and a rising queasy excited feeling in my tummy and lower down – a rising liquid excitement.

It was – it is – amazing what that man's touch can do to me, even after weeks and months. Just his glance or the sound of his voice can have the same effect. My rational, mathematical mind sometimes finds it annoying – annoying in theory, but not in practice.

"This book has a fascinating history of the development of astronomical instruments," I said, "It shows how the astrolabe developed over time. Which is truly, when you think of it, rather intriguing, because as the ..."

"Your collarbone is a marvel of design." Still kneeling next to me, he kissed it. "This little dip here is sublime, and the way your flesh is sculpted over it, the light and the shadow, it is perfection itself."

"Like I was saying, the navigators used the astrolabe to ..." I swallowed and licked my lips. My tummy fluttered. My heart raced. This was unfair! How would I ever finish my thought about the astrolabe if James insisted on driving me to distraction?

"Ha, ha!" Wicked James kissed his way along my collarbone. This was pleasant, but it was exploding my concentration into tiny little floating bits of ungrammatical nonsense, star-struck fragments of an imploded self. Me – splattered all over the place. I took a sip of the Chablis. I turned a page. I cleared my throat. "You see, James, you could calculate where you were, even far out at sea, out of sight of land, by using the astrolabe, to estimate ..."

James was on his knees, examining every bit of me. *The naming of parts*, Kate used to call it.

"Your ribcage is beyond beauty."

Oh, annoying man! This is ridiculous! I shifted sideways as his lips tickled my ribcage, tingling along and playing a little tune, just above my diaphragm. With the tip of his fingers, he began to trace the undercurve of my breasts. "Oh, come on, James!" I wanted to say, but I didn't. I frowned, I licked my lips. I trembled. My nipples were erect – traitors!

"You have superb breasts, darling Gwendoline," he said, as if he were discovering my breasts for the first time. Hmm, I thought: Maybe this is the formula for eternal youth – eternal randiness, the eye of desire forever alert, and eternal love – the rediscovery of every feature and every quality of your lover's body with each and every touch, redefining and reinventing your lover's body each time anew, as if there had been no before and as if there would be no after: every instant an eternity, as if he had forgotten everything he learned the night before – maybe continually reborn lust is a form of craziness, of amnesia, of the eternal present, of Nietzsche's eternal recurrence, captured in each instant, the eternal merry-go-round of instantaneous desire.

"Well, yes, as I was saying, James, what I was saying was – before you so rudely interrupted my train of thought – what I was saying, or trying to say, was that, with this astrolabe thing, eons before GPS, you know, you could calculate, from the position of known stars, or the angular altitude of the sun, where precisely, more or less, you were and you could set your sails for ..."

"Cupcake breasts," he nibbled and licked, "true champagne glass breasts. They are perfect, rich, substantial, firm, elastic, bouncy, yet delicate in their precision and charming decorum."

"Decorum? That's silly." I shivered with tingly, antsy lust. I frowned. I licked my lips. I was trying to keep my mind on a steady keel. I didn't want James to capsize my little boat of reason and concentration. But my body and my imagination were chafing at the bit, pawing the ground, snorting, running riot.

Now, oh, wicked man, he was teasing one nipple with his incisors, little nibbles, tiny sharp nips, and counter clockwise twisting tugs, followed up by a whispering kiss and a soothing lick. I trembled. Oh, annoying, maddening man! I was staring – trying to stare – at a photograph of an astrolabe used by Arab navigators in the 14th Century in the Arabian Sea. It made me think of the Arabian Nights and, as James caressed me, and as the ragged edge of my mini-shorts tickled my thighs, I yearned, for an instant, to be a cabin boy, tossed up on the shores of Zanzibar, say, or Illyria, say, and, yes, there he was: James, the bold wicked slave trader, with a sword in his hand and an eye patch, and ...

"So, the question is: how did this astrolabe work, exactly?" I said, clearing my throat and turning the book on its side. The explanations were not very clear. "Some writers should learn how to write." I frowned. "It has gears inside, I think."

"Your nipples and areolae are unique," he whispered, tickling me with his breath.

"Unique? Oh? How so?"

"And your areolae, stippled in such a regular fashion, and of a skin tone that is perfection itself. You are a whole world I am only beginning to discover. And I am doing so without an astrolabe."

Part of me wanted to guffaw, and mutter "Oh, Pshaw, Master! You are a total, absolute idiot!" But I didn't because of the rest of me was riding high on a wave of suppressed excitement; his fingers and lips were extremely savvy, and I was flattered by the idea that I was a whole world he was discovering, like he was Columbus or Magellan, and perhaps he would sail everywhere, and possess everything, and take all of me, creating an empire upon which the sun would never set, little red-white-and-blue flags flapping in the breeze. Part of me, a shrinking part, was still trying to figure out the astrolabe. A few lines from a poem John Donne occurred to me. And so, I murmured:

I wonder by my troth, what thou and I
Did, till we loved? Were we not weaned till then?
But sucked on country pleasures, childishly.

My fingers were wandering in his hair. He has such beautiful thick hair – this dark, handsome, mysterious stranger.

"Your nipples stand out, and they spring into action so easily, so readily, like just now."

"Yes, like just now," I said. My nipples were shameless. I'd given them strict order to behave, and yet ... "Do you know how an astrolabe works, James?"

"An astrolabe?" He nibbled at my lower rib, threatening to invade my tummy and attack my totally vulnerable, absolutely undefended bellybutton. "Not exactly," he murmured, looking up at me, "I think you could use it, let us say in the vertical plane, to read off the angle of the sun above the horizon, how high above the horizon it is, and the angle of various stars, say the North Star, Polaris, above the horizon. Therefore you would know, from the angle to Polaris, how far south or north you were, at what latitude; and maybe, in the horizontal plane, say in a 360-degree circle, if you had a starting point, say due west, you could calculate where the sun was supposed to be, in which constellation, depending on the time of year, and the phases of the moon, and the seasons which the astrolabe would also allow you to calculate ..."

I cleared my throat. "Well, it's very interesting, the way they were able to represent the heavens and the passage of time with such a small instrument and use it to navigate by the stars. It indicates centuries of accurate observation of the seasons of the year, and of the – ah – corresponding evolution of the heavens, the stars, planets, sun, moon and constellations, observations going back to Ancient China and Babylon and beyond. All of this was centuries – even millennia – before the telescope had been invented. It was all done with the naked eye. Human beings are very ingenious."

"Yes, they are. I adore your bellybutton."

"You do? You truly do?"

"Yes, I absolutely do. The sacred whorl and whirl and maelstrom, and center, navel, the turning point, the still point, axis of the world, source of wonder, origin of it all."

"Holy Moly, James! What has gotten into you? You wax poetic."

"Indeed, I do." He looked up and into my eyes. "It's you, Princess, that's gotten into me."

I frowned. "When I was a kid – out on grandmother's farm, or trailing around after mother in hotels and motels and nightclubs and cocktail bars – my belly button gathered fluff and lint. But it doesn't anymore. I don't know why it stopped gathering fluff. Maybe there isn't any more fluff. Maybe my bellybutton just grew up and put aside childish things." I looked down at my belly button and at his thick slick black head of hair; he was concentrating on my belly button and on my belly.

"Oh? No more fluff. Well, I wouldn't worry, darling Gwendoline. As presently constituted, and fluff-less, your belly button is sweetness itself."

"I just read that some people don't have bellybuttons."

"Really? I didn't know."

"There's this famous model I just read about in the *National Enquirer*, and she has no bellybutton."

"The *National Enquirer*?" James was kissing my belly and caressing my thighs. "You're reading the tabloid press?"

"Yes, I am. I can't avoid it. Every time I open my computer,

I learn about something called 'wardrobe malfunctions.' A gazillion clicks are harvested because somebody's bra is showing or somebody's tits get to go on air. People's imaginations are starved. I like people, but I can't resist feeling they are desperate for a little tickling and titillation and touching and Tender Loving Care. Anyway, it said she had no belly button."

"Poor girl! She will be without such sublime beauty as I am now beholding and kissing." James kissed my belly and worked his way around the bellybutton, a twirling spiral of smudgy smackeroo tender little kisses.

He looked up at me, one eyebrow cocked. "How was the embryo fed, then, because the umbilical cord is the lifeline, if I remember correctly, and without the umbilical cord ..."

"Hmm, I don't know. They didn't say. Maybe she had a belly button, but it went away. Maybe it was ashamed to be a belly button. Some belly buttons, I imagine, are shy."

"And your thighs are so white ... so perfect, thighs of muscular marble."

"Muscular marble, ugh ..."

"Yes, but smooth as silk, glowing like satin, moist like a fresh, dewy rose, exquisitely sculpted, joining nicely to the neatest, perkiest bum in the whole wide world," he said. "You have a cute asshole, too, absolutely perfect." He looked up at me. "And the vulva, has anyone ever discoursed upon your labia, your vagina, and your clitoris, the hood of your clitoris, the slope, and architecture of your mons veneris?"

"Hmm, Martine has said some nice things about how sweet the whole ensemble is, and I, of course, have praised hers to the skies; and Kate was very poetic about my "Heart of Darkness," as she terms it, or my "Bermuda Triangle," which she baptized in a special ceremony involving champagne and Swiss chocolate. She, in fact, gave it many names. And Martine has some especially cute words in French ... But let us have a look at this drawing of an astrolabe. I wonder how you used it exactly. Let's see ... "

He sat up. He kissed me on the nape of the neck, his nuzzling warm breath stirring strands of hair and tendrils of ticklish desire, lust, horniness, soaring absurd fantasies, his hand sliding down my spine, his fingers playing on one vertebra at a time, like he was tickling my ivories or fingering a flute; he slid his palm down to my backside and gave me a sweet vicious little slap on my right buttock – the neat little shock reverberated right through my shorts.

"Ouch!" I kissed him. "Ouch!" I whispered into his mouth. Our lips and tongues mingled. "Ouch!" I murmured.

"Off with your shorts," he said.

"You are excessively annoying today, Master. With you around, a girl can't concentrate on an astrolabe and the wonders of astronomy and the infinite mysteries of this vast – perhaps unending – expanding Big Bang starry cosmos within which we find ourselves. But since you insist ..." I stood up and slid out of my shorts and laid them carefully on the back of the divan.

"That's a good girl," he said.

"You too, then," I said.

He stood up, and I pulled his shorts down, until they were crinkled up around his ankles. "Now step out of them, Master," I ordered, and he did so.

Then he was again on his knees. "Your bum is sublime," he said, "It is nectar to the gods."

"My bum! *Nectar to the gods!* That is ridiculous!"

"Not at all," he said. He kissed my backside. "Your bum is uplifting, aerodynamic, about to take flight. Your gluteus maximus, gluteus medius, and gluteus minimus are a fabulous team, all pulling together. And, around here, just down below, the butthole is one of the best-designed, exquisite buttholes ever seen."

"Pshaw! Enough of this!" I made a face. "Let us see who is most beautiful, who is most admirable," I said, "Lie down on your back, Master."

As I commanded, he lay back on the divan, and I knelt on the rug and faced him. I touched his shoulders and ran my fingers along his collarbone. "Let us have a look at this." I concentrated. "Ah, yes, man is truly a work of art – the measure of all things. Now, here we have very broad shoulders, and we have very nice curly black fur, pure virile animal energy, here we have brawn and sinew and muscle! We have man himself, and he has the nicest nipples perched right on top of his perfect pectorals, streaked with very cozy virile straight black hair that streams down so beautifully and makes exquisite patterns, Master, particularly when you are soaked in water, naked in the rain or under the shower or rising up like a sea god out of the Mediterranean."

"Hmm." He twisted his lips.

"Now," I leaned in closer, going slightly cross-eyed, I know. "Here we have the cock – the luscious cock."

"Okay, Gwendoline. Enough!"

I glanced up at him. "People object to the cock. True, true, people do not like to talk of the cock." I kissed it. "The cock does not come up in polite conversation. The cock violates decorum. The very world cock makes people antsy as if they were being nibbled by bedbugs." I tickled the cock and ran my fingers over my master's hard, smooth belly – great abs – to his rib cage, up to his pectorals, and I slid my finger along his collarbone, oh, elegant collarbone!

He levered himself up and kissed me on the forehead.

"People," I said, "At least some people, prefer penis."

"Really?" He puckered his lips and kissed my lips.

"Penis is puny."

"Hmm. Puny?" He looked down at himself. "Cruel wench."

"Penis does not hack it. Penis has no bounce, Master. Penis is insufficiently imperious."

"Okay, okay, Gwendoline!" He was grinning.

He looked so delicious, so frustrated, lying there, that I couldn't help myself; I couldn't stop. "And dick is disreputable. There is the private dick and the public dick, and then there was Dick the President of the United States, and throughout history, it must be said there have been many dicks, known and unknown, none of whom have merited acclaim." I was giddy. I hadn't had a drink. I hadn't smoked marijuana; I hadn't sniffed coke. I don't know what had gotten into me.

James kissed me again. I think he wanted to shut me up, but I was not going to stop; this was, I suddenly understood, a crusade: this was feminism in action: if you can objectify me, I'm going to objectify you!

He stroked my hair and stared into my eyes.

I pursed my lips and then, in my best professorial tone: "And, if we mention the phallus, we have to admit, ladies and gentlemen, that the phallus, though heroic, is too abstract. Puffed up and pompous and classical is the phallus, like a Doric column, a hangover from ancient times. If we are going to use it, we have to dust it off, a feather duster, perhaps."

"Gwen ..."

"Shush, shush, little man, shush!!"

He looked down, adorably abashed. If he had been a blushing man – which he isn't – he would have blushed.

I put my finger vertical against his lips, and I continued. "And wee-wee, to admit the bare truth of the matter, is limp and pre-pubescent and childish and will let us down and do us no favors."

"Yes, alas."

"Shush, Master, shush!" I kissed him and turned my attention to the thing itself, proud floppy little cock, not yet aroused, maybe even timidly mortified. "But, oh, the cock is outstanding. Cock, cock, cock, tick-tock, tick-tock, goes the cock, back and forth, waggle-waggle."

"You're giddy, Gwen."

"Indeed, I am." I licked my lips and slurped a lascivious sloppy slurp, letting my tongue hang out a bit longer than necessary. "Ah, now it is awake. It is standing straight up, out of its little forest bed with all that nice crispy underbrush that smells of Irish Spring. A blossoming flower of flesh! What a sublime little pecker! Peter Piper picked a peck of pickled peppers ..." I beamed at it. "There it is, all upright, an outstanding citizen."

I began flip and slide my hand around his cock, as if my hand were a fighter aircraft strafing the ground, and I made a buzzing sound like a World War II Spitfire or Messerschmitt, buzz, buzz, buzz!

I zoomed down towards his cock, buzz, buzz, buzz: "Cunt calling Cock. Cunt calling Cock. Come in, Cock, Come in! Buzz, buzz, buzz!"

Weird, eh, I thought, and then I realized it must have been because I'd been out on the aerodrome at Duxford and seen the Lancaster bomber and the Hawker Typhoon fighter. "Buzz! Buzz! Buzz! I'm coming in for a strafe: putt, putt, putt, putt, bang, bang, bang!"

James laughed. "You are an absolute goof!"

"I know. Buzz, buzz, buzz!" I was so close to him now; I was really cross-eyed. "Cunt calling Cock! Cunt calling Cock! Come in, Cock! Are you there, Cock?"

James gave me a grin spiced with an evil glint and leaned up and kissed me.

I began to flip the cock – the magisterial imperial phallic-patriarchal patronizing cock – back and forth. "Wiggle-waggle, back and forth, it is like an elastic pendulum, Master. We could construct a clock, tick-tock, tick-tock goes the cock. I wonder, Master, if you could create an astrolabe with a swinging cock. Let's see, you'd have to paint the signs of the zodiac, here, and here, and ..."

I bounced up and down on his leg. I leaned over his cock, cross-eyed. "A cock-clock! Cock, cock, cock, little cock, huge cock, monstrous cock, adorable cock, nasty cock, aggressive cock, imperious cock. A rose is a rose is a rose is a rose. Have you ever noticed, Master, how repetition takes the magic out of a word? A taboo is no longer a taboo, an icon no longer an icon, a fetish no longer a fetish. The magic fades. Meaning evaporates. The word becomes an empty puff of air. The nymphs depart. Enchantment is gone from the world!"

"Oh, giddy idiot. Oh, Gwendoline."

"A kissable cock! A lickable, likable, loveable, slurp, slurp, cock. An ice-cream-cone candy cock that comes in many flavors – chocolate, vanilla, lemon ... A candy-floss cock. A midway fairground display cock. A cock like a cock of the walk or a revolutionary cock, a tricolor French Revolution cock. A biteable cock."

"Dear Gwendoline, by my troth, your mockery is robbing a man of his inestimable mysterious glory, the last vestiges of his dignity."

"I wouldn't say that, Professor, I worship the cock and the phallus and the ground they walk upon." I squeezed the cock. I kissed the very point of it; I patted it and stroked it. "It is, indeed, a most adorable cock."

He sighed.

"And have I expatiated upon your abs, dear Professor? Breathe in, and tense up, Professor, for I am about to give a mighty speech, objectifying your tummy muscles."

"By the gods, Gwendoline ...!"

"Oh, oh, oh! Don't fuss, Master. Don't fret." I kissed his belly button.

"You are an intolerable Renaissance wench, a frivolous irreverent female!"

"And I have not even begun to lecture upon your tight little male warrior ass. Why, let me count the ways ..."

"Darling, idiot, please shut up."

I stopped, took a deep breath, and gazed at him in studious adoration. "All this time, all I wanted to do was to talk about the astrolabe. The angular motion of the sun and the stars and how people found their way about the cosmos and high seas in ancient times by measuring the movements of the moon and the sun against the constellations and the height of the North Star up there, above the horizon."

He sat up, and seized my arms, pinned them to my sides, and lifted me up, brought my face to his, and shut my mouth with a deep hard, unforgiving kiss.

"Oh, Professor," I sighed.

His hands slid down my back, and he began to sermonize: "Let me, dearest, repeat the favor. Such admirable shoulder blades sculpted in white marble, and a beautiful curved spine, even when walking barefoot, as if you were wearing the highest of high heels, or carrying a marvelous load of bananas balanced on your head, or babies bouncing upon and hanging from your breasts, and then there are the two perfect, wonderfully welcoming and elastic, dimples just in the small of your back, and then your ass, your ass is the most wonderful ass, your bum the most curvaceous impertinent bum, and your bum's undercurve is sublime, uplifting, spiritual, a curvaceous symphony, an arc of ecstasy, a –"

"Oh, Master, shut up." I stopped his mouth with a juicy slurpy kiss; I arched my body against his, curving myself tight into him, into his warmth, into his tense conquering muscles.

"You will be the death of me, Gwendoline."

"Pshaw, Master, such gallant cockamamie blarney codswallop as you spout when you get going, like an incorrigible true gallant of old. Your grandiloquence makes a girl blush, brings tears to her eyes, and reduces her to a sodden lump of soapsuds." I plunged down towards him, breathless, mouth open, ripe for another kiss.

"You know, Gwendoline, you get adorably cross-eyed when you concentrate."

"I do not!" I whispered into his mouth and gently pounded with my fists on his chest. "I do not!"

"You do so!"

"Well, maybe a little."

"A lot!"

"Well, Master, then it is because of the intensity of my worship, the fire of my passion. I just go all cock-eyed gazing upon the divine cock, on this patriarchal phallic wonder, this obelisk, this lingam, this intercontinental rocket, this guided missile, positively Biblical and Prophetic in its glory."

"Gwen, the clown! For the party next week, we shall dress you as a jester."

"That sounds peachy cream, Master. I shall be the joker in your pack." It must have been hormones or something. I exaggerated my cross-eyed look and knelt before him and looking up at him I kissed the impertinent upstanding self-righteous cock, and licked it carefully so that it shone and glistened, the skin tense and thin and translucent, as if varnished, the bluish and red veins glimmering, and the little cap at the top, a tender circumcised mushroom cloud. His cock was peaked, slick, and helmeted, like a First World War British trooper, and neat as an arrowhead. Lick, lick, I bestowed upon it my favors with my pink liquid eager tongue. "Now! Lie back, Master."

He lay down on the divan, which was firm but offered just the right amount of bounce. I straddled his hips and carefully, artfully, lowered myself down, and guided him into me. His hands – fingers masterfully spread – grasped the two cheeks of my ass. I leaned back, cantilevered myself against him, my wild bronco, and I reached for the sky, stretching my arms straight up, and crossing them like a twirling ballerina. I leaned back further, increasing the angle, and swayed with some sort of primitive inner music and heartthrob drumbeat. He was the pivot and axis of my world, the turning point upon which I moved. He levered his hips, riding me from below, his hands on my waist now, squeezing me, conquering me, and constraining me. Inside me, he seemed enormous.

Oh, the cock, the cock, the beautiful cock!

Divine cock! Oh, Phallic God!

Well, I do get carried away! Sometimes.

He was straining, squeezing my waist, forcing me back, and down, so I was leaning farther and farther backward, a tight arc of trembling, taut, female flesh. A shudder rose, rippled through my belly, and as the pressure mounted, it swept through my legs, my tummy, and my thighs, my whole body, leaning back, stretched like a sail snapped to attention by a sudden ocean breeze ... Everything went black, stars swirled, the ceiling swayed, my master cried out in a choked, strangled voice, "Oh, darling, Oh, Gwen, Oh, Gwendoline!" I shuddered. Stars shot across flashes of darkness; my loins melted, all of me was liquid, muscles dissolving. Suddenly – in a great explosive rush – I came, he came, we came ...

"Oh, oh, oh ..."

The aftershocks echoed and echoed. Each echo shaded into innumerable quivers, softening diminuendos, sensual ghostly shades of voluptuous polychromatic abandon, and utterly painful excruciating pleasure. I bent forward, brushed my breasts against his chest. My lips touched his. I kissed him. His eyes stared up – his dark laughing eyes, wrinkles at the corners, dark lashes, gold sparkles of mica in his pupils, gateways to the soul. I wondered that such perfection could exist on this earth.

We disengaged, sank down together, exhausted.

"Whew," I lay still, bathing in the luxury of it: We two were glued together, merged in our sweat, cum, saliva.

I kissed him again, and again and again.

"I could eat you up," I whispered into his ear, "I could eat you all up and not even leave the bones behind. I am a famished blood-soaked cannibal on a desert island. I am a naked savage. I want to consume you, break you. I want to have you all for me, every bit of you, and all the tiniest fragments of you. Yummy, yummy!"

He growled a low throaty growl, nuzzling my ear. "I will eat you up, you appetizing, delicious morsel. Ah, look at the nape of your neck, its delicate swan-like fragility, it begs to be bitten." His fingers began to play a tune on my vertebrae.

"You're ticking," I said.

"I am?"

"Keep going – I like it!"

This silly poetry could go on forever. My fingers played in his hair while the fingers of my other hand snuck down and played with the now limp cock, slick with liquid, no longer the cock of the walk, no longer the window-shopping dandy, the strolling all-conquering *flâneur*, but a timid, shy, retiring, satiated little hangover of a cock, about to fold up and go to sleep, maybe I should sing a lullaby.

Oh, no! I spoke too soon. It was waking up, standing up for itself, once again raring to strut its stuff. His hand was down on my Heart of Darkness, my sweet forested little valley, my infamous vulva, known around the world, the labia still wet, already newly moist, was waking from its brief slumber, and beginning, once again, to yearn ...

Whew! I lay back and stretched, feeling like a naked nymph in some voluptuous 19th Century French painting. I sighed. This continual rutting had to stop. We were two totally insane rabbits; if I hadn't been on the pill, we would have litter upon litter of bunnies or cute little piglets. Oink! Oink! Oink! Or adorable little human babies, pink all over, with round little eyes and round little toothless mouths blowing a stream of glossy little bubbles, and I would produce gallons of milk to keep them all happy – *oh, the thought of it!*

It was time for a breather.

We lay together, dazed. I rolled over, sprawled, on top of him, all my defenses down, my mind and senses utterly open – all the little sounds drifting freely in; a light, perfumed breeze coming from the terrace, the lazy rippling awning on the terrace, the gentle rustling of the terrace plants and leaves; the wail of a police or ambulance siren from far away, probably from Lungotevere which was the road that skirted along the Tiber, only a few steps away, under the dusty and mottled plane trees that lined the river's embankment, and then a church bell rang, somewhere close, a thin, tinkling echo, probably coming from across the Tiber, from some slender church tower soaring above the crowded tangle of narrow, crooked, cobblestoned streets known as Trastevere. Then there was the undefined general hushed humming sound of a great city; somebody shouted, "Fiori, Fiori!"... "Flowers, Flowers!" I lay my head on James' shoulder and closed my eyes.

I woke with a start, dazed. Where am I? Who am I? My eyes blinked. I remembered. Bits and pieces came flying back – the jigsaw puzzle of memory. I put the pieces together. I am me. I am here. I am with James. I was lying on his warm, breathing flesh, my cheek against his chest, with his arms around me. We are on the divan, in the living room. I could hear his heartbeat. His breath was even and steady, his eyes were closed; he was asleep.

Cautiously, I disentangled myself from his embrace, levered

myself up, stepped off the divan, and tiptoed, barefoot and naked, into the kitchen. I looked out at the bright sunlight, ate an apple, sat on a stool, and thought about the stars and the sun and the moon, while the coffee was brewing. I came back, carefully balancing two brimming cups of café latte. I perched next to him. I didn't make a sound. I waited.

His eyes opened, fluttering, innocent, confused, almost for a moment, it seemed, the eyes of a child; then there was the dawning light of understanding. He was once again the alert warrior male. I held out the cup of latte.

He sighed. His smile lit up the room. He took the cup and sat up. I sat down next to him. We didn't say a word. He put his arm around me, and we drank the coffee, hot steamy, and strong – double shot latte, one of my favorite things.

His fingers ran up and down the nape of my neck – just a light feathery touch, light as the breath from a kiss. We began to leaf through the *History of Astronomy* together. We discussed how the astrolabe worked. And I got out a sketchbook and drew a diagram of the thing. What interested me was how primitive humans on this little spinning planet – which for thousands of years we thought stood absolutely still at the center of the universe – how we two-legged upright little simians, wandering out of Africa, managed to go from just looking at the dazzling display of lights in the sky – the sun, moon, planets, stars – and all the mysterious changes of the seasons, and the weather, how we got to our present knowledge of the universe. What observations and thoughts led us from dazzled and awed ignorance to knowledge? How did we construct an idea of what was happening and how all those heavenly lights were related to earth and how they were related to us here on earth, to us puny little big-brained bipeds? How did we come to develop to a picture or model of the solar system, with the sun at the center and the planets in orbits circling around it? And, from there, how did we develop an idea of the universe, of galaxies, and of our own galaxy? And then how did we move on to build full-blown theories of cosmology – cosmic mechanics and then to theories of the birth of the universe in the Big Bang and knowledge of distant galaxies, and black holes, and the speed of light, and the possible existence of parallel universes, and so on ...?

"You are a curious creature, Gwendoline." said James, as I turned a page.

"And you too, I think can claim that title, Master. You are positively weird." I pressed close and allowed my body to dissolve into his. "You are deliciously weird."

That night we ate at home. I made clam spaghetti with a garlic and chili pepper and parsley sauce; James put together an arugula salad with prosciutto and figs and thick slices of parmesan.

We ate on the terrace and listened to the sounds of the city. Somebody was giving a concert in Piazza Farnese. The music came to us, distant, romantic, and muted by distance and by the maze of narrow cobblestoned streets and big old buildings.

≈

The next morning, we were still talking about cosmology while we showered and got dressed. I pulled on ragged short shorts and a T-shirt and sandals. James outfitted himself in jeans and a T-shirt and sandals. We decided we would lunch at Alfredo's.

I phoned to reserve a table on the terrace but under an umbrella, ideally, and sheltered from the sizzling sun. Alfredo assured me he would hold the very best table just for us.

I brought along the *History of Astronomy,* and we traded comments about it.

Outside on the terrace at Alfredo's, we were drinking mineral water and eating a light salad since both of us intended to work in the afternoon, and wine in the middle of the day makes me sleepy – and goofy and horny. A clear head is a marvelous thing! It was a warm sultry day, with the humidity building up towards a storm in the afternoon or evening.

"Tonight, there will be rain," James said.

"Yes," I said, "and I want to give you a very special shower with a very special massage."

"Ah," he said. "You are big on liquids, Gwendoline."

"Yes, I am." I speared a leaf of lettuce and held it up. "Oil massage, mud baths, chocolate baths, body paint, body soap, rolling in the wet or dry sand, splashing in the surf, soap suds, raindrops ..."

"Speaking of chocolate, there is a scene in a very old movie, *Sweet Movie* ..."

I inserted the lettuce in my mouth and began to munch on it. "The one where Miss Universe, the beautiful Quebec actress, Carole Laure, bathes in Swiss chocolate ... It gives me the shivers."

"Yes. You really are an encyclopedia of arcane erotic and perverse knowledge, Gwendoline. Wherever did you see that film, when did you get the time?"

I was about to blush, but I kissed him instead.

When lunch was over, and we'd paid the bill, I slipped the *History of Astronomy* into my backpack, and we decided to head home by an indirect route, taking a leisurely stroll, hand in hand, down the narrow streets, with the darkening stormy sky above, and a rising, menacing sense of electricity in the air.

We stopped to look in shop windows and to watch some kids dressed in shorts splashing each other with the water from the drinking fountain on Campo de' Fiori. The gloomy statue of Giordano Bruno loomed over them – right on the spot where he had been burned to death by the Inquisition. Each time I saw the statue, I imagined what it must have been like.

In this quiet, tense stormy afternoon, I felt cocooned. Being with James, I was living in a little bubble of safety and happiness, walking hand in hand. Any secret I had, I could share; any desire I felt, I could confess; any wandering thought that passed through my mind, I could say out loud. and he would make it his own.

I hoped he felt the same. The fear he didn't, was the one thought I didn't want to share with him. I was afraid my fear would make him afraid, and if he was afraid, he would leave me.

When we got home, we went right to work. I loved this, our home: James working at his desk, and me, just a few feet away, working at mine. It made me feel safe, safe from all the things that tear people apart, all the things that empty the meaning out of people's lives; the things that destroy everything, even love, even friendship.

CHAPTER 7 – SUPERGIRL SLEEK

Two days later, James had to go to New York. Luckily Martine was in Rome shooting a superheroine action film with Philip out at the film studios of Cinecittà. *Inferno's Revenge* was the second in a series of the *Girl Inferno* series. The first film, *Gates of Inferno*, was going to premiere in a few weeks, and they were already filming the second. Martine invited me out for lunch – and to visit the set at Cinecittà and see what they were doing.

I took the tram to the outskirts, to Cinecittà, the City of Cinema. The studios had been built by the Fascist dictator Benito Mussolini in the 1930s to promote the Italian film industry. Ever since, many famous films, hundreds of them, had been shot there.

The tram rattled its way past tall apartment blocks, desolate box-like high-rise developments from the boom years of the mid-20th Century, it went down broad empty avenues, and finally it came out onto a vast dreary-looking highway, and then I saw, not far away, the yellowish ochre walls of Cinecittà. Finally!

At the gate, a security official confirmed that I was expected. This made me feel important. A young woman said I should follow her. Inside the walls, it was like a little city, with the studio buildings set among umbrella pines and avenues running this way and that.

I met Martine on the set. It was in the famous old Studio 5, which was huge, and which was where Federico Fellini and many other famous directors had shot their films. Martine was looking super-sexy in a skin-tight lustrous black leather-and-latex super-girl catsuit, with a close-fitted ribbed black rubber bustier; it displayed her figure in the most exact and flattering way.

"I can hardly breathe." She kissed me on the cheeks. "And it's so tight and complicated. I'm not allowed to take it off when we go for breaks," she said, "Peeing is an agony of organization. And the boots and bustier are impossible to get off by myself. I'm a prisoner. I might as well be hog-tied."

"It looks cool. I'm jealous."

"Well, if you want to suffer, maybe we can cure you of your jealousy, darling." She gave me a kiss, right on the lips, and turned it into a deep, long kiss, and then drew back and looked at me and laughed. "I'll fit you out in one of these things – then you'll know what it's like! You will be my fellow prisoner."

Philip, handsome, and looking harried and disheveled, came up, smiling, shook my hand, and kissed me on both cheeks. He couldn't join us for lunch because he had a couple of production meetings, he said, but he would be delighted if I could stay around for the afternoon.

Martine and I went to the canteen. "We'll get one of these torture outfits modified for you, and we can go to the press party, like twins, with James and Philip. It will be a nice publicity stunt."

"Really! Wow!"

"Would you like that?"

"Absolutely cool. I'm dying to wear one of those things." I was beginning to get confused and was even thinking that I was some sort of superheroine starlet, well, in a way, in a very ephemeral way, I guess I was – I was Martine Aubin's dark shadow, her other side.

≈

The press party for *Gates of Inferno*, the first film in the series, was a few days hence. I went for a fitting in the studio. They had several copies of Martine's outfit for Martine's doubles and in case of accidents. The design was very similar to that worn by luscious Kate Beckinsale in the *Underworld* films – and, boy, was it tight; but it was certainly cute.

"Your derriere is divine," said the fitter, as she patted said latex-wrapped derriere and polished it with some sort of liquid spray.

"Really?"

"Absolutely."

I stood up and looked at myself in the mirror. So, there I was, outfitted as a girl warrior. It was dangerously sexy. I like disguises and make-believe, and this costume was intoxicating. I strutted around. The boots made a creaking and a clip-clop sound. I was a futuristic superheroine warrior. Every tendon and muscle of my body had been reinforced and morphed and sharply defined.

It's amazing how the uniform transforms – and creates – the man or the girl. Slip me into something diaphanous, and I would just float around, liquid and fluid and lascivious. Outfit me in a suit of armor, and I will slay a dragon! Fit me up in woolly khaki, wrap-around puttees, studded leather boots, and a Tommy's steel helmet, and I'd crouch in a muddy trench, shoulder a Lee-Enfield, and start shooting away. Now, sleek in leather, I was all tense muscle, eager to fight! I was ready to pull my scimitar out of its scabbard and smite all the villains and vampires and aliens and zombies in the whole wide world! What is that old expression, "The habit makes the monk"? Well, the uniform makes the soldier.

The day came for a press party and presentation. The first film in the *Inferno* series was about to be released in Paris, London,

New York, Berlin, Rome, and Moscow, as well as Tokyo and Shanghai.

James was back from New York and was delighted by this little bit of show business. He was in the audience, watching, when Martine made an entrance onto the stage of the Press Center with her leading man on one side and me on the other, which was sort of interesting and made me wonder.

What am I doing here?

The photographers were shooting like crazy, and the video cameras were whirring. Martine was being interviewed in three or four languages. I stood there, next to her, feeling like a dummy, a stage prop; my eyes were getting wet. If another minute went by, I might even blush. I was totally irrelevant.

I was about to move away, and move off stage, when Martine tightened her grip on my arm, turned to me, and kissed me and hugged me, and announced, "And you all know my very special friend, the mathematician – the *famous* mathematician – Doctor Gwendoline Clermont. She was Philip's inspiration when he was writing the script. Gwen is a math and science prodigy, and she's also a real devil and an acrobat, and so she was the model for Sabrina."

Suddenly people were interviewing me. Video cameras, film cameras, and cameras were flashing and concentrating on the two of us. People remarked on the contrast – Martine blonde, buff, and tanned, and me, jet-black hair, and vampire-pale, chalk-white skin, Martine with sparkling blue eyes, all sunny clarity and sweet reason, and me with demonically dark eyes, like the gates to paradise or hell, or, as one of the journalists put it, "like the *Gates of Inferno*."

Philip stepped forward. "Gwen has been essential to this project. The character as you know has extraordinary mental abilities, like Gwen, and Martine had learned a great deal sharpening her wits with Gwen who, as Martine said, is a world-class mathematician, among other things, she teaches at Cambridge and lectures at Columbia and at the University of Paris, and at the *École de Guerre*. So, we thought it would be fun to have Martine and Gwen both dressed up as Sabrina, who, as you know, in the plot is a brilliant mathematician. Her talents expose her to extreme and present danger, so she is forced – against her will – to become a superheroine. So, as I said, Gwen, in several important ways, served as a model for Sabrina."

I whispered to Martine, "Is that true?"

"Yes, darling, I'm a vampire, I have been secretly sucking ideas out of your bones and marrow and blood, and so has Philip. When he was writing the screenplay, he and I were observing you carefully, your tics, your habit of lecturing, the way you lick your lips when you are eager, the way you narrow your eyes when you are thinking or about to say something serious, the way you put your hands on your hips and stick out your chin when you are about to lose your temper."

"I never lose my temper!"

"Sometimes you almost do – but you always pull back, just in time. I can see the emotion boiling."

"Really?"

"Yes. And remember when Madam Nicole dressed us up, and we went to Alfredo's, and then we went on – sort of naked more or less – to the Lesbian Bar."

"That's when we met."

"And that was the precise moment Philip had the idea of a sort of super-sexy prodigal superwoman nerd – so you were the origin of the whole *Inferno* series."

"Gosh!"

≈

"Did you know they modeled Sabrina on me?" I asked James.

"No. But I did suspect something. Philip kept asking me about your intellectual interests – your curiosity, why you seem to be an encyclopedia, how you seemed to know everything about everything, and how, sometimes you turn into a –"

"How I turn into a nerd, geek? An utterly boring bluestocking pedant?" I leaned up and kissed him. It felt like a very sexy gesture in my superwoman costume. The boots were virile. The leather was tight, and with my every move, it squeaked.

"I was about to say how you are admirably informed and informative," James said, and put his arm around my shoulders.

≈

Then, we were at a cocktail with all the film folk, a crew party, after which we were to go to Alfredo's, still in costume, where a table had been reserved on the terrace.

I didn't think I could eat very much squeezed as I was into this rubber and synthetic leather costume, with the tightly laced armored bustier, but it was sort of fun to stomp about looking like I could easily kill anybody. There were instructions on how to get me out of it, which James had to study. He would be the engineer in charge of the delicate operation of extracting me later that night.

Photographers got the usual shots of us arriving; then, we were able to settle down and eat. "To us," Martine raised a toast, and we all drank, "To us!"

Martine said that she thought that she and I should soon do something spectacular together; several rather risqué charity balls and dinners and performances were coming up in Paris; it would be nice if James and I were in Paris – and we might well be – if we could take part. "I want something particularly spicy," Martine said, "And very, very dramatic – spectacular and indecent."

I was quite happy to strut around in the skin-tight superheroine costume; it made me feel like a sexy metallic robot or an alien warrior from some distant galaxy. "It suits you," Alfredo said, when I went in, with Martine, to get some antipasto.

He insisted that the two of us step briefly into the kitchen so the cooks could get a look. They were mostly Egyptian, very sweet, though frantically busy, but they were nice enough to take the time to give us a quick ovation and cheers, plus a few appreciative comments, ogles, and winks.

CHAPTER 8 – OBJECT OF DESIRE

After the *Gates of Inferno* interlude, things settled down. James and I went back to our routine of working all day and playing at night.

Late one evening, with a storm roaring outside, and when our workday was winding down, we went out onto the terrace and sat down on the deckchairs under the awning.

The awning was flapping wildly, the storm was roaring around us, and the rain swept down only a few feet away.

"Did I ever tell you how much I like your shoulder blades?"

"No, James, I believe you never did, not in the last five minutes, at least."

He lifted off my T-shirt, leaving me in ragged shorts, and he began kissing my shoulder blades, a whole series of sliding little nibbling caresses and kisses.

I was getting a lot of worshipful attention these days. It made me nervous. Was James falling in love again, too much in love? Was he becoming obsessed? Would he panic, as he had before, and suddenly bolt and run, fearful as always of love, of permanence, or that horrible thing we women call "commitment"?

I steeled myself for the inevitable.

I had decided to stow away my worries and put my fears aside and plunge into each moment and taste it to the full.

Carpe diem. Seize the day. Live in the instant; the only eternity there is, is *now*; the only life we have is *now*!

I recited a litany of slogans of impermanence. I would submit to the drift of events; I would go with the flow; I would allow destiny to take its course; I would be easy, oh, so easy; I would abandon all pretense of control, all priorities, and planning; I would allow myself to be an utter slave to my master's caprices – though, in truth, his caprices so neatly matched my own, and he was so careful of my feelings and so attentive to my desires, that such slavery was pure expansive pleasure. They were really *our* caprices, *our* fantasies.

Yes, I loved playing the servant, the cabin boy, the girl in chains, the woman held down on a bed or on a mattress on a terrace under the pounding rain and under the weight and energy and thrust of my master's body. But I also loved being the boss, being the master, and the mistress! I loved sitting astride him and bending his will and his body to my every whim. So, right now, at this particular moment in the onward rush of the universe, I felt I needed to take the initiative. "Now, dear James, dear Master, you need a massage."

"You think so?" He blinked at me.

"Yes, I do."

"Well, then ..."

"No, clothes, man, I want you naked." I stood up, hands on my hips, my most imperious pose.

His lips curled in a thin smile. But he obliged. Off went the T-shirt, the jeans, the underpants, the sandals, and there he was – the thing itself, bare naked man. "Ah, my Princess," he sighed, "you are too good to me."

"I aim to give good value, Master. I shall change, and I shall return." I disappeared into the bedroom, peeled off my shorts, but left my underpants, an austere, tiny, black almost non-existent string thing. I picked up a bottle of creamy oil, specially concocted for the most heavenly of intimate massages, or so it said on the label.

When I returned, my master was standing, looking out at the rain, naked, and he turned towards me, one eyebrow raised, a neat, patriarchal quizzical expression.

"Lie down, there, Master, on your sacred patriarchal tummy, if you please."

"Of course." He lay down on his stomach on the flat mattress, where I had laid it out sheltered under the awning. Just a few feet away, the rain continued to thunder down.

I slipped out of my panties and poured the creamy oil into my hands. "Have I ever told you, Master, how much I adore your ass? You have the most spectacular butt."

"No, darling, you have not told me in so many words. You have hinted, of course, and once you began to make a very flowery speech to that effect, but ..."

I slapped him on the butt, plopped down a huge gob of oil and spread it, and massaged his butt carefully, thoroughly; then, I climbed onto him, and smoothed the oil on his back. "I must count the ways in which you are perfect, Master, a perfect object of contemplation and adoration. Your shoulder blades are exquisite, and I tremble with pleasure when I think how broad your shoulders are, and the way your back tapers to a very fine and thin and trim and extremely masculine waist gives me the little-girl shivers." I leaned forward, the tips of my breasts brushing his oily back. I swayed against him. I kissed him on the nape of his neck. "And your neck! What can I say about the nape of your neck! It is sublime, James, truly sublime!"

"You are objectifying me, Gwen."

"Why, yes, I suppose I am!"

"You are a total goofball, Gwendoline, but ..." His voice trailed

127

off sleepily as if I were lulling him into dreamland. I kneaded his shoulder muscles. I slapped his bum. I rode him as if he were my captive stallion and I his heroic Amazon rider.

My master dozed off. I rode him, warm and wet with desire, I held him tight between my thighs; I pressed myself down into the small of his back. He growled. He stirred. "I can feel your warmth," he mumbled into the mattress. "I can feel the wet hot heart of you, Gwen, the damp, wet, hot, yearning heart of you." His voice trailed off; he was half asleep.

I stroked him and massaged him and slithered my body back and forth over his back.

Ah, ah! That got his attention!

He woke up. "Lie on your belly, Goddess," he commanded, turning over, sitting up, and kissing me on the lips.

"Really, Master?" I had the bottle of oil in my hands.

"Really! Down you go!" He took the bottle from me.

"I am your humble servant, Master." I lay on my belly. He soaked me in oil, and he began to cover me with caresses; then he began to massage my muscles and tendons, and he went on and on, until he had touched every inch of me, every millimeter, inside and out, every curve, every fold, every surface, and every orifice.

"Turn over, Princess."

I groaned and turned over and lay on my back, looking up at him through wet lashes and dazed eyes.

Again, he detailed each feature of my body, in a soft, whispered, feathery voice, which was more than soothing. He massaged every aspect and facet of me. It was exciting and dreamily soporific. I was dozing off, drifting into dreamland, and, at the same time, I was aroused and eager to leap up and grab him and carry him down with me and into me. I was half in a dream-like state, and I was, equally, utterly aroused. How confusing! Oh, well ...

The massage session ended with both of us soaked, covered in glittery dripping oil. I felt like a Greek salad sloppily drenched in extra virgin. But James was not going to stop. The kisses came thick and fast. And extra massages. "Lie back, wench," he said.

I lay back and stared up at him and above his head at the striped white and blue awning, which was rippling under the pounding impact of the rain. I'd almost forgotten about the rain, though it was coming down heavier than ever, a glittering silver wall, just a few feet away from us.

James had decided that my vagina and my mons pubis and my clitoris needed a delicate multi-facetted many-sided feathery back and forth up and down and sideways type of ecstatic slow-and-fast motion massage and which involved his index finger and his little finger and the palm of his hand and then his tongue, so and it began to build, and build ...

"You are being quite intimate, Master," I gulped, trying to put on a dignified face and control my panting, the deepening huskiness of my voice, and the flood of saliva that had filled my mouth and was dribbling out of one corner. I think, given the circumstances, that I did quite a good job.

"Really?" he glanced up at me, and then disappeared between my legs, back to work, his tongue darting, hither and thither, truly a busy little bee, harvesting honey here, there, and everywhere.

"Really ..." I sobbed, in a choked desperate voice, "Very extremely intimate, oh, oh, oh ... Master, Master, Pity, Master ..."

"Ah," he said, looking up from between my thighs, "Well, then, you had better help me."

"Help you?" I sighed. I was choking, panting with a suspended avalanche of passion that just needed the slightest touch to rush down the slope and engulf me and carry away everything in its path.

"Yes, darling," he went back to task in hand, ducking between my thighs, "Would you mind, awfully, darling, if it's not too much bother, caressing your breasts, the tips, the nipples, both of them, squeeze them, twist, caress them, that would be awfully nice of you."

"Oh, my God! Yes, Master!" I tried to lick back the flooding drool of saliva dribbling from my chin, "I think I might just manage to do that." I began to squeeze and twist my nipples; both were tense, engorged, shamelessly straining, and oh so totally erect. Oh, the traitors! They instantly reveal all. They are utterly without stoicism or honor. "Ah, ah, ah!" I groaned. I wanted to scold the two of them: They had no self-control, absolutely no self-control. All flags flying, all passions manifest – they might as well be lacquered in glowing scarlet, the rascals! My own touch seemed to act like an extra electric shock.

It was strange. I was totally trapped in wild desire, in bodily sensation, but I was adrift too: I could see myself, caressing my breasts, twisting my nipples, but it felt as if they were James' hands, my master's hands, or Martine's hands, or Kate's, or an amalgam of Kate and Martine, and, in this folly, this craziness, there was my master, James, the real James, his tongue and his hands leading me, dancing me along the razor edge. I was in a state of utter abandon, even the humiliation of me caressing my breasts in front of James. It was as if I were on a stage masturbating in front of him ...

Oh, oh, oh! I was on a stage, performing, and I was out there somewhere, beyond the footlights, beyond myself, out there in the audience. And, also, in the audience were my master, James, Martine, Kate, Philip, and ...

The gaze of the "Other," male or female, is an explosive thing.

Objectification, exposure, shame!!

Oh, oh, oh!!

I came ...

It was a shuddering rippling, oh, oh, oh, tidal wave, rushing up and down my body, echoing in every muscle and nerve and tendon, and only slowly did it finally subside. I was exhausted. James peeked up from between my legs, he was watching me.

"You bastard ..." I muttered, "You lovely cruel, loving vain, beautiful, patriarchal, phallic, narcissist bastard."

He smiled, pulling himself away slightly. "Now, darling, I want you to do it to yourself, entirely you, just you, nothing but you."

"Really, Master?" I was still trembling. I sighed and raised an eyebrow. "You mean do-it-yourself masturbate, Master, an exclusive onanistic performance, in front of you, all greased up and dripping with oil, and exhausted and burnt out and in ecstasy and totally humiliated from what has just happened?"

I hiccupped.

"Yes," he said, "Just you, entirely you."

I hiccupped again.

I was hiccupping, soaked, limp as a rag, and shaking. "I am not sure if I can, Master." I was lying flat on my back. I was under the illusion I was no longer in the mood. All passion was, in a sense, spent. A girl can only manage so much in a single stormy afternoon.

"I shall get us two glasses of wine. I think that will help." He stood up, glittering in oil. And, like an ancient god of gold, he padded off, barefoot and naked, toward the kitchen and refrigerator. I was alone on the terrace, sheltered by the awning that was still being pounded by the deluge

The hot rain poured down.

Gusts of warm wet air bathed me.

I hiccupped. I burped. I was as limp and discombobulated as a soggy noodle.

Lightning flashed, illuminating in a flare of bluish light, the vases, the plants, the deckchairs and garden table, the awning, statues along the balustrade.

Thunder rolled in, a slow, inexorable drumbeat tide, shaking everything; it was greater than anything human. I dissolved into humble awe before the unleashed force of nature.

I lay on my back in the clammy damp heat on the mattress only a few feet from the pounding silver curtain of rain, and I thought: *Hmm. I think I can, I think I can, I think I can ...*

Yes, I think I can, I think I can ... I'm a little red train, chugging along, determined to get up that damned hill.

I think I can, I think I can ...

I touched the nipples, lightly, just a little fingertip caress. Oh, yes, they were alert as ever. They had been eavesdropping, the scallywags! They had minds of their own and were excited by the idea of self-exhibition and more do-it-yourself tactile stimulus. I caressed my breasts, a lazy, circular motion. They seemed quite bouncy and full, as if they too had increased in volume. Was this possible? Had I been fed hormones? Had James put something in my drinks? Surely, I wasn't pregnant? On that point, I was exceedingly careful ...

James was crouching beside me.

Where had he come from?

He handed me a glass of wine.

It was an unbreakable plastic glass.

"I see we are being cautious with the glasses, Master," I slurred, drooling, spilling the words. My attempts at cool irony were feeble and fading.

Dreamily, as if drugged, staring into space, I twirled and twisted one nipple. Currents of electric desire, lineaments of lust, of self-lust, mixed with James's lust, Martine's lust, and Kate's lust, and the whole history of my own lust, all rose to the surface. The roaring current raced and bubbled and swirled along my belly and down my thighs.

Every fiber of my being was trembling. But I did manage to take a sip of wine from the glass James held out.

I spilled some of course, and of course, he licked it from my lips and from my chin and my shoulder. He bent low and kneeling over me, he touched my labia with his lips, caressed with the very tip of his tongue, the clitoris, which seemed to have awakened from its short slumber, like the girl in the fairy tale who only needed the touch of the lips of her princely lover to spring into action, wake up, and say, eagerly, sweetly, "What's next, my Prince!?"

"Now, Gwen, you mustn't neglect your clitoris," my Master said, withdrawing from me – and leaving me, for an instant, on my own, while he hovered less than a foot away, looking down on me like a torturer, like a lover, like a god.

I moved my hand down my belly over the smooth, gentle swelling – which gesture suddenly caused the bizarre idea that I would like to be pregnant to spring into my head; it was an instantaneous epiphany, which I had never had before; I had a vision, a truly mystical vision: me with an immense billowing belly, sailing on the wind, like Titania, Queen of the Fairies in *A Midsummer Night's Dream*.

The idea was violent, inebriating. I was breathless, dizzy, at the thought of me, big-bellied, a fully laden Spanish galleon, all sails billowing, plowing through the stormy sea, heavily freighted with new life, twins or triplets perhaps, sustaining new life, and my breasts suddenly mightily ponderous with milk; and now I was being suckled by some marvelous baby, no, by two marvelous babies, hanging, both of them, avid little creatures, their warm wet toothless mouths slurping away and clinging and grasping my flesh, and me on all fours like a she-wolf, suckling my very own Romulus and Remus! Gghhhr!

Oh, Oh, Oh, Yes, Yes, Yes! I began to caress myself. I imagined my Master was doing it. He stroked my side. He touched the one nipple I was neglecting. He squeezed it. I squeezed and twisted the clitoris. He caressed the nipple lightly, playfully teasingly, and I caressed the clitoris, light, feathery, teasing. He twisted his fingers around the nipple, and I twisted my fingers around the clitoris with a delicate touch, as he directed me, our gestures in counterpoint, part of one rhythm, perfectly coordinated and complementary. He delicately twisted the nipple, as if the nipple were the steering wheel, and then, when he began to stroke my ribs, and move up and down my sides, I caressed and pinched the labia, and they burst with life and eagerness, famished, starving, yearning; they wanted to suck me in, they wanted to totally possess me.

I imagined that I – my hand, my body – that I had become the dreadful patriarchal masculine cock, that I, the cock, was going to be sucked in, eaten up, consumed and possessed by the hungry, famished voracious vagina, origin of all things, origin of the world, from which all human life springs. Then, when my master suddenly went back to the nipple, and his finger twisted it, I returned to the clitoris. I squeezed and twisted it, and I raced across it, strumming with quick feathery strokes like the stings of a wild gypsy guitar. Oh, my God ...

I came, and I came, and I came, under the eyes of my master, obeying his directions. He was the director. I was a puppet, a doll, a slave, an exhibit in a sex show on rue St. Denis in Paris, a traveling carnival freak, a ...

Boom!

It was an explosion – an explosion of wetness, of stars in my eyes, of sudden blackness. For an instant, I was blind. Then there were stars. Then I could see – I was not blind after all.

My body arched up, a tense violin string, vibrating with some divine melody. Oh, God, Oh, Love, Oh God! Oh God! Slowly, slowly, it ebbed.

"Oh, boy, Oh, Master," I breathed. The waves of excitement exploded, exploded, exploded, and then, slowly, began to recede;

the tide ebbed, riptide, backways, swaying waters, up and down, up and down. I closed, then I opened my eyes. Sounds came back. The world came back. A wall of rain poured down just a few feet away.

Suddenly, my master was on top of me. His lips were on mine. He plunged like a sword into me. No warning, no words, not a glance, not a touch. I held onto him, I desperately grasped him. I pulled him deeper and deeper into me, close to me, and, as we were both still covered in oil, we were glued together, we were sticky, vacuum-sealed, one divine package, one being. My orgasm had hardly subsided, and now it began again. Is such a thing possible?

Oh, wonder of wonders. I was lifted on a rising tide of excitement. I shuddered and I came in the same instant. My master came too, and together we shuddered, and we both cried out, shaking, trembling, in convulsions. We were in an agony of pleasure that peaked into pain.

Just a few feet away, the rain poured down. Suddenly there was a great blinding flash of lightning. The thunder rippled through us. My master lay half on me, half off. His breath was ragged; he sighed, "Oh, darling, oh darling Gwendoline, oh darling."

"Yes, darling Master" I caressed his hair, my fingers exploring and separating the thick dark strands. I felt I was comforting a child. I was happy. I was delirious. I had become the Earth Mother, the Mother Goddess, fertile, and fecund, broken up and scattered to the four winds, pollen and spores and tumbling leaves, my seeds cast everywhere. I felt as if I had already been pregnant, fertile and rotund as a goddess, and had given birth to a litter of my very own delicious hungry divine little piglets or brave furry little wolf-cubs that sucked and suckled.

I lay splayed out, my nakedness open to the world, my eyes half-closed, the light of the terrace lamps filtering between my eyelashes in vague rainbow flickering patterns; the rain drumming on the awning, which smelled of fresh wet canvas; and the deluge, splashing, pounding on the terrace, on the plants, and on the deckchairs making a violent melody as if the whole world were being flooded with sensation, feeling, and touch. Every inch of my skin was being drummed upon, a patterned tattoo of divine music.

I swallowed. I drew a deep breath. "I'm not so sure that was entirely dignified on my part, Master, being supine, naked, face exposed, oily, rutting wild and bestial like that, wide open, offering myself, in onanistic ecstasy, as a sacrifice to your objectifying masterful phallic-patriarchal male gaze. What do you think?"

"I think, Gwen, that you were sublime – a pagan goddess returned from ancient times."

"Well, it *was* exciting, that's true." I blinked at the awning and turned my head to look at the rain. Silver-gray sheets of water obliterated everything. I ran my hand over my tummy. It was gluey with oil, slick with sweat, lathered in cum. I had been painted over with passion. "James, tonight, we will need a great deal of soap."

"Yes, my darling, we will."

Neither of us moved.

We lay there and the rain – just out of reach – redoubled in fury.

CHAPTER 9 – FEAR

The next few days were uneventful and exquisitely serene in that particularly splendid Roman way: blue skies and warm sun – with only a few little clouds looming on the horizon. Those clouds concerned my work and James's business – and, also, Kate.

I was afraid.

I was afraid for James and Kate.

Kate was in West Africa. The situation was more and more alarming: the new version of the Ebola virus was spreading through jungle villages and out onto the semi-arid savannah and the Sahel; and at the same time the fanatical religious group – so-called Jihadi Warriors for the Caliphate – was spreading its tentacles westwards towards the plague zone.

What would happen, I wondered, when the jihadi chaos and tyranny met the plague? And what would happen if the jihadi attacked the United Nations medical outposts? What would happen to Kate?

Kate's research and hospital facility were right in the path of both the spreading plague and the jihadi rebels rumbling forward in their SUVs and Toyota Land Cruisers and pickup trucks.

To keep my eye on things, I subscribed to various specialized sites and blogs which were tracing developments; and I hacked into some intelligent nets and some of the jihadi sites and added automatic translation apps and programs so that I would be able to read what they were saying.

I used my crime-network analysis program, which is like a program to trace the spread of diseases, to make a series of predictions about the spread of both. This would be only very rough – and totally hypothetical – because I didn't have access to enough on-the-ground real-time information. Probably nobody did, though drones and satellites were keeping tabs on the jihadi advance, and, super-hacker that I am, I was able to piggyback or hack into the information flowing from some of those.

I was worried about James too. He was interested in buying a company that had cutting edge biological and electronic capabilities. Some of these technologies could be used as weaponry. As we knew, one company in the Czech Republic was also being targeted – as I was able once again to confirm – by a Russian arms dealer and drug- and people-smuggler Sergei Platonov. I began to trace Platonov's networks, superimposing all the grids and information I could find, to see who Platonov associated with, where, and how. There had been other murders of people involved with the company – Martin Stern, the brave investigative journalist, was not the only victim.

While we worked, James and I were like a normal couple. I sweated away at my computer – or scribbled equations and ideas on endless reams of lined yellow notepaper – and James, aside from his outside business appointments, toiled at his computer.

He was often on the phone or in conference calls and would walk up and down, talking on his cellphone, in shorts or jeans or with a towel wrapped around his midriff, sometimes wandering out onto the terrace in the sunlight to catch the light breeze that came from the hills and the sea and refreshed the Roman afternoon or early evening.

With James close, I felt safe and totally comfortable. When

I got antsy from sitting too long at my computer, I'd kiss him and go out and work at one of the little cafés on Campo de' Fiori. Sometimes James would join me and bring a book or newspapers or reports he had to read and his smartphone – his office was wherever he was – along with his base in New York with Allison keeping tabs – and sit with me while I toiled away writing, calculating, inventing different methods of separating out "noise" and "static" from real "information."

James would put his hand on my knee; I'd look up and let my mind drift; I'd study the pigeons, the changing light, the fruit and vegetable vendors, the passers-by, and the constant relaxing buzz.

Campo de' Fiori – The Field of Flowers – is almost always busy. In the morning, it has the fruit and vegetable market; by about two in the afternoon, the market stalls are folded up, the cobblestones are swept and hosed down, and it becomes just a square with the statue of Giordano Bruno, and some fountains, a metal drinking fountain, kids hanging around, teenagers hooking up, and, along the edge of the Campo, lots of cafés, wine bars, restaurants, and shops.

Many of the little streets and alleyways near the Campo are named for different medieval, and ancient crafts and trades – the comb-makers, the cross-bow makers, the jacket-makers, the hat-makers, and the key-makers – and the Campo itself still has a sense of the medieval about it, and of the Renaissance, with the beautiful Renaissance places set down, here and there, in odd haphazard places, with fountains, and monuments, amidst the higgledy-piggledy little medieval streets, and, sticking up here and there, are 2000-year-old bits of Ancient Rome. At one end of the Campo, there is a weird high irregular building; it was built on the remains of Pompey's Theater, which was opened in 55 BC; Pompey was a Roman general and rival of Julius Caesar; and, a few steps away, is the place where, a little over ten years after the theater opened, Julius Caesar was stabbed to death, on 15 March 44 BCE.

Often, early in the morning – if we were up early – James and I would shop in the Campo, drink an espresso or latte at the corner café, and then come back to the flat and work.

James liked to cook lunch and sometimes dinner. If he cooked, I did the dishes, and he dried them. If I cooked, he did the dishes, but I liked drying them. It wasn't often that we used the dishwasher, though it was always there, waiting, brand-new and state-of-the-art.

Still, amid all this reassuring domesticity, I did worry about James and his projects as I traced the overlapping criminal and corruption networks in Eastern Europe and in Russia and the Middle East.

I routinely hacked into and followed a great many sites and blogs and monitored traffic in various directions. I had a lot of automatic alarms set that would warn me when there was action.

And, while sitting, at my computer, naked as James liked me to be, and now waxed to total nudity since it was high summer and I liked the breezy naked feel, I delved deep into the murky world of half-legitimate holding companies and totally illegitimate and invisible holding companies; and I came upon something.

I glanced over at James. He was reading some annual reports and skimming the news with his iPad. I felt the patina of sweat on my skin, desire, a suppressed ripple of erotic excitement, and I felt fear, I sensed danger. As I went deeper into the murky networks, I found something I didn't like, something I most definitely didn't like.

"James?

"Yes?

"You know that high-tech Czech biotechnology company, Czech Synthesis Futures, you want to buy?"

"Yes, very talented group, just outside Prague,. They have some key patents, strategic assets. I'm not sure they realize how strategic."

"Well, as we suspected, there are other people interested in purchasing that company – and they already have some shares."

"Oh."

"Look."

He came over and glanced at the screen.

"They have bought 15% through a cover company." I pointed.

"What's that symbol – who are they?" James pointed at clusters of letters on the screen.

"I have my own symbols. This one is for the Russian-Georgian Mafia. I think that the Russian-Georgian Mafia, the Vladimir Clan, now run by that guy, Sergei Platonov, are the ones behind Swiss Synergy Enterprises, the SSE symbol, here. I'm not 100% sure, but, say 99 % sure. Swiss Synergy Enterprises has acquired 15% of the Czech company. And, if you look here, on this flow chart I've set up, you can see the Swiss Synergy Enterprises shareholders – these little red boxes; they are based in Cyprus, and they are proxies for a thing called Moscow Trading Ventures, that's this big box MTV symbol here, which is based in Saint Petersburg, and MTV is owned by this big green box here, Asia Trade Link, ATL, here; and these little violet boxes are legal firms based in Mumbai, Toronto, Vancouver, London, and Cape Town, and they own Asia Trade Link, and they are, essentially, the whole chain of shadow companies, fronts for the Russian-Georgian Vladimir Clan, for Sergei Platonov, post-office drops more or less. All the individuals are relatives – uncles, cousins, lovers – of the treasurer and boss of the Vladimir Clan, our old friend, Sergei Platonov. These are dangerous people. You remember the Oblomov case? And then there is the Martin Stern murder – and a few others."

"You worry too much." He put his hands on my shoulders and massaged. "I noticed you were grinding your teeth in your sleep last night."

"I was?"

"Yes. You were lying on your back, growling and grinding your teeth. You'd tossed aside the covers and were lying face up like a statue of white marble in the moonlight, the steel-blue shadows sculpting your body, just so – shoulders, breasts, belly, and hips, shimmering in ghostly blue light. And you were going, *Grrhh, Grrhh, Grrhh*. It was sexy and sweet. I was tempted to wake you, make love to you, quiet you down, comfort you, and tame you, and then insist you wear a bridle and a bit."

"Hmm." I kissed him and growled.

"Tension?" He was still massaging my shoulders. "Still worried?"

"Yes." I frowned. "Yes, I am worried – I'm worried about you. I was wondering when to tell you about my suspicions – so this morning, I checked them out, and I'm pretty sure I'm right. The same group kidnapped Ivan Oblomov and killed him – remember. He was trying to corner the Moscow meat market. They cut him into little pieces, while he was still alive, and fed him to pigs in a stall in the Caucasus. Their sense of poetic justice, I guess."

"And then the pigs went to market in Moscow, I imagine."

"I guess so. The poor pigs! But this is serious, James."

"I'm sure it is." He kept massaging my shoulders, kneading deeper and deeper.

"Sergei Platonov is no laughing matter. He almost certainly arranged the Stern assassination and a few others."

"I know that."

"He also likes to torture women – particularly women with tattoos."

"He doesn't like tattoos?"

"No, he loves tattoos. It's a fetish with him. He sometimes has his victims tattooed before he kills them."

"Oh. Does he tattoo himself?"

"No, he doesn't, but for his victims, he apparently hires the best artists – full-body tattoos. He's a connoisseur."

"Gwen, your arcane knowledge is wondrous. I am in awe."

"This is serious, Master!"

"I'm glad you have told me of your fears, darling." He bent down and kissed the nape of my neck, stirring all the little tendrils. "One of the reasons I wanted to buy Czech Synthesis Futures – CSF – was to get it out of the hands of raiders like Moscow Trading Ventures and Sergei Platonov. I didn't realize they'd already acquired some shares. I'll have to move quickly. I'm pretty certain Moscow Trading Ventures – and Platonov – also have links to terrorist organizations."

"Yes," I sighed. "There's that too – and they have links to some intelligence services as well – the ones that have connections with their supposed enemies."

"Yes." He was pressing down on my shoulders, kneading the tension out of my muscles. "And some of the Czech research could have military or terrorist applications – particularly bio-weapons."

"Yes, I figured that out. You'll be careful." I reached up and put my hands on his hands, "Promise!"

"Yes. I promise. I'll be extra careful."

"Good. I'm going to monitor this. I can hack into most of these communications lines."

"Why did I fall in love with a girl genius?" He knelt beside me and kissed me and kissed my shoulder, and my breasts, warm nuzzling little kisses, almost feline.

"Hmm," I said. I was beginning to feel aroused. Being in the same room with him, and being naked on command, kept me, always, on the trigger edge. Excitement was only a touch away. Somehow though, it didn't destroy my concentration; it provided mysterious extra energy. James was all the danger I needed, and with his presence – and the guarantee of adventure – came a sense of serenity. Then I thought: "*Love!*" OMG! He had used the word *love*! He said, "*fall in love.*" It made me nervous. *Love*, he had used the word love! *Love* – the thing he feared most in the whole wide world!

CHAPTER 10 – DISPLAYED

Later that day, I emailed the draft of my latest article to my supervising committee. There were members in Oxford, Cambridge, and MIT, plus an advisor at the University of Paris, and a specialist in Berlin. Professor Ho Chan Lee – who had introduced me at the fellowship speech in New York – where I had shown my naughty naked and fetish photographs – was in Shanghai on sabbatical and not officially on the committee but I sent him a copy since he had followed my work and inspired some of what I was doing.

I waited to see what they thought.

I knew within two days.

The results were satisfying. Everybody approved of the article. A few had suggestions. Professor Ho Chan Lee pointed out some extra literature I might refer to, and proposed I put in an extra paragraph on one of the aspects I had barely touched on, just alluded to. "I think you could make an extra real and original contribution here, Gwen. Just push a few of those concepts and equations further, and you'll open a whole new field of exploration." It was a good idea, and so I did it. And then, after three or four careful proofreadings, I sent it to the *International Journal of Mathematical Discovery*. The answer came back immediately: "We have been looking forward to this paper, we have seen it in draft; our committee has accepted it and is eager to see it published."

"We should celebrate," James said.

"Celebrate? Celebrate what?"

"Your upcoming *International Journal Mathematical Discovery* article. That is a great honor. Philip is in Paris, but Martine is in Rome and alone. Maybe she can join us."

"That's a great idea," I stood up and threw my arms around him and hugged him and kissed him. Martine had told me she was in town, but she had been out at Cinecittà and busy with fittings and rehearsals, and I had been busy with my article; until now, we had not had time to get together.

≈

So, that evening we were to celebrate. I had been out shopping and working at a shaded table on the terrace of a café on Campo de' Fiori, and had just come back, a bit sweaty and dusty and a bit greasy from a drippy over-ambitious hamburger I had grabbed on the Campo at one of the wine bars and eaten, carelessly, while reading a book and not watching where the fat drips were going, which was mainly down my chin and T-shirt and onto the crotch of my shorts.

"Welcome, famous goddess," James said, "Now we must get ready for tonight's celebration, but first ..." He paused and favored me with an imperious and knowing look.

"First, Master, what is first?"

"First, we shower, and you strip naked as you always do when great events are portending. I have a surprise for you."

"A surprise? Oh, dear! Oh, well, yes, Master." I put the groceries and my laptop down. I stowed the fruit in the refrigerator and in the fruit bowl. I wondered what the surprise would be – something truly shameful and utterly degrading, undoubtedly.

We showered. It was a comforting all-over, extremely intimate, totally relaxed, two-person shower, with a little iced dry vodka martini – in plastic glasses – added, to give the hot steamy downpour extra spice and sharpen the senses, as we soaped each other and explored the nooks and crannies and wonders and promises of each other's bodies.

I stepped out of the shower feeling extra alive.

James insisted on toweling me down. He took his time; he was gentle and thorough. Each stroke of the towel was a caress; he interspersed the toweling with kisses and ended it up with one long lingering embrace, our two naked bodies pressed against each other.

"Now, while you dress me, you, Gwen, you, Goddess, remain naked."

"Absolutely, Master." I wondered what was coming next. Marvels in this household never cease, which was a delight for a curious kinky little person such as I.

I was keyed up in the nicest dreamiest of ways, every pore a sparkle of sensation – and anticipation. It had been a creative day. I'd done a lot of work sitting in the Campo, and I'd watched people go by, a pleasure in itself, and which, strangely, increases my concentration. A little floating attention is great, it seems to me, for generating new thoughts. Distractions give the old thoughts, the old ideas, time and mental space to dance and laze around, to flirt with other ideas, to send out fuzzy tentacles, explore new connections and outlandish analogies, and hook up with new dancing partners and – eureka – from two old ideas, or even three or four old ideas, one sparkling new little baby idea is born! If you are stuggling to solve a problem, pause to drift and daydream – that's my advice.

As he applied the towel, James was treating me delicately yet forcefully, handling me like his princess-slave, which combination – tenderness and brute strength – was more than stimulating. I wanted to make love right away, hippity-hop, lickety-split, *tout de suite*, *pronto*, without any exhausting preliminaries. I had lusty girl-fever: I was naked, freshly scrubbed, perfumed, spick-and-span, stripped down, and raring to go!

But ...

But ... I am a good and obedient servant, and patience, they say, is a virtue. So, I sighed in frustration and prepared to dress my master, not leap on him. At that moment, just as I was patting his biceps, I caught sight of us in the big wardrobe mirror, which graciously had just swung out. There we were, the two of us, full-length me, chalk-white and totally naked, like something a 19th Century French sculptor, toiling away in a bucolic and mythical genre, might have carved out of virginal white marble; and there he was, my master, tanned dark gold, lean and muscular, and stippled with beautifully patterned hair, muscles neatly delineated everywhere, with a powerful chest and not an ounce of fat to be seen. I swallowed and licked my lips: I was itching to leap on him, but he was to be dressed, and not to be possessed.

I held out my master's underpants – those cute gold and black striped boxer shorts – and helped him pull them on. I pulled his T-shirt over his head and pulled it down and patted his iron-strong stomach, and I stroked the lean muscular small of his back, which for some reason, I find particularly moving. I picked up his jeans, helped him pull them on, and buckled up his belt.

"Now, you are fully and magnificently clothed, Master, and I am naked and awaiting my orders." I stood at attention, heels together, and my arms straight at my sides, ready to serve.

"Yes, my darling, you are naked."

"Hmm, so now, what's next?" I allowed myself a sip of the frosty, dry martini.

"We equip you."

"Okay." I wondered what equipment would be involved this time – a fishnet body stocking, or a ...?

He held out a transparent tanga or mini-thong, two cords with a fine weave net triangle attached. "Oh," I said.

He knelt and slipped it onto me and helped me adjust it; it went very tight up my ass. "Ouch ... oh, oh, oh ..."

"Snug enough?"

"Yes, Master, quite snug enough."

He gazed at me, and then slipped a frilly transparent scarlet baby-doll teddy, which had been ripped open at the front, over my shoulders. It made me more naked than when I was naked.

He held out a pair of high-heeled scarlet pumps that were easy to slip out of and which made a flip-flop sound each time I took a step.

"Walk," he said.

"Yes, Master. Like this?"

"Yes."

I traipsed around the flat in the tanga and fluttery teddy with the pumps going clop-clop-clop. It gave me an agreeable sensation, a frisson, the forbidden thrill of being a true slattern, a sloppy, ill-kempt whore, a negligent floozy, oozing insouciance and sinful abandon, an icon from some old pulp fiction paperback cover, ancient movie poster, or an old, dog-eared, coffee-stained, second-hand paperback picked up in a leftovers bin. I felt I should have scarlet lipstick and a cigarette dangling from the corner of my mouth, and a bottle of Johnny Walker trailing in my hand, but I wasn't wearing lipstick; I've never smoked, and I rarely drink whiskey.

"Let's go out on the terrace and have another drink," James said.

"Yes, Master," I said, feeling deliciously irresponsible and voluptuously slutty, and, as I said, much more naked than when I was naked. Naked, after all, is natural. It has no context. But if you add a few trinkets to nakedness, you create a whole scenario, you transform the natural animal into a cultural icon, a symbol, soaked in meaning and insinuation. Just think, what – added to a naked body – a black rubber or leopard skin jockstrap can do, or a black or scarlet velvet choker with great-great grand-mother's Edwardian cameo, or, for that matter, a garter belt, with the straps dangling free, and nothing else, or perhaps just one silk stocking instead of two, one leg tamed, the other free. Sex is soaked in symbols – raw nature and tame civility duking it out. Sex, as some wise person once said, is all in the mind.

While I schlepped around the terrace, in the slippery high-heeled pumps, with the breeze fluttering and tickling my skin, and playing havoc – and hide-and-seek – with the few remaining tattered scarlet rags of the beautiful, frilly, chopped-up teddy, my master disappeared into the flat to prepare our double martinis. I felt deliciously and playfully exposed. I was flirting with the night air, with the city, with the universe. The night was luscious and warm. Caught in a dream-like fantasy, I mused how luxurious it would be to drive out to the beach and go for a skinny dip in the Mediterranean, by moonlight, down at one of the little sea-side towns south of Rome.

As I twirled around and mimed a waltz, dreaming of James swinging me around in his arms, this way and that, to the tune of Shostakovich's deliciously sublime, melancholy "Second Waltz," I wondered if James and Martine were planning to take me to Al-fredo's and parade me around like this – virtually naked in glowing minimalist rags. If we went to Alfredo's, pasties to hide my shame-less nipples and areola would be in order – even at Alfredo's totally exposed nipples, and areola were, just barely, out of bounds – unless you were nursing an infant; then, all was forgiven; then, even be-ing a female human was forgiven; then, you could be as florid and expansive as you wished, you could bare all. Babies, in Rome, made breasts respectable, and if the baby crawled diaperless around on the tabletop amid the bread baskets and wine bottles, so much the better. Maybe I could rent a baby the way people rented dogs so they could hook up with socio-economically suitable dog owner bipeds in public parks, and I wondered if I could artificially stimulate lactation without going through the bother of being pregnant. That way, I could properly service the rented baby and keep it deliciously deliriously happy and thankfully quiet; I had heard of such things, but I wasn't sure they really existed.

So – and this is truly, truly shameful – my fantasy was running riot. I was becoming, out there on the terrace, in my mind, in my own private swirling, high-stepping, waltzing Bacchanal, a shameless shamanistic Earth Mother, losing myself in my own imaginings, my arms outstretched embracing my imaginary lover, bathing, as I swirled around, in the sensual night air, becoming ever more brazen and fecund, becoming a wolf mother, with a whole brood of hungry little mouths hanging from my multiple swollen breasts ... At that moment, James came out onto the terrace, and, bowing gallantly, handed me the promised martini – cutting short my transformation into a She-Wolf-Mother Goddess. The martini was extra strong, extra good. He toasted, "To you, the math genius, Gwendoline."

I returned the toast, "To you, Master."

"Let us begin," he said, giving me a nice neat little peck on the cheek.

"Begin what?" I bit his lip and grabbed a quick sip of the very dry, exceptionally good martini.

"You will see, or, rather, you won't." He kissed me. And then he led me by the hand into the master bedroom where he opened a drawer. In his hands, suddenly appeared what looked like rope and several sets of handcuffs.

"Lie down on the bed, Princess, spread-eagled, face up."

"Yes, Master." I grabbed another gulp of the martini, then a second gulp, and put the empty glass on the bedside table. I slipped my feet out of the pumps and lay down on my back. I spread my arms, crucifix fashion, and my master leaned over and fastened the handcuffs to my wrists and then to the bedstead, which was of steel and strong enough to restrain an elephant.

"Spread your legs."

"Yes, Master."

He took my legs and opened them, so that I was truly tummy-up spread-eagled. He attached cuffs to my ankles and linked them with the cords – stretched tight – to the bedstead.

"The classic approach," I said, blinking at him.

"Yes," he said, "do you mind?"

"Not at all, Master," I said, "Traditions are fine things." I was totally suspended, splayed out, tied down tight, in the spread-eagled sacrificial crucified position. If anything happened now, I would not be able to free myself – totally impossible.

I was still wearing the transparent tanga; it was tight, sensuously, uncomfortably tight, up my bum, and the frilly transparent scarlet baby-doll teddy open at the front, and nothing else.

James turned the lights down low, and he put on music in the next room. The doors from the bedroom to the terrace were open. I could feel the night breeze on my skin, gently fluttering the ragged teddy.

James returned, bent down, kissed me, and said, "Now, we shall make you naked, my prisoner and princess, or almost naked."

"Yes, Master."

"First, I'll take off your teddy."

"Yes, Master."

He cut what remained of the teddy with scissors. The cold metal of the scissors pressed on my flesh in a series of slow strokes and metallic caresses, as if the cool blade were going to cut into me and not the cloth. My master pulled the teddy from me, in small, rough gestures, as if he were tearing it from my body.

For just a second, I saw into the heart of the violence of the man. I felt a tinge of fear. He was so strong. He was so mysterious. I was absolutely at his mercy. Anything could happen. It was thrilling. A tingle of fear – and a hot flush of shame – went up and down my spine.

"Now, you belong to me."

"Yes, Master," I whispered, "I belong to you."

I was naked except for the tanga; stretched wide, I could hardly move a muscle.

"Now, I think we will add a blindfold." He held out a black velvet and leather blindfold.

"Yes, Master." I tilted my head up. He slipped the blindfold over my head. It covered my eyes entirely, blinding me utterly, but it did leave my mouth and lips free. My heart beat faster and faster. I was tented in darkness. I licked my lips. What would he do next? Feathers, ice cubes, a whip, his tongue, an affectionate Burmese python ...?

My master was silent.

I lay there, wondering.

"Master?"

Silence.

What was he doing?

"Master?"

Silence.

Sweat broke out. I could feel it, slick sweat, beading my arms, belly, and thighs. Silence. The tension rose – and a rising tremulous sliver of fear. I was wet with desire – and with fear. My mind began to wander, to speculate: what would happen next? I was entombed in darkness. The sounds became enormous – the clock, ticking – tick, tick, tick – the squawking and cawing of a flight of seagulls flying up the Tiber, the gentle rustling of the terrace awning and the fronds of the terrace plants, the wafting whisper of the white muslin curtain and murmur of the big city out there – Rome, Caput Mundi, Capital of the World, the Eternal City – and the vast sky. Where was my master? What was he doing? Then, I felt a hand, his hand, on my foot, caressing the sole, the instep, the heel, my ankle, each toe at a time; he began to caress my leg; he worked his way slowly up the calf, slowly, slowly. Each touch was electric with suspense, like a drama, where was he going to go next?

Then his hand was on my belly.

Then his lips were on my stomach.

Then he moved upwards, to my breasts.

Silently: Not a word did he speak.

Oh, oh, oh. I shivered. I trembled.

He kissed my nipples, cupped my breasts; his hands caressed the inside of my thighs, twitchy and damp in excitement and tense with anticipation. He ran his fingers along the string of the tanga, which was tight transparent plastic; he caressed the triangle of the tanga itself, softly, and then less softly, pressing down, knowingly, giving me an insidiously savvy massage, pushing precisely the right buttons; I was soaked, trembling with painful yearning; I whispered his name, "Master." He put his finger across my lips, meaning "silence." I bit my tongue and said nothing.

I wiggled my thighs. I ached to twist and rotate my hips, I lusted to swivel and rise up, I yearned to spin around, with him inside me, my hips were famished, greedy to seize him; my vulva, my labia were dripping creamy beads of honey, I could feel it, my vulva was starving, starving; and I was ravenous, I needed the touch of his lips, I would die for a kiss. I wanted to seize him, pull him into me. But I was tied down, helpless, stretched out, blind. Helpless, all my sensations were multiplied. I was skin only, a surface of epidermis, a taut drum of tingling sensation, a spirit of soaring desire.

Finally, oh, finally – he kissed me on the lips; and he began to caress and touch me with kisses, with his hands, and he was the most delicate of musicians, strumming every nerve, gifting me, arousing me, with small feathery light caresses, promises of more to come, working his way from my neck and shoulders downwards, caressing my underarms, and up the soft underside of my upper arm, and, breathless, down my sides, and then again my breasts, each nipple, a soft feathery caress and then a kiss, and a lick. I held my breath. I was not supposed to talk. The silence of the room was immense. Beyond the room were the sounds of the city, coming from a distant and different universe.

I licked my lips. I swallowed. My heart was beating faster. My pulse throbbed. What animals we are! How painfully delightful it was, to be helpless, excited, a primitive creature, powerless in the hands of – and at the mercy of – this man I didn't even know existed three years ago. Now he possessed my body, he possessed me, he filled my soul, and he mastered every fiber of my being.

He kissed my tummy, sculpting my belly button, and nibbling at the gentle swelling, and blowing on inner whorl of flesh with his lips; he teased with his fingertips my nipples which were, of course, straining erect, as always when my master was near, betraying my utter sensual slavery, my drooling, dribbling, breathless servitude, my abnegation, and my exaltation. What an abyss I am! He touched, with the lightest of touches, the triangle of the tanga, pressing on the – again – freshly totally waxed and naked mons pubis, soaked with the sweat and secretions of desire. It was warm in the room, and the soft sea breeze was damp; it was a hot summer night ...

I wiggled. He slapped my tummy. "Don't move, Goddess, you are a statue, you are lifeless, utterly immobile."

I swallowed.

He lifted the tanga up, stretched it. The strings cut into me and tightened in the crack of my ass ... Sodomy, Sodomy, oh! Take me, take me! Oh, yes, ass, ass, ass, ass, ass ...

He pulled the tanga away, slipping it, tightly, down my thighs, and then just above my knees, with the cold steel blade pressing against my flesh, he cut the tanga's strings – snap, snap – and lifted it away. He plunged and touched me with his lips; he opened his way to the clitoris, delicately, with the tip of his tongue; he twirled the clitoris; it blossomed like a flower, like an explosion of fireworks, like a billowing cloud of lust. Oh, if I could only cry out! I choked it back, I gurgled, deep in my throat, I gurgled. I was no longer me, no longer human.

He twirled and licked. His tongue expressed the artistry of the cosmos. I saw swirling galaxies, whole universes slowly rotating. I saw vastness, and I sensed the center, the center where I was, reduced now to pure sensation, no longer me, no longer human, twirling around, spinning, spinning into ecstasy, pure trembling desire. He kissed me on the lips, his mouth rich with the taste of me, as if I were united somehow, through him, with myself, a serpent curling in a circle, biting its tail, and, as he kissed me, he guided himself slowly into me, just touching me with the tip of his cock, his mushroom-shaped cap, a guided missile, just teasing me, entering, then retreating, entering, then retreating, each time deeper, each time slower. I wanted to cry out, "Oh, you evil Master, you, Oh, how could you do this to me!?" But I was mute. I had my orders. My lips were sealed.

Tense, spread-eagled, pinned down, suspended in taut

immobility, every nerve, every tendon, every muscle of my body was straining for control. He entered deeper. Each time, he seemed to get larger, immense.

He kissed me.

I tensed, making a supreme effort at control. He plunged deeper. As he plunged deeper, his kisses were deeper too. Then he was deep inside me, thrusting gently at first, and kissing me; then he thrust faster and faster.

I tried to raise my hips to meet him, to help him split me open, cleave me in two, devour me, possess me, break me!

Then, in a shuttering exhalation and gush of desire, I came! Defeat, surrender, annihilation!

But, Oh Glory, Victory! Revenge! In the very same instant, he came – a long shudder that swept up and down his body. I felt it with every muscle and tendon and nerve. It was as if our bodies were united, fused into one body, one fireworks explosion.

It went on, and on, and on ...

Silently, I gave thanks: "Oh, Master Oh, Master, Oh, Master!"

His withdrawal was artful, and tender – long and slow and delicate with many returns and many delicate echoing playful after thrusts, as if the aftershock would continue forever and ever.

"Ah," Enveloped in darkness, in pure sensation, no longer me, but just nameless trembling, I sighed.

He lay against me. He kissed his way along my body, and he caressed me.

"Oh, boy," I whispered, "Oh, Master."

"Yes, Princess," he said.

"Oh, boy," I breathed.

His hands moved over me slowly, exploring: the vulva, wet, soaked; the belly; the rib cage, and the breasts and shoulders. I felt sweat bubbling, forming a slick patina on my skin, stars bursting from the pores and settling into a mist. He kissed me on the lips and whispered, "Martine is going to pay us a visit."

"What?"

"She'll be here in a few minutes."

"Untie me now!"

"Don't you want her to see you like this?"

"Not particularly."

"Well, then ..."

"No, let me think about it."

"In the meantime, I think you could use a glass of wine."

"Yes, Okay, a glass of wine," I sighed, overwhelmed by a surge of voluptuous surrender. I imagined it: Martine would witness me, spayed open and naked, drenched in the aftermath of sex, and helpless. Did I want this?

The weight shifted on the mattress as my master moved off the bed, and stepped away from me, and his gentle naked footsteps whispered as he left the room; from afar, I heard the fridge door open. Already, I could taste the cool white wine.

Do I want Martine to see me like this? Hmm? The idea of such intimate, exposed humiliation was exciting.

But I'd want my revenge.

Would Martine allow me to tie her up the way my master had tied me up? That would be even more exciting. We would exchange roles, she and I. I would be the master; she would be the slave.

It would be a luscious scene: Her, my very own blond goddess – manacled and shackled down on her knees, or tied up and splayed out, helpless and exposed, so I could play with her to my heart's content and coddle and comfort her and feed her and give her drinks to drink ...

Hmm ...

And so, I lay cocooned and bound in silken darkness, blind to the world, spinning my own little fantasy cinema, featuring Martine Aubin, my very own star.

My master was back. He pressed the wine glass against my lips. I tried to raise my head and of course, blind and tied down, I only managed to dribble the liquid. He licked it from my lips. He poured more on my breasts and drank and licked my nipples, my breasts, my ribcage.

"Yes, Master, Martine can see me as I am," I said, "but she must not touch me unless I give her permission, and you must release me if and when I say release me. And only Martine, no one else, not even Philip, is to see me reduced thus, as you have reduced me, Master, to a total abject object, bound and blind, your helpless plaything."

"As you command, Princess," he said. "In any case, as you know, Philip is not in town."

"Well, this will be perfect then." I licked my lips, "just the three of us."

He offered more wine, and I drank, in small, chilly sips, and it was delicious. It wet my lips, and it wet my chin. I was parched.

The doorbell rang.

My master padded away, invisibly, to open the door. I heard Martine's voice. I heard her say, "Oh, really?" and I heard my master's reply, "I'll get some drinks, and leave you two alone."

Then I felt a subtle perfume, a waft of air.

Martine was in the room; I could not see her, of course, but I felt her presence. She said, "Hello, darling Gwendoline."

"Hello," I gulped, realizing suddenly how sublimely ridiculous I must look.

"Oh, Gwendoline," she said, "You have been naughty, I see." I felt the mattress shift as she sat down.

"May I touch you?" Her voice was soft, a whisper, almost as if she were in awe.

"Yes, go ahead," I swallowed, suddenly yearning for her touch, her mastery, her delicate command of the mysteries, and arts of sensual and sexual excitement.

Her hand went to my breasts, and then down my ribcage to my belly, to my belly button. She played with my belly button, feathery swirls, circles, narrower, then wider. Her fingers had a lighter, more tentative touch than James, a fine-textured little dance, and with the points of her fingernails, she mimicked a scratching, as if, like a cat, she wished to scar me with her claws.

"Oh, navel, oh, origin, oh omphalic center," she whispered, "so sweet, so rich, and gently rising perfect fertile fruitful belly! Oh, dear Gwen, I should so like to give you a spanking!" She caressed her way down to my vulva. "Here, the rivers flow, and here the mighty are made prisoner. Here is the beginning of the world, *L'Origine du Monde.*"

Her caress was soft, savvy, insinuating, and too exciting – a wave of desire and lust surged up. I quivered like a violin string. Slowly, cautiously, Martine eased off, patting me gently, letting the tension subside.

She leaned forward and kissed me on the lips.

"I want to do this to you," I whispered, my voice throaty and trembling.

"Oh, you want to do it to me. Hmm, that is a fine idea. What if we were to do it to each other?"

"Yes." I coughed, trying to clear my voice, not succeeding; it was still throaty, choked with desire, rising excitement. "Yes, yes. Let's do it to each other!"

"Is that a promise?"

"Yes, it's a promise."

"Good. I'll hold you to it." She kissed me on the lips, and then on the nipples, and she said, "I think I'll release you." She shouted, "May I release her, James?"

"Yes, if you wish," James shouted back from the kitchen. "But you might leave the blindfold on, and she does need a shower. Perhaps you could help her."

Again, I felt a thrill of voluptuous abnegation and abjection. They were talking about me as if I were not there. I was an animal. I was not human. I was a pet. I was their pet, their shared pet. I was a creature. I was no longer a person, no longer a subject. I was an object. Oh, how luxuriously wanton – to be an object, how reposeful! They would feed me and pet me and groom me and look after me. I wanted to stretch out like a cat and revel in my servitude, but of course, I couldn't. I was manacled tight, wrists and ankles, to the bed.

"I have no objection to the blindfold," I managed to say.

Teasingly, a piece at a time, Martine undid the cuffs that held me pinned down, and then she guided me up until I was on my feet. She kissed me on the lips. Her hands ran down my sides; she led me by the hand to the bathroom and to the shower.

"Shall I help the creature shower?" Martine shouted.

"Yes, of course, if you wish. I think that's a splendid idea," James shouted, "I'm cooking."

"Then I must disrobe too."

"Yes, of course, Martine, that's another splendid idea." James sounded pleased: Two naked females in his cave instead of one.

Martine led me into the shower cabin. She left me, and stepped out; I stood there. I groped for the shower levers, and I turned on the water. It came gushing out and pouring down; I stepped towards it gingerly. Suddenly, I was under the deluge, still blindfolded; I felt Martine's hands on me, and I felt her body, now naked, move close to mine, and her voice, a whispering insinuation in my ear, "Now, my darling Gwendoline, I shall give you a good scrubbing!"

She began to shampoo my hair – her fingers plying my scalp,

back and forth, up and down, a hypnotic rhythm, with thick creamy warm foam flowing down my face, over my ears, down my neck.

She set about scrubbing my back vigorously, with a little brush, and my backside. She was grooming me, like a good pony. She was careful and caring with my breasts and belly and all the tender, intimate parts.

She was thorough. She went everywhere on – and in – my body, a body she knew just as well as her own. It fired my imagination, feeling her body, naked, brushing against mine: her nipples brushing my nipples, her belly touching my belly, her leg sidling smoothly up to mine, her leg pressing itself between my legs. She embraced me, rubbing herself against me, like a purring cat, our wet soapy skin sliding and slipping, surface on surface, skin on skin, wet, warm, and intimate. Finally, nibbling my earlobe with her lips and sharp, perfect teeth, she whispered, "You might as well do me too, darling,"

So, blindly, I poured shampoo into my hand, and I shampooed her. I scrubbed and caressed her everywhere; and, as my hands moved blindly over her body, it occurred to me what a sacred thing the body is, particularly the body of a person you love, how full of mystery and promise it is, what a delicate tender thing, and how honored I was to be her lover; and, entombed in hot, wet, silken darkness, I imagined how our two bodies must look, utter opposites, a vivid contrast, glowing in the steam, her tanned golden body, and my chalk-white body. I imagined her cold blue Nordic eyes upon me, the crystal-clear eyes, the blond hair, and the dark, dark lashes of a Norman-Italian beauty. Even when I couldn't see her eyes, I felt the power of their gaze; I knew it so well. But I could not return her gaze. It gave me a sharp thrill – being defined by her gaze and in its power; and helpless to return it, though I was defining and possessing every curve and slope of her body with my hands and my fingers – warm, tactile intimacy. I trusted both Martine and James absolutely. I felt secure and comforted in that trust, with an almost infantile exaltation.

We stepped out of the shower. Martine toweled me down, and I toweled her down. Finally, taking the towel from me, and with a lingering kiss, she whispered, brushing her lips against my ear, "I am going to put on a bathrobe, but you, dear Gwendoline, you will remain naked."

"As you wish, Mistress Martine, and if my master so desires, I shall remain naked."

"Master, how do you wish your princess and slave to be dressed?" Martine shouted.

"As nature made her!"

"So, it shall be. Come, Captive Princess, follow me." Martine took me by the hand and led me out onto the terrace.

And that was where we dined, the three of us, in the evening air, which was warm with a slight evening breeze, the "ponentino" of Rome, which James had described to me when he first introduced me to the mysteries of the Eternal City.

Being blindfolded, shrouded in darkness, made me extra-sensitive to every caress of the perfumed air, to every nuance of smell and taste. The food was delicious.

James had prepared a marvelous spaghetti primavera, with the carrots, onions, red and green peppers and tomatoes, and zucchini that I had bought in the Campo de' Fiori market that very morning.

"Gwendoline is now allowed to be human," said James.

"Yes, indeed, whatever is your pleasure, Master," said Martine.

"You may, Martine, if Gwendoline agrees, lift off her blindfold."

"I agree," I murmured.

Martine carefully, slowly, lifted off the blindfold. I blinked at the night air, at the candles that were flickering on the table, at Martine, kneeling next to me, her eyes bright, her hair still glowing and wet, her skin lustrous and golden, wrapped in a big fluffy white bathrobe, and at my master, sitting across from me, handsome and austere in his masculine beauty, with a nice stern five o'clock shadow catching the evening light, but smiling, and his blue shirt, open at the chest. "Welcome back, Princess," he said.

He stood up to fetch more wine.

"Whew!" I sighed. It was a pleasant feeling, both humiliating and exalting, to be sitting, primly naked, with my sight restored, and being served by my two fully clothed ultra-civilized lovers.

Martine had to leave early. She asked me to help her dress, which I did, as her naked barefoot servant, pulling on her panties, slipping her T-shirt over her head and smoothing it down, pulling on her jeans, kneeling to fit her shoes, buckling her belt, zipping her zippers.

Caring for her this way was something I adored. Once, when Martine had a bad flu, several months ago in Paris, and while Philip was away shooting in South Africa, I served as Martine's nurse and constant companion: I held her when she was throwing up, I consulted with her doctor, I bought supplies, I made chicken broth, and I cooked for her and washed for her, and tended to her every need. I adored doing it, particularly since she was a very easy and grateful patient, amused at my ministering and scolding, and ironic about her own whining and complaining.

On the threshold, I kissed her and held her.

"I love you," I said.

"And I love you, Gwendoline." She kissed me again, and patted my bum, a nice sharp little slap.

Martine was no sooner out the door than I ordered my master to take off all his clothes so that we would once again be equals.

He did so, and we sat drinking and talking late into the night, like two philosophers in Ancient Athens.

I thanked James for such a wonderful "celebration." He promised me another, more public celebration, probably at Alfredo's, al fresco.

As we talked, the warm, humid Mediterranean night breeze made its mark upon us – brightening our skin with gentle luminous pearls of sweat – and we gazed into each other's eyes.

Then, together, we washed the dishes and dried them.

Exhausted, we went to bed, and I lay in his arms for a long time, and played with the phallic god ... All bodies are sacred, and all people too. And I played a gentle little tune.

Penis

Cock

Wee-wee

Phallus

A rose is a rose is a rose ...

And all the temples and idols came tumbling down.

Well, not quite ...

The sacred phallus stood erect, performed a comic pirouette, and made one last bow. I patted it down, and sang it a closely whispered intimate lullaby, punctuated with soft loving little kisses.

Then we both slept, or all three, or all four of us, I'm not sure, for, as the poet said, we all contain, each and every one of us, multitudes. And he was right, was he not?

≈

When I woke, the delicious fragrance of fresh coffee drifted into the bedroom. James had prepared breakfast on the terrace. I slipped out of bed and walked barefoot and naked to the terrace.

"Breakfast for a princess," James, my master, was already civilized, dressed in a crisp blue shirt, blue jeans, and sandals.

"Thank you, dear sir." I sat down.

"You shall remain seated, Gwen, just as you are, your Highness, and be served."

"Indeed Master, your wish is my command, and it pleases me greatly that you, my Master, serve me thus."

"Yes, just as you are: Aphrodite just risen from the foaming billowing sheets," he said, "Naked as the light of dawn."

"You are exceedingly poetic this morning, Master." I flapped my eyelashes, gave him my best flirtatious glance, and spread some marmalade on the hot buttered croissant. My mouth was watering. I took a big crisp, creamy, luscious bite. I picked up the folded copy of *The International New York Times* – delivered by Giuseppe every morning – and glanced at the headlines. It was the beginning of another splendid warm, clear, sunny Roman day.

"It is you who are the poetry, my dear," said James, pouring more coffee into my cup.

I half-closed my eyes and grinned, caught between delight – and, because of his extreme care for me, fear. Could it be that all of this was an illusion, the deceptive calm before the storm? Could the man, who so feared love, truly be in love, and really be this calm, this accepting, this happy?

CHAPTER 11 – MISTRESS NICOLE

Three days later, James was in Moscow for a week; Martine had returned to Paris. I was alone in Rome, a sexual and spiritual orphan. I knew that I had better keep my mind and libido well occupied while I worked. Otherwise, I'd go crazy and do something indecent.

I decided to set out on foot and explore the city. The weather was so splendid – seemingly endless hot dry sunny days – that working inside seemed a crime, and working outside on café terraces was a constant temptation and pure pleasure. I put my laptop in my ancient backpack – inherited from grandmother Claudia and her hitchhiking days – and I wandered – across the river to Saint Peter's, along the Tiber to Testaccio, which was near the river Port of Ancient Rome, and which contained, among other things, a mountain of ancient crockery and amphorae, and many cute little restaurants and cafés, and I dawdled my way through the little streets and alleyways of Trastevere, the bohemian quarter of Rome; I went everywhere and anywhere my fancy took me.

Early one bright sunny morning, I decided to explore the Borghese Gardens – known as Villa Borghese Gardens. The gardens are a big park. It overlooks Piazza del Popolo and also gives onto via Veneto, the street which was once, long ago, way back in the

1950s and 60s, famous as the center of the dolce vita, the sweet life; it thronged with film stars, paparazzi, and was rich in sex and scandal, and Rome produced 300 or 400 feature films a year, and was known as "Hollywood on the Tiber."

I worked for a couple of hours in the park at a table on the terrace of a café, sitting in the gently shifting shadows under the umbrella pines; there was a soft breeze; the light changed by quick, subtle gradations, with the changing humidity in the air; it was sensual, like being in the Garden of Eden, at one with nature, with no frontier between the body, the gentle breeze, and the golden, luminous day. I sipped a latte and concentrated on my netbook screen and on making notes. From time to time, I looked up and watched some kids running back and forth along a pebbled pathway between rows of weathered and lichen-covered gray marble busts of famous personages, most of whom had certainly long been forgotten. I cast sneaky glances at two fashionable young women, drinking tea and gossiping and laughing at a table not far from mine. And I concentrated my attention on a young man who was painting the slender columns of a delicate metal pergola with white paint; he smoothed the white paint on with gentle slow regular strokes. He was topless, muscular, deeply tanned; his abs, pectorals, and biceps rippled in the sunlight; his faded, paint-spattered blue jeans were slung low, sagging from a thick black leather tool belt. I watched him, dreamily, and I thought of James, and his body, the muscles of his back, which I loved to gaze at and would have loved to touch. The world – and I sighed with pleasure – was – is – full of beauty – and temptation.

Finally, after an hour or two, I set off again, and walked to Villa Medici, a fortress of a place perched on a hilltop overlooking Rome and which houses a colony of French artists and writers, and to the Church of Trinity of the Hill, which towers up at the top of the Spanish Steps. Then, lugging my backpack,

I traipsed down the steps – past the magnificent displays of flowers and tourists sitting everywhere – to Piazza di Spagna, and I headed down Via Condotti, a narrow pedestrian street, with the famous Antico Caffè Greco, and which is one of the world's gold standard streets of expensive shopping, like Fifth Avenue in New York, or the Bahnhofstrasse in Zurich, or Avenue Montaigne in Paris, or Ginza in Tokyo. Lined up next to each other were all the famous names – Gucci, Christian Dior, Prada, Armani, Valentino, and so on ...

I stopped in front of a luxuriously outfitted store window and examined some shoes – extravagant stilettoes with an emerald reptilian pattern, like a bright jade-colored snake on stilts; next to the emerald masterpiece, and up on a little rotating platform, were some fashionable black fetish boots that laced up beyond the knees; then there were some feathery black stilettoes, like wearing crows or ravens on one's feet; and standing in a corner was another stylishly fetish-like pair of black boots, with a red stripe down the side, and red-and-black lacing; they went all the way up the thigh.

I thought they might be worth trying on. Maybe I could try out the stylish over-the-top dominatrix look. James would be pleased.

There were some playful looking ballet slippers, with tassels and little bells – the court jester or Harley Quinn look. I wondered if the jester slippers came with matching jesters' caps, floppy horns, bells, and maybe big donkey or bunny ears. I mused about whether I should go in and try some on – maybe the slippers, or the thigh-high boots. Femininity is a masquerade, n'est-pas? Hmm!

No, I stiffened my resolve. I'd continue my stroll, find a place for lunch, open my laptop, and get back to work. As I turned away from the window, I saw an elegant woman who, like me, was window shopping. She had short jet-black hair, and was wearing a light, black silk jacket, a black pleated skirt, dark stockings, and high-heeled black patent leather shoes, and she looked, for some reason, exquisitely neat, the kind of image of perfection that steps out of a fashion magazine. So self-contained, so ideal, it looked as if her feet hardly touched the ground.

There was no way I could measure up to such a beauty. I was dressed in frayed and bleached blue jeans, with a ragged hole at one knee, a black baseball cap, a white T-shirt, and leather sandals, with the old leather and canvas backpack; I looked like a waif hitchhiker who belonged in a youth hostel. The stylish apparition – a sort of ideal of feminine elegance – almost certainly must be an executive, I thought, a banker or the sales director of one of the big fashion houses. At that moment, she turned towards me and smiled. I instantly recognized her. It was Madame Nicole.

"Gwendoline," she exclaimed, "Gwendoline Clermont!" Her smile was radiant. "You have become quite famous."

We shook hands. I thought, oh, what the heck, I really do like her! I embraced her and held her and kissed her on both cheeks. "How are you?" I looked straight into her eyes.

"Wonderful. And you?"

"Pretty good," I shifted my backpack and felt it was a lame thing to say; suddenly, I felt like a bashful schoolgirl faced with a forbidding headmistress. I realized I didn't even know her last name. But I was curious about her, so I took a deep breath and asked if she would have time for tea or coffee. After all, she was my mentor – she had introduced me to Martine, and to many forms of entertainment it might have taken me a long time to figure out on my own.

"It's lunchtime," she said. "Perhaps," smiling, she fixed me with her sparkling dark gaze, "if you are free, we could have lunch."

"Yes." I almost blushed.

"What about Babington's Tea House?" She nodded towards the end of Via Condotti. "It's just up the street on the Piazza di Spagna, right next to the Spanish Steps. They serve marvelous light lunches, with the most delicious tea."

"Let's go!" I shifted my rucksack to a more comfortable position.

She took my arm, and we headed up Via Condotti to Piazza di Spagna and across the piazza – close to the fountain where James and I had splashed each other that hot Roman night over two years ago – and we entered a cool shadowy corridor and then we were in the tea house.

"This place is an institution," Nicole said, as we sat down. I looked around. There was wood paneling everywhere and discreet little mirrors on the walls, little wooden tables and chairs, and an air of old-fashioned gentility. The waitress who took our order for tea – English Breakfast for me, Earl Gray for Nicole – seemed to know Nicole very well. Nicole suggested we choose sandwiches. The waitress nodded and smiled and made a little note. I glanced at the menu. It looked very classy – and delicious! Nicole chose the Scottish smoked salmon sandwich, and I chose the chicken and bacon club sandwich. Yummy!

"I'm a regular," Nicole said. I was reminded, from her accent, that she was French. She glanced around with a wistful, almost proprietary air. "Babington's has been here since the 1890s; it was set up by two English ladies."

I again noticed the simple wooden chairs and tables. It did have the air of a place that had been around for a long time, and that was proud of its traditions.

"They offer over thirty kinds of tea, I believe. And during Mussolini's dictatorship, in the 1920s and 1930s, anti-Fascist intellectuals used to meet here. It was a polite little island of opposition." She took a delicate sip of tea. "It has retained, I think, a romantic whiff of resistance and daring, combined with a slightly antiquated air of English gentility."

The light inside the tea house was muted, but limpid; I realized, examining her closely for the first time, that Nicole was extraordinarily beautiful.

"How did you, ah ...?"

"How did I get into the business of training and equipping naughty young ladies such as yourself – and occasionally naughty not-so-young gentlemen?" She laughed. Her dark eyes sparkled. She took another sip of tea, tilted her head sideways, and looked straight into my eyes, almost a challenge.

I licked my lips. She was, I guessed, in her forties, and she radiated self-confidence and sensuality. I felt a quiver of admiration and desire. Like Martine, she was charismatic – animal magnetism, beauty, and high intelligence combined.

"Well, Gwendoline, the truth is I began in prostitution." A wistful, slightly melancholy smile hovered on her lips. "Luckily, I was an upper-class prostitute, a call girl, as they say. I had – I still have – a rich, usually quite refined clientele who paid – and pay – very well."

"Wow!" I whispered, but I still felt like an idiot; I should have guessed; but somehow her avowal was, I don't know, moving.

"My background was entirely different – old French aristocracy, terribly snobbish, money and land going back to Louis XIV and beyond – back to the Middle Ages. When I was a child, and then when I was an adolescent and student, mother and father didn't approve of me, particularly father. They kept me on a very tight leash or tried to. I was rather naughty." She glanced around the room. "My family, well, they are the sort of people – or they were – the type is rather rare now – the sort of people who think the French Revolution – well over 200 years ago – never happened, or never should have happened. The family is extremely Catholic, ultra-traditional; they insist that Mass be said in Latin; generally, they are boring, and stuck-up, and insufferable; they are anti-Semites, too, most of them, and Fascist sympathizers. Though I did have a charming great uncle, the classic black sheep of the family, who fought for General de Gaulle's Free French Forces in the Second World War, was in the Resistance, and married a very beautiful, exquisitely intelligent Jewess and moved to New York where he made a lot of money, a fortune really, in banking."

"Brains ..." I said.

"Yes, he certainly had brains – and guts. He liked risk, heroism, making the grand gesture. I see his great-grandchildren when they come to France, or to Italy, and one of the girls stayed with me for a year in Paris when she was studying at Sciences Po."

She topped up the tea in my cup and smiled. "We do have – well, my parents have – a great deal of inherited money, wisely, cautiously invested, and a very beautiful château, in the Loire Valley, with lots of land attached. Our family, my grandparents – except of course for the wicked uncle – were against the Allies during the Second World War; out of long family tradition, they hate the English; and they were anti-de Gaulle, pro-Vichy, and even pro-German, or, to put it bluntly, pro-Nazi." She took a sip of tea; her gaze for a moment was far away. "Really intolerable and often hateful people, and of course they are my flesh and blood. The ancestors passed their prejudices down to my father. He married a woman from a family with the same ideas."

"Pretty stultifying for you, I imagine."

She smiled. "Well, it was not easy, though it was an extremely privileged upbringing; and they did love me in their own way, aside from rather frequent beatings my father indulged in – a whipping on my naked ass with a whip, even when I was a teenager, even after puberty. Daddy did seem to get great pleasure out of it, and I of course realized – as children and young people will – that he took pleasure out of it and was excited by it in some strange way I didn't understand at the time, and which was vaguely frightening – and also exciting and tantalizing in a perverse terrified sort of way. In many ways, children are geniuses as psychologists. We are more perceptive when we are young, more open; later, we learn to tell ourselves lies; we learn to be blind to what we don't want to see. We put things in categories, and we forget what it is like to really *see* them, to really *feel* them for the first time, or *as if* it were for the first time. When you're a child, you see so much, it's hard to absorb – and of course, as a child, you do not have the words to describe such things. Perhaps, as adults, the words blind us. Words are judgments, after all." She half-closed her eyes. "Perhaps I inherited Daddy's sadistic tastes, or maybe he conditioned me to find pain and shame and humiliation exciting, to associate such feelings with sex and with sexual pleasure, even ecstasy, a sort of sublime abandonment of self. I don't know." She looked up.

The waitress was hovering, smiling at us, and holding a small tray. Our sandwiches had arrived.

"Thank you," we said, and accepted the delicacies.

Nicole lifted a triangular bit of sandwich to her mouth, and hesitated. "As I grew up, I became the black sheep of the clan, left-wing, an intellectual in a modest teenage sort of way, passionate about ideas and about debating ideas and politics, with Muslim and Jewish friends. Passionate, too, about sex. I went to the Sorbonne and did quite well. I was doing postgraduate work, and attending the art school, the École des Beaux-Arts and I had a Jewish boyfriend – this was beyond the pale, absolutely beyond the pale. Daddy and I had a huge fight. I was shown the door. "I disown you. You no longer exist," those were Daddy's very words, and his last words to me. It was rather melodramatic: out in the country, in the château, far from any town, a dark and stormy night, which was certainly appropriate. I suppose God was displeased with me too and arranged for the downpour, though I'm sure the farmers were happy; it had been very dry, and they needed the rain. I walked to the nearest train station, waited for hours, and got to Paris at 2 am and slept in the railway station and then, when the police roused me and told me I couldn't sleep there, I went to an all-night café and nursed a single café-crème for hours and read the newspapers. My mother, who came from a slightly less reactionary family, had wept during the scene in which I was disowned but she said nothing and didn't defend me; she was – she is – afraid of my father. I had already broken up with my – beautiful, witty, intelligent – Jewish boyfriend, but I didn't tell my parents that. I decided to pay my own way through art school. I had a girlfriend – Brigitte – another art student, a sexy, beautiful girl, from a very fine family near Bordeaux; she had – has – a spectacular body. She earned money as an artist's model. I moved in with her, and I became an artist's model too; then, one wintery evening – it was drafty in the studio I remember – we were offered money by a famous art dealer – for entertaining – and having sex with – some of his most important – richest – clients, two Japanese gentlemen, who had just arrived from Tokyo. It seemed a quite good idea, and it was an easy transition, in the good old 19th Century tradition of artists' models sliding into the world of prostitution or the demi-monde of being some rich gentleman's mistress. Brigitte and I thought we had discovered a gold mine: we managed to put together a small list of clients: Businessmen, international civil servants, a few gentlemen from the Middle East, Saudis and Iranians, our Japanese friends, and some Chinese and South American millionaires." She looked away for a moment. Her eyes were far away. But the dreamy smile still hovered on her lips. "Why did I go the way I did? Why did I choose prostitution? I was a rebel. And I liked sex – or thought I did – and I wanted to experiment. And I discovered that, in fact, I really did like sex and all its quirky kinky perverse and bodily sides and aspects, even those that are, frankly, quite unpleasant." She glanced at me, that same intense stare, hungry and amused. "I do like sex. I liked the power it gave me – and still gives me – over men, and over women. It is, relative to lots of other things, easy money. I like the thrill of the 'forbidden,' which I suppose comes from the powerful repressive Catholic upbringing that lingers in my background and, of course, from Daddy's spankings and punishments which were, in their own perverse way, quite thrilling. So, I like what French philosophers sometimes used to call 'transgression.' It's a pretty mild and very bourgeois form of transgression, or misbehavior, or violation of taboos, of course, not exactly designed to overturn the social order, destroy capitalism, save the planet, or bring about the workers' paradise, or eliminate neo-colonialism or racism from the world; but I like it. Also, I like the insight this life gives – exploring people's needs and imaginings, their secret longings, their multiple hidden selves, and secret stories, and the stories they tell themselves: it is very rewarding. And, of course, I learn about myself at the same time."

"Power." I concentrated on my sandwich. "You like the power?"

"Absolutely. I like to dominate, but, like you, Gwendoline, I like to be dominated too, though only by certain types of people. I choose my masters or mistresses carefully. Sex is certainly about power, though lots of people with romantic ideas don't want to recognize that aspect of desire – and then, ignoring it, they sometimes find they are in for a big surprise. Ignorance is not always bliss."

"But as a call girl ...?" I gave her the classic Gwendoline stare, dark, dark eyes, from under the thick, arched black eyebrows.

"Was I at the mercy of the clients?"

"Yes, that's what I want to know."

"Not often, not really. Many of the clients want to be dominated – not all, mind you. There are men – sometimes very important men – who are into extremely rough sex, violent sodomy and violent restraint, and whippings. They must be held within limits. Otherwise ..."

"Dangerous guys."

"Yes, they can be dangerous. Even when they don't want to be dangerous, they can lose control – they can slap you, hit you, punch you, try to strangle you. They are like caged tigers; they wear expensive suits, and often have refined tastes, knowing all about Renaissance art or German Lieder or Christian theology or something like that, but inside – inside, there is a wild, barely tameable beast. You have to be very clear with them, what the boundaries are, what the 'safe words' are – that is, how to tell them to stop. And they must obey the rules, and I set the rules. We need a discreet, safe, organized environment with lots of safeguards. But, generally, at least in my case – or in the case of people like Brigitte – the call girl is not the person without the power. Many of the clients – even the very rich ones – are extremely needy. If you are skillful, they are, in a sense, at your mercy. Some of them want to be dominated, some want to dominate, to play master and slave ..."

"James and I ..."

"Yes," she smiled, "James is definitely the dominant type, but he's also very gallant, and he worships you. He is one hundred percent man, though I think you are also a proxy for his feminine side; you are part of him, I imagine, and he is part of you. Many of our clients want, more than anything, to be touched, or coddled, or caressed, or just treated to a good time, or they want to talk, or they want, maybe, to try out a kinky idea or two. Brigitte and I had the luxury of choice. Almost all our clients were very easy, very nice, true gentlemen really, very quirky and perverse sometimes; but who isn't, secretly or not, quirky and perverse? And we quickly got rid of the bad apples. We were lucky – we were educated; we weren't addicted to drugs or booze; we didn't have a pimp or exploiter. We both kept going to school. We were exceptions, that's true, we had the luxury of choice; not all women do. Choice is a luxury."

"That's an understatement."

"Yes, it is. In fact, most women don't, even now, have the luxury of choice. I'm not talking just about prostitutes – about the kids who've been seduced into taking drugs, the young women captured by smuggling rings and who will be killed or mutilated if they try to leave, or, if they are from some other country, back home, their families will be killed. People trafficking is a huge problem, but it's not the only problem. I'm also talking about women in general. A lot of power is still in the hands of men, so, even in marriage, there is a lot of slavery, though it may go by another name."

Nicole lifted the cup to her lips and paused. I could see she was savoring the aroma, enjoying the sensation. Her nostrils flared, she sniffed, delicately. The point of her tongue passed over her lips. Her eyes narrowed. "Couples are difficult. That's true of gay, trans, lesbian, or straight, I think. It's not easy for two people to live together, to desire each other, over a long period of time. Power is always involved. And all the trappings of power – of dominance and submission – are often present, implicitly and unspoken, unrecognized, in the most normal of marriages and couples. Just under the surface, complex games are being played."

"So, you're saying that people who do play – explicit – games are recognizing something that is always there?" I asked, taking another bite of my sandwich. It was delicious.

"Yes, I think so. Yes, in a sense, yes. I think people – couples, lovers – should recognize the power dynamic, and, when it works, have fun with it." Nicole's eyes twinkled as she gazed straight into the heart of me. She took a sip of tea. "Like you and James, Gwendoline. You play it out."

"Yes, we do. But wouldn't recognizing the power games rob from the romance, the sacred sense of union, at least for some people?" I took another bite out of my sandwich. "I mean: love is based a lot on illusion, isn't it?" As I said this, I noticed two very distinguished-looking gentlemen, in finely tailored suits, enter the tearoom. One of them waved to Nicole, bowed slightly, and winked, and she smiled and waved back.

"Yes, maybe you are right, Gwendoline. For some people recognizing the balance of power in a relationship might destroy the romance. Perhaps. But power is romantic too. Seduction is power. Even romance is power: the candles, chocolates, fine food, wine, cognac, exotic vacation spots, the powerful car, beautiful clothes – it's all a *mise-en-scène*, it's theater and illusion – and therefore power: it's about money and status. Wedding dresses and showers and all the ritual – it is power. The priest and the vows – that is an expression of power. All these things keep people in their roles, anchor them; the rituals, whether they're secular or religious, give people recipes, telling them *who* to be, what *role* to play, and instructions on *how* to behave. Just like being able to hypnotize someone is power. There is a lot of illusion involved in all relationships in society. I consider myself, really, a sort of producer. It's all showbiz. As the Bard said, 'all the world's a stage and all the men and women players.' We humans do insist on dressing things up, frills and coverings, furs and silks, wigs and medals, and jewelry. The body, after all – even the most perfect body – is always flawed."

"True," I said, chewing.

"We humans have had inculcated into us a sort of platonic,

ideal, almost mechanical idea of perfection and beauty – machine-like, glittering, strong, and polished. No human body is that perfect. We need illusions."

"Yes," I said. "We piss and we shit, and we drool, and our eyes run, and we leak snot and sweat, and we sniffle and sneeze, and we get fat and develop aches and pains and cellulite and deadly and chronic diseases and dandruff and have acid reflux and burp and belch, and we fart and ... Absolutely, we need illusions."

"Gwendoline, you are a true philosopher!"

"The other day, James farted."

"Really?" Her eyes opened wide, and she grinned, suddenly looking like a little girl. "How dreadfully inconsiderate of him."

"I said, 'James, you farted!' 'Oh, I did?' said he, all wide-eyed and innocent. 'Yes, you definitely did.' 'Dear Gwen, I thought you wouldn't notice.' 'Well, I did notice.' And he said, 'Gwen, I'm in despair. I'm done for. I've destroyed all your illusions.' 'Not really, darling,' I said, 'it was a cute fart, a delicate sweet little hiccup fart.' And he said, 'It wasn't too noisy, darling, not too intrusive, or sulfurous?' 'No, darling,' I said, 'it was a perfectly well-rounded not too smelly modest little fart.'"

"You and James make up a perfect sparring-match couple – just the right degree of warfare. I'm jealous. He's a handsome man, and I think he's just intelligent enough to handle you." Nicole took a bite from her sandwich and nodded towards the two gentlemen who were now ordering their lunch. "Those two men are among the most intelligent people I have ever met. One is an economist at the Bank of Italy and the other is a professor of geophysics at the Rome University La Sapienza. He also has a high-tech company. One is divorced. The other is a life-long bachelor and a bit of a Don Juan. They went to high school together, and they have lunch once a month, usually here. They are both occasional clients. Often when they have to entertain people from abroad – from the Middle East and Africa and China – and the States – they come to me. I'd say that in a way we've almost become friends. More than anything, they like the freedom to be able to talk about anything. And they like the company of young and beautiful and intelligent women, and I can provide that. It's a taste, for some older powerful men, of immortality, the feeling of being young again, of being appreciated by youth and beauty, and the feeling of status of course that comes, for an older man, from possessing and displaying – even if through payment – a stylish, intelligent, beautiful young woman. The sex is almost secondary."

"I think that's often true. I mean, I suspected as much. People are often lonely because they can't talk about some of the things closest to what they really are. And it's often difficult to talk to the person closest to you."

"Yes, you're right, Gwendoline." She paused and patted her lips with the serviette. She frowned, as if in concentration. "My job, partly, is to know instinctively what people desire, what they need, without their telling me. And I have a number of girls who are students or young professionals and who are glad to earn extra money – and even grateful for the experience and the contacts. I'm pretty good at putting the right people together and in knowing who needs, or wants, what – I'm not sure why, but I think it's because I have had a great many unruly desires – and inner conflicts – myself, so I can see the clues and the cues in other people, men, and women. Often, like those two men, it's the talk, and the teasing, and the mental intimacy – the no-holds-barred ability to talk of anything and laugh at anything – that is what they like. And, of course, an occasional wild weekend somewhere – or evening – with a beautiful and obliging young woman who has imagination and taste. Then, of course, some men like to be tied up, or to be a transvestite for an evening, or act as the maid, or nurse, or schoolmarm, often the scenarios are quite elaborate, and they must be just right. At its best, catering to such tastes is an art."

I patted my mouth. "People have complicated identities; I mean each psyche is a sort of ramshackle, slipshod, accidental, improvised, many-layered house of cards."

Nicole gazed at me for a moment, as if I were a prized pupil, which, maybe, I was. She smiled. "Yes, that's true. The outer self, the social self we present to other people, the self we allow them to see, it is usually a pretty limited and heavily censored version of who we are or who we might be. It's a sort of moving, shifting front line, or compromise, between what we might really be, the circus inside, and what we are permitted to be. So, to make up for the deficit of fulfilment, as it were, in our private lives, we unleash our fantasy lives, our Walter Mitty existences, or Marquis de Sade existences, or Story of O existences, or Harlequin Romance existences, we imagine, we embroider, we play games in our minds: we are Napoleon or Marilyn Monroe or Tiger Woods. When people act out their fantasies, well, lots of the scenarios are parody and exaggeration, and irony. People playing at what they are not – and they know, of course, that they are playing at what they are not, at least what they are not socially, outwardly, or in their bodily form. Biology and anatomy don't always match desire – or felt identity – or imagination."

"But imagination and reality can intersect, pretty deeply, it seems to me." This was a topic that interested me as a mathematician. My work was to try to imagine reality – and how math could decipher and structure reality so we could better understand it.

"Yes, you are right, Gwendoline. After all, you are the mathematical virtuoso and philosopher, not I. Reality – particularly social reality – is largely constructed in our minds – and by our minds. Stories – religions and myths – hold the whole thing together. Nationalism is the same. Someone called nations 'imagined communities,' if I remember correctly, so our social lives are constructed around imagined entities, around stories, around fantasies."

"Yes – fantasies. Certainly much of social reality is constructed that way."

"Stendhal saw the emotion of love – and it could equally be desire or infatuation or lust – as the result of what he called 'crystallization.' He meant that all sorts of desirable ideas crystalize – cluster the way a crystal builds up – around the figure of the loved one, a sort of projected aura of ideal images, conscious, semi-conscious, even unconscious, that gather around the person you have glimpsed or just met, all workings of the imagination. The awakening can be pretty brutal."

"Infatuation," I said, "Associating all sorts of delicious ideas – a whole new life, a whole new self – with the idea of the loved or desired person."

"Yes, that was Stendhal's idea: all sorts of wonderful ideas cluster around the image of the person you love – as if drawn by a magnet – and so you become infatuated with desire – with lust embroidered with all sorts of wonderful images. It's about transforming and changing yourself as much as possessing the loved one. It's a bit like lusting after a new purse or a new pair of shoes. By buying the shoes, you will transform yourself, invent a new you. It's a form of redemption. A Louis Vuitton handbag takes the place of Christ the Redeemer. But it's always only a temporary fix."

I smiled. "Obstacles to redemption or to possession help. Satisfaction delayed is satisfaction redoubled."

"Yes, you're right: obstacles stimulate – often create – desire. Romantic comedy and mating rituals are all about obstacles. As

Stendhal pointed out, this crystallization process – attaching all sorts of desired ideas to the loved one – works best if you are not around the lady or gentleman all day; indeed, it's best if they are far away, unattainable, in some way taboo. That's why, for some people, adultery is so seductive. You are going for what you can't – and what you shouldn't – have. You are risking, and gambling. The desire is more intense – and the imagination liveliest, the crystallization more powerful – when you don't or can't possess the person in question, or only possess them intermittently, imperfectly. Risk and danger are inebriating – the fog of lust is like the fog of war: who knows what will happen? When you truly, finally, possess the desired one, the risk is over – and much of the fun."

"Or when you buy the shoes or the purse."

"Precisely." Nicole took a dainty bite from her sandwich. "You are right. Dreaming, in that case, is often better than possessing. Once the shoes are bought, it is an anticlimax. They get put away in a cupboard, whereas religious redemption can provide you with a permanent charge. Christ is within you, and yet never fully possessed – salvation and paradise are always just out of reach."

"A literary critic at NYU once told me that in romance, the story is over when the girl and guy get together. Marriage wraps it up. After that, the plot stops; nothing literary or interesting happens."

"Yes," Nicole smiled. "Though, of course, a lot happens. But the mating game is the essence of romance and comedy. And it is all quite formal and coded, underneath, if you look closely. In Shakespearean comedy, the last act is the act where the hero and heroine get married. It is a bit anticlimactic. As you said, nothing much can happen after that. The fun is in the chase, in the dance, in the struggle, the showing off, the enticing and seducing. We are hunters, and we are like peacocks, doing a performance, strutting our stuff. Obstacles, as you said, are important. Rivals are important. Mystery adds spice. Ritual is crucial – the flowers, the champagne, the expensive car, the stag party, the $100,000 wedding."

"Ouch! If I got married, I'd just want to go to City Hall, and then we'd elope. That's my idea: The two of us scampering off to a beach somewhere, or some city we've never been in, or a farm in the middle of nowhere. Anyway, like courtship and weddings, perversion is ritualized too." I poured us both some more tea, from the two little pots. I like tea. I didn't really understand why I didn't drink more of it; I suppose coffee is my first love, and tea comes second. But I should really try tea more often.

I glanced at Nicole – so precise, so perfect, the sculptural delineation of her nostrils, her lips, her silky eyelashes, so precise, so dark, jet-black, each one of them.

She laughed. "Absolutely, Gwendoline, Perverse scenarios are complex, ritualized and repetitive, like religious ceremonies. They are stories and miniature myths, acted out. Every little fetish is a story, every kink or icon involves stories"

"Stories?"

"Yes, every fetish is a story, or set of stories, unconscious or pre-conscious stories, and sometimes conscious stories, forms of acting out. High-heeled shoes suggest a myriad of ideas and scenarios. A studded leather collar or an Edwardian choker, ideally with a cameo, evoke a whole world. But I think that this is true of so-called ordinary sex too. A simple caress is more than a caress; it's a thought, it's a half-conscious scenario, it's a promise – it's a gage and measure of things to come, it touches a nerve, it touches memories, it triggers expectations; that's why caresses are so tantalizing, so intense, and so frightening. A kiss is the most powerful of caresses. Well, it's one of the most powerful. A glance is the same – it offers a gateway to the soul, to the future, to a possible adventure – all of which implies danger as well."

"Yes," I said. "A first kiss, like when you are a teenager, is particularly exciting. It can also be scary. A lot is at stake – maybe your whole future! You have to decide what you want to do – or not."

"Yes."

"What about costumes – corsets, feathers, veils, all that sort of thing. Even the Bible and Salome knew about those."

"Well, the Ancients – the Jews, the Greeks, the Romans – and I presume all the others – were wise in the ways of the flesh. A lot of fripperies, veils, and feathers create a 'distancing' effect – a puzzle and a mystery – that's one effect of a lot of these trappings. Another is to emphasize sexual attributes – or to symbolize them, the feathers, the spangles, the beads, the glitz, and the glitter. The bustier – or corset – for instance, is a marvelous invention. It emphasizes, and it hides at the same time; and it is also a form of bondage, subtle enough, and flattering; often it narrows the waist and widens the hips, evoking ancient archetypes, evoking procreative possibilities, turning a woman into something like a fertility object, a procreator, fecund. And such symbols are signals, a form of advertising, saying, 'Here, take me, I'm a sexual object, I want you to desire me, I want you to possess me, I challenge you to try, if you will, and if you have the guts, to possess me, to conquer me, go ahead and try.' It's an offer, and a challenge. It's like throwing down the gauntlet."

"It makes you exotic too."

"Yes, exoticism is a useful erotic tactic. It is a way of avoiding the incest taboo, or at least that's what some of Freud's followers thought. If you are fitted out in feathers or spangles or a belt of bananas, you are, symbolically speaking, probably not the chap's mother or sister. You are 'other.' You are outside the tribe. You are, on the level of the pre-conscious or unconscious, an exotic animal, to be hunted down, captured, and tamed. As an exotic creature, you can be sexual in a way a close relation cannot be. Also, in banal terms, you can be categorized as a 'loose woman' of 'fallen woman.' So that makes you fair game. Exoticism, which overlaps sometmes with racism, allows desire to wander outside the tribal boundary and usual decorum."

"Hmm! Yes."

Nicole gave me a look that was sweet and almost predatory. She bared her teeth. "I'm getting even more jealous now." She laughed. "You and Martine Aubin, well, well ..."

"You shouldn't be," I said.

"You are a nice plaything, a beautiful toy, Gwendoline."

"Yes, I am." I sat up extra straight, a bit prim.

Nicole laid her hand on my wrist. "Darling Gwendoline, I think it must be a pure delight to subdue you!"

"I suppose it might be," I speared another olive. Nicole was, in her cool, precise, intellectual way, a very commanding and animal presence. She was dangerous. There was a tension of desire – an unspoken power struggle – between us, that was impossible to ignore.

We finished lunch. Nicole insisted on paying the bill, and as we stood up, she asked. "Would you like to come back to the shop? You could see our new inventory."

I hesitated. I really should work. I was about to hem and haw. But then, without really thinking about it, I said, "Yes, I'd like that."

"Wonderful!"

I checked my cellphone for messages or texts from Kate or James. But there was nothing – Just some routine emails from a mathematician in Oxford, a nice lady whom I had not yet met, and a Jesuit friend in Paris who was sending me a couple of references – copies of rather rare articles – I had asked him about.

We walked across Piazza di Spagna, down Via Condotti, across a side street to via Frattina, and then into a small side street, or dead end, and through a doorway into the little cobblestoned courtyard that I remembered from two years before. Nothing seemed to have changed. Time, here, stood still. The antique bookstore was still there; the entrance to the apartment block was unchanged; the flowers were still in pots sitting on the cobblestones, the bluish light from the sky still filtered down, luminous, dusty, and glamorous, into the small sheltered courtyard.

In the window of Nicole's *La Petite Boutique Rouge* – I glimpsed a deliciously tight, wasp waist corset and several whips, displayed in a little arc, and framed by panels containing illustrations by fetish artists, such as John Willie, Stanton, and Guido Crepax; there was also that classic Allen Jones poster depicting voluptuously virile legs sculpted in what looked like steel-gray leather or latex.

Hanging in the door was a neat little sign in red-and-black Gothic script. It indicated that the shop was closed for lunch, but would open again at two o'clock. I glanced at my wristwatch. It was precisely two o'clock.

Nicole unlocked the door, and opened it. The little bell tinkled. She turned the closed sign around, so that it now said "Open." The open side featured a black-and-red cartoon image of a smiling voluptuous female devil, with horns and a tail, who, with a lascivious wink, invited the customer to enter. We entered, and the door closed smoothly behind us.

Once again, I was in the fairy-tale boudoir, where James had brought me to have my first "lesson" and where I first met Martine and Philip.

I breathed it in. It was a mini-trip back in time, a dizzying gulp of nostalgia; it took me back to the old me – two years ago.

The small plush room was unchanged; the gilt Louis XV chairs, with their ornate armrests, the cream-colored ormolu dresser with its elaborate gilded handles, all stood in the same place; the anonymous miniature 18th Century painting of naked frolicking nymphs and the large reproduction of Fragonard's *Happy Lovers* were precisely where I remembered them. It was all the same, and it still smelt and looked fresh, like a summer breeze. Red roses stood proudly in a ceramic vase on the dresser, and the thick cream curtains still indicated the way to the change room. And there were the two full-length mirrors with gilt frames. The effect was intimate, like a boudoir. There were iPads and old-fashioned paper newspapers in a rack, and magazines, *Vogue, Harpers, The Economist, Le Monde*, the *Frankfurter Allgemeine Zeitung, Corriere della sera, la Repubblica, El País*, the Japanese, *Asahi Shimbun*, and so on.

"I can show you our collection, if you like, Gwendoline, and you might even, if you have time, try some things on."

Try some things on? I licked my lips. I almost purred. Hmm, the temptation was luscious. And I had been working hard! I did deserve a break!

"Yes," I said.

"Come." Nicole indicated the way. We stepped through the thick velvet curtains into the change room. I now discovered that, behind the change room, was a hidden steel door; it led to a minimalist ultra-modern spiral stainless-steel staircase. We went down the staircase.

"Oh!" I opened my eyes wide. We were in a large empty white room lined with rows and rows of built-in wardrobes flat to the walls. There was a platform or stage at the far end of the room, and hanging on the wall behind the platform were chains and manacles. Spotlights shone down from the ceiling. Brightly lit, in the center of the platform, were what looked like wooden stocks – the sort of thing they would put witches and gossips in and pelt them with rotten apples, pig slop, and mud.

Nicole took my arm. "We could chain you up down here, Gwendoline, on the stage, perhaps for a party, or lock you naked in the stocks, if that would please you."

I narrowed my eyes and licked my lips. Would that please me? I wasn't sure. The exquisite ambivalence of public humiliation and shame – just the thought made me antsy. "Perhaps, maybe, someday, for a private, very select, party ..."

Nicole put her hand on my shoulder and rolled back one of the inbuilt sliding doors; hangers trundled out; they contained lines and lines of corsets, in different colors and materials, hanging close together, dozens and dozens of them.

"So, if we were to chain you up on the stage over there, we could use black leather, say, a hood, or a fetish outfit ..."

"Or leave me naked."

"Yes, that would be pleasant. I do like it when you are naked, Gwendoline. You are really designed to be naked and kept in a cage. We could start with you dressed. Then we would strip you slowly ... bit by bit, piece by piece."

"That might be cute."

"It could be a piece of performance art."

"Deconstructing Gwendoline."

"Exactly." Nicole patted my cheek. "Speaking of being naked, Gwendoline, why don't you take off your clothes? Then you can try some things on."

"Right, okay," I said. "But won't you have other clients?"

"Oh, it's a slow day – and, if there are other clients, you won't mind, will you? I'm sure they, whoever they are, won't mind."

"Depends," I said. But, nothing ventured, nothing gained; it would be fun to try on some of this stuff and ... "Okay," I said, "I'll strip."

"Wonderful. We'll have fun." Nicole pulled out another corset. "Here you have PVC, or polyvinyl chloride. It is glossy and shiny, and a bit tacky, in my opinion. Young neophytes looking for a thrill are often drawn to PVC. Of course, it can be used to ironic effect – combined, say, with the frilly little-girl look, or with a long Victorian nightgown. But the line between sophisticated irony and simple kitsch is often thin, and much depends on the culture and eye of the beholder."

I nodded. I began to think I was back in university. Nicole was a fine lecturer.

"Rubber is thicker, less shiny, and more matt – subdued and understated if you like, but often heavier, more restrictive, and enslaving."

While Nicole talked and displayed the corsets, I lifted off my T-shirt and put it on a hanger. I unbuckled my belt and slipped out of my jeans and folded them over a hanger. Then I took off my panties. If I was going to be naked, I would be naked. Gwendoline does not do things by halves.

"Wristwatch too," said Nicole, holding out her hand.

"Yes, Mistress," I whispered. Just saying the words gave me a shivery little thrill that rippled up and down my back. I slipped my wristwatch off, and she took it.

"I'll leave your phone here, on this chair, just in case someone calls, but I'll put your clothes and backpack in a safe place," she said, and disappeared with them – and with my sandals – through a door, and I stood, barefoot and naked, exposed and vulnerable, just as I wished to be. So, there she was, Gwendoline Clermont, once again naked as the day she was born.

"You certainly don't need clothes, Gwendoline," Nicole said as she came back, carefully closing the door behind her. "As I said, you were born to be naked."

I stretched, went up on my toes, and pirouetted around. I did feel free.

"But, that said, you could use a collar and leash, Gwendoline. I don't want you running wild on me."

"Okay. Attach me."

She removed a thick leather collar from a hanger in one of the hidden wardrobes. The wardrobe was a cornucopia; it contained a whole array of collars – rows upon rows of them, thin collars, thick collars, metal collars, leather collars, colored collars, classic black collars.

She held the collar out. "Is this acceptable, Prisoner?"

I took the collar. It was thick leather, rather heavy, and quite high: it had a large ring at the front, and an extra ring at the back, probably for a chain to link handcuffs. "This is definitely acceptable, Mistress Nicole."

As she fitted it around my neck, the silk lapels of her jacket brushed against my breasts. Her breath was perfumed and sweet. She buckled the collar into place, tight but not too tight. She stood back, contemplated the effect, and then attacked a leather thong leash to the collar's front ring, just under my chin.

"So, Prisoner Gwendoline, shall we continue our tour?" She tugged lightly on the leash, swining me around to follow her.

"Yes, Mistress."

Nicole opened one large wardrobe and drawer after another, giving me an in-depth tour with lectures on everything and every aspect of sensuality: she pulled out one walk-in drawer, and showed me the section dedicated to sensual aromas, with row upon row of little bottles and vases and vials: musk, lavender, rose, banana, vanilla, sandalwood, licorice, cucumber, and cardamom. She showed me the section devoted to total body coverings – Japanese style zentai, and catsuits of various kinds, with hoods and without. I didn't realize there could be so many designs and textures and fabrics: latex, spandex, rubber, nylon, etc., etc. It was endless!

She tugged on the leash, drew me close to her and kissed me on the shoulder, and looked up into my eyes. "James should take you someplace – some tropical island – where you never have to wear a stitch."

I felt a trickle of sweat form under the collar and wander down my backbone. As she kissed me, I was suddenly acutely conscious of my nudity. Pearls of sweat formed on my skin, even though down here, underground, it was cool – like in a vault. I was a sweat-pearled body in a vault full of phantoms.

"You don't need any excuses to be who you are, Gwendoline." She pulled me closer. She kissed me on the forehead. "You are perfect, Gwendoline, just the way you are. You don't hurt anybody, and you give pleasure and love to lots of people."

"You are very kind, Mistress Nicole."

We stood for a moment and just looked at the display. The cat-suits and zentai hung in rows – I fingered a few sample materials.

I looked down at myself. Her elegance and my nudity were both statements.

"And this is the shoe section. Try on these pumps." She lifted a pair of very high-heeled black mules from a shelf of shoes – there were stilettoes, high heels, pony-hoof shoes, and bondage boots, almost all in black.

She knelt in front of me, and I slipped my feet into the mules. Suddenly I was three inches taller and cantilevered into the sexy stiletto pose.

"How do they feel?" Still holding my leash, she stepped back.

"Voluptuous."

"They are made of the finest leather." She knelt and buckled and locked them so I would have to bend over to liberate myself, and I would need a key.

She slid another large door aside "Here, we have makeup, and body paint, and false tattoos." On the shelves were aligned bottles and spray bottles and brushes and then hundreds of tattoo designs were lined up and on display: dragons, serpents, hearts, plants, flowers, demoiselles, castles, and purely abstract patterns.

"And here we have long gloves." Nicole pulled out another hanger. And there they were: long gloves, in satin, silk, lace, latex, rubber, in black and in all sorts of colors. "Some of these are bondage gloves," she showed me two or three samples. "These versions turn your hands into paws."

"Hmm, Gwendoline, the panther," I whispered.

"I think, Gwendoline, that you might find these leather binding sleeves particularly interesting. Have a look. As you can see, the arms are bound together, zipped into this single tube, and then constrained by these laces. This one goes behind your back and can be attached to your collar. Would you like to try it, dear Prisoner? I would love to see you try it."

"Yes, Mistress." I bowed my head.

She pulled out the long tapered black leather "glove" and held it up. "I think it will do nicely. Put your arms tight together, behind your back."

"Yes, Mistress." I put my arms behind my back and she wrapped the "glove" around both arms, and zipped it shut, scrunching my arms close together. I was surprised. It was so fast, and unexpected.

"It has a zipper?"

"Yes, a zipper and laces, double security."

I felt a little frisson of helplessness. She laced up the crisscrossing cords, tightening them, locking my arms even tighter together, pressed close behind my back; the tension pulled my shoulders back, sharply, tightly. I couldn't move my arms, not even a little bit.

"Now, we shall just anchor this restraint to your collar." She lightly brushed her fingers against my shoulders as she attached the "glove" to the ring at the back of my collar and locked the two together.

"How does it feel?"

"Tight." I bit my lip.

She walked around me, circling me, considering her work. She tugged the leash, slowly pulling me to her. She touched my breasts with the tips of her fingers, cupped one of them, stroking it softly, and kissed me on the lips: our eyes, wide open, stared into each other.

She could do anything with me she wished to do. She drew back and grinned. It was a sudden grin like a bright beam of light and made her look like she was a mischievous, naughty teenager, not a sophisticated professional 40-year-old.

"Now, darling, in this section, we have various other bits of equipment." She pulled out a series of slanting trays that displayed a whole array of special equipment. "Here are pasties or clamps for the beasts – we might try some of those on."

"No clamps, please, Mistress."

"No clamps? Why, Gwendoline, you surprise me! I thought you'd like to suffer." She touched my cheek with the tips of her fingers and kissed me, slowly, deeply, on the lips, and it was a nice soft, warm kiss, and her hand was moving, lightly, softly, warmly, on my bum. "Well, then, dear Prisoner, glue-on pasties it shall be – you choose."

I considered the lineup of pasties. "Those." I nodded, indicating my choice with my chin. "The black-and-red ones with the little dangling jingle bell tassels.

"So – it shall be as you indicate, Gwendoline. Jingle, jingle, all the way!" Nicole opened a small drawer and pulled out a flask and a small ball of cotton wool. She poured clear liquid from the flask onto the cotton wool.

"What are you doing?"

"Getting you prepared. Your tits need to be ready."

"What is that stuff?" The little flask looked sinister. What was she going to do to me now? Lacquer me all over? Turn me into a painted icon?

"Skin cleanser."

"Oh."

"To make sure the pasties stick." She pulled over a chrome-colored stool and sat down in front of me. Concentrating closely, she began to clean my breasts, carefully moving the cotton swab over my nipples and areolae and around both breasts and underneath. "You have first-class breasts, Gwendoline," she said, tracing the undercurve of one with the point of her finger.

"I think they've gotten bigger." I frowned.

"Yes, I think so too. Before, they were neat little cupcakes. Now, they are, how shall I put it, showier, bouncier. All that excited estrogen pumping. They are full, magnificent, ripe."

"Ripe!" I pouted. I was an ageless nymph; I wasn't *ripe*! I would never be *ripe*. I'd be Peter Pan forever!

The cleanser tingled and tickled. It was warm, then cool as it evaporated. My nipples were erect, engorged, straining.

Nicole glanced up. "You are so responsive, Gwendoline. Every pore, every muscle, every gland, every secretion reacts precisely on command. Working with you is very gratifying."

"Hmm!" I frowned. I'm a windup toy, a sex doll!

She put the adhesive strips in place on the back of the pasties, then she positioned the pasties carefully. Each touch of her fingers was electric. She licked her lips as she was doing this, as if I were a piece of luscious smooth vanilla cake topped with icing, and she was applying cream puff curlicues. I sensed that she wanted to bite me, and eat me – it was, for me, a delicious sensation. On my skin, I felt her breath, moist, desiring, and warm.

"Yes, Gwendoline, you *are* delicious. Yes, I *do* want to eat you." She smiled and looked up and pressed the pasties into place. She cupped her hands under my breasts, lifting them, jiggling them. "Now, you can shake and shimmy and jiggle and juggle and leap up and down and run around all you want, Gwendoline, and they will stay on."

"You mean I'll be stuck with them forever?"

"No, my silly darling." She stood up and put her cool hands firmly on my shoulders. Her face approached mine. Her lips – playfully, tentatively – brushed my lips. Her tongue, moist and cool and pink, flickered out. I parted my lips. Her tongue met mine, touched it. The tips of our tongues did a slippery tactile wet little dance, forward, back, and up to the middle and down to the back, hoop-la!

"Very good, Gwendoline," she said, stepping back slightly. "Don't worry about the pasties. We can peel them off easily."

She stepped further back, narrowed her eyes, put her hand to her chin, and examined her work. "I tried to line them up to be perfectly symmetrical. Now, let's have a look at you, Prisoner. Let us contemplate our artistry." She stared at my breasts, caressed one, then the other, jingling the bells, and smiled. "Yes, absolutely right."

She took up the leash and pulled me around so I could see myself in one of the full-length mirrors. There I was, framed in the flattering light of the mirror: in patent leather stilettos, imprisoned in a stiff, high, black leather collar that forced my chin up, keeping my head rigidly erect. I looked as if I had no arms; they were pinioned so tight behind my back, they were invisible; and, then, adding to the ridiculous effect, were the pasties, red-and-black, and star-shaped, with dangling, bright red tassel bells that swayed and tinkled and glittered. They went jingle-jangle each time I moved. It was true: My breasts did seem extra bouncy. *Ripe!* Pshaw!

Nicole, standing beside me and holding the leash, was

perfectly dressed and coiffed, in Armani chic, as if she were about to preside the Board of Directors of the Deutsche Bank.

"I think James will love this look." She put her hand on my shoulder. It was warm and dry, and roused me just by its touch. "Later, Gwendoline, if we have time, we should endow you with a Goth look, I think: Lots of makeup, a few false piercings. Perhaps try out a corset or two."

At that moment, my phone, which Nicole had placed on a chair, so I wouldn't miss a call, began to buzz.

"Shall I?" Nicole raised a quizzical eyebrow. It was clear I couldn't answer – I was pinioned and helpless.

"Yes. Answer, please, Mistress." Sweat trickled down my back; I was at this moment very much in fear of bad news – from James, from Kate, from Martine ...

Nicole picked the phone up, pushed the button, and held it to me.

"Hello?" I said.

"Hello, darling," James' voice was warm and intimate, as if he were breathing into my ear. "How are you?"

"More important," I said, "how are you?"

"I'm fine. I'm just concluding the real estate deal I came to Moscow for, simple really; I should be home tomorrow evening – we can dine out, if you wish, perhaps at Alfredo's."

"I'd love to. I'm just getting some lessons from Nicole – at her shop. She's showing me her collection."

"Ah, Nicole!"

"She's allowing me to try out some things."

"Oh, that sounds, very spicy, very enticing. Are you wearing something now?"

"Not much."

"How interesting. Perhaps Nicole could describe you. It is always amusing to have the third person point of view."

"Hmm, yes, okay."

Nicole put the phone on speaker. "You are on speaker, James."

"Good. I'll comment where appropriate."

"Well, Gwendoline and I ran into each other and had lunch. And right now ..." And Nicole described what I looked like, using the word "prisoner" and not my name. *The prisoner is wearing a very tight three-centimeter-high leather collar; the prisoner is naked and has her arms pinioned tightly behind her back ... the prisoner is wearing pasties, the prisoner ...*

"I wish I were there." James sounded pleased.

"I will take my revenge when you get home, Master," I growled.

"I'm looking forward to that." He laughed. "I'll be there, if all goes well, about seven o'clock in the evening."

"I'll be waiting."

"I'm counting on it, my love," he said. "Goodbye, Gwen, goodbye, Nicole." And he was gone.

"Shall we continue our tour, Gwendoline?"

"Yes, Mistress."

She opened another door and slid out a rack on which hung dozens and dozens of corsets and other treasures. She held up a corset. "I rather like this one, dear Prisoner."

"Yes, Mistress." I concentrated, like a good schoolgirl.

"You will note, Gwendoline, how each detail of color and design – degrees of nudity or not – and each fabric – resonates differently, feels unique, and has a variety of erotic connotations."

"I am in awe, Mistress."

"And so, you should be, Prisoner. These objects have been invented for your pleasure." She opened another slide-out drawer. "Now, we have dildos."

"Dildos?"

"Yes, don't be obtuse, Gwendoline! Some come with special positioned double vibrators to give the clitoris and the G-spot some double fun. There are lots of new and ingenious designs on the market."

"Yummy!" I slurped goofily with my tongue and lips.

"You are rather frisky, aren't you, Gwendoline."

"I try." I grinned.

She put her finger under my chin. "I think, Gwendoline, that you must be punished."

She held up a miniature U-shaped vibrator – It was one of the so-called G-spot and clitoris combined things; it looked like a little U-shaped pink flexible plastic magnet. Nicole smiled. "This is remote-controlled."

"Oh?"

"It allows your Mistress or Master to give you an orgasm while you are standing in line at the baker's or giving a speech to the Chamber of Commerce."

I had a vision of myself reduced to slobbering incoherence being paraded down the streets of Rome and forced to have continual remote-control orgasms every few cobblestones.

"As I said, it works by remote control – and it can be operated with a computer, so that, say, James could be in Singapore and via his computer and your computer – with Blue Tooth – he could give you an intimately modulated, fine-tuned orgasm, while you are, say, in Amsterdam or Rome."

"Wow! I mean ..."

"I'm tempted to insert it now, dear Prisoner, and take you up into our little piazza and give a public demonstration. I could buzz you around the square like a toy airplane."

"Oh ... " I shivered. Me! There I am! I can see me, vibrating with a remote control orgasm, bound and pinioned, in front of *La Petite Boutique Rouge*, and next to the climbing vines and the potted plants, or standing, howling, in front of the antique bookshop – an attraction for tourists, publicity for Nicole.

"Yes, I thought you might find such an experience amusing." Nicole put her hand on my bum and squeezed. "I think I shall put this little item – in its pink version – away, wrapped as a gift, free, for you and James. Perhaps, darling Gwendoline, once James has taken you on a few test flights, you could write a testimonial." She whispered the last words, her breath warm against my cheek, and ticking my earlobe, and she caressed my backside delicately, sculpting and kneading all the nerve endings; her every touch, her very fingertips, displayed mastery and art. She leaned forward and kissed me on the lips. It was a sweet, prolonged, exploratory, and deep kiss. Her silk jacket pressed against my breasts. My nipples strained under the pasties. The little bells jingled. With my arms pinioned, I was totally in her power. I was wet and trembling with anticipation and trepidation.

She tapped me on the bum three times, and then she moved back slightly. "Shall we continue your education, Prisoner?"

"Yes, please, Mistress."

"Now, here, my dear helpless Gwendoline, we have butt-plugs. This is a whole world, a variant, as it were of the dildo. They come in various forms – with tails or without tails, fluffy tails, animal tails, and brightly colored tails."

"Hmm – brightly colored tails?"

"And here we have ball gags and bits – for naughty little pony-girls and occasionally, for disobedient ponyboys."

"Interesting."

"We might try a gag." Nicole lifted one up.

"A gag, I don't know."

"Come, Gwendoline, darling, I insist."

"Okay, but ..."

"Open wide. This won't hurt."

"Well ..." Then like an obedient little idiot, I opened my mouth wide. She slipped the rubber ball of the ball gag into it, forcing my mouth even wider open. She strapped it in place. Three thick rubber straps went around my head and two over. The gag was equipped, I realized – but too – late – with attachable blinders. These she fastened on either side of my eyes, so, like a horse wearing blinkers, I could only see straight ahead.

"Ghhmph!"

"If you slobber, dear Gwendoline, I shall be forced to spank you!" She tightened the gag.

"Ghhmph!"

"That's right, Gwendoline."

"Ghhmph!" Saliva was building up. My tummy rippled in excitement – and flooded with a delicious tingling frisson of panic. How is it, dear Gwendoline, that you always manage to get yourself into these dreadful fixes?

"Perhaps, Gwendoline, you need a tail."

"Ghhmph!" No way, I waggled my head, my breasts juggled and jingled, the bells tinkled, my backside swayed back and forth in protest: No way would I sport a tail!

"One of these?" Nicole held up a bright bushy yellow-tailed butt-plug and wagged it in my nose.

"Ghhmph!" I shook my head as vigorously as I could, jingle-jangle, jingle-jangle: No, no, a thousand times no – not now, at any rate.

"Quite right. We'll save the butt-plug fluffy tail for later."

"Ghhmph!"

"I think we should add some perfume – the sexiest muskiest over-the-top animal-in-heat smell might do."

"Ghhmph!" I protested.

"This will be fun." She slapped my bum – a playful little slap.

"Ghhmph!"

She brought out a small vial with a spray top, and she sprayed some on my belly and around my breasts and then on my ass.

"Ghhmph!"

I sniffed. I suddenly smelled like an overpopulated whore house in heat – but it was a nice, sharp, rich, spicy hormonal smell, and it made me as horny as hell.

"Exciting, *n'est-ce pas*?" She stepped over to a drawer and brought out a cat-o'-nine-tails, contemplated it for a moment, and then whisked it gently over my backside, the points and braids caressing my skin, and then she moved it up and down my belly, flicking it gently, just touching the skin, applying a danger-ous, teasing, feathery caress. She circled me like a leopard circ-ling her prey. I was wet with fear and lust.

The front door bell tinkled, I looked up at the monitor, the door to the shop opened. A tall young woman in black jeans and a black T-shirt came in. She looked around and then headed for the back of the shop.

"Ghhmph??" I snorted. It was not hot in the basement, but sweat streamed down my back, sweat-pearled in sliver sparkles on my breasts, sweat beaded, making a luminous patina on my belly.

"Oh, don't worry, Prisoner. You are perfectly presentable."

"Ghhmph!"

"And you smell delicious!"

"Ghhmph!" I stamped my high-heeled foot.

"Good enough to eat. Yum, Yum!"

More sweat beaded down my back; it pearled on my breasts. The breast bells jingled. I realized, not for the first time, that I am an idiot; I deserved to be branded and driven naked out of the city; at the thought of it, a delicious hot frisson of shame and humiliation spread up my lower belly, and down my thighs. I shivered in horrified delight. My breasts bounced; the breast bells jingled – jingle, jingle, tinkle, tinkle!

The young woman clambered down the spiral staircase. I

turned to look at her and saw her framed between the two blinkers as if she were framed by a camera. She had jet-black hair and a tanned complexion and looked like a model, in a perfectly molded black T-shirt – no bra I noticed – tight black jeans and stylish black boots. She was wearing a heavy backpack, of the kind tiny Kindergarten tots use to tote their monstrous textbooks and computers.

As she took in the scene, her eyes went wide, and she flashed a huge smile. "Hi, Mom! I didn't realize you were busy." She went straight to Nicole and wrapped her arms around my mistress.

Blinkered as I was, I had to turn my whole body to follow the action. The woman kissed Nicole on both cheeks. *Mom?* Did Nicole have a daughter? Was this her daughter? Oh, boy! I could feel saliva dripping seeping past the gag, dribbling from my chin.

"Justine, let me introduce you." Nicole turned to me. "This is my daughter, Justine. Justine, this is Gwendoline, Gwendoline Clermont."

"Ghhmph!" If I could have frowned, I would have.

The young woman's face lit up. "Oh, Gwendoline! Gwendoline Clermont! Mom has told me so much about you." She clapped her hands in delight, slipped out of her backpack, and put it down on the floor. She straightened up and gazed at me with eyes so dark they were like burnished coal, and then she put her warm hands on my naked shoulders, taking possession of the prisoner. "It looks like you two are having fun!"

"Ghhmph!" I stamped a foot.

"Oh, Gwendoline," she smiled, her hands still on my shoulders. "I saw the video of your conference at MIT, and I read your article on stochastic models and the fallacies of prediction. You are so totally, absolutely brilliant."

"Ghhmph!" My breasts swayed and bounced – and chimed and tinkled – jingle, jingle!

Nicole brushed the ticklish stinging tips of the cat-o'-nine-tails across my backside. "Gwendoline and I are trying out a few things. Have you got time, Justine? Would you like to help? Gwendoline may need a few extra lessons in deportment."

"Help? I'd be delighted. I'd be honored. Oh, since I heard of you, Gwendoline, and your work, I've always wanted to meet you – and to talk to you. And now, here we are!"

"Ghhmph!"

"Oh, this is delicious!" Justine's hands were still on my shoulders. She slid one hand down to the curve of my breast, and then she flicked and tinkled the little bell with her finger. "Oh, this is so cute! Little tinkle bells and pasties!"

"Ghhmph!"

She flicked the dangling little bell again, making it swing back and forth, jingle, jingle, jingle. "Gwendoline, I really do want to talk to you if you have time. I'm doing molecular biology at MIT – postgraduate and on my way to my PhD. But I think some philosophical and methodological problems overlap in all the sciences. For instance, there was the paper you wrote on 'Scientific Models and Paradigm Shifts.' It was absolutely super!"

Her hand was stroking the underside of my breast and absent-mindedly tinkling one of the little bells.

With her right hand, Nicole was stroking the cat-o'-nine-tails. "Gwendoline and I ran into each other window shopping on Via Condotti. We had lunch at Babington's, and we've been discussing the philosophies of desire and sex and perversion."

"Super!" Justine put out a finger and touched the drool on my chin, and stroked it, spreading it along my cheek. "Oh, how liquid you are! It's delicious." Her hand moved down my belly – leaving a cool, warm gooey tattoo. "Drip, drip, drip. You are just so perfectly yummy." She spread her fingers wide on my belly, pressing down, possessing me, branding me, making me hers.

Nicole picked out several corsets and held them draped over her arm. "I thought we might take Gwendoline upstairs to the showroom and help her try on some of the corsets."

"Super," said Justine. She took her hands away and rubbed her fingers on her jeans.

"Justine is a great makeup artist," Nicole turned to me. "She's worked on quite a few of the stars – and also on some big film and TV productions."

"I've been helping mom since I was a kid," Justine said. She took the leash from Nicole and tugged me towards her. "Let's go, little pony, let's go, little Prisoner." She slapped my buttocks – they vibrated, bouncy, responding to her mastery touch. My breasts swayed; the pastie bells jingled. I was a circus pony. The only thing I didn't have was a tail.

"Ghhmph!"

"You can neigh all you want. Little good it'll do you."

"Ghhmph!"

"I totally adore her when she is high-spirited." Justine gave me another slap. My buttocks, I felt, were patterned red with finger-prints, blushing. Her imprint and brand were on me.

As we headed up the staircase, Nicole led, carrying the sheath of corsets, I followed. Justine was right behind me, slapping me on the bum and tickling me with the cat-o'-nine-tails. The high-heeled pumps made of each step a very self-conscious effort, and caused my hips and ass to sway, making me acutely conscious of the wet tensions and antsy desire in my lower belly. My breasts swayed; the bells tinkled. "She has an adorable ass," said Justine, flipping the cat-o'-nine-tails against my bum, lightly, playfully, stinging each millimeter of skin.

We got to the top of the stairs and entered the boudoir show-room. "Will you have time for lunch sometime?" Justine asked.

"Ghhmph!" I wagged my bum, nodding my assent.

"That's great. Hyper-super! I'm so totally thrilled. There's a great restaurant near Piazza del Popolo with a super terrace. It'll be my treat!" She slapped my bum and then left the palm of her hand on the stinging skin.

"Ghhmph!"

I snorted and wagged my head. My breasts swayed, the bells went crazy – jingle-jangle, tingle-tangle.

I was standing in the middle of the boudoir showroom, in full view of the little courtyard. I caught a brief glimpse of myself in the full-length gilt-framed baroque mirror. Oh, boy!

I turned blinkered eyes from the mirror, and, through the two old-fashioned show windows, on either side of the door, I could see outside – the shadowy courtyard was bathed in the warm, tender, smoky bluish light of a Roman summer afternoon reflected down from the sky.

A young couple was standing in front of the antique bookshop across the way. They turned and crossed the courtyard and stopped to look at *La Petite Boutique Rouge*'s window display – the corset on the mannequin and the fan-like exhibition of whips. I saw the woman look up – and she pointed. The man looked up. They gazed at me and exchanged some remarks, which seemed to add up to something like, "Wow!"

Nicole noticed this. "Perhaps we should tether you outside the shop, Gwendoline. It would attract interest and add new lustre to your reputation."

"Ghhmph!"

"If we supplied a G-string, you would be legal, I think, and much better than a neon sign." Nicole curved her hand under my left breast and made its jiggly little bell bounce and jingle.

"Ghhmph!" I shivered. Both jiggling bells jingled.

"Yes, mother, she would be legal," said Justine, "Section Seven of Paragraph 325 of the B-3 law of 1908."

"Definitely, better than a neon sign," said Nicole.

I was wet with excitement and pearled in sweat – a weirdly exhilarating mixture of shame, fear, humiliation, and desire.

Justine caressed my backside, scraping her nails across my bum, and then, withdrawing the threat of her nails, she slapped me, gently, twice, a truly amorous caress. She slid her hand around my hip and down my belly to my pubis – still totally waxed and naked as a virgin – and she pressed gently, subtlety, on the downslope, and then gently opened the way to the clitoris – and began a subtle, subtle massage. Oh, but the girl was savvy! Twirl, press, pinch, stroke, slip sideways, slip up and down, and all around ...

I trembled. I swayed. I groaned. I swore I would not snort. No, I won't snort. I won't neigh. I won't whinny. I won't give her the satisfaction. Saliva rushed to my mouth; I tried to swallow; saliva bubbled up, pushed its way around the tight ball gag, and began to drip. I shuddered. Saliva spurted. I couldn't hold it back. I snorted.

"Ghhmph!"

"Ghhmph – Wheeehhugg!" I neighed. I trembled. "Wheeehhugg!" Sweat beaded my skin, everywhere. The bells tinkled and jingled, my breasts – they seemed to be getting larger and heavier by the minute – and swayed back and forth. Jingle, jingle, jingle

I was soaking wet and still trembling. The impact echoed in my thighs, my loins, my belly, my womb, my ass, and my heart. Oh, oh, oh, oh ...

"Oh, that was marvelous. A spontaneous orgasm! A true gift!" Justine put her hands on my shoulders, and, sliding her hands down my breasts and ribcage and belly, she knelt down, and planted a long, savory, warm, intimate kiss on my sweat-pearled tummy.

"Well, darlings," Nicole said, "that was splendid. You are a true artist, Justine."

"Thank you, mother."

Justine kissed her mother on the lips. Nicole returned the kiss. They were rather intimate for mother-daughter, I thought.

"Now, let's try on some corsets!" Nicole was crisp once more, all business. "I think we must liberate Gwendoline if we are to dress her anew."

"May I have the honor?" Justine bowed her head.

"Yes, of course, Justine, the prisoner is yours."

Justine unlocked the ball gag, and slowly, carefully removed it from my mouth. And she pulled the blinkers away from my eyes. Saliva overflowed.

"Oh, naughty Gwendoline," she said, and wiped it with a soft cool white cloth that seemed to have materialized from nowhere.

"Thank you," I said.

Slowly, taking her time, Justine unlaced and unzipped the arms harness, and I was able, finally, to lift my arms out of the contraption and flex them and touch myself. I was wet with sweat, as I have said, and also, damp, to say the least, with excitement, in a post-orgasmic daze.

"I need a shower," I said.

"A dry shower might be more fun," said Nicole, "right here where you can be appreciated."

"Great, yes, I'll do it!" Justine seemed eager to do whatever she was going to do. She disappeared.

"Justine will remove the pasties and their cute little bells," said Nicole. "You, dear Gwendoline, don't have to do a thing. Just be! Perfectly Zen, perfectly still. Now, which one of these corsets strikes your fancy?"

She laid them out on the desk and on the two Louis XV chairs, and I contemplated the choices.

Justine came back with a large fine-grained sponge and some spray and thick bubbly dark turquoise liquid which she took pleasure in pouring over me – and then she scrubbed and brushed – she seemed to be enjoying it. I stood there, a pony or cow being rubbed down, or an idol being serviced, I wasn't sure which. Justine was thorough. She took a humiliating interest in every nook and cranny of my modest self. "Hold up your arms. Yes, like that!" "Open your legs. No, open them wider." "Bend over! That's right. Touch your toes! Don't be shy!" Foam and soap were everywhere. Justine dried me off, and she carefully pried off the pasties – *ouch!* – and worked with a tiny soft brush on cleaning my nipples – they, of course, responded. She took her time, being very coquettish with each nipple. Finally, she toweled me down.

I did feel fresh and clean and smelt like a rose.

The couple in the window had watched this performance with interest. I stared back at them, but they didn't seem in the least intimidated. I saw the man glance at his watch. They drifted off, but not before waving. I waved back.

Nicole handed me one of the corsets. It was black, made of a satin-like material, and had what looked like metal stripes on the front, and embossed bits of metal on the sides. "This looks like a piece of armor," I said, turning it around, "something a warrior would wear." It was stiff and reinforced by whalebone or the equivalent. The buckles looked like latches to a door.

Justine wrapped the corset around me. "It is armored. Corsets are like armor. Now let's just fit this to you. Nicole has taught me well, I think."

Nicole lifted some glasses out of a drawer; they were large, with thick black frames. "Here, put these on."

I did. I adjusted them. They felt heavy, and it was like looking through goggles. I looked at myself in the mirror. "Hmm, yes, I see ..."

"Oh, I love that look!" Justine clapped. "You should always wear them – even if you don't need glasses."

Nicole stood back and gazed at me. "Now, Gwendoline, if, say, you were a blonde, and your hair was up in a severe, tightly controlled bun, and perhaps we'd add black patent leather high heels. A certain degree of formality helps."

I stared into the mirror. "I'd be an old-fashioned fantasy schoolmarm, but naked and vulnerable: Every old-fashioned, 20th Century schoolboy's dream."

"Exactly." Nicole stepped forward. "Pin her arms behind her back, Justine."

Justine unwrapped the corset from my waist and put it down on a chair, and she took my arms, and, with me offering them, she pinioned them tight behind me.

Nicole considered the effect. "Yes, with your arms pinioned behind your back, our old-fashioned schoolboy would undoubtedly get even more excited. You'd be his – to do with what he willed. You would be the symbol of female authority reduced to servitude."

"Ouch."

"You like it." Justine squeezed my arms harder.

I grimaced. I was surrounded and outnumbered.

"Let us take this little experiment a bit further." Nicole lifted a man's dark blue striped necktie out of one of the drawers and began, carefully to tie it around my neck.

Justine squeezed my arms still harder, twisting back my shoulders. I could feel her breath on the nape of my neck.

Nicole finished tying the necktie and patted and smoothed it down with a lingering caressing touch.

Justine let go, but I kept my arms pinioned behind me. I thought the armless effect might be more striking. I looked at myself in the mirror. The heavy glasses and the necktie did confer a certain cachet, a certain je-ne-sais-quoi.

"Now, if we were to replace the necktie with a black tie, or a polka dot bow tie, then the whole effect would be different."

Nicole stroked her chin and contemplated the image in the mirror.

Justine fondled the corset and matched it against my body. "You and this corset will be a perfect fit." She opened the corset up.

"It is cute. I like the frills." I ran my hand over the frills.

"It's a black, under-bust corset. See, it leaves the breasts entirely free, but it emphasizes them. Do you want to try it on?"

"Yes."

Justine opened the corset. I stepped into it, and she slid it around my waist.

Justine began to tighten the laces.

"Ouch," I said.

"I'm going to make this very tight, totally snug." Justine pulled harder on the laces.

"Now, here at the front, we have six busk clips," said Nicole. "The clips have a double notch, so they are a bit tricky. You need nimble hands."

"You both have nimble hands, and sweet lips," said I, displaying my independent, pert, impertinent side.

"Perhaps I should spank you, Gwendoline. I have a nice soft cat-o'-nine-tails here." Nicole lifted it up and trailed it across my backside.

I was now in the frilly little topless wasp-waist black corset, but other than imprisoning my torso, it felt open and free. There was indeed a sweet disorder in my dress. My breasts and buttocks were free – exposed, offered. Nicole ran the tips and straps of the cat-o'-nine tails gently over my buttocks. "Do you mind?" She stepped forward and offered her lips.

"No, not at all," said I. I was eager for her touch.

She kissed me, and then flicked the straps of the cat-o'-nine-tails gently against my backside.

"Are you going to whip me?"

"Of course, darling," she whispered, and she did, very softly – whap, whap, whap!

"May I have a go too," Justine reached for the whip.

"Of course, darling," Nicole handed Justine the whip.

Justine flicked it back and forth, with a bit more energy, and then let the little tangle of sharp thongs rest lasciviously, cruelly, on my tingling backside.

"Yes." Nicole gazed at me. "You have a voluptuous ass, actually, Gwendoline. It's magnificent. I can see why James goes mad for it." She slapped my buttocks lightly.

Justine stepped back and then added to my ensemble a black velvet choker with an ivory cameo at the front and a small silver ring to which a leash could be attached.

The wasp waist of the satin-like black corset, which Justine had tightened, made it tricky to breathe. The black frilly top of the corset curved under my breasts, tickling them with little bits of feathery pointed black lace but leaving them fully exposed. The bottom fringe, like the top, was frilly, and left my pubis and hips naked and entirely free.

While Nicole watched, Justine helped me pull on a pair of silk stockings which had an oily slippery silken sensual feeling and were black and sheer and without a seam; she clipped them to the garters which hung from the bottom of the corset.

I was barefoot in the stockings.

Nicole said, "Now for a new pair of shoes. I think black satin stilettos with little locks will be just right. Justine, could you get me a pair of the five and a half inch stilettos in size five, please."

"Yes, right away, Nicole," Justine clattered down the spiral metal staircase.

"How does the corset feel?" Nicole circled around me, lightly caressed my bum with the flickering soft tips of the cat-of-nine tails.

"Perfect," I said, "just tight enough to be voluptuous torture."

"It does make you aware of your body, doesn't it?"

"Yes." I shivered with a voluptuous little wiggle of my haunches. It sure did. The frilly top tickled my breasts and excited them, my nipples were erect, and the frilly bottom swished lasciviously over my backside. Just breathing made it move – swish, swish, swish.

I turned around. The garter suspenders, tight along my thighs, made every movement self-conscious. "There's inner eroticism," I said, "and outer eroticism."

"Indeed." Nicole ruffled the frills under my breasts and put her hand on my shoulder. She gazed at me – and kissed me on the lips. "You are perfect for this. If you had more time, I would love to use you as a model. We're doing the costumes for an opera in Paris, and beginning work on it next week. It's a rather daring production – lots of nudity and lots of quick change."

Justine appeared with the shoes. "I'll put them on," she said, and she knelt, and I lifted one foot so she could slip the stiletto on. It looked luscious.

"I'm keeping you away from molecular biology," I said.

"Oh, no, not at all," she looked up at me. "I needed a break, and I adore helping mummy with her friends and clients. Mummy often uses me as her model, too – so I know what it's like on both sides of these little performances. Don't I, mummy?"

"Indeed, you do." Nicole said, and turning to me, she added, "Justine is a superb model, very patient, very understanding of my whims and caprices."

Justine buckled the shoe and locked it, and then I slid my foot into the other shoe, and she buckled and locked it.

Now I was imprisoned in the topless-bottomless corset and in the stilettos. I walked back and forth, a doll-like martial stride. I was a toy soldier. Such high heels – these were five and a half inches – certainly do transform the body's sense of itself. I wiggled my backside – the frothy frills brushed back and forth, swishing on the skin, a feathery tickly caress, as if indeed I had a sensuous, fluffy tail.

"It tickles my backside." I shivered and wiggled my bottom, to illustrate the sensation.

"Yes," said Nicole, "tickling and titillation, they're closely related."

Nicole and Justine stood back, mother and daughter, and gazed at me with expert appraising eyes: Was the doll up to scratch? Was the store window mannequin complete?

Justine touched my arm. "I think black satin gloves, going up above the elbows, might be quite nice."

"Yes, that would add a definite touch," said Nicole.

"I'll get them." Justine disappeared through the curtains.

"Meanwhile, I shall add a little touch of makeup." Nicole took a small makeup kit out of the desk drawer; she pondered, licked her lips, and selected a tiny brush; she sat down on one of the two gilt chairs, and, concentrating like a true artist, she began to paint my nipples and areolae a blushing scarlet red – at first I felt a cool astringent tingling and then a warm tightening.

"You are wicked, Nicole."

"Of course, I am. We are playing at being wicked, Gwendoline. In fact, I know that you are totally loyal and quite chaste – in your own fashion – and that your passion – and love – is exalted and truly romantic and reserved for very few people." She lifted away her brush. "You are a fine person, Gwendoline, even if you don't believe it."

"Yes. Thank you." I swallowed. I turned to look at myself in the mirror. Then I turned back so Nicole could continue her work.

At that moment, the bell tinkled, and the door opened, and

two young women came into the shop. One was black, and the other was white and blond, a pure Nordic or Germanic type.

"Hi Jo, hi, Marlene," said Nicole, putting the finishing touches on my nipples and areolae.

The black woman was spectacular. She had extraordinarily long gleaming legs, a high forehead, a neatly trimmed Afro, steel-rimmed tinted aviator glasses, a frilly semitransparent 18th Century-looking white blouse, with a high ruffled neck and a loosely knotted pink tie, over the blouse she was wearing a natty, well-worn, scruffy, brown leather antique Second World War aviator jacket, hanging open at the front, and pink spandex short shorts, white bobby socks, and phosphorescent pink oversized running shoes with purple laces. Her skin was as black as anthracite and looked as smooth as silk, like polished ebony. She was breathlessly beautiful, with high cheekbones, full lips, and beautiful teeth. She smiled, looked at me, and said, "Oh, if this isn't the whitest bit of white, I've ever seen. Why this girl is so white, she looks like pure Carrara marble."

I gave her the look, from under my stormy black eyebrows.

Her aviator glasses stared back at me, but her mouth flashed an enormous grin. "May I touch you, darling? I want to make sure you are real."

"Of course," I said, "touch ahead."

"Touch ahead," she repeated, "Touch ahead!" The smile got brighter. "She's a card, this white girl you got. She's got a tongue on her, and she's a beauty. Where'd you dig her up?" She slid the tinted glasses up onto her forehead. Her eyes were big, startlingly beautiful, and strangely sad – like the eyes of a world-weary and wise old man, someone who has seen too much suffering.

She touched my shoulder. Her fingers moved along my collarbone, and then she touched, very lightly, my right breast, and just brushed with the tip of her fingers the nipple, which was painted

216

scarlet and quite erect. She pinched it. "Well, sister, I'll say this: You certainly are for real."

"So are you, apparently." I touched her cheek, and then her lips, running my finger along her lower lip; it was rich, full, and sensual – and she wasn't wearing lipstick.

"Touché," she said, flashing the huge smile. Her eyes remained serious, wary, calculating.

"What do you think?" She turned to her companion. "She might be the right one."

"Yes, she might," said the blonde. "How much do you charge, sister? It would be for a performance, a work of Performance art. It would be in Paris, all travel expenses paid. It would be messy, very physical, and involve nudity and touching."

"Let me see," I said, trying to look thoughtful and wondering what sort of gig this might be – messy and nudity and touching sounded promising.

Nicole put her hand on Jo's arm. "Gwendoline is not a professional; she's not a model. She's a friend, and a very valued customer."

"Gwendoline?" Jo looked me up and down. It was an appraising glance, like she was going to purchase me in the cattle market – or perhaps the white slave market. For just a moment, a delicious little frisson of imagined servitude swept up my back. I half-closed my eyes and composed the picture: Jo was a rich African princess about to purchase me, a poor European slave, captured by the pirates of, say, Algiers, or Casablanca. I could feel the tangy Mediterranean breeze, the hot North African sun, the lash of a slave master's whip, the weight of chains on my wrists and ankles, the iron collar around my neck, and the burning desire of her eyes upon me as she calculated precisely what price she would be willing to pay to have my wonderful cool helpless northern flesh at her beck and call. Sigh! My, but the girl's fancy does take flight! All that racialized imperial-colonial fetishism! And just in an instant! Poof! I was back in the Roman boudoir.

Jo looked me in the eyes. "Ah," she said, a light dawning, "you're that math wonder, Martine Aubin's squeeze, her floozy, her playmate, and girlfriend – the genius nudist who plays soccer naked ..."

"That's me," I said.

"Wow! Delighted to meet you," Jo said, reaching out her hand.

I shook her hand, and then I shook Marlene's hand. Both had firm, frank handshakes, and elegant hands, with long slender fingers. Marlene was giving me a calculating look. She murmured to Jo, "I agree. You're right. Even if she's a math prodigy, I really do think she'd be perfect for *Black on White/White on Black*."

Nicole put a protective hand on my shoulder. "Gwendoline is just trying on some corsets. Gwendoline, as you can see, has exquisite taste."

Justine appeared, carrying the satin gloves.

"Hi, Jo. Hi, Marlene." She gave them both a kiss on the cheeks, and then she handed me the gloves and helped me put them on.

"I think we should add a frilly little maid's cap, that would make her very special," said Jo, giving me that appraising look – matched by the big smile.

I gave her the look: Jo liked to play games. It might really be fun if ...

She grinned. "Don't fight it! You'd make a perfect French maid. And yes, Marlene, you're right: she's perfect for *Black on White/White on Black*."

"That was exactly what I just said. But, still, control yourself, Jo. She's not yours to play with." Marlene shot Jo an indulgent and proprietary – but stern and Germanic – schoolmarm look. "Jo is easily infatuated." Marlene gave me a sunny, blue-eyed smile, her chin slightly raised, with a tiny, steel-sharp Germanic edge: *This is my girl, baby! Watch your step!*

"Just saying," Jo drawled, and winked lazily at me. She lifted off her aviator jacket and sat down in one of the gilded Louis XV chairs, and leaned back, crossing her long satin-black legs, and once again gave me the once-over. I glanced at her and blinked. Impertinence, I decided, was her style; it was cute and provocative; it suited her; I liked it. Her eyes were anatomizing every detail of me and of my costume. With a little help from Justine, I had just finished pulling on and smoothing down the black satin gloves, they were smooth and tight, like a second skin, and went up above my elbows – and, yes, they were exquisitely sensual. I turned around, looked at myself in the mirror, and swung back towards the ladies.

"A little frilly cap," said Jo, "Or rabbit ears. What do you think?" She was looking at me intensely, a searching probe. She uncrossed her legs, leaned forward, and put her elbows on her thighs, her knuckles under her chin. It was a very manly posture, a coach watching a football team.

In that instant, I realized who she was. She was a dancer, lived in Paris, did modern dance, avant-garde "Performance art," choreographing her own performances, and produced retro cabaret shows, 1920s and 1930s style, where she slicked her hair down sideways, wore skirts made of bananas doing Josephine Baker imitations in vaudeville cabaret revivals. James would be thrilled to meet her. He'd showed me photographs of her performances and suggested that when in Paris we should go to see her show.

And her girlfriend was a famous German artist – from Munich I think – who painted big slashing semi-abstracts and brightly colored expressionist nudes, and who drew too, exquisitely drafted and hyper-real drawings of straight and gay sexual entanglements, and who also created installations and performance pieces which were usually both chic and scandalous, retro-feminist references to the sexual revolution and the scandalous anything-goes 1970s, with lots of challenges to both the milquetoast conformist and the militantly intolerant twenty-first-century versions of political correctness.

"I think a frilly cap would be best," I said, "bunny ears can be for another time. Hugh Hefner's not really my thing."

"That's my girl," said Jo, slapping her thigh, "Impeccable taste."

"I definitely think she would be just the person for *Black on White/White on Black*." Marlene put her finger under my chin and tilted my face up. I suddenly realized I was surrounded by females. There was not a man in the house. I began to think I would like an objectifying male gaze to spice up or calm down with a dose of lofty patriarchal phallic testosterone this escalation of estrogen.

"Now, I'm going to add an extra few touches," said Nicole, and, with Justine's help, she began to applying makeup to my face.

Jo and Marlene watched. On went the foundation, on went the cheek powder, on went the eyeshadow, thickly applied, and on went the lipstick. It is fascinating how fascinated women are by female transformation – clothes, accessories, makeup. There were instructions and suggestions from the gallery – Jo and Marlene. I did feel as if I were a mannequin, a pure object, being designed and put together by a committee of intense female esthetes. It was playtime, and the girls were busy with mommy's makeup kit. Finally, I seemed to have been adorned and painted to everyone's satisfaction. I was allowed to look at myself.

What I saw was startling. Truly, it was the vampire-vamp version of me: The cheek shadow made my face look thinner, almost gaunt; the eye shadow, a wide upward turned slash of silken turquoise black, made my eyes bigger, hungrier, hypnotic in their intensity. The black lipstick lent a cadaverous, purplish tone to my skin. The dust of purplish shadow hollowed out my cheeks, making them look skeletal and glamorously anorexic. This was deliciously gothic. Even I was afraid of me.

Jo and Marlene circled me, touching, commenting, standing back, gazing. I suspected they were treating this as my audition for their Paris project. I wasn't sure about the project – whatever it was – but I was tempted. "You're the one," said Marlene, giving me the look, "You are definitely the one!"

"Would you be willing to shave your head?" Joe was circling me, closer and closer, like an impatient panther.

"Depends," I said.

"Coward," she said.

"Maybe," I said.

"Wishy-washy, milquetoast, middle-of-the-road, pasty-faced white liberal, whey-faced, false consciousness, fragile, pseudo-feminist," Jo said. Her teeth showed a big smile, absolutely glorious. "You're a scaredy-cat."

"Exactly," I said.

"And you're a secret push-over." She winked.

"I know," I said. "But ..."

"Ain't no buts allowed." Jo hooked her finger in the collar ring, tugging me close to her, face to face, so close we could kiss without moving a muscle. "Ain't no buts between us, sister, no buts at all, ever!"

"I will consult with my advisors," I whispered in a breathless little-girl voice.

"Advisors?"

"Yes."

"You do that, honey," Jo said, and kissed me. She made it last.

The purple-black lipstick, I discovered, was truly non-smear.

≈

When Jo and Marlene had gone, and Justine had settled down in a corner upstairs, minding the shop and working her way through a big fat book on molecular biology, Nicole took me back down the spiral steel staircase. I was still in my leather collar, frilly constraining corset, stilettos, and shadowy vamp makeup – and she introduced me to the universe of the "French maid."

I had expressed an interest in this scenario, thinking that James – and quite possibly Martine and Philip – might find it interesting.

"The French maid, Gwendoline, is a classic fantasy," said Nicole, as she pulled open a folding wardrobe and revealed a glittering and shiny array of samples, lined up on pull-out hangers, and neatly classified. "Now, for this, we can have shiny PVC, or latex, or leather, or best perhaps black satin, with whalebone, and ruffles, and the classic color scheme is black-and-white." She appeared to very much enjoy lecturing me on the French maid fantasy. "Your hair has to be neat, perhaps tied in a ..."

≈

When I stepped out of *La Petite Boutique Rouge* – freshly showered and scrubbed clean of all traces of makeup and costumed debauchery – the sun was still in the sky, and the sky was still blue. Only four hours had passed since I ran into Nicole! It seemed a lifetime. I had to get back to my life – my so-called real-life life – math, and streets, and people, and Maria, and the flat.

Waving goodbye to Justine and Nicole, I set off into the sultry late afternoon heat. I was once again in jeans, a T-shirt, and toting my ratty old canvas and leather backpack, looking like a typical student; but now I was encumbered with a large shopping bag containing the booty from Nicole's shop – a French maid's costume, several pairs of silk stockings with garter belt attached, and a small collection of catsuits, plus one close-fitting red-black-and-white jester's hood equipped with floppy horns and with bells at their tips – plus of course, courtesy of the house, wrapped up in a special pink box with a pink bow, a remote-controlled suavely sculpted pink silicon dildo and its remote control and Internet empowered and Blue Tooth app. From Singapore or Cape Town, thus equipped, my lover could, by touching a few buttons, give me an orgasm in London or Berlin or Moscow. Globalism on steroids.

The shopping bag was big and bulky, so I hailed a cab. The cab took me down via del Babuino – the Street of the Baboon, apparently named for a very ugly statue placed there in 1571 – to Piazza del Popolo and then down to the Tiber and along the riverside drive, Lungotevere. The sun was bright and gold in the plane trees that line the river's embankments.

I glanced at my phone. There were texts and messages. A text from Kate in Africa: "We need more real-time information, so we're heading towards the front line of the plague. Rebels are heading that way too. Death toll rapidly rising. Don't know what will happen. I'm in a convoy in a dust cloud. Can't see a bloody thing! Hot as hell. Locals are brave, generous, and wonderful. Talk soon. Smiley Face. Love you!"

And there was a text from Claudia. 'Darling Gwendoline – do let me know about your latest round of mischief. I am always curious, as you know. Living vicariously is one of the things we old people do! It's what children – and grandchildren – are for. You know that clever French saying, *Si la jeunesse savait, si la vieillesse pouvait.* If youth only knew, and if age could only do. But do be careful! I care for you very much, you know, Gwendoline, and I think of you every day. Much love, Claudia."

I glanced out the window. Kate was headed into dangerous territory. I clenched my fist around the phone and blinked out the cab window at the passing spectacle.

Rome always puts on a good show. The brilliant late afternoon sun filtered down, gold, sizzling, hot light, coming through the plane trees. The huge Palace of Justice – built in the 1890s and first decade of the 20th Century – loomed, massive and dark, on the other side of the Tiber. It drifted by, sleepily, in the dazzling afternoon light. We rounded a bend, and there, to our right, also across the Tiber, was the tomb Emperor Hadrian built for himself in the years 134-139 CE. So much history concentrated in such a little space. The tomb perches right on the edge of the Tiber and is now known as Castel Saint Angelo; it's a massive squat round brick structure that had once been covered in marble and topped by a small forest of cedars. The popes turned it into a fortress where they could hide when a hostile army invaded Rome or when the populace rose up in revolt against Papal rule. Hadrian's monument swept behind us, and I was almost home.

The taxi left me off at the corner, and I walked the last few steps to our building. Maria was standing in the shadow of the large arched entrance – fanning herself.

"Ah, Signorina Gwendoline, I see you have been shopping."

"Yes, I have."

"Wicked things, I imagine," she giggled, half-covering her mouth, looking like mischievous a little girl.

"Absolutely wicked things." I displayed the shopping bag with its cavorting red-and-black female devil, *La Petite Boutique Rouge* logo. "I will give you an exclusive fashion show, just you and me, if you like."

"Would you?"

"Absolutely!"

"Oh, that is wonderful. And as your reward, Signorina, I have made a new pesto sauce. You and the Professor will adore it. Just a minute! I'll get it." She hurried back into her lodge.

Maria was a superb cook, and she kept giving us gifts. She had also learned quite a bit about my escapades – everybody in Rome, which is a village, seems to learn everything about everybody, while being very discreet about it all and not at all self-righteous. "Live and let live" is Rome's motto and operating principle. After all, the Romans have had 3000 and more years of experience of human folly and quirkiness – and they have long memories: realism dictates the wisest of choices – tolerance. Being judgmental, in Rome, is in extremely bad taste. As for me, I had certainly not been hiding my lights – or my nudity – under a wicker basket.

Maria was particularly fascinated by my relationship with Martine Aubin. This, as I have mentioned, got me into the tabloids and gossip and show business sites on the Net, not to mention scandal sheets and even high-class fashion magazines. Maria had also come across a photo of me – unrecognizable in my black spider girl costume – in an Italian magazine and had pinned it up in her lodge. Her favorite was a series of black-and-white glossy and glamorous photographs of Martine and me being naughty in a restaurant, smooching, and clowning for the camera. That series, she told me, Giuseppe particularly liked. So ...

She returned with the pesto, in a small plastic container and, thoughtfully, in a plastic bag, so it would be easy to carry up in the elevator.

I put down the giant *La Petite Boutique Rouge* shopping bag and hugged her, and kissed her on both cheeks. She and her husband were like family, and they rather liked, I think, this perverse wayward niece, this scandalous waif, the Professor – the very distinguished James Hewitt Spencer – had somehow picked up and brought home, once again, fully reconciled, as a private pet trophy.

"Thank you! Darling Maria. I'll show you some of my wicked treasures tomorrow, before the Professor gets home."

"Oh, that is wonderful, Signorina! I can hardly wait!" She put her hands together, as if she were praying, and as if I were a sacred icon in some ancient pagan temple or perhaps a profane version of the Virgin.

We sealed the bargain with another warm embrace – slightly sweaty on both sides, but pleasantly so – and Maria disappeared back into her lodge.

I went up in the creaky little metal and wood cage of the elevator and got out at our landing. And just as I was putting the key in the door, my cellphone rang. "Oh, damn!"

I left the key in the door, fumbled with the phone, managed to answer, and utter, "Hello!"

I took a deep breath: it was Doctor Joseph Hansen; he had a Nobel Prize in Physics; he explained that he and his wife were in town, just for this evening; they were wondering if James and I were free. I was struggling with the key and with the phone under my chin, and I explained that James was in Moscow; Doctor Hansen said, "Well, it was really you, Doctor Clermont, that we wanted to meet, so if you are –"

"Yes, I'm free," I said, "and please call me Gwendoline; everybody does." And it was true; even people I met in the streets called me Gwendoline, and my students seem immediately to call me Gwendoline. After all, in some ways, even if only visually, almost everybody was already on excessively intimate terms with me.

"We do not know Rome very well – could you suggest a restaurant where we might meet?"

I suggested we meet at Alfredo's and I explained how to get there.

I hung up, got inside the door, shut it behind me, and set down the giant *La Petite Boutique Rouge* bag. Now, I thought, what shall I wear? A Noble Prize is not to be trifled with. After an afternoon of spiritual exercises – dominance and submission – and fashion fittings – and lectures on perversion, I wondered if I would have the energy to face a Nobel Prize.

It turned out I did.

≈

The evening following my pleasant and enlightening dinner with Doctor Hansen and his wife, I was in an enjoyable tizzy. After almost two weeks in Moscow, James would be home in an hour, perhaps less. I put flowers in a vase over the fireplace. I watered all the plants on the terrace. I brushed and polished and scrubbed. I put his favorite white wines in the refrigerator. I was trembling in anticipation. I was like an anxious puppy dog, a girlish girl. My man had been away too long.

As I prepared the meal – skipping around in the kitchen barefoot and with only a skimpy frilly ticklish black apron for attire – I went back over the night before, which I had spent with Joseph Hansen and his wife; it had been, I think, a success. I dressed in black jeans and a black T-shirt, and I clipped on the black velvet choker with the black-and-red Marquis de Sade cameo, and added black patent leather shoes with very high heels. I hoped I had struck the right balance between bohemian casual, scholarly sobriety, and subtle intimations of satanic depravity.

When Doctor Hansen and his wife arrived, I was already seated at Alfredo's, out on the terrace, and chatting with a waiter. It was a beautiful summer evening; the restaurant was crowded with long-legged models and chic and glitzy fashion people.

At first, Professor Hansen and his wife seemed rather dazzled by the glossy, tanned, bare-skinned, daring, Italian glamor of the place, which I presumed must be rather different from their own ultra-respectable sophisticated Metropolitan Opera and Nobel Prize crowd. Oh dear, I thought, Oops! Wrong choice! I immediately feared they would feel out of place.

But Alfredo was his genial self – and soon, Professor and Mrs. Hansen felt like they were old friends and part of the family.

Doctor Hansen's wife, it turned out, was Simone de Zegher, a well-known French philosopher-sociologist, and she was, in fact, quite glamorous, though in a subdued, austere, and cerebral way, reminding me of Simone de Beauvoir. One result of dinner was that I got an invitation to give a lecture on "conceptual models and their limits" in Paris, and to give two lectures and two seminars on science and statistical methods at MIT. This was excellent, well worth shedding my nudity and putting on jeans and a T-shirt and venturing out into the world.

After dinner, I took them for a long stroll through Rome, showing off my favorite places: Campo de' Fiori, Ponte Saint Angelo, and Piazza Navona, and all the little tangled streets and alleyways that lead from one place to another. As we went, I gave them a sketch of the history of each place. Just taking a walk in Rome is like seeing with X-ray eyes or plunging deep into the past in a time machine. And, then, since the center of Rome is really a small village, we met an artist's model I knew and her husband; and we came across two other friends, a gay couple who lived close to Piazza Navona; and, finally, we ran into my two Carabinieri friends, the lieutenant and the colonel, and had coffee with them at a late-night bar near Piazza Navona, Saint Eustachio, il Caffè. The talk turned to criminal networks, and how math and science could be used to analyze and combat criminals and terrorists. The Professor and his wife seemed delighted by their casual "Roman" evening with its unplanned encounters, which is, I think, one of the great pleasures of "villages" like Rome or Venice or even, some neighborhoods of Paris and New York and London.

The next morning, I slept in, and, in the early afternoon, I took a break from work, and had lunch with Maria – some of her delicious pesto with fettuccini. And, for dessert, I showed her my newly acquired treasures. I modeled a fire-engine red catsuit, and a black lacy semitransparent corset and a few other trifles and trinkets. Maria had to help me get into the catsuit and corset, which caused her, I think, great delight, but possibly a twinge, too, of nostalgia.

"Oh, if I were only young and beautiful like you, Signorina Gwendoline!"

"You are not old, and you *are* beautiful, Maria."

"Well, Giuseppe tells me that, you know," she patted her hair, "but I never believe him."

"You must believe him, Maria! Giuseppe is right. You are exquisite. And he is a man of impeccable taste."

"Oh, Signorina, you are a darling!" Maria said. Stepping back, she cast an appraising glance on my appearance. "Now, shall I help you get out of that corset?"

"Yes, Maria. I couldn't do it without you!"

Several hours later, when James arrived, dinner was almost ready, all set up in the fridge, with the poached salmon waiting to be served. I was sure it was going to be delicious: spaghetti with aubergines and with a side dish of cool, delicate, light, and fluffy gnocchi bathed in Maria's pesto sauce. I was becoming an accomplished cook, particularly after talks with Maria and after my frequent visits to Alfredo's kitchen, where Alfredo and his chefs were very generous and taught me some of the secrets of making excellent pasta al dente.

"Master!" I curtsied as I greeted James at the door. I was dressed in my newly purchased French maid's costume: high-heeled black patent shoes, net stockings, a short frilly pleated skirt, a wide black belt, a white-and-black frilly apron, a tight corset, a choker with a Queen Victoria cameo and a frilly white cap, and long satin gloves, and I was standing smartly to attention – ready to serve.

"Oh, Gwendoline!" His face was tired; he looked worried. He put down his suitcase, stared at me, grinned, grabbed me, lifted me in the air, and kissed me and held me and then put me down and stood back and stared at me and said, "Oh, what a divine creature you are, Gwendoline!"

I curtsied. "Will you shower, Master? Will you have a drink, Master, perhaps a dry martini, or a glass of wine?"

"Perhaps, Froufrou, I shall have a glass of Chablis."

"Froufrou?"

"Tonight, dressed like that, my darling Gwendoline, my princess, you are Froufrou."

Froufrou! This was thrilling – why hadn't I thought of it?

"Froufrou is your slave and servant, Master," I said. "Froufrou will fetch your wine this instant, Master." And, with her heels clicking, Froufrou hurried off, in provocative, swaying, classic Froufrou style, towards the kitchen.

Froufrou served her master the Chablis, in a very fine glass, made of plastic, because he was going to the shower while drinking from it; Froufrou most definitely did not want her master to cut himself. While her master showered, Froufrou finished preparations for the meal. And when her master emerged from the steaming mists, his dark skin glowing, his shining black hair slicked back, a tiny white loincloth of a towel knotted casually around his waist, he said, "I think, Froufrou, I shall dine like this, more or less naked. Is that acceptable, Froufrou?"

Seeing him naked – except for the loincloth – and seeing him steaming and tanned and hearing him call me Froufrou – it sounded as if I were a poodle dog – again gave me that funny, taut, shivery, lustful little thrill, a tickly goose-bump frisson that blossomed in my belly and worked its tremulous playful way up to my breasts, tingling intensely, almost painfully, in the very tips of my nipples, and then radiated back down, like a flush of shame, flooding over my back, down my spine, and running like tingling fingers of warm ice, along my inner thighs. I swallowed a sudden gush of saliva and licked my lips.

"I will be delighted to serve you thus, as you are, attired or un-attired, Master."

Thus, it was that James, my master, sat at the table on the terrace – in all his steamy masculine splendor. I brought the food out on a carefully balanced tray. I clip-clopped in with the ice bucket and the wine, and as I served him the steaming hot food, he declared, "Oh, Froufrou, this is delicious."

I stood to attention by his side while he ate. I put my black satin gloved hand on his shoulder. "Do you mind, Master?"

"Not at all, Froufrou. Your slightest touch gives me infinite pleasure."

"Oh, Master!"

"Now will you feed me, Froufrou? Sit here, next to me. It will be easier."

Perched on the edge of a seat, I fed my master, carefully, worshipfully, a forkful at a time, and a sip of wine at a time; my master was very gracious and allowed me to wipe his chin if a bit of sauce remained, like a varnish on his wonderful lips or in his divine manly dimple. I stood up to serve my master a second course.

"Now, Froufrou, you must eat too."

"Yes, Master."

"Sit down – right here next to me."

So, I sat next to my master – his towel had fallen away, and my master was naked, which sweetly exposed his softly vulnerable divinity. Night had come. The sounds of the city were muted. I bathed in the sultry, sensual, perfumed air, and in the glory of seeing my master, aka bold and foolhardy venture capitalist and millionaire James Hewitt Spencer, defenseless and naked, while I, his slave, Froufrou, aka Gwendoline Clermont B.A., B.A., PhD., was fully dressed, albeit in scanty servile garb. It made me acutely conscious of myself and of him, and I thrilled at the paradoxes of our respective roles. But, as always when James and I were together, particularly if we had been separated for some time, the games and role-playing and make-believe quickly faded, took on nuance, and merged into real daily life; our mundane selves burst out of their imaginary cocoons and emerged like richly striated multi-colored fluttering butterflies from the husk of our multiple half-imaginary selves. So, as we ate, we began to talk of our work, of our lives, of the people we knew and what they were doing, and of politics – Italian, American, French, and Russian – and even of religion: I felt my sexuality had a mystical side and wanted to explore it. I told him about my lunch with Nicole and how I had offered myself up as a doll-like mannequin, trying on corsets, ball gags, and bondage gear, how Nicole had subdued and teased me, how she had tickled me with the intercontinental remote-controlled dildo, which she had given to us as a gift for our future long-distance flights of fancy, and how Nicole's daughter Justine had arrived to assist her mother in my humiliation, and how there was a weirdly sensual complicity – spiced with some edgy competition – between mother and daughter, and how both were very sensual and sexual and provocative with me, taking turns playing the dominatrix, and how Jo and Marlene had arrived – "Ah, Jo Delyle," James said, "and Marlene Richter, they are a famous, slightly scandalous couple, united in life and work."

I told James how Jo and Marlene said they wanted to use me as a model – with Jo – in an art performance in Paris that Marlene and Jo were planning: *Black on White/White on Black*.

"I am sure that it will be exciting." James kissed me, caressed the nape of my neck, and kissed me again. "If their past performances are anything to go by, it will certainly involve a lot of nudity and quite a bit of mess."

"Mess! Nudity! Yummy!" I shivered in a Froufrou parody of delight.

James grinned, kissed me on the lips, and again ran his finger down the nape of my neck in that particularly savvy insidious way he had. I shivered again.

I told him about a new statistical model I had developed. It could be applied to the spread of epidemics and the dissemination of information or rumors. And I discussed some of my thoughts about predicting the future – a very tricky subject of course; I told him about my dinner with Doctor Harsen and his wife, and how they had both asked after him. "Ah, yes, I met Joe and Simone in Singapore a few years ago, one of those conferences on the future of biotechnology." When he said this, I hummed a little tune from the song about "the future's not ours to see."

"Ah, yes, Froufrou, the future – *che sara, sara*, what will be, will be – the future's not ours to see," James said, as he served me three large dripping, fork-and-spoonful, scoops of pasta. "It is a problem. In fact, right at this moment, I am trying to figure out what these Russians want – whether I should walk away from the Czech deal or whether I should stick with it. They are playing complicated games."

"Dangerous games, Master? Remember those murders and assassinations!"

"Yes, Froufrou, these games are dangerous, even very dangerous. Perhaps, Froufrou, you could apply your pretty, chock-full, brilliant, analytic little head to doing an update on who these Russians are, and who they are connected to, and what their real agenda might be?"

"Froufrou will apply her pretty little over-stocked head to just that, Master."

We finished eating. I patted his mouth with a serviette. "Oh, Master, you are truly a thing of beauty, an epitome of the male of the species, a very pinnacle and masterpiece of nature." As we stood up, I kissed him.

"Thank you, Froufrou, I think you shall now cease to be Froufrou, and you shall be ... ah ... my cabin boy! Would that please you?"

"Oh, yes, Master, but you must release me from my outer female semblance and my sexist chains. I am frozen in a pose of female domestic servitude! But you will liberate me, Master."

And liberate me he did, very slowly, very deliberately, taking apart the maid's costume carefully. He took off the corset, the shoes, the stockings, and the panties, leaving me naked. "I think we shall leave the choker," he said, "it looks like a collar." James grinned and rubbed his hands.

"Oh, yes, Master."

"Now, boy, we shall begin."

And so, we did.

≈

A week later, James suggested we transfer for a month to Paris, to the Left Bank flat, which, thanks to James, was now mine, but which would serve both of us as our headquarters in France.

I agreed, obviously – I could work from anywhere. And, in Paris, Martine and Philip were available for extra entertainment.

I had the bright idea that Martine and I should both be dressed as French maids and prepare and serve dinner for James and Philip.

Nicole provided me with an extra French maid costume, and Justine, who was coming to Paris, brought it with her and delivered it when she and I had the long lunch we had promised each other at La Coupole. We talked mostly science and biotechnology as well as peppering our conversation with a few allusions so to our sweet afternoon together.

Justine also told me how difficult it had been, at first, to be Nicole's daughter, and then how wonderful. "She was a very stern disciplinarian – study, study, study. I had to be the very best – math, literature, history, science, philosophy. I revolted. I went wild – boys, pot, and booze, dancing all night, sleeping in the rough ... Nicole threw up her hands and let the leash go, and, suddenly, my little period of revolt was over. We were reconciled. She treats me totally as an adult – confides her fears, her weaknesses, and I reciprocate; I tell her everything. We're more like sisters now, though, you know, I'm still in awe of her."

The new French maid costume had a few special adjustments that would make one maid more vulnerable and naked and exposed than the other; such are the subtleties and nuance in dominance and submission. It's almost like politics.

When Martine dropped by, I was barefoot, holding a dripping paintbrush – I was touching up some cupboards – and dressed in ragged short shorts, and in a paint-spattered scarlet tank top, while she was elegance itself, dressed in a black velvet jacket, a black string tie, a cream ruffled satin shirt, tapered black velvet trousers, and high-heeled black pumps. I apologized for being a slob. Carefully avoiding the wet paintbrush, she kissed me on the lips. "I love you exactly the way you are," she said. I explained my plan: we were going to treat our men to a super meal, and we would serve them, dressed as French maids.

"Really!" She favored me with the cutest of doubtful pouts. "Both of us servants! And to our men! This is counter-revolutionary! This is feminism going down to total defeat! You, Gwendoline, are becoming kinkier by the minute."

"Yes, I truly am." I put the paintbrush down in its tray, carefully sloshing it with paint thinner. "I have had excellent teachers in the science of kink." I opened the French maid wardrobe. "Here,

Let's look at these costumes. They're really fine – and very expressive." I handed one of the costumes to her.

"You're kidding, right."

"Not at all."

She looked at the costume and held it up.

"What do you think?" I was eager for her approval.

"This one has no bottom; it opens at the back, leaving the poor maid utterly defenseless."

"Yes."

"Brilliant – so who gets to be naked?" She turned her dazzling blond smile at me – the full glare of the headlights.

"I figure we flip for who is most naked."

"You are wicked, Gwendoline."

We flipped, and I lost. So, it was decided. I, Gwendoline Clermont, would have the naked ass.

"You cheated," said Martine. She licked her lips like a cat contemplating a bowl of milk.

"No, really, I didn't."

"Yes, I'm sure you did. You want to flaunt your ass. And it is an adorable ass, that's true!" She moved close, gave me a kiss and a sweet slap on the backside.

"Okay, let's flip again."

We flipped again. She lost. Her ass would be naked.

"That's better," she said. "Someday, Gwendoline, if you are really, really good, I shall be your slave for a day, or maybe a whole week."

"Luscious idea," I said.

"I thought you'd like it."

"And for the magic evening, we cook for our men," I said.

"Okay, we cook." She narrowed her eyes. "I'm quite a good cook, I think, and I know you are excellent!"

When the magic day came, James was out of town, so Martine and I had the flat to ourselves; we cooked, and we had lots of fun goofing around, gossiping, talking about movies, anatomizing the latest Paris scandals. And, you might be curious. Did we wear any clothes while we cooked? That is a very good question. We did wear frilly aprons, and high-heeled mules, which made an echoing click-clack with each step we took. We were little girls wearing mummy's high heels. Giggling is undignified, but we giggled.

"I want you to try this chocolate." Martine fed me dark thick liquid Swiss chocolate and then licked it from my lips and kissed me, and the deep kiss mingled with chocolate was smoothly darkly delicious.

It was dark when James and Philip arrived, almost at the same time, to find their women dressed as French maids; Martine's costume was open at the back and, from the back, she was almost totally naked; her costume could easily be slipped off too, so, at the twitch of a finger, she could be made even more naked. We provided the gentlemen with drinks while we finished preparing the meal.

Finally, when all was ready, the two gentlemen sat down, to a candle-lit dinner, and Martine and I served.

Philip could not resist giving Martine a friendly slap on the bum. "Oh, Monsieur!" she cried, covering her mouth and giggling a perfect skittish French maid giggle.

Finally, as the meal progressed, we two were invited to join our masters, to sit down, and to eat with them, a great honor when you think about it. Philip proposed that one of the two maids should be truly naked, or almost, and that his choice fell on Martine. James concurred, saying that, in this regard, Philip had precedence. I was assigned the task of disrobing the French maid.

I carefully removed what remained of her uniform, while our two masters watched. And then, as an added touch, I attired her in a sparkling G-string, another product of Nicole's cornucopia.

We sat down, Martine essentially naked, except for the G-string and a velvet choker, while we three were dressed. "You are wicked, all of you," she said, consuming us with a fiery glance, "Soon, I shall have my revenge. I shall do such things – such things I shall do! As yet, I know not what they be, but I shall do things that neither man, nor woman, can imagine, nor can the heavens conceive."

"Behold this beauty – behold these forms," said Philip, standing up to make a speech, gesturing towards Martine, and laying his hand, lightly, on her shoulder. "Behold this divine spark, behold this divine sculpture. Man is born to worship woman."

"We too often forget that fact," said James.

"Yes, too often, we forget that our role, as masters and gentlemen, is to worship women." Philip raised his glass.

Martine gave him a sharp look, a flicker of a smile, and bowed her head in acquiescence.

James smiled. "To the eternal and divine feminine."

"May we two lowly maids drink to that too?" I asked.

"Yes, absolutely, Goddess, both of you goddesses, you can drink to that."

We clinked our glasses, and we drank.

When we finished eating, we sat at the table, by candlelight, talking for a long time. James put on some old dance music. We danced until quite late, Martine in the choker, G-string, and high heels; I peeled myself out of my French maid costume and joined her, in the same costume, choker, G-string, and high heels, and so we danced, Martine and I together, while Philip and James watched; and then Martine danced with Philip, and I danced, sleepily, with James; finally, when Martine had dressed again – in her street clothes – Martine and Philip said goodnight, and they were gone.

Later that night, I asked James if he wanted the Paris apartment back. He kissed me and said, No, it was mine, forever mine, just as he was mine – forever.

"Forever, forever," I whispered. I clung to him, and I kissed him. "Forever, forever, forever."

Inwardly, I frowned. I wanted to bite my nails. Never say "forever"! It was one of my mottos: never, never say "forever." After all, nothing is forever, but, that time, I made an exception. I said, "forever." I repeated, "forever." I repeated it again – like an incantation, like a prayer. Perhaps, I thought, I will live to regret this.

CHAPTER 12 – PERFORMANCE ART

A few days after the French Maid Show, I received an email from Jo. She and Marlene wanted to have lunch with me in a little bistro just off Place de l'Odéon. The idea was that we would discuss their project, Black on White/White on Black.

When I set off for the rendezvous, it was a chilly day with a pale blue sky. A brisk raw breeze was blowing out of the west. I was dressed in white jeans, a broad white leather belt, soft white leather boots, and a big woolly white turtleneck sweater, and a zipped up white canvas vest. The bistro was tiny, rustic, with only six tables of unpolished wood; it was cozy, with a fireplace crackling away merrily in one corner. Marlene was dressed in tapered skin-tight black leather pants, a black T-shirt, and a black leather jacket. When Jo took off her ankle-length black leather overcoat, she revealed that she was wearing a short slinky black silk 1930's type dress that left little to the imagination since she almost certainly was wearing nothing under it.

We did the cheek-kissing thing, and then we sat down at our little rustic wooden table. The owner, a vastly overweight man with an oversized white and blond handlebar mustache and wearing a well-used, sauce-spattered apron, came out from the tiny kitchen to take our orders. I ordered pâté and toast and onion soup and a glass of red wine; Jo copied me exactly, and

Marlene ordered the classic steak-frites. Then, we sat and looked at each other. After a moment, Jo reached out, ruffled my hair, and said, "We're gonna shave it all off."

"Oh?" I took a sip of wine, good simple raw strong red, perfect for a raw, windy day with a chilly intimation of autumn and winter already in the air.

"You'll look good bald. You have a cute skull."

"Really?"

"Yep. *Really.*" Jo half closed her eyes, tilted her head back, and stared at me in a most charmingly lascivious way. I felt I was being propositioned – right in front of her girlfriend.

Marlene put her hand on Jo's arm – a sort of order to calm down. "I want to explain the idea," she said. "*The Black on White/ White on Black* performance we are planning."

"Okay." I took another sip of wine. Marline looked ultra-serious, truly Teutonic, perfectly Prussian, and quite beautiful in a sharp-featured pitiless way. I wondered: Would I survive lunch?

"It will involve you and Jo. You may be aware of Jo's work."

"I am," I widened my eyes and giving them both my best, my biggest smile. "She's a true star. I love her work. And I'm aware of your work too, Marlene – it's magnificent!"

Until a few weeks ago, I had not been at all aware of Jo or her work – except very vaguely – nor of Marlene and her work, again, I had a vague, misty idea. When I confessed my ignorance, James, who was a fan, made a face. He declared he was appalled by my unlettered ignorance. While massaging my shoulders, he treated me to a quick in-depth seminar on Jo, aided by lots of YouTube clips.

The performances were impressive. Jo was more than cute; she was, as I had seen in Nicole's shop, beautiful. She was muscular, lean, fine-boned, and subtle, with a body as fluid and elastic and quick as an electric eel. She usually wore a moderate Afro, but to play Josephine Baker in a cabaret revival, she'd greased down her hair, slipped into a skirt made of bananas, put on a variety of flimsy slinky period dresses, and sung some of Josephine Baker's great songs from the 1920s and 1930s. Looking at all the clips James was showing me, I could see that Jo was ultra-quick, saucy, playful, hugely talented, acutely intelligent, and lots of fun; in short, she was an aggressive, opinionated, unpredictable, talented, goofy handful of a woman.

As James gave me his little lecture, I discovered that he was extraordinarily well-informed about contemporary art – and not only of the kinky variety. He knew about Pop art, Earth art, Performance art, Feminist art, Graffiti art, Postmodern art, Installation art, and so on, and on, and on. He gave me a quick course on Marlene, her work, and her place in the contemporary German, Feminist, and International art scenes. Marlene was a severe sort of expressionist, with lots of postmodernist theoretical trimmings. In her paintings, she was expressionist-representational – you could actually glimpse the garter-belts, sky-scrapers, tanks, napalm, and burnt bodies, anti-riot cops, in the swirl of gesture, in the painterly layered graffiti-like surfaces; in her performances, she was overtly theoretical – lots of big words in the manifestos – and openly perverse, playing with that old philosophic concept Martine and I love so much – "transgression."

With all of this under my belt, I had come – somewhat – prepared. While I slurped up the thick, gooey, steamy onion soup, Jo and Marlene explained what they wanted to do. *Black on White/ White on Black* would be a sort of performance – involving mud wrestling or something approximating thereto – and it would embody and deconstruct, as Marlene said, racist and sexist and power clichés and master-slave relationships and give the public recipes on how to overcome them, with a parody of Hegelian-Marxist dialectical change whereby the stereotypes and clichés and signs and symbols which structure our conscious and unconscious lives – and determine our identities – are integrated into a critique of the same stereotypes and clichés, and are thus transcended in a transversal Hegelian-Marxist semiotic dialectic of freedom – or something like that. Like, the only way to get rid of a prejudice or cliché or racism is to flog it to death by over-use, to excoriate, excise, and exorcise it by irony and postmodern playfulness.

"Wow!" I said. I gulped a huge gooey spoonful of onion soup and washed it down with an equally huge gulp of red wine. I decided that I'd probably be drunk after this lunch. If the wine didn't do it, the words would.

Jo and I would perform together. It would be on the frontier of parody: a black woman and a white woman, mostly naked, wrestling for supremacy, several times reversing roles of dominance and submission, meanwhile elaborating on a critique of what they were, in fact, doing. *Hmm, mud wrestling! Yummy!* The images evoked sounded lusciously perverse. But I thought that the frontier, in this case, between parody or critique, on the one hand, and just plain racism or sexism or exploitation might be a wee bit thin, dangerously thin, in fact. I imagined the critics and feminists and ideologues howling at us and tossing rotten tomatoes and burning us in effigy – or in real life.

"This project is really racist," said Jo, favoring Marlene with a big grin and popping a chunk of onion soup-soaked bread into her mouth. She chewed noisily and seemed to be enjoying it.

"It is racism as a critique of racism," said Marlene with a very severe Germanic straight face, "meta-linguistically speaking, using stereotypes to criticize stereotypes."

"Maybe I should wear the banana skirt."

"Like in your Josephine Baker number?" I looked up from my onion soup.

"Yep, she's my namesake, or I'm hers," Jo grinned flirtatiously at me. "I can never figure out the proper meaning of 'namesake'."

"This is a critique of racism and sex and class-exploitative relationships," said Marlene, "The performance work, being merely a statement, is not in itself exploitative, though it will be seen as such, racially and sexually, which is part of the point, isn't it?" She lifted a savory dripping piece of steak, speared together with some helpless fries, to her mouth, ate, and began to chew. Like Jo, she had beautiful teeth. The better to bite you with, I thought. I was getting tipsy.

I frowned. Did Marlene have a sense of humor? I dipped a piece of bread in the gooey soup. She was beautiful, that was a fact. I tried to imagine Marlene and Jo having sex. Yes, it was certainly easy to imagine, all too easy. I tried to imagine Marlene telling a real joke. That was not so easy. I wondered what mischief Jo and I could get into. Then I told myself: Stop that, Gwendoline!

"We're all racist, Jo said.

"That is true," said Marlene. "At a certain level, we are all imprisoned in stereotypes, tribal and racist or racial stereotypes prominent among them. Not all stereotypes, or racial stereotypes, are negative. Some stereotypes stimulate lust, desire, even love." She put her hand on Jo's arm.

Jo winked, turned to me. "Do we want to do this?"

"I leave it up to you," I said. "I'm not sure about shaving my head." I thought the project they had described was certainly in questionable taste, and could go entirely wrong, we might be accused of racism and lynched by the press and by academics and ideologues, but it would be sexy and fun – maybe.

Jo looked at me. "I'm gonna shave my head too," she said. She put her finger under my chin and tilted my face up. "It will be fun to enslave you."

"Really?"

"Yes, really." She grinned. She looked like an enthusiastic five-year-old. Her skin shone – shades between anthracite and deep, dark, liquid, fine-grained Swiss chocolate – flawless, and her body glowed; yes, it was a dancer's body, thin, muscular, lithe, and perfect. All in all, she was a succulent temptation. She displayed all the *lineaments of desire*, as the great mystical poet said. Eros can lead – no doubt about it – to transcendence.

"This will be fun," Jo said again, pursing her lips slightly, half closing her eyes, staring at me.

"Well ..."

"Let's do it." She grinned.

"Okay," I said. "I guess we will do it." I pursed my lips, put on a thoughtful, scholarly air, while, inwardly, my little red demons – having escaped from *La Petite Boutique Rouge* – were jumping around celebrating: *Now you've done it! Now you've done it! Now you're committed! Now you're trapped! Whoopee! You can't back out now!* Oh, Gwendoline, how easily you surrender, how easily you give in to caprice, how easily you are carried off course by the slightest whiff of desire, by the slightest suggestion of naked mischief!! Oh, Gwendoline!!

At this point, the owner of the restaurant came out, rubbing his hands on his big dirty apron, and asked how we had enjoyed our meal. We said it had been excellent. He offered us dessert. His daughter came out from the kitchen and began to clear away our plates.

"You, Gwendoline, will play a chap, an imperialist capitalist pig."

"Peachy keen," I said. How super! I'd be a chap, openly transvestite. Costume balls were among my favorite things. It sounded like fun!

Marlene went on, explaining about the class struggle and

the race struggle and the anti-colonial, anti-imperialist struggle and the feminist struggle and the lesbian-gay-trans-polymorph-I-don't-know-who-or-what-I-am struggle, or the ecological struggle, and how all the struggles intersected – *intersectionality* – in various forms of alienation, exploitation, and conflict, some of us being branded by all sorts of stigmata, being a woman, being gay, being trans, being black, being *racialized*, being poor, being pregnant, being a mother, being single, being stuck in a bad job, being unemployed, being stuck in the wrong family, wrong neighborhood, being fat, being skinny, and so on, others less so, less branded with the stigmata of intersectionality, that is, and thus less discriminated against, exploited, and stigmatized. I kept my mouth shut and ate my crème brûlée. The bistro was muggy, warm, comfortable, dimly lit, and full of earthy smells.

The owner's daughter hovered next to the table. She was pale, with skinny arms and legs, a wistful triangular face, a big mouth with fine lips, mouse-colored, fine-textured hair, all in a tangled, fuzzy mess, a high clear forehead, and leaden circles under her thin gray eyes which had extraordinary long, dark lashes.

I allowed myself to gaze at her. She was intensely, whimsically, attractive, in a fragile waif-needs-to-be-rescued sort of way – a precocious, perverse, secretive, skinny urchin. And, yes, she was androgynous, wounded, and gamine. I had an impulse to take her in my arms. I would comfort her, caress her, and make her smile.

Her eyes were open wide, and her mouth was hanging open. She bit her lip, self-consciously looked down at the floor, and then looked up. She seemed awe-struck or star-struck or something. I thought she must be an admirer of Jo or a fan of Marlene's avant-garde art. Or maybe she was just simple-minded, abashed, and scared. She was staring at me. When I glanced at her and blinked, she blurted out: "Aren't you Martine Aubin's girlfriend?"

I was so surprised that I almost sprayed a mouthful of crème brûlée all over the table and into the girl's face. I gulped, swallowed, and patted my mouth with my serviette. I must have looked bug-eyed. I swallowed again and cleared my throat. "Yes, I am."

"Would you tell Martine that I absolutely love her – I love her and her work, absolutely!"

"I will, absolutely, I will."

"May I have your autograph?"

"Me? Me?" I frowned. This had never happened before. "Ah, well, yes, sure, I mean, yes, I guess."

Jo grinned, and Marlene looked severe and disapproving: this interruption to the dialectic, particularly since it involved mere showbiz and commercial movies, movies which made money, since Martine Aubin was big – very big – at the box office, was untoward and unwelcome. I fished a ballpoint pen out of my jacket pocket and scrawled my signature on a menu. Then I thought better of it.

"What's your name?"

"Claudine."

"Well, then, Claudine," Above my signature, I wrote: *To dear Claudine with love from her friend Gwendoline.*

Claudine looked startled, then infinitely grateful; she held the menu pressed against her chest. "Thank you, Gwendoline, Thank you!"

"You're welcome, Claudine." I gave her my best smile and put my hand on her arm: I really did want to comfort her, to take her home, wrap her up in a blanket, feed her chicken soup, and make her warm and happy. James, I'm sure, would approve. He had a weakness for waifs. Maybe I should bring Martine and Philip and James to this place – the food was excellent. Martine's fan would be in seventh heaven!

"So, let us continue," said Marlene, her attractive lips thinned into a lusciously intimidating Teutonic schoolmarm pout.

"Yes, let us continue! The dialectic waits on no man, nor woman neither," said Jo, her mouth widening into a glorious smile. She winked at Claudine. And Claudine smiled, looked down, bit her lip, and hurried away.

"Well, then ..." And Marlene began to explain how Jo and I would indulge in various forms of physical as well as dialectical struggle, black against white, white against black. Apparently, we would be wresting.

"We won't actually hurt each other," I said, "Right?"

"No, of course not," said Marlene.

"Oh, I don't know, darling. I love to inflict pain," Jo narrowed her eyes, tilted her head back, and gave me the look, "And you, Gwendoline, are very naughty; you need correcting."

"She's joking," said Marlene.

"Right," I said.

Marlene put her hand on Jo's wrist – a gesture that was both affectionate and restraining – and continued her disquisition on how Jo and I were to rollick and frolic.

A light dawned: So, this was where the title of the performance came from: *Black on White/White on Black*: Jo would paint me in black latex, and I was to paint her in white, entirely. The paint was latex, very clingy and opaque, but easy to wash off. Luckily, I didn't have an allergy.

"Hmm," I said, frowning. Blackface desecration, on the one hand, and *Black Skin, White Masks*, by Frantz Fanon, on the other; that was a pretty explosive mixture. Watch out, Gwendoline, I thought. I put a gob of butter on the end of a piece of baguette and began to munch. I could see the lynch mob coming, and they would be right!

Then we would, painted thus, and naked, me black, her white, both of us with shaved heads, and perched on the edge of the stage under highly focused spotlights, discuss with the public what had just occurred. Was this blackface or not? Were we idiots or not?

Were we exploiters or exploited? Were we insulting and demeaning people and each other, or not? Improvising from a skeletal script, we would field questions, and argue about racism and about the symbolism and the fetishism of race, we would talk about "white privilege," and "micro-aggressions," and "racialization," and "othering," and we would boldly confront the question of whether our performance was exploitative, racist, and trashy-fetishistic-erotic-kitsch, involving our naked bodies offered up as commodified sacrifices, which I thought it certainly delightfully promised to be – a trashy, but interesting sex show – or militant and semantically useful in a revolutionary perspective, in a newly *woke*, consciousness-raising, and utterly woke *manner*, which it would really be, Marlene insisted, since, as Marlene patiently explained to me, the whole shindig would have the effect of collapsing *signifier* and *signified* into one primal pre-symbolic, pre-Oedipal, pre-Phallic cascade of imagery, the Other merging into the Self, which would be an image of prelapsarian paradise – like we were back fooling around in the Garden of Eden – all cavorting totally unconscious of the privilege of being mindless naked dumbbells, shameless and without self-consciousness. In paradise, Jo and I would merge and exchange identities, and then exchange again, and again.

"Right," I said. "I see. She is me, and I'm her. She *others* me – makes me see myself, and define myself, through her gaze, and I attempt to *other* her – make her see herself, and define herself, through my gaze."

"You got it, sister," said Jo.

Marline continued; the event would also, in total contrast to the mindless paradise depicted in Genesis, reveal post-lapsarian hell and *abjection*, as analyzed by Julia Kristeva, the blurring of frontiers, the loss of the distinction between "me" and "you" and the violation of taboos, the contagion of symbolic pollution, since, as utterly fallen and abject and very self-conscious and shame- and guilt-ridden creatures, we would be tossed down, into the muck of indeterminacy and the blurring of frontiers of self and other, the overlapping of fluids and boundaries, the shattering of taboos, which is the very definition, according to the best anthropologists, of obscenity and pollution. The name of Mary Douglas, the author of *Purity and Danger: An Analysis of Concepts of Pollution and Taboo*, also came up.

"Okay," I said, "Heaven and Hell in one package. We start in mindless heaven, we end in angst-ridden, mutually alienating, racist Hell."

"Nice summary. This kid is smart," said Jo, blinking at me from over her espresso cup.

"Undoubtedly," said Marline, rather dryly. She continued for another half an hour to explain the complexities of the dialectic and of the world economic system – finance capital, that is banks and their ilk, dominating everything – and how it intersected, on multiple levels, with racism and massive capital accumulation in the white, Western World, which had been made possible by the international and Atlantic slave trade, by the sugar and cacao and cotton plantations, based on slave labor, and by the gold and silver extracted – also using slave labor – by the Spaniards from the New World, and by the conquest and appropriation of vast tracts of land in the New World and in Australia and New Zealand, and by the exploitation of the rest of the world through colonialism and its avatars.

Whew! Lots of this was interesting, and some of it I knew, but Marlene was relentlessly didactic, and professorial. She made me, Gwendoline, look like a rank amateur in the preachy bluestocking stakes.

Whatever it was, it would be an interesting sex show, with Jo, a delightful and delicous partner, or that's what I thought. And we might be lynched, which was also an interesting prospect.

≈

James that evening, while dumping the spaghetti into the colander, told me that, in his humble opinion, I was selling my soul to a posse of cockamamie Germanic Left Bank intellectuals with big next-to-meaningless vocabularies and that it was a very fine and splendid thing indeed; and would teach me a few lessons. In particular, he liked the idea of striptease and naked wrestling. And seeing me with my head shaved and being covered in black latex paint, in front of a lot of complicated highfalutin talkative Parisian lefties would, he said, be a stimulating experience. And, while shaking the spaghetti, he added, "Also, behind all the highfalutin theory, Jo and Marlene are onto something – racism is real, it is complicated, and it permeates everything, in ways that range from the crudest to the most subtle and insinuating; it sneaks in where you think it would be absent. It's global and it's micro; it's systematic and it's intimate. We are all part of it. And, this performance will be stimulating!"

"Stimulating? For you or for me?" I poured pesto sauce onto the steaming spaghetti while James held the bowl.

"For both." He looked pleased with himself.

"You want me to shave my head?" I mixed the pesto sauce into the spaghetti.

"I think that would be delightful." He sampled a gob pesto sauce on the end of one finger.

"Well, I guess, if you say so." I kissed him on the cheek. When Sampson was shorn of his locks, he was shorn of his power. Was I being castrated? Would all my seductive female power evaporate when my egghead noggin was revealed, naked, for all to see?

"I say so." He grinned and slapped me on the bum, which was most gratifying. I slapped him back.

"Now, Master," I said, "let's eat."

That night, the lovemaking was deliciously normal, slow-motion teasing, and it went on, and on, and on ...

"The mere idea of art inspires you, Master."

"It does, Gwendoline. Indeed, it does."

≈

Jo and Marlene and I had more planning sessions, and as I suspected it would, the "concept" evolved as we worked on it. In other words, despite Marlene's elaborate theories and rationalizations, we didn't, in the beginning, have the slightest idea of what we were doing. But, I'm told, that's art – improvisation all the way. Just create a mess, and then try to climb out of it. First, you *do*, then, if you're lucky, you might possibly figure out what you *have done*; if not, some critic will explain it all to you – usually in impenetrable language that requires even more exegesis than the original incomprehensible thing-in-itself. Meantime, I boned up on Franz Fanon, James Baldwin, Jean-Paul Sartre, and a pile of fascinating brilliant writers and thinkers, like Peggy McIntosh on "white privilege" and Laura Mulvey on "the male gaze" and Erving Goffman on "The Presentation of Self in Everyday Life" and R. D Laing on "The Self and Others." I tried to unpack the concept of "white privilege" and I analysed all the multiple ways I myself am privileged, and there were certainly lots of those, and being white and American was pretty central to most of them, and then of course there was, along with social class, the unmentionable, essential one – *money!* I looked into "microaggressions" and Jo and I did a bunch of exercises, acting them out, alternating roles, exploring all the seemingly small ways people can, often without realizing it, demean and dehumanize and stereotype another person or whole class of persons, with a glance, with a word, with a snub, with a gesture. Jo explained to me how she had to "navigate" her relationships, even just saying hello on the street, or buying groceries, or entering a building, because she is a black woman living in a world which is essentially white. "Every day, in every way, I have to pay attention to every move I make, every glance, every gesture, every word, I have to make sure I'm not misunderstood, and I also have to make sure I'm not misunderstanding other people. It can get tiresome, and very, very stressful, particularly for other black people, or 'racialized' people – because I'm pretty well known, and I go, mostly, where people already know me. I stick, as much as possible, to a safe zone. For black guys, it's really, really difficult. In some places they can get shot just for crossing the street or driving in their car. Navigating all this is exhausting and really, really difficult." We talked for a whole afternoon, Jo and I, about "Intersectionality" – the way different identities are constructed, in complex combinations, and the ways prejudice can form, and distort, in multiple ways, one's identity – as a black woman, say, or as an unmarried black woman from a "difficult" part of town, so that various forms of prejudice can pile up and reinforce each other. With Jo's help, I began to unpeel racist attitudes and mythologies – and casual racist and cultural fetishisms – inside my own stormy little personality. We certainly are complicated creatures! Hmm!

Here we were, in another restaurant, gabbing away. The art scene in Paris seemed to have a lot to do with food and wine and endless talk, which was okay with me.

"Whew," I said, staring at Marlene and trying to absorb all the theoretical Marxist and Hegelian talk that defined what we were going to do on stage.

Then after we had talked for maybe two hours, Marlene stood up. "I have to run," she said; she kissed Jo on the lips and slipped out the door.

Jo and I finished our coffees and paid for the meal – which was surprisingly cheap – trust artists to find the best cheap places in any city, even Paris – and then I was out on the street alone with Jo, in the raw west wind. It so happened we were going the same way.

"I think this could be fun," I said. I really did think so, although it would undoubtedly absorb too much time.

"I wanted us to mud wrestle at the end." Jo took my arm and pulled me close, "But Marlene vetoed it."

"Really?" I said. "You'd win. You're in better shape than I am."

"I'm not so sure, but anyway, it would be rigged and staged, you know. We'd choreograph every little detail."

"Sounds super steamy," I pulled her closer, warmth, and intimacy in the raw, blustery Paris afternoon. "It would certainly be intimate: we'd be skin on skin."

"Exactly," she said.

"Exactly," I echoed.

"Maybe we can do the mud wrestling another time." She snuggled even closer and kissed me on the cheek.

"It's a date," I said.

≈

That night – when we were dining at a small bistro not far from the Seine – I explained it all to James, including Jo's fancy that she and I do a mud wrestling session.

"Every boy's dream!" he exclaimed, "I'm totally with Jo on this. She is a true artist."

"You might be jealous."

"Certainly, I will be jealous. But you and I can mud wrestle another time. And I know just the place. About two hours north of Rome, there is a very fine mud puddle, hot sulfurous volcanic mud, with a hot natural waterfall out in the fields. You can sit outside in the hot mud, or hot water, and, if it is winter, watch the rain, and even, sometimes, the snowflakes come down. We can splash around like infants or piglets in the mud, under the stars."

"Hmm, sounds lusciously romantic." I sucked dreamily at my straw. I stared at him; he was indescribably beautiful. "This *Black on White/White on Black* thing is feminist theater as well as art," I said. "There will be a montage of images of oppression, sexist and racist, so it will be pretty ideological. Agitprop for the twenty-first century."

"Just what the world needs," said James, and leaned across the table and kissed me.

≈

Later, after we returned home, James told me he most definitely thought this "performance piece" would be worthwhile. Me getting stripped and sloshing in paint with a beautiful black ballerina – whom he already fetishized – was just his cup of tea.

"You are an absolutely wicked boy," I said. "You realize these are post-imperial exotic and erotic racial stereotypes and fetishisms you are indulging in. You are a mashup of imperialist white male clichés!"

"Yes, I realize," he said.

"Maybe you should come to the performance in a pith helmet and slapping your jodhpurs with a stiff riding crop." I was astraddle him, on the bed, looking down at his tangled, tousled hair, his amused eyes, his strong chin, his fine mouth, his perfectly symmetrical chiseled nose.

"I believe a tuxedo will be sufficiently offensive." He gazed at me out of half-closed eyes.

"Will you love me when I'm old and gray?" I sighed.

"By the time you are old and gray, I will either be dead or be Methuselah, and I'll be so blind I won't notice you are old and gray."

"You are so totally an idiot." I lifted myself up and lowered myself onto him, welcoming him into me, and, bending over, I kissed him on the lips, arching my back so that my breasts just touched his chest, teased his skin, caressed the virile chest hairs.

≈

Rehearsals for *Black on White/White on Black* were exhausting. We had to get our timing exactly right, and there were lots of lines to learn. And I had to master the subtleties of the philosophical and critical jargon we were going to spew when we were improvising. I wondered if I'd made a mistake in agreeing to do it. But as we went forward, I found it was more and more fun and – I adored Jo. She smelled of spices and tropical breezes, and she was ultra-affectionate as we swiveled sensuously around each other, held each other, tossed each other, practicing dance steps, wrestling moves, and rehearsed how, precisely, we would paint each other's bodies.

Martine dropped in a few times and said she was going to get so jealous she would have to punish us both.

"But I'm not sure of which one I am most jealous," she said. We both gave her beatific smiles: being punished by Martine, we agreed, would be a fine experience.

≈

The morning of the performance, Jo shaved my head. She insisted on doing it herself. "I'm an excellent barber," she said. She sat me down in a chair, backstage in one of the change rooms. "No looking," she said. She snipped and snipped with scissors. I felt the locks falling away. Then she used clippers, and the buzzing felt vaguely sensuous and quite frightening. Then, with hot water and a shaving brush and a razor, she went to work. She rinsed the result and toweled me down "You can look now, baby," she said

I looked in the mirror.

"Wow!" Never, I thought, have I been so naked.

"Very sexy. You look like a beautiful boy." Jo grinned, ran her hand over my shiny, utterly smooth skull.

I did look like my master's dark-eyed cabin boy, after said boy had been shorn of a cargo of pirate lice.

James dropped in, ran his fingers over my squeaky smooth bald pate, kissed me on the crown of my head, and said I was the sexiest creature in the universe.

I kissed him desperately, hungrily, for I had feared that – once he saw the bald me – he would stiffen and scream. But, no, he seemed enchanted with the new cropped, unsexed Gwendoline.

≈

The show was crowded; it was a small space – and contained about two hundred people.

When the applause finally died down, Jo and I disappeared behind the curtains. "Whew," we said, and fell into each other's' arms. "That was exhausting," I said. "You were terrific," Jo said. "You were more than terrific," I said. We kissed, and the kiss lingered – two contrasted painted bodies and faces, one black and one white, clinging.

Marlene was out front, almost certainly being brilliantly didactic, talking to the public.

"She'll be a while," said Jo.

"Yeah, I figure," said I.

Jo and I felt our way down a cluttered, ill-lit corridor to the narrow little shower cubicle that was adjacent to the gaudy richly mirrored dressing room, and, squeezed in close and splashing like mad, we helped each other wash off all the paint. It was a giggly intimate experience, a sort of spontaneous extension of the performance, spiced up with a few interestingly varied kisses and lots of little teasing caresses. Finally, we came out of the shower and toweled each other dry – this was done carefully, ritually, with great mock respect and considerable gallantry – and we changed for dinner.

Keeping with the *White on Black/Black on White* theme, I was dressed in a semitransparent black catsuit, wearing a black beret, and black stilettos. Jo was encased in a semitransparent white catsuit and wearing white high heels and a white beret.

We went – both wearing thin silk jackets, mine black, hers white – to the after-show dinner which was at a crowded and very fashionable restaurant in Montparnasse. It was attended by quite a few art critics and artists. James was by my side, and Martine was next to us with Philip and Jo and Marlene.

I was a bit flushed by it all, all bright-eyed and bushy-tailed. Martine winked. "James and I really must put you on a leash."

"Oh, my dear children," I sighed, "I am already on a leash. And I love it!"

≈

The press was mixed: The whole affair was blatantly exploitative, it was sexism and racism, merely a pretext for a titillating striptease and wrestling match by two naked women; it was the very incarnation of the racist white privilege patriarchal male gaze it claimed to criticize; but some of the press went into raptures: It was a bold experiment in mixing genres and attitudes; it brilliantly poked fun of all the stereotypes; it daringly transcended and defied our present poltroon-like, head-in-the-sand, politically correct conformism; it brought us to a new level of healthy ironic playfulness in recognizing our own racism and sexism; the performance "outed us all as racists and fetishists of race and racism" in the words of one critic; Jo Delyle was stupendous, the papers said, her gleaming athletic body, and her hieratic goddess-like beauty admirably capturing, with marvelous elasticity and humor, each reversal of emotion, each comic nuance, each shift in mood; and Gwendoline Clermont, sex artist, and prize-winning mathematician, turned out, as a neophyte performer, to have impeccable comic timing and superb acrobatic skills. She was a perfect and superb foil to Jo's virtuosity.

"Well, well, sex artist," said James.

"Hmm," I said.

"Superb acrobatic skills." He put his arms around me.

"Hmm." I licked my lips.

"Shall we put some of those superb acrobatic skills to the test?"

"Hmm, yes, Master, let us do that."

There followed a memorable night. It included a pillow fight and a naked dancing session by candlelight and some romantic 1930s Italian tango and gypsy music and a calm interlude which involved cooking a huge heap of pasta and eating; and also drinking a very powerful home-brewed health drink – a heady mixture of herbs and spices and spinach, and, if my memory does not betray me, a pinch or two of vodka.

≈

As I've said, one of the unintended consequences of being a shameless hussy, and identified as such, was that I became, as a sideline, a sort of model.

Recently in *Vogue France,* there had been a series of photographs where Martine and I posed in lascivious attitudes in a series of revealing playfully – ironically, self-referentially, fetishistic outfits – a new line from a Parisian designer who was following in the footsteps of Jean-Paul Gaultier, with echoes of Madonna, and Lady Gaga.

And there were requests for me – even me alone without

Martine – to pose in costumes or without costumes – for charity events, or commercial promotions.

I didn't have time for much of this since, normally, I was putting in six hours a day working on math and methodology and the use of mathematics in tracing underground criminal networks, smuggling networks, financial fraud networks, and in studying, with similar mathematical tools, patterns in the spread of epidemics, and in the spread too of ideas – clichés, stereotypes, or as they call them 'memes' and terrorist ideas – and terrorist patterns of recruitment.

≈

James had to go to Moscow again and then to Tbilisi for meetings. He'd asked me to read the company reports and to do some more background checks – his cool way of suggesting that I do some computer hacking and spying – on the Russian group that was competing for the biotech firms he wanted to take over.

"As I said, I'm not sure you want to mess with them," I objected, "There are some murderous vultures out there." I had traced some of the partners. One of the partners was linked to a gang of Georgians and to some of the Russian Mafia.

I had access to all sorts of data, and people in the intelligence and security worlds – including Interpol – did tell me things since I was for them a very useful occasional problem-solver; they could call on me, and I could depend on them.

I tracked the networks as deep as I could, and by some ingenious hacking I was able to get some intelligence material: my old nemesis, the one I had already identified, Sergei Platonov had his fingers in a lot of pies; as we already knew, he was ex Russian special forces, and he had his headquarters in an independent republic, the Republic of Transbeckistan, south of the Russian Federation; the Russians did not like him, in fact, the Russian

President hated him, but Platonov was difficult to get rid of. He had set up his own little empire in a fortress complex, and – through blackmail, intimidation, favors, and corruption – he had "bought" protection from the local government.

"But the company has some superb technology," James said, "and the original partners are totally on the up-and-up."

"Yes, but they have had to take in as silent partners some unsavory guys, and some really tricky financial backing. Sergei Platonov is involved, I'm sure of it," I said. "These guys are really, really dangerous."

"Yes, darling, that's the point: I want to pry the company away from the bad guys and the dangerous guys," James nodded and tapped his finger on the palm of my hand. "If I can buy them out, or get rid of them, then the company can make a real contribution. Not only an economic contribution but a tactical and strategic one too."

I knew what he meant; some of their inventions and patents could be weaponized – electronic weapons, and chemical and biological weapons. It was dangerous stuff. "What if the bad guys don't want to be bought out?"

"Well, I might give up." James frowned. "But I do have some friends who could put pressure on them."

"Aren't you playing a dangerous game, here, James? I don't want anything to happen to you."

"I'm pretty savvy, Gwen."

"I know."

"I'm even pretty tough."

"I know."

He frowned. "But you are right, Gwen, and you, of course, spotted the nature of risks, as I knew you would. Platonov is the key. You're better than the CIA and MI-6. I always see things more clearly after talking to you."

"Thank you." I gazed at him. "I would die if anything happened to you."

He grinned at me. "You've given me a pretty good map of the dangers, Gwen. I *am* worried. I'm even afraid. But I don't want to give this one up."

"Okay." I kissed him. "You are free, Master. Do what you have to do."

And off he went to Moscow.

≈

I mulled and stewed. I bit my knuckles. I paced the floor. I took a hot shower, and then a cold. He would be away, he said, for a week, maybe two.

CHAPTER 13 – A MAID'S TALE

While James was away in Moscow, Philip was away too, in London, organizing a co-production with India and doing some storyboard work with the Indian screenwriter.

Martine and I were alone in Paris. Martine came over often – partly to console me and keep me company, and partly so she would not be alone. We spent a lot of time just being together, in silence, like an old married couple. She would curl up on a sofa and read scripts or novels or scribble notes.

Martine was already a TV and movie star, and now she was beginning to get a reputation as a short story writer. It was annoying! Why do people have to be so intelligent and accomplished, and with varied skills that seem to have nothing to do with each other? Sometimes it gives me the pips! I growled Ghhrr! Ghhrr!

It was a rainy, cold Parisian night, the wind tunneling down the long straight boulevards and whistling against shutters and windowpanes.

Marine was lying on her tummy on the rug in front of the false fireplace, well, gas fireplace. She was wearing very tight jeans, and a white, almost transparent T-shirt, and she was scribbling, writing by hand, in a spiral notebook she carried almost everywhere.

I was toiling at my computer, and I had just received an email from Kate. I scratched my head, which was still short, dense stubble from the *White on Black/Back on White* performance.

The scratchy scrappy baldness made me antsy, and I was jittery too because I was afraid for Kate – she was heading deeper into danger.

Kate's latest note was not reassuring: "Dearest Gwen, how is your love life? How is James? How is Martine? I am jealous of both. I have no love life down here. We are at the new forward base I told you about. Recent reports from upriver, from the interior, are more than alarming. As you know, the new version of Ebola seems to be mutating, faster, and faster. We suspect that it is now being carried on the air, and transmitted by sweat and saliva and coughing, which is really bad news; actually, it is potentially pandemic end-of-the-world bad news. Also, rebel forces of the Anti-Western, Anti-Education, Universalist African Islamist front are advancing, getting close to the infected area. If the rebels reach the infected area, all the medical personnel will be evacuated, and then all bets are off as to what will happen next. My darling, I do not want to be witness to the end of the world! I want to be back in Paris, and I want to meet Martine – I've seen lots of images, and I am jealous – and I want finally to meet James. By the way, Doctor Robertson and Doctor Sekibo and the team are using the new diffusion of the epidemics program and simplified apps which you developed and sent me, and they are proving very useful. The problem, as you have been the first to point out, is to get the right inputs, the on-the-ground information, that we need, to make the model work at its best. But, as you anticipated that problem, your model is still much better than what we had before. Robertson and Sekibo send thanks and greetings – to you, dear prodigal. And, as for you personally, darling, do send me an email – and perhaps next week we do a video call, I want to see your face, and maybe all the rest of you too!

I miss our cozy little nest in Boston with the sun deck and the poplar trees and your room piled up with books and you and me, just the two of us, walking around being silly throwing pillows at each other. All my love, your friend forever, Kate."

"You know what?" said Martine, looking up, the light from the fire glowing in her blond hair, reflecting on her golden tan.

"No, what?" I swiveled around in my chair.

"I'm jealous." She displayed a very pretty pout.

"Really? Of whom? Of what?"

"Of you and Kate. Of you and Jo. Of you. I want to pick a fight."

"Pick a fight?"

"Yes." She licked her lips and sat up. "I want a wrestling match! I want to wrestle you to the ground and hold you down and kiss you and make love to you."

"That sounds exciting. But you are not supposed to get any bruises or scratches. Philip was very clear about that. He even gave me a very stern lecture. You are filming in Berlin next week. And you are going to be very exposed. Love scenes, sex, and lots of skin, so no scratches or bruises."

"So – you'll have to surrender."

"That is absolutely unfair." I stood up and stretched.

"Let's see." She stood up, put her fingers to her chin, tilted her head to the side, and sized me up. "You'll have to surrender and be my prisoner tonight."

"Hmm." I frowned and turned off and closed my laptop. "Darling, just decreeing that I must be your prisoner is not fair. Let's flip coins or something like that. After all, we can't fight, though that would be fun. We don't want to leave any bruises or scratches on your beautiful body – it is so valuable. And I might get carried away."

"That's true. You're right. I am shooting next week. And Philip would be furious." She thought for a moment. "Okay, coins."

"We'll flip coins – and make it strip poker. She who loses is the slave."

"Strip poker. Sounds sufficiently harmless. Okay. Let's do it."

So we flipped coins, and we slowly stripped and the one who was naked first would lose and would be the prisoner for the evening; we stipulated that if I won I was not to whip her scratch her or bite her or to otherwise leave any marks on her body or on her face which would cause the film production and makeup people and insurance company and completion bond people to go hysterical and have conniptions and give Martine and Philip no end of trouble. Besides, Philip would be seriously annoyed, and he could be very stormy and – for days at a time – unsettlingly morose – which was very distressing and would upset Martine no end. She sighed, "I can't stand it when he's in a mood!!!" These were eventualities to be avoided.

While we played strip poker, we took our time, sipping two very strong very dry martinis which I had concocted – and we talked of all sorts of other things. It was weird, and very intimate. In a way, we were schizophrenic, adults on one wavelength, and silly naughty children on another. Still, it was thrilling.

We got down to panties. We were tied!

We had finished the martinis – a very pleasant buzz.

Before the suspenseful last flip of the last coin, we decided we should open a bottle of wine.

I went to the refrigerator and got out a chilled bottle of white wine, and we sat and drank a glass each, and we talked about what we were doing, and she described the scenes she would be shooting next week – scenes which sounded pretty sexy and in which she would in truth be showing a lot of skin – stark naked except for a little glue-on triangle – so we really had to avoid scratches and bruises. For the sex scenes, the guy, she told me, would be wearing a woolly sock.

"You're not using a double?"

"Nope, no double." She grinned. "Philip insisted. Authenticity, he calls it."

"Okay, now," I said. I handed the coin to her.

She balanced it in the palm of her hand.

"Heads, I win," I said.

"Okay," she said. And she threw the coin in the air. Up and up it went, seemingly in slow motion, and then down and down it came, flipping over and over and spinning, and then it landed in her hand, she closed her fist and opened it. I stared at it. There it lay. I stared at it and grinned.

"Heads," I said, "I win."

"No, that's not possible." I thought she'd be pleased, but she seemed truly chagrined. "How could you win? You're supposed to be the prisoner." She glanced at me and wet her lips. Her eyes flared, cool blue Norman fire, Viking blood merged with suave and subtle Mediterranean sensuality – a challenge and a promise. The flickering light from the fireplace made her body look like burnished gold, and her finely sculpted features, perfectly symmetrical, made her look like a goddess, a blond goddess who had just stepped out of some northern Nordic forest.

"Well, I won," I said. Now I had to figure out how to be the master. "Take off your panties, now, right now, tout de suite, Prisoner."

"Do I really have to?" She stuck out her lower lip, and looked down, feigning a charming childish pout.

"Absolutely, you have to. No, on second thought, I'll take them off for you." So, I slowly slid her panties down, and caressed her hips and her thighs and her labia. She wiggled a bit, but did not protest, and she put her hand on my shoulder.

Delicately, she stepped out the panties. I threw them on the little pile of clothes. I licked my lips. This was yummy. I put my hand on her arm. "Now, darling Prisoner, let me look at you. Turn around. Yes, that's right. Up on tiptoes. Yes. Stretch your arms up. That's nice. Hmm, I wonder if we should dress you up and go to La Coupole or Brasserie Lippe or Balzar on rue des Écoles. What sort of costume would be best? Or no, Costume at all. What do you think?"

"I am your prisoner, Mistress." She lowered her eyes, and then looked up at me, blinking. This was fine! I could get used to this. Why is this so exciting? I wondered. And Martine, at that very instant, said what I was thinking: "Why this is so exciting?"

"Power is exciting," I said.

"Yes, that's it – power."

"Power over somebody you desire."

"Yes." She again lowered her eyes, and glanced timidly up at me, "Or being in the power of somebody you desire – or someone you love."

"And who desires – who loves – you." This was luscious, but new. She was, I was, openly, admitting to love. Love is a very big word. I tried to make light of it. "It's all very Hegelian and dialectical as Marlene would say. It takes two to tango. You see, according to the dialectic, I define you, darling; you define me, darling; we *are* part of each other. Your desire is integral to my desire." I gave her my most masterly fiery dark glance of possession and dominance. I thought for a moment, and said, "Well, then, Prisoner, undress me, please, with your teeth, and on your knees."

She sniggered. The wench sniggered.

She put her hands on her hips; I could see revolt brewing; well, I would scotch this in the bud. I put my finger under her chin. "Don't worry, Prisoner, we'll do it on the rug, so you don't bruise your sensitive and valuable and heavily insured knees."

"Yes, Mistress." Her smile was shy, but also sly. She narrowed her eyes, and carefully got down on her knees in front of me;

she leaned forward, bared her teeth, and seized my panties, and began to pull them down. Her lips, breath, and teeth touched my skin. "Now, Prisoner, no hands. Your hands stay behind your back," I said.

She nodded and put her hands behind her back.

So, there she was, the luminous star, on her knees, hands clasped behind her back, slowly tugging my panties down to my ankles. It was not as easy as it sounds. She risked falling flat on her face, but, luckily, she was as buff and flexible as an acrobat. I lifted one leg to help her and then the other.

"Good, Prisoner. Now keep the panties clenched with your teeth and stand up."

She did so. She was staring at me, her blue eyes bright, her blond hair in dark strands plastered on her golden cheeks, which were flushed. The black-red-and-green lace panties dangling from one side of her mouth gave her the look of a dog who had re-trieved something for her master – or, in this case, mistress.

"Let us dance, Prisoner." I put on some music, and we began to dance – me leading – cheek to cheek. Her breasts were against my breasts, and I rubbed my belly against her warm, smooth belly. I looked deep into her blue-blue eyes. She looked beautiful and deliciously silly with the panties – they featured a little design of sparkly red roses and sequined green leaves – hanging from the side of her mouth. Finally, I lifted the panties from her mouth and threw them off to the side.

"Now, kiss me." I offered my lips.

Her lips met mine; we kissed; electricity sparkled. Our loins and breasts rubbed together, softly, slowly. Our bodies were perfectly matched. We are almost the same height. Her breasts brushed my breasts nipple to nipple, and her belly pressed my belly, and I pulled her closer to me; we kissed again – no masterly martial order was required this time – and so we danced around the living room, our bodies softly interlaced. And then, deciding to up the ante, I said, "Kneel before me, Prisoner. But first, I shall fit you with a collar."

I went to the sideboard where James kept the equipment, reached into a drawer, and picked out a nice thick high black leather collar, with a large iron ring at the front. I fastened the collar around her neck and snapped it shut. I sat down on the divan. She knelt before me.

"Do your duty, Prisoner," I said. She looked up at me with those wonderful bright eyes. She leaned forward and licked and nibbled at my breasts, her savvy tongue – where she learned to do all these things I don't know – twisting my nipple and licking and transforming everything – and me – into liquid excitement. She kissed and caressed her way downwards, to my belly. Slowly, gently, she spread my legs. She kissed and explored my smooth, waxed pubis, the clitoris, and the labia, and she liquefied me, my loins, my innards, and kissed the clitoris. I felt the excitement rising, and I put my hand in her hair, clutching at it as if to guide her, but she needed no guiding.

"Oh, you, oh, oh!" I yearned for more.

Slowly I slipped off the divan. We were both on the rug. I stretched over her, so my tongue could reach her, the heart of her, the golden stippled, naked, waxed, or laser-smooth heart of her.

I licked and kissed her.

Her absolute nakedness brought my excitement to a fevered pitch. She licked and kissed me. She was already wet, as was I. We kissed and licked and nibbled. She plunged and kissed me deeper and deeper. The excitement rose in a wave. I could feel her muscles tensing, just as mine were. The tension soared like a symphony. It flooded up to an unbearable intensity. Her hands were everywhere, just as mine were. Her tongue was savvy, just as I hope mine was. Then with a shutter and two muffled cries, we came, both of us, at the same time, and it was a long, rippling shudder; she screamed, and I screamed, and the orgasm, slowly, echoing in aftershocks, subsided and echoed.

"Oh, my God," she whispered.

We curled around so we could kiss on the mouth. I gazed into her eyes, and she gazed into mine. She passed her hand over my head, caressing my raspy stubble, reminding me of my baldness. I shivered in pleasure. Our bodies, slick with sex and sweat and desire, mingled, melted, became one. I knew I was feeling what she was feeling, and she was feeling what I was feeling.

I ran my hand up and down her body. I wanted to touch every inch of her. I grabbed her hair, gently, and I pulled her face to mine. We kissed, and her hands cupped my face. We kissed again and again; and again, she ran her hand over my skull.

"I love you," she whispered.

"I love you," I whispered.

Now, we'd said it; we'd known it for a long time, but now we'd said it, said it seriously, breathlessly.

We kissed, and again we kissed.

Finally, we sat up and faced each other. "You are still my Prisoner," I said.

"Yes, Mistress. Until the stroke of midnight, I am your Prisoner."

"What shall we do now, then, Prisoner?"

"You are the mistress, Mistress. You must decide." She pushed a strand of damp blonde hair away from her cheeks, which were still flushed. Her eyes were extra bright.

"Well, then, Prisoner, perhaps you can tell me of your sexual feelings, your romantic feelings. I wish to possess your soul. I want you to confess. I command it."

"Confess? Must I confess all, Mistress?" She sighed and leaned down, kissed my thigh, and then locked up, and put her arm around my shoulder, moving close, so our thighs and arms were touching. She put her finger to my lips. "Well, my dear vampire-pale mistress-confessor, who wishes to possess my soul, the first confession is this: I love playing like this. Being your prisoner is exciting. And making you my prisoner is even more exciting. It's hard to decide which is most exciting. And, as you know, I love you." Her voice had gone throaty, dreamy, and her fingers were playing in my stubble, caressing it, stroking it, my almost naked skull. It was unbearably arousing.

We slid to the floor and rolled over. I pinned her down. I bit her left nipple, just a delicate nip and twist, and lingering lick and kiss. Remember! Leave no marks!

"The silliest things arouse me," she whispered, her teeth tugging my earlobe.

"Like what?" I slid off her body, and lay beside her, both of us now on our sides, face to face, only a few inches apart. "Like what?" I repeated, kissing her, and running my hand over the curve of her hip, and cupping her backside.

She took a deep breath. "Certain gestures you make drive me crazy."

"Me?"

"Yes, like when you reach up to put the curls at the nape of your neck back in place, or when you just touch the nape of your neck. Or when you tilt you head down and look up from under your eyebrows that are coal-black like arched arrows in flight. Or like the way your English accent in French is sometimes just a bit awkward, and you make adorable little tiny mistakes in French grammar – and you're half-aware of it – and I want to touch your lips and correct you by kissing you. And then – and this is unbearably beautiful – the excitement makes me breathless – there's the self-conscious way you sometimes walk, looking down as if abashed at the cobblestones just in front of your toes, particularly if you are wearing very high heels, as if you are self-conscious of your sexual vulnerability, as if you were shy, and retiring, a vestal virgin about to be sacrificed, a timid, self-conscious child. And then there's the way your shoes are always so neat and impeccable, even when it is raining, or muddy. I don't know how you do it! I want to get down on my knees in front of you and worship! Everything about you is neat, and self-contained, and as if it had been just polished."

"You are crazy, my love – and for such poetic excess, my dear Prisoner, I bestow upon you a kiss." I kissed her.

"And then there is the way you get crossed-eyed, when we are very close, like now. It's absolutely adorable. Oh, my Mistress!"

"You are a naughty prisoner, pointing out my faults!"

"It is not a fault, Mistress, it is beautiful, sublime, it makes you look so intense, and also slightly goofy, and I am totally in love and totally enslaved."

"And Philip is not jealous?"

"No, he's not, he likes our dalliance, and even our love, he calls me his 'little wild one.' He knows I love you; he knows that I am *in* love with you. And he says that you are like a twin to me and that you and I are made for each other. We are sisters, he says, incestuous sisters, but sisters. We complete each other. He's a libertine, of course, and has a whole philosophy about it."

"Exactly like James – he is not jealous. And, yes, he has his own libertine philosophy, the Marquis de Sade, and *The Story of O*, and so on."

"Yes. It's part of a program. After all, the two of them set us up to meet, and in a rather provocative and promising setting, chez Madame Nicole. They put us on stage, already wound up, and ready to go."

"Yes, they did, me naked and painted and depilated absolutely smooth, and you stripped down and trying on that frilly corset." I ran my finger along the wonderful, curved, smooth, plow-blade-like line of her hip.

"Men!" I sighed.

"Men!" she echoed and kissed me.

"I'm delighted they did it," I whispered.

"Me too, absolutely," she deepened the kiss.

"How did you meet Philip?"

"Oh, my darling Mistress, it is a banal story, going back to Heloise and Abelard, the teacher and his pupil! The maestro and his acolyte! The sculptor, and his clay! I'm almost ashamed of the pure clichéd nature of this modest tale."

"Still, tell me, I command thee! Unveil this banal clichéd tale."

She feigned a pout, lips pushed out, and crossed her eyes and put her finger on the tip of my nose and pressed slightly, delicately squashing my nose, which was very bold of her, since I was her mistress and she was my prisoner; she knew full well pushing on the point of my nose with her finger would make me cross my eyes, and thus rage within at this my imperfection; my prisoner is a master of cruel tactics and intimate psychology. And, so, she began her tale: "Philip was my mentor. And he had absolutely no respect for me, while I, of course, had a very high opinion of myself. I had studied French literature and English literature at the University of Paris, and also I followed courses of Italian and Italian literature, since my mother is Italian, and I speak Italian just as well as French; after university, I enrolled in the Acting Academy in Paris and studied in London too; I had performed, when I was just a teenager, in Moliere and Shakespeare and Schnitzler at the Comédie Française. So I was considered a sort of prodigy – just like you, I guess, but in a very minor way; you are a genius, I'm just – well, I guess, 'talented' is the word, and I have the *physique du rôle*,' the looks and the body for the stage – and also for the camera. So, I was quite snotty about it all, with a very exalted idea of myself. As I said, when I was just a teenager, I was on stage at the Old Vic in London, and then in the Festival in Avignon. Philip came to give a lecture and hold a series of workshop-seminars, a whole season, at the Acting Academy in Paris, where I was studying. I didn't like some of his advice and told him so. "Really?" he said. He was clearly annoyed. He made me play some scenes from a Jean Genet play, "The Maids," and also, he made me play Irma, the madam of the brothel in Genet's "The Balcony" and then some Moliere, and Shakespeare in French. I had to do Viola, and Portia, and also Hamlet. Bits and pieces."

"Ah, Hamlet, I played Hamlet too, and Kate was Horatio. It was amateur theater, of course, not professional."

"You would be a marvelous Hamlet, my dear cruel dark mistress, dark and brooding, cross-dressing, vampire-like, stormy, a murky, murderous, sensual, sexually ambiguous Hamlet."

"Hmm. That is an intriguing idea, my dear, dear Prisoner: me – a vampire Hamlet. And you, a delicate, hysterical, diaphanous Ophelia." I slapped her gently on the bum, three times, and kissed her, "Perhaps we should suggest this idea to Philip."

"Thank you, Mistress! I adore it when you spank me." She stuck out her tongue and gave me the sweetest smile. "Do it again!"

I gave her another pair of slaps – she has the most adorable resonant bum, elastic and firm. Each slap echoed. She favored me with a swooning look through half-closed eyes. "Well, Philip was very critical of my acting; he was cruel, even sadistic, and in front of the others too. I was annoyed, and, oh, so totally pissed off! I wanted to kill him."

"Poor little mouse." I favored her with a kiss, first on her forehead, then on the tip of her nose, then on her mouth.

She sighed. "I was a roaring mouse, really, and a wounded mouse, inside at least. Philip had struck at the core of my idea of myself, at the very heart of me, at the whole meaning of my life. He made me feel like I was nothing, and worth nothing. And he was a cult figure already. I thought he was showing off and full of himself. A real asshole."

I caressed her hair. She returned the favor by running her fingers over my stubble. Her eyes sparkled, sleepily. She blinked and wet her lips.

"After that, in each session, he bullied me – he picked me out and pounced. I was beginning to doubt myself. I became nervous, even neurotic. This was totally unlike me. I am usually totally self-confident, even arrogant. His nattering, nitpicking cruelty kept me awake at night. I could hear his voice in my head. If he asked me to improvise, I'd break out in an awful sweat."

"You fascinated him – so, to defend himself from his fascination, he decided to be cruel." I reached over to the bottle – in its ice bucket on the rug – and filled her glass – my prisoner was permitted to drink – and held the cup to her lips. She drank, and drank, gulping it down, and then continued with her tale.

"Yes, maybe. Maybe he was trying to defend himself. In any case, he was dreadfully and incessantly cruel. Once, after a workshop – it was a stormy winter night – I went to the school canteen alone, everybody else had left. There was nobody in the room. There was a damp chill in the air, even inside. I took a cup of coffee and clutched it between my hands and drank. I was shaking. I had decided to quit the course and maybe quit acting. But what else would I do with my life? It was silly, I know, but I felt like jumping off a bridge into the Seine. Everything I had done up to that point was useless; my future, which once seemed so bright, was empty. It was a blank. It was cold and rainy and dark outside and even, while wanting to end my life, I didn't even dare face the weather. I was so shaken. I wanted to crawl under the table and roll up into a little ball. Then Philip entered the canteen. I watched him, feeling for some reason terrified, absolutely terrified. He got himself a cup of coffee and sauntered over – totally casual – and sat down at my table, facing me. I just looked at him. I was trembling, and I thought I was going to break into tears. I said, 'I think you were wrong about Irma in *The Balcony*.'

'Oh,' he said, 'You think I'm wrong? Who are you? Who are you to think I'm wrong?'

"We got into a fierce argument. I told him what I thought of him. 'You are an asshole' I said, 'and a bully, and you are picking on me, and I do not understand why. Do you only feel good when you are tearing somebody apart?'

"His face went red and then pale. I swallowed. He is going to kill me right here, I thought. And at the very least he is going to give me horrible marks. Instead, he stood up, like he was going to leave, turned his back on me, then turned to look at me and said, 'You are intolerably opinionated and stuck-up for such a young woman.'

"I stuck out my tongue.

"He turned his back on me and walked to the door. Then he turned and came back and said, 'I think we should continue this over dinner.'

'Dinner? Really?' I was still furious.

'Yes, really' he said, 'Enemies should always talk.'

"I was fuming. I glared at him. But I said, 'Okay, then, if you think it is a good idea.'

"We went to a tiny bistro, just off Boulevard Saint Germain. It was crowded and noisy, but we managed to get a corner table, and we also had a very nice bottle of Bordeaux and heaps of the steamy boeuf bourguignon, ideal for an icy, rainy night.

"The fight became more relaxed. He knew movies by heart. And since I'd seen every movie I could, especially the classics, I could match him reference for reference. We talked Ernst Lubitsch and Stanley Kubrick and Woody Allen and Sergio Leone and Jean Luc Godard and Alain Renais and Eisenstein and about acting styles and directing styles.

"And, then, when we were on the sidewalk, under the rain, and about to say goodbye, he said, 'Do you want to come to my place for a drink?'

'For a drink?' I raised my eyebrows and gave him a look.

'Well ...' he almost stuttered. He looked abashed.

'Well, then,' I said, and I took his arm, 'Yes. Let us go to your place for a drink.' It was raining harder now, an icy wintry rain, and, as you know, Paris can be very inhospitable in the wintry rain, all the windows closed, all the shops shuttered, all the lights low, the long boulevards are like wind tunnels that seem to lead straight off to some infernally cold, lonely infinity.

"I slanted my umbrella into the rain, so he and I were close together, my arm under his, and we walked through the icy wind and rain to his building.

"We did have a drink, Glen Grant, I remember, on the rocks.

"His flat was a labyrinth high up under the eaves of a building from the Haussmann era, the 1850s or 60's and the flat had been carved out of a lot of little separate flats and occupied two floors. The rain was pattering on the roof. From the living room window, I could see Notre Dame – lit up and wrapped in mist and rain. I examined his books. They were piled high and everywhere, and movie posters, and DVDs and old VHS tapes, scripts, cameras, etc. He had an old-fashioned Hasselblad and brought it out – and I thought, *Oh, oh, here we go* – and, yes, he wanted to photograph me, with clothes and without clothes, and I said, 'Later, maybe, if you behave.' And he said, 'So be it.' He smiled and winked at me and put the camera away.

"His bed was piled with books on one side. I said, 'I think we should continue our discussion in bed.' He hadn't touched me except for a very light kiss just before he prepared the drinks – which I found delicate and delicious and quite promising. So, the question of whether we were going to have sex or not was hanging in the air. I had decided that I was going to have sex with him. It would be a form of revenge. I'd prove I was worthy of him, maybe better than him.

"As I said, the flat was a real warren of a place – the bedroom was far off in one corner. The bed was an antique brass bedstead. I punched the mattress. It was lumpy. The bed creaked and bounced. This is not promising, I thought: I doubt he's ever brought a woman to this bed; no self-respecting woman would put up with it. Maybe he's gay, I thought, or maybe he's a neuter, consumed by his creativity, locked in his vanity, a narcissist-artist who does not need sex or friendship.

"I tested the mattress again – disgraceful! I much prefer decent hard surfaces, a little resistance. Leverage does help if two bodies are trying to come to grips with each other.

"I turned to him: 'So shall we accomplish the evil deed? Shall we be the beast with two backs?' He nodded. I think he was a bit taken aback, and he certainly thought I was a touch forward.

"I took off my skirt, a pleated green-and-black tartan skirt, and I hung it up on a rung in his wardrobe, and then I took off my blouse, and I hung it up too. I was dressed rather conservatively, with a black bra, and a black garter belt and black stockings, and black patent leather high-heeled shoes. I looked at some of the books.

"During my demure little striptease, Philip had not made a move towards me. He stood and looked at me. Finally, he said, 'You are a very forward young woman.' 'Not always,' I said, 'not usually.' He cleared his throat. 'I'm honored,' he said. 'I suppose you should be,' I said, and then I added, 'but I too, Maestro Philip, am honored.' I took a volume out of the bookshelf. It was *The Citizen Kane Book*, with a long essay by Pauline Kael.

"Philip stepped closer to me. And I said, 'So, Maestro, tell me about the story-within-the-story structure of Citizen Kane,' and holding the book between us, I kissed him, and I said, 'And tell me about the lighting and the shots – the visual style.'

"He began to talk. I pressed myself to him and bit him his lip, gently. 'Ouch,' he said, and rubbed his lip and looked sorrowful. 'Oh, poor dear,' I said.

"He described some of the shots, how shadows were used, how the *contre-plongée* was used, I don't remember the word in English for *contre-plongée*, oh, yes, a 'low angle shot,' with the camera looking upward, so the characters look like giants and you see them against the ceiling or the sky, it turns everybody into a god or a hero, or a fearful monster, there are some similar effects I think in Fritz Lang's *M* about a child murderer; and so, the poor dear, while I nibbled at his lips, he went on in a fairly interesting way about how Wells had learned from the German expressionists, such as Lang.

"It was raining harder now; the rain was beating against the windowpanes. Up there, high in the old building, we were surrounded by night and rain. It felt warm and cozy and sheltered, with the smell of books and photographic paper and old rugs and old wood.

"I put *The Citizen Kane Book* down, and I unbuttoned his shirt, and I kissed his chest. 'Talk,' I said, 'talk.' So, responding to my whim, he went on talking; he talked and talked and talked, giving me a very neat lecture, with lots of parentheses and asides, on German Expressionism, on the Russian school, Vertov and Eisenstein, on Hollywood in the 1930s and 40s and how Orson Wells fitted in, or, really didn't fit in. How, in Orson Wells, genius and self-destructive excess were intimately mingled to the point, almost, of suicide.

"I lifted off his shirt, and I unbuckled his belt. And I ordered him to step out of his shoes. And I pulled his trousers down till they were around his ankles, and I left them there. Making a man slightly ridiculous is a useful tactic, I have found, and some men, if they are very self-confident, don't mind playing the clown – a little bit anyway.

"If a woman seems strong, or is strong, then conquering her is more piquant, or spicy, the trophy is more valuable, as it were; if they look upon us as prey, as many men do, and most men, even the most loving and benign, do see us as prey, then the more difficult the prey is, the more skillful and flirtatious and playful and demanding, the more exciting the prize. It's a rite of passage for men. They must go hunting, and we are what they hunt.

"I kissed him again, and I put my hand on his underpants, on his crotch, and he was erect, very erect, an admirable erection, which gave me great pleasure. 'Yes, he desires me,' I thought. Power. Yes, power, the power to arouse, the power to elicit desire, the power to be liked, to be admired, to be desired. It is a bit like being drunk." Martine stopped talking, took a sip of wine, and gave me an adorably half-drunk, half-asleep look, a declaration of love, I think, yet another declaration of love.

"And were you already drunk?" I asked. I was stroking her hair. I loved her telling me her story like this. I kissed her lightly on the lips. "I love you," I whispered. Her breath was sweet like sunshine, like lemons and honey.

"I was just a bit tipsy, Mistress. But not really drunk."

"Were you watching yourself as you confronted Philip, or were you totally immersed?"

"Oh, my dear mathematician philosopher and mistress, always thinking – and thinking about thinking, which is really quite extraordinary – I was mostly immersed, but there were moments when I said to myself, 'Oh, look, Martine, you are beginning an affair with this famous, talented older man. Oh, look, you are being terribly brazen. Oh, look, it is a romantic rainy, cold night in

Paris; you are flirting with and sailing very close to becoming a cliché. Here you are, my dear Martine, playing in a scene out of a cheap novel: student falls for professor, acolyte tumbles for maestro. And we know how cheap novels end: Oh, look, poor naïve, darling, corrupt, slut Martine, he may bed you, and then toss you out, and humiliate you even more than before. But, oh, then, dear Machiavellian Martine, you really don't care. You don't give a damn. You've already leveled the playing field: he desires you; so, you have already scored a major point. Even if it ends now, you have totted up a notable advantage!' Part of me thought, too, of the movies I'd seen – and how, if it were done the right way, the scene might be worthy of a movie, ideally shot in moody old-fashioned black-and-white, like something from the 1950s or in the style of the Nouvelle Vague of the 1960s. So, yes, my Mistress, I did have a certain reflective, self-conscious *distance*. But I was excited, too, and immersed in the instant, to use your word, Mistress, I was *immersed* in the moment – I was wet with excitement. But I wanted it to go very slowly, a sort of slow-motion film; I pressed myself against him, I slipped my hand into his briefs, and I squeezed and twisted. He kissed me, this time fiercely; I held the kiss; for a long time, I didn't let him go; we stood like that. Now, if I zoom back to that moment, I think how strange and comic it was. You, Mistress, I am sure you can see this and appreciate it, if we zoom back, we are faced with a ridiculous tableau: the man and woman standing, facing each other, the man, his cock being squeezed, the woman, pressed against him, still in her high heels, still in her bra, and still in her panties and garter belt; it's a tableau, suspended in time, an old sepia or silvered-over photograph. We were like two boxers or wrestlers, facing off, not yet ready to plunge into full attack mode. I caressed him, working on his excitement, bringing him closer and closer to orgasm, teasing, torturing him as best I could.

"Then I said, 'Remove my bra, please, Philip.' 'Philip,' I said, using his first name for the first time.

"'Yes, Martine,' he said, using my first name for the first time. Up to this instant, it had been 'Maître' or 'Maestro' or 'Monsieur le Professeur' and 'Mademoiselle Aubin.'

"He was deft with his fingers and quickly unhooked the bra. 'You'd better hang it up,' I said.

"He blinked at me, bowed slightly, and carefully hung it up, where and as I indicated he should.

"Then I pulled his underpants – or briefs – the terminology is confusing and annoying – down, so he could step out of them. Naked men are quite vulnerable, I find, don't you, Mistress?" She blinked at me, almost a childlike grin.

"Yes, Prisoner, I do find it so." I kissed her and held her and looked deep into her eyes. "It is perhaps for that reason they can, occasionally, become overbearing and once naked, wish to act quickly and get it over with so they can pull their pants back on and hide their vulnerability and scoot away or smoke a cigarette and fall asleep. Continue, Prisoner."

"Yes, Mistress," She kissed me on the end of the nose and then kissed my left breast and looked up at me through half-closed eyes. "Yes, Mistress, your every wish is my command. Well, he, the Professor, the Great Film Maker, the Maestro, was naked, and I wasn't. It was the sort of little imbalance that I like and that I know you like – tiny shifts in power, symbolic more than real, but real just the same. After all, we are such stuff as dreams are made on, are we not? We are made of performance and symbolism. Iteration and variation of performances make us what we are – man or woman, master or slave, as I believe some of those feminist philosophers you so adore like to say. A cigar is a cigar, certainly, but never merely a cigar, as Professor Freud allegedly pointed out. So, there we were, power having shifted, temporarily, a little bit."

"Just like now," I said, "you are my prisoner, and I am your mistress."

"Yes, just like now, Mistress Mine, oh, Gwendoline." Her eyes blinked, and she touched my lips with her fingers. "You can observe a person carefully, objectively, when they are naked. And he, the Great Man, was naked.

"So we kissed, and I caressed him, and then, frankly, I wanted to kneel before him, which I did, and I licked and caressed him, and sucked him, but gently, because I didn't want him to come in my mouth; and I wanted it to last, and I wanted it to be romantic, I wanted it to be mutual between us, as equals. His self-control was admirable, and at a certain point, when he was getting very tense and trembling, he said, 'Gently, now, gently, Martine.' He lifted me up and kissed me on the mouth. 'Undress me,' I said, 'Strip me naked,' and I bit him, lightly, on the under lip. 'Yes,' he said, and then he began – I helped him – to unhook the garter belt, and to unhook the stockings, and he knelt and unbuckled the shoes, and I stepped out of them, and I rolled down the stockings, and he watched as I wiggled out of the panties.

"And so, finally, I was naked. I stood up straight and stared at him, just stared, and I smiled, I don't know exactly why, but I smiled.

"He looked at me for a long minute then, without moving, he said, 'You are too beautiful.' It was almost as if he were dismissing me. He put the emphasis on the 'too.' 'You exaggerate,' I said, 'besides, you, Maestro, are too beautiful too.' 'And too old,' he said. 'Well, Maestro, I shall be the judge of that.' I took a step towards him; I reached up and kissed him, and I pulled him and held him to me, squeezed him close against me; of course, he was still erect, and I was ready, more than ready."

Here Martine took a deep breath; her eyes were far away, dreamy; she blinked and touched her finger to my cheek, drew it down, along the line of my chin. I gave her a little peck on the lips. "And at this point, Prisoner, were you detached? Did you see yourself and your lover from a great, divine distance? Did you zoom back for a panoramic view?" I was watching her closely and caressing the curve of her hip, and the soft slope of her belly, and touching, lightly, the delicious smooth swelling of her mons veneris, lightly pressuring the clitoris.

"No, Mistress, I was not at all detached." Her eyes went blurry; she wet her lips. Her voice was throaty; saliva shone on her teeth.

She cleared her throat. "I was, I think, in love, or infatuated, yes, certainly infatuated."

I brushed her lips with mine. "And then?"

She cleared her throat. "And then, we moved towards the bed. We cleared off the books. Some of them looked interesting. The whole bed was a rumpled, tossed. creased mess. I think I spotted breadcrumbs. 'When did you change these sheets?' I asked. 'Oh, I don't know,' he said, 'maybe two weeks ago.' 'Do you have a cleaning lady? Or, to be correct, a cleaning person, or, to be more correct, do you hire personal space renewal cleaning personnel?' He looked at me wide-eyed. 'Well, yes, she comes once a month – she's Russian and very thorough – but I don't let her touch anything where the books are. I laughed. 'The books are everywhere, Maestro. How can she do anything at all?' 'Well, she does the dishes, and the floor, where she can find it.' 'Buried under the books,' I said. 'Yes,' he frowned, 'buried under the books.'

"So, with the books gone, we crawled and fell into the bed. 'This bed is too bouncy,' I said. I felt I was going to fall or be bounced out of the bouncing bed. Being bounced out of the bed and onto the floor would not be romantic. We struggled with the bed for a while, me on top of him, then him on top of me, but we kept bouncing around, and slipping off each other, and the bedstead was groaning, and the springs were creaking and twisting, and the mattress was lumpy.

"I said, 'I can't do this.' 'What?' he said. He sounded appalled. 'I don't mean you, silly, and I don't mean the sex. I mean the bed.' 'Oh,' he said. He grinned and kissed me, and I kissed him back, and we were facing each other, on hands and knees and kissing, and the bed got so bouncy it almost tossed us both overboard. 'Enough of this,' I said. So, we got out of the bed. And I got some blankets, and I laid them on the floor and put some pillows around the blankets, like a little wall, and I said, 'Now, Maestro, let us try again.' And we did. We had found a solid place. Philip is a splendid and patient lover; he took his time. It was as if he was an explorer, and I was a new continent he had to explore and map everywhere, all the little plateaus and valleys and hills and mountains. And I, of course, wanted to be explored and to explore. You know that poem by John Donne, the one about the lovers being two hemispheres. Well, it was like that, Philip was like an explorer, and so was I. And I discovered that, yes, indeed, he was truly a wonderful lover."

"Like James," I said, and kissed her.

"Yes, I imagine James is very good, kinky, but good."

"Kinky like me," I blinked at her.

"Yes, Mistress, kinky like you, but also kinky like me, and Philip is very French, so by definition, he is kinky. It goes with the territory. It is stamped on the passport: *The French Republic of Kink*. It's part of the brand. That's why we sell perfume and lingerie and tours of the Eiffel Tower. As you know, Philip has read the Divine Marquis de Sade and Anne Desclos's *The Story of O*, and the erotica of Anais Nin, and Dangerous Liaisons, and Henry Miller and D. H. Lawrence, and Boccaccio and Casanova, and Krafft-Ebing, and so on, so he has explored the psychology of power and sex, and of course, he writes scenarios and directs films and plays about the shifting power relations of sex and class and race, including that film he made about terrorists and sex – how young women are entranced by the idea of being a slave to some presumptuous and immature bearded fundamentalist warrior idiot, and the film about the beautiful Somali girl, Ayaan, and her affair with a rather caddish rich Italian and how she managed to turn the tables on him and make him truly fall in love. I really think that underneath the roses and candlelight and violins, and behind the waiters or waitresses pouring champagne, and behind the wedding bells, sex is about the raw naked body, sweaty, and salivating, and shitting and peeing, and it's about the self, and ego and vanity, power and appetite and chemistry – personal chemistry. Transcendent chemistry, if you like. Sex is dynamite. Civilization tries to tame it."

"Dynamite like you," I brushed her forehead with my lips.

"Flattery, Mistress, will get you everywhere. And, in fact, I think you have been everywhere; already, you've explored every aspect and orifice of my body, I believe." She blinked and looked down and blushed prettily, a slight rose tinge spreading under her golden tan, and she added. "And, Mistress, you do know how to push – how do you say it? – all my buttons."

"Continue your tale, Prisoner," I said. I wondered at myself: A little less than three years ago I was a graduate student in mathematics in a house just outside Cambridge Mass, and now I was in Paris, and I was the mistress and the lover of a famous French actress, Martine Aubin, and the lover of millionaire adventurer James Hewitt Spencer. Three years ago, I didn't know either of them existed. One can travel a long way in a short time.

Marine licked her lips and caressed my shaven, stubbly, androgynous, girl-waif skull, running her fingers over it, teasing the scratchy surface; then she touched the curve of my ear, delicately, and tugged slightly, teasingly, at the earlobe. "And so, it began, dear Mistress, that glossy rainy night in Paris, with his silly bed and us among the books on the floor, making love, and then – when we were totally exhausted – we did sleep in the bed. I got him to change it soon afterward. I had him solder the brass bedstead and reinforce it so that it was solid and not creaky, and I had him replace the wooden slates with steel cross-braces, and I bought a new, solid, hygienic, firm mattress. And I laid down a firm rule: no croissants or sandwiches or food in bed – coffee, yes, wine, yes, but no crumbs, please. And a maximum of two books on the bed at any one time."

"Oh, you are masterful, my slave-for-an-evening." I favored her with a long, lingering, nibbling, vampire-like kiss.

"Oh, Mistress Gwendoline," she sighed, "you are most kind – and most cruel!"

"Yes, I am, Prisoner – so continue your tale." I tugged on the ring in her collar, as a gentle reminder of who was boss.

"Yes, Mistress. And, so, Philip did take photographs of me, naked, dressed, indoors, outdoors, everywhere. And he has directed me in five films. We live as if we were independent, but we are virtually always together, and most nights when he is in Paris, we sleep together, either at my place, which is more comfortable, or at his place, which is more interesting."

"And you are happy?"

"I am happy and even happier since I met you, Mistress. People say that young women are inevitably victims if they have a relationship with an older man, a powerful man, a maestro; they say that a teacher and a student should never be lovers – even in university when both are adults. I think that is stupid patronizing cowardly nonsense. How do you say it, bullshit?"

"I agree," I said, "I think young men are too immature, often, for young women, and that young women need the experience, sometimes, of an older man. Of course, you have to find the right older man. Young men could use some experience with older women, too, I think."

"Yes, I agree. An older woman can teach a lot. And young men do need mentors – but often they are too proud and too immature to accept lessons. Though I understand from an older woman friend of mine, she's an art director, that young men are very interested, now, in older women; she has had a few affairs, recently, with young guys; so, things are looking up!" She took a breath, her eyes seemed oh, so deep. She continued. "Young women, particularly if they are good-looking, but even if they aren't classically good-looking, even if they are what used to be called ugly, but if they are confident of their power and appeal, such young women have immense power – they should use it; it doesn't always last. Charisma, sex appeal, is something you can cultivate. We are throwing away the wisdom of the ages by not learning to use our sexual power while we have it – and to use it with older men too. Older men can be very interesting. You can learn a tremendous amount from an intelligent, experienced older man. And one can tame them – it just takes guts, self-confidence, and savoir-faire. And, if they are mature – not all older men are – then they can teach much, and that is very useful."

"We share this strange taste for mature men." I kissed her. I let the kiss linger. Our eyes open. I truly felt I could see her soul.

"Yes, we do, Mistress. I learn so much from Philip. He does know a lot. I have learned, I am learning, a huge amount from him. He is a wonderful director of actors. He is kind and considerate, and very brave, and I love him. I love him totally. I think I have helped him too, in his art, in his work, and also in his intimacy, in the way he knows and thinks of himself. So, for me, it's been great, for my career, and for me, personally ... And you ..."

"What about me?"

"I hesitate to say it, Mistress."

"Speak, I command you."

"I wanted to touch you the first moment I saw you."

"It was a shared desire, Prisoner."

"You know the myth Plato used to explain love and desire; that lovers are one soul and one body that have somehow been separated and they search and search for their other half, and, when they are finally united, it is as if two halves have come back together to restore wholeness. Well, that is the feeling I have for you, it is as if I have always known you were there, and now I've found you."

"It is true for me too. The instant I saw you, I wanted you." I touched her forehead and brushed a strand of hair from her eyes. I kissed her on the lips. "It is almost seven o'clock. Now, what shall we do?"

"I could offer you a massage, perhaps, my Mistress."

"Yes, Prisoner: that does sound delicious, a massage."

I turned up the gas fire in the fireplace, and I lay on the rug, and we both had glasses of wine, and she lowered herself onto me, and sat on my back. I could feel the heat and moisture between her legs, the wet heart of her, pressing into the small of my back. She began to massage my shoulders.

"Oh, so tense, Gwendoline!"

"Well, I've been thinking," I said.

"And what have you been thinking?" Her hands were delicate and strong; she seemed to be kneading each muscle and each tendon; she seemed to know, too, where all the tensions were and precisely how to relieve them.

"Ah," I sighed. I reached out one arm and played with the texture of the rug. "I'm worried about Kate."

Martine gave me a little slap on the bum. "Ah, Mistress, I am jealous!"

"And I'm worried about James."

Another little slap. "Ah, Mistress, you are cruel to me, your prisoner. But tell me. Why are you worried?"

And, I told her: Kate was on the front line in the struggle against the new form of Ebola, and she was in danger from the spreading plague – which was probably mutating into a much more contagious form. And she was in danger from Islamist rebels who had sworn to execute and rape and torture and mutilate any westerners, men or women, who fell into their hands, and I was worried about James. He was trying to rescue a very interesting Czech biotech firm from some very dangerous criminal and Mafioso types – Russian and Georgian gangs and arms dealers – who would not hesitate to kill anybody who got in their way.

"Whew," Martine whispered, "You do have a lot to worry about – and, Mistress, if you are worried, I am worried too. What can we do about this?" As she said this, I felt the moist warmth of her, delicious and intimate, glowing hot in the small of my back; her hands were kneading my shoulders and tracing the lines of my shoulder blades – I felt I was a damp lump of unformed clay; her fingers were magically giving me life.

"Nothing," I said, "For the moment, we can't do anything."

"Ah, I see." She slowly worked her way, massaging, down almost to my waist. Then she lifted herself off my back – I suddenly felt naked and bereft – I had grown used to the moist warm glow of her sex, intimate, for me alone, in the small of my back.

She crouched beside me, massaging my bum, very nicely too, like she was kneading fine dough to make a very nice loaf of bread; she worked her way down both legs.

I lay in a stupor of gratitude and sensual abandon. Her touch was magic. And just the image of her, naked, crouched next to me, running her hands over my body, had an almost mystical intensity, an exaltation of desire and comfort and thankfulness.

"Now, you are done, Mistress," she slapped me on the bum.

I rolled over and stared up at her. I think she must have seen the pure look of adoration in my eyes. She smiled a huge warm, welcoming smile. I sat up. Now we were sitting, cross-legged, facing each other.

"I do like serving you, Mistress," she said.

"And I like serving you, too, Martine." I pushed her down on her back on the rug. And, plunging forward, on hands and knees, doggy-style, I crawled on top of her, my hands pinning down her wrists. I kissed her on the lips. She struggled weakly, smiling up at me, and half closing her eyes. I held her down, and I kissed her collarbone, and then I kissed her breasts and teased and kissed each nipple cupping her breasts and caressing them, and I sucked and teased the nipples and as I touched her and kissed her and nibbled at her and licked her, her hands, now free, began to move over the stubble of my skull, and she signed, and murmured "Oh, oh, oh, Gwendoline!' And I kissed my way down to her tummy and kissed her belly button, and with one hand I massaged her between the legs, I teased and kneaded her golden stippled pubis, I teased her nipples, I touched and opened the little hood and with my hungry, hungry tongue, I teased the liquid clitoris. She cried out, low, just a whisper, "Oh, oh, oh, Gwendoline, oh, Mistress!!" I kissed the inside of her thighs, working my way down, then up, until with my lips I again opened her labia, and licked and kissed and teased, and then I flicked and twirled and turned the clitoris, that fluid little magic dial, and flick-flick-flick, back and forth, with fluttery little kisses and blowing on it once or twice as if I wanted to light a fire from kindling, and then lick-lick-lick, and then suck, suck, suck, as if I needed sustenance, I yearned to milk her of all her desire. She was trembling. Her knees went up, and she squeezed me between her thighs, her legs tensing, tightening, and her fingers holding my head, caressing, stroking the stubble, touching my ears, caressing the lobes. I licked and licked, and twirled now, my tongue hungry, my whole self, wrapped up in my tongue, and in my hands stroking, kneading, teasing, and caressing her breasts "Oh, oh, oh," excitement was rising in her, convulsive now; she was soaking wet, and trembling, more and more. I was caught up in her excitement, feeling the excitement rise inside me like a tidal wave, my tummy trembling, my saliva dripping, my labia soaked with lust, and then, in a crescendo the excitement peaked, but for a moment it was suspended there, in some sort of infinite space, it seemed suspended there, unbearable; and then she cried out, "Oh, oh, oh," and she came in a spasm of wet trembling shaking quivering exaltation, and I too was on the edge, and I worked at it, I wanted it to be so intense that she would not be able to stand it, and I kept going, my own trembling and excitement so intense so strung-out so vibrant it was painful and, as she came, her thighs clutching me, letting go, clutching me, pressing me, crushing me between them, and she cried out "Oh, oh, oh, Mistress, Oh, Gwen, Oh, Gwendoline, Oh, darling, Oh, my love, Oh, my divine love, Oh, what are you doing to me, Oh, Gwendoline, Oh stop, stop, stop! No, no, no, Gwendoline, don't stop, don't stop, don't stop, don't ever stop ..."

We both came, my orgasm echoing hers, overlapping tsunamis, sweeping us away, sweeping us both away.

"Oh, Martine," I cried out, "Oh, my darling, Oh, my love!" I licked, and I kissed her, I nursed and coddled with my lips and my tongue her clitoris, I comforted it, and slowly I said goodbye to it, a fond farewell, and I kissed my way up her body – sweaty now, trembling now, glowing in the firelight, golden silken iridescent shimmering smoothness. I kissed her breasts, and I sucked and suckled each breast; I teased each nipple. I kissed her on the lips. Her eyes were closed; her hands grasped my head and pulled me to her.

We kissed again, and her eyes opened and gazed into mine. Her lips were slick with saliva, mine, and hers. She kissed me again, and she whispered in a choked, throaty voice, "Look! You've got your adorable cross-eyed look!" "Oh, you," I said, and I grabbed her wrists to hold her down and punish her, but she surprised me and pushed me back up and rolled us over, so I was suddenly under her. She raised herself up and bent over, and slipped down next to my body, and crawled back down and kissed my hips and belly; then she got up on all fours, so she was above me, doggy style. She gazed down at me, stuck out her tongue, whispered, "Oh, Gwendoline," and she kissed my labia and then teased with her tongue my clitoris, and she turned around and crouched down on me, putting us in the sixty-nine position, and I licked and kissed her labia, and she licked and kissed mine, and then we were making love, once again, now mutual, her savvy tongue and lips consuming me, raising me to a height of painful trembling ecstasy, absolutely obliterating me, and I was kissing and licking her and plunging into the musky wetness of her, the fertile, fecund earthy wetness, the fluid fleshy liquid lips of her, and grasping at her legs and her buttocks, as she nuzzled, sucked, kissed, licked her way deep into the heart of me, and then, as if in a single instant we both trembled, grunted, snorted, heaved, licked, trembled, cried out, buried our muzzles and snouts deep, deep, in each other, cried out, licked sucked, grunted, groaned, whimpered, and then, yes, then, we came, simultaneously we came, in a great rush, in a trembling screaming crying rush.

"Oh, Gwen, Oh Gwendoline, Oh ..."

"Yes, Prisoner ..."

"Oh, oh, oh!" She sighed turned over, and, lying on her belly, she stared at me dreamily, and fingered the rug. The fire in the fireplace sculpted satin reflections on the silken curves of her backside and shoulders, glimmering in strands in her golden hair. "I really like this rug," she said in a throaty half-whisper. "This is an amazing rug." She smiled at me, a silly, goofy, wide, little-girl smile.

"It is indeed a fine rug." I crawled close to her. We lay there, staring at the fire, both of us on our bellies, my hand on her backside, her hand on my backside.

"Mistress?"

"Yes?"

"We are a bit rank. Perhaps we should take a shower."

Yes, Prisoner, a shower – that is a fine idea."

The shower was a sensual and relaxing experience; there was lots of room for both of us, and so we cared for each other with sponges, washcloths, little scrub brushes and fingers and hands, and lots of shampoo and liquid soap

We came out of the shower wrapped in towels; we dropped the towels on the divan, and we sat down on the rug in front of the fire.

"Now, Mistress, I must make a confession." She crouched down on all fours, lowering herself in front of me.

"A confession?"

"Yes, my confession, Mistress, is this: I worship you. You are not only my Mistress; you are my Goddess." As she whispered this little declaration, her eyes sparkled with mischief. "What do you wish your prisoner to do now?"

I crawled to her on all fours, and I kissed her. I thought about it for just an instant: "Let's go out," I said.

"Out? Hmm. Like this?" She licked her lips. "Naked? That would certainly be good for our reputations – such as they are!"

"No, not like this." I kissed her shoulder and sniffed at her perfumed skin; I closed my teeth, delicately, on the soft surface of her shoulder, being careful not to leave a bruise; I wanted to gobble her up. "Let's see. There must be something that will fit you. In fact, almost everything would fit you!"

I got up and rummaged in my sex carnival supplies – the very large wardrobe and set of drawers James and I – I had become a collector too – always kept very well stocked – and found a tight black latex skirt and frilly top, which could be used, I thought, to create a cute Punk-Goth ensemble.

"I'm going to turn you into the opposite of what you are," I said.

"The opposite?"

"Yes, you will cease to be a blond goddess, and you are going to become, for this evening, a classic Punk-Goth Freak."

"Oh, well, Mistress, if you wish it, then your wish must come true."

I had fun making her up. I carefully applied a thick ultra-smooth white foundation; it turned her sunshine golden tan into a luminous, ghostly, white, ceramic pallor; I added purple-black lipstick, and then purple and black eyeliner; her delicious sleepy eyelids I did in a glorious purple, and added to the lashes, and then curved shaded charcoal up to her eyebrows, which are naturally jet-black and which I filled in and curved outwards towards her temples. I painted heightened bluish-gray shadows on her cheeks, giving her the classic, hollow-cheeked, famished, blood-thirsty cadaverous vampire look. Nicole's and Justine's lessons in makeup were proving invaluable! Then I attached large circular earrings to her ears – they clipped on tight. "Ouch," she whispered, but it was a very soft "ouch." And then, I inserted a rather large nose ring. It was thick and looked like iron, but it was ultra-light and made of plastic and had a clamp which pressed on the septum and kept it neatly in place.

"Maybe a wig," I said.

"A wig?"

"And colored contact lenses."

"You've got colored contact lenses?" She laughed. "By all the gods! Gwendoline!"

I fitted a snug jet-black Louise Brooke-type wig over her head; the sunny blonde disappeared except for the blue-blue eyes.

I put in the contact lenses – dark eyes, with pupil and iris merging in blackness – like a soulless demon.

"Ouch." She winced. So far, she had been passive, accepting my every ministration. She had not yet caught a glimpse of how she had been transformed.

"You look perfect," I said. "Look. Here's a mirror." I held it up.

"Holy Cow! Bugger!" She stared. I had transformed the sunny tanned blond goddess into a shadowy creature of the night – a Goth vampire. She was unrecognizable. Her grimace was comic.

"You are beautiful," I whispered, patting her on the bottom.

"If you say so." She stuck out her tongue at her own image. And then turned and kissed me, lightly, with the point of her tongue.

"I say so." I sighed, "And the lipstick and makeup are non-smear. You can kiss away!"

She gave me a deeper kiss and then drew away. "And you, Mistress? How will you be attired? Will you come as you are?" She looked at me with an appealingly sly expression. I was naked.

"Oh, I shall dress in black jeans, and a black T-shirt and boots, and we'll go to Henri's."

"And I shall be exposed to the glances and mockery of the whole world. Me, the golden girl, as a pallid ghostly Punk-Goth!"

"Yes. Exactly. That is the point."

"You are cruel, Mistress. But – trust me. I shall take my revenge in grand style." She kissed me on the lips and pressed herself against me. I wrapped my arms around her and kissed her. It was so delicious we almost decided we wouldn't go out for dinner.

At that very moment, Philip phoned. He'd just arrived back from London. He was in Paris. Martine told him about our little game – confessed in detail to our love-making – and described how she'd been transformed into a Punk-Goth Vampire, and that she was until the stroke of midnight my prisoner. Philip said that, if the Punk-Goth's Mistress didn't mind, he'd join us at the restaurant.

Martine glanced at me. I nodded. I didn't mind. I was pleased. Martine phoned in the reservation.

I instructed her to help me dress. Which, as my prisoner, she did. I adored every caressing touch of her hands, every intense glance. Her eyes were beautiful, even disguised as they were now. I basked in the focused attention she bestowed every part of my anatomy, every detail of my clothes, and the infinite close-focused care with which she buckled up my belt.

I got out the collar and the leash, attached her, and led her to the restaurant. The weather had turned. It was a damp, warm Parisian night, and the air in the streets and boulevards under the plane trees glowed with humidity.

People walking by glanced once – then twice – at Martine. She was an apparition.

Several people stopped to gawk. She turned to stare back at them and smiled. One woman said, "Aren't you Martine Aubin?" Martine said, "Yes, once I was Martine Aubin, but no longer – this beautiful sorceress, the evil witch Gwendoline, has cast a spell, transforming me into what you see before you."

Philip arrived at the restaurant just as we did. We were given a table out on the heated and sheltered terrace. There were a few photographers who took shots of the famous Martine Aubin dressed in elegant S&M Gothic Punk style and being led around on a leash by her notorious freakish girlfriend, Gwendoline. Philip was pleased – lots of publicity. "You had fun, then, I imagine," he said.

"We did indeed," we said, almost in unison, almost as a chorus.

"James and I risk becoming obsolete, I fear," he grimaced and poured himself some more wine.

"No," we said, in unison, "You will never be obsolete, dear gentlemen, we need you, and we love you."

"You speak with one voice, I see," said Philip, gazing at us with the look of a benevolent uncle.

We had a great time. We talked about Martine and Philip's new film; I told them about James's adventures in Russia and the Czech Republic; and I told some stories of Claudia, my grandmother, and her rather wild and adventurous life – and how, in many ways, she and her ex-husband, my grandfather, had been – and were still – my mentors, and my parents. Martine was curious about Kate and pretended to be jealous. I gave them a description of Kate's latest adventures confronting the plague.

"It sounds extremely dangerous," said Philip.

"Yes, it is dangerous," I said. "More dangerous than Kate is willing to admit – maybe even to herself."

"But if she's in danger, you will ride like the cavalry in those old films to the rescue – right?" Martine glanced at me, her dark glowing eyes eerily framed in ceramic white and silken black, flames of ink-black and scarlet-turquoise flaring towards her temples, the steel nose ring catching the lamplight, the bright, perfect teeth, and her full glossy black lips, ripe, rich dark grapes, dying – begging – to be kissed, to be nibbled, to be drunk – dry, to the last drop.

"Yes, I figure I'd try to save her," I said. But I wondered what I could do.

"We'll all help," said Martine. "I think I'm in love with Kate, just hearing you talk about her."

"Ah, you wonderful girls," sighed Philip. He kissed Martine, being careful not to smear her makeup – which was non-smear in any case. It was a passionate kiss, and passionately returned. During the kiss Martine, her strange dark eyes wide, blinked over Philip's shoulder, staring straight at me. I realized I was not jealous at all; no, I was excited, and I was moved – I was moved by the fact that this man loved and protected Martine and by the many ways in they gave so much to each other; I was moved by the way neither of them minded me, and by the fact that, even in the midst of her passion for Philip, Martine kept a space for me – in fact, in some way, with her glance, she was telling me that we shared everything – that I was her, and she was me, even in that instant, even when she was kissing Philip.

Finally, it was time to go home. They walked me back to my building, and then, after I gave Martine and Philip instructions on how to remove the makeup, instructions they really didn't need. They flagged a cab. When they got into the cab, they were arguing – in a friendly, bantering way – about whether they were going to Martine's flat or Philip's flat. She preferred his, and he preferred hers. I watched them disappear down the street, and around the corner.

CHAPTER 14 – OWL

Martine did get her revenge for her evening of servitude – several weeks later; it was spectacular – it got press coverage everywhere.

It all began three weeks after our Goth interlude, at my Parisian flat.

"Owlish, you look owlish." Martine shot me a calculating stare over her dark-framed glasses. Dressed in ragged black jeans and a white T-shirt, she was lying on the cream-colored divan, her bare feet on the cushions, a script propped on her knees; she was making marks with a yellow highlighter and going through the lines, mouthing them silently, sometimes closing her eyes.

I was working on my computer, but from time to time, I glanced at her. This little domestic scene, this totally natural intimacy, gave me a thrill; I was crouched over my trusty high-powered laptop, turning some complicated mathematical models – drug routes, terrorist networks, and Mafia clans all superimposed – into simplified graphics, so that I could present this rather complex package of information to an upcoming conference in London in as succinct and clear a way as possible. The mathematical and graphic analysis of illegal markets and networks can be very illuminating. Illgeal networks tend to overlap in their logistic networks – transporting people and goods – and in their financial networks – laundering and investing income and profits – because they have similar problems – avoiding the law, obtaining illegal goods, transporting illegal goods, which can be arms, prostitutes, slave labor, drugs, and distributing those goods at the retail level, and then recycling the profits or financing the operations, which means they have to hide the money and ownership trails as much as possible. Organizing the data as multiple overlapping schematics and databases also facilitated the work of Artificial Intelligence, when it went searching for patterns and relationships.

James had just gotten back from a quick two-day trip to Moscow, and he had popped in to say hello to both of us, and then he had gone out to shop for dinner. Philip was flying in from Rome and hoped to join us if he could. We were going to cook at home.

"Owlish?"

"Yes, darling, you look like a studious owl." She chewed the end of the yellow plastic highlighter while staring at me with that bright, thoughtful, intense blue gaze that could almost be frightening.

"I do not look like an owl."

"It's a compliment," she said, still staring with that unblinking stare – a cat contemplating a mouse. I could see that some thought, some bright, intense, and certainly perverse idea, was germinating in her beautiful, ingenious cerebellum.

Yep – that was it! She was cooking something up!

"I have a fabulous idea, darling!" She suddenly grinned, still staring at me, as if I were a morsel she was about to swallow in one gulp.

"Oh, oh," I groaned. "It will involve me taking my clothes off, I bet."

"Precisely! You will be utterly and totally naked." She swiveled around, put her feet flat on the floor, and leaned forward, intense, elbows on her thighs. "You know that big party, the charity ball that they will be giving down on the Loire, at the *Chateau Illusion et Mirage de Bonheur*. It will have some pretty risqué stuff, fashion defiles and so on, some nudity, some S&M and tasteful bondage, naked dancers and acrobats and so on, to raise money for the *Refugees from Religious Fanaticism and Hatred Foundation*."

"Yes," I said, drawing out the "yes," expressing doubt and hesitation, and thinking – No, knowing – I'd be tempted, if she wanted me to be part of it, which I was certain she did. Being naughty with her – or with James – was always an extra exciting delight. "What exactly are you thinking, my love?"

"You remember the scene in *The Story of O* where O appears in an owl mask, but otherwise naked?"

"Yes, yes, of course, I remember it." I cleared my throat. *The Story of O* was a classic of sadomasochistic literature. It was written by a French woman who had been in the French Resistance in the Second World War and who was part of the post-war Parisian literary elite and existentialist scene. Her name was Anne Desclos – she was bisexual and had men and women as lovers. Anne, I had read, was a very serious translator and critic, and she could appear rather prim. She wrote the novel – one of the greatest erotic novels ever – after her very masculine lover Jean Paulhan, who worshipped the Marquis de Sade, told her no woman could write an erotic novel. "Oh, really?" she said. So, she wrote her masterpiece. *The Story of O* caused a huge scandal when it was published in 1954. It was the utter – almost mystical, almost religious – apotheosis of love and desire, of abnegation and masochism, of abasement and abjection, the utter abolition of the self. In the story, elegant, proud, chic, cool O allows herself to be transformed into a total object, a zero, an orifice, an empty spot, a slave, a void and vacuum, defined by others, labeled by others, possessed by others, and destined, in the end, for the final annihilation, which is death. The book was a masterpiece.

The owl scene? How could I forget the owl scene?

I half-closed my eyes: O is a successful Parisian professional woman, a fashion photographer; one day she is taken by her lover, René, to live in "the château" and, in this closed, sadistic, monastery-like space, of her own free will, and because she is in love with her lover and will obey his every order, O allows herself to be reduced to total sexual slavery. She becomes a passive sexual object for her lover and for the other men he offers her to. The climax of her destruction comes when, at a glamorous soirée held in the garden of the château, O is offered up to the multitude, naked, her pubis waxed and pierced with a ring, and with a chain attached to the labial ring. She is led, chained by her sex, by a beautiful young girl, who – perverse young thing – aspires to be a total object, a fetish, just like O. And, thus O is led, by a potential acolyte, naked, but her head feathered, and her features masked by an owl's mask, and thus she is exposed to the elite crowd, to gentlemen in tuxedos and women in splendid evening dress. For me, *The Story of O* was sublimely erotic in its totem-like abnegation and destruction of self. When I first read it, it was, frankly, orgasmic, a hot, sweaty, focus of my deepest nocturnal imaginings, even when those occurred in the afternoon at siesta time! Being turned into an owl, a totem, was O's apotheosis. And it was mine. To be nothing and to be everything, a totem, the focus of all the gazes – to be the object of desire, of envy, of distain, of worship, of disgust, of horror, of secret identification, and of utter estrangement. I, like O, often felt most real when I was a thing, an icon, nothing, nil and null, a cipher, zero, the nadir and the zenith, all in one.

"Well, here is my idea." Martine jumped up and came over and knelt next to me where I sat perched in front of my computer. She kissed me. "You will be O, and I will lead you by a leash."

"Attached to my labia?"

"Yes. Just like in the story."

"And, how, dear Martine, will we arrange that? I do not wish my labia – I'm very fond of them – to be pierced and tortured. I wish them to remain intact, seemingly virginal, and user-friendly."

"I'm sure we can do it – I know the most marvelous makeup people. It will be perfect! Nothing permanent ..."

"And you? I'll be naked, an owl, hmm, and you will be ..."

"I'll wear a tunic, but it will be transparent, or something like that, so I'll be effectively naked, not quite as naked as you, of course, and perhaps I'll wear a collar ... Let's see ... Maybe James and Philip will have some ideas."

"I'm sure they will. Those two gentlemen are extremely fertile in ideas." I returned her kiss. "Let me think about it."

"What is there to think about, darling Gwendoline? You will be divine! And you do secretly desire to be O, do you not?"

≈

In bed that night, James held me. It was still raining, a hushed splashing against the windowpanes, which made being in bed even more delicious. "You are sure you want to do this? This *Story of O* thing. It's quite a production."

"Yes, I'm sure I want to do it." I lay beside him, quiet in his arms, stroking his shoulder softly kissing his chest. "James, do you think I'm crazy?"

"We are both crazy, darling," he said.

I slid up onto his chest and put my fingers to his lips. "I do love you, James, you know that."

"Yes, I do."

"Does it make you afraid, James – are you terrified?"

"Absolutely." He stroked my back. "It is terrifying to be loved and to love," he whispered, "and it is the most exciting inebriating thing in the world. And the most dangerous." He kissed me. I lay quiet for a long time listening to his breathing and to the rain against the windows and against the little window balcony just outside our bedroom.

Out beyond the curtains, beyond the window and the shutters, was Paris, the city of light, sunk in the deep dark night, with rain sweeping down the Seine, rippling on the fast-flowing water, falling on the ancient stone bridges and their shining lampposts, falling on the two islands, on the Ile de la Cité and on the Ile Saint Louis, falling on the snouts of the lonely, grotesque stone gargoyles, high up in the spires of Notre Dame, falling on Napoleon's Tomb at Les Invalides, falling on the domed Pantheon high up on its hill in the Latin Quarter, with all its buried heroes and heroines; the rain was sweeping down on the cobblestoned streets near Les Halles, on the rue St. Denis, and on Place Pigalle, where the prostitutes – often Africans and Brazilians – were certainly out late, sheltering in doorways or under umbrellas, plying their trade, calling out to passers-by, and where the neon signs were reflected in streaks of rain and in rivulets of red, yellow, blue, and green, as the water ran gushing in the gutters, and swirling down out of sight, and where late-night restaurants were still open, champagne being served, oysters being shucked over racks of ice at open wooden benches by men and women in rubber aprons, giving off, into the rain and over the sidewalks, the salty briny odor of the sea, restaurants still crowded with customers, where people were still entering and leaving, bending against the rain, unfolding their umbrellas, where taxis and cars were lining up, their steamy exhaust rising ghostly into the rain, and so life goes on, as it always goes on, no matter who tries to stop it. Then, before I knew it, I was asleep. I dreamed I was an owl, deep in a forest, lonely as perhaps owls are lonely, and with bright staring yellow eyes, waiting for ... waiting for something, but I didn't know what. "Too-wit, too-woo," I cried, "Too-wit, Too-woo."

≈

The charity ball and the art show – some performances would include naked ballerinas and nearly naked acrobats – was to be held, as Martine had explained to me, in a 16th Century château in the Loire Valley, the Château *Illusion et Mirage de Bonheur*. The proceeds would go to a variety of charities, including one charity set up to help the victims of religious persecution, in particular for people persecuted for professing no religion at all.

The great day arrived. We drove south towards the Loire Valley. No sooner were we outside of Paris than it was decided by a vote of three to one that I – the pre-ordained sacrificial lamb – should get into the spirit of the thing – which of course, meant me getting naked.

So, as we drove down one leafy tree-lined rustic road, just outside a very picturesque village, I was ordered by the Central Committee to take off my long white T-shirt, which was all I was wearing. "Yes, dears," I said, as I pulled the tight T-shirt over my head and wiggled out of it. The others seemed pleased. Their puppet had complied. I was their plaything.

Whoopee! Exhilarated and vulnerable, I had not a stitch between me and nature, nature that was whizzing by in the form of high feathery white clouds, deep blue sky, tree branches heavily laden with leaves, mottled and ancient and deliciously sensual tree trunks, each with a story to tell a perfumed breeze, and fields with waving wheat or green with grass and spotted with browsing cows. Under my bare backside, the leather of the car seat was at first cool and sticky, then warm and sticky; my naked legs and breasts flickered, like a pagan sacrifice in the flames, in the racing speckled sunlight and hot wind. My skin displayed shivery mystical goosebumps from the thrill of it all. The breeze from the rolled down windows of the topless Porsche played tattoos and patterns of light – filtered by the swiftly passing leafy trees – that rippled on my skin. I was dissolving into nature, into light and air and wind, into the leaves and the fields and the high drifting cumulus. I stretched my arms above my head – I felt drunkenly, sublimely, at one with the whole universe. I was Ariel, flitting about, running errands for a divine Prospero. I was wearing nothing but phosphorescent scarlet plastic flip-flops. This was comical and hardly a suitable costume for an aspiring mystic, and I am sure that was the effect James – who had orchestrated this part of the overture to our performance – wished to achieve. He liked to bring out my inner – naked – clown; and, natural goof that I am, I am always pleased to oblige.

"This is humiliating," I said brightly.

"Precisely, darling," said Martine; she was sitting next to Philip in the back seat, and she was naked under a long black silk T-shirt which was fluttering mightily, whipping this way and that, and went only midway down her thighs. She was wearing sober black plastic flip-flops, not phosphorescent scarlet, much more dignified.

"If you want to be clothed, we shall clothe you," said James.

"No," I said, "Yes. No. I mean, No."

"Ah," Philip sighed, "the complexities of the human heart. The girl knows not what she wants. Or maybe she does."

"She does," said Martine.

So, racing along, we drove down some pleasant and picturesque country roads. Inns and small villages flashed by. I sat there, offered to the breeze and to the sun, naked, my chalk-white skin almost shiny, like plastic or marble, in the sunlight that blazed through the windshield, allowing my usual ornery self to melt into delight in the wind in my hair which – after the head shaving performance – was now growing out to its normal and proper length.

At least there was that – I was not going to perform bald.

Just before we arrived at the entrance to the château grounds, the Central Committee allowed me to shimmy back into the long white silk T-shirt. I suddenly felt over-dressed, though, as I said, it only went down to my thighs. We parked the car, and then, along with Martine in her fluttery black T-shirt and James and Philip, splendidly attired in tuxedos, with highly polished shoes and bright red carnations in their buttonholes, such as is required by male dignity and the phallic-patriarchal power structure which imbues us all – male and female – with its unspoken assumptions and informs our every gesture, we headed towards the château. Holding hands with Martine, I traipsed along, in my pavement-slapping, glowing, scarlet flip-flops and my flimsy T-shirt, up the steps that led into the central part of the château.

Upon entering, we were ushered by a very impressive looking butler type – whom I was tempted to address as "Jeeves" – through a magnificent hall, guided down several mirror-lined corridors, and finally led into the charge rooms, which had been set up in the Grande Salle – the huge Reception or Ball Room.

The ballroom was divided into sections by folding screens. Other performers were changing into costumes, getting makeup applied, doing last-minute rehearsals. It was strange to see this nomadic, backstage, greasepaint, circus atmosphere, and to be oneself in a skimpy state of almost complete undress, and wearing tasteless sticky bright flip-flops, in this vast, formal, seventeenth-century reception room, with its highly polished parquet floor that smelled of delicious fresh wax, its lofty gilded ceilings, its huge gold-framed mirrors, and its giant French doors that looked out onto the gardens and forests of the estate and onto the rippling sheen of the river Loire itself. Fluttering cupids and goddesses cavorted high above us on the arched ceilings; tables and mirrors were set up for the makeup and costume people;

movable metal clothing racks for costumes, parked every which way, stood everywhere. It looked like a film set, which, I suppose, in a way, it was. The white canvas partitions were minimal and placed roughly here and there and didn't hide much of anybody or anything. There was virtually no privacy. I licked my lips. I loved to look, and I certainly didn't mind being looked at. Age will come soon enough, Gwendoline, I thought, enjoy your sparkling show-off youth while you can; if you survive long enough, you can play a bit part, a cast off, naked, wrinkled, sagging, witch-like crone; or perhaps I'll be a skinny, weathered, sun-blotched, flirtatious, bitchy, old seductress, or a worldly-wise, winkled sophisticate, or a crab apple rural recluse. Or maybe I could be glamorous, and ageless, like grandmother Claudia. Who knows? Time ripens all.

Two women, totally shaved, bald and hairless, and naked, were being painted – one in silver, and the other in gold. They kept giggling and making jokes. Their makeup artist – a very serious, tanned, wiry-looking, white-haired French guy with a white, tobacco-stained walrus mustache, a black, paint-stained canvas vest, and baggy black corduroy pants, and tan leather cowboy boots – kept scolding them in his gruff grandfatherly voice and ordering them to stay still.

There were two guys in elastic sort of G-strings and two girls in the same costume; they had fine-boned, lithe-limbed athletic dancers' bodies. A very intense-looking young woman with steel-rimmed glasses and dressed in black short shorts and a black halter top, was spraying them with some sort of sprinkle dust. This was a big production. Martine and I weren't going to be alone – or unique – in our nudity.

"Isn't it rather old fashioned," I turned to Martine, "I mean, this whole concept? I mean, *transgression* of this kind is rather *vieux jeu, n'est-pas?*" I loved bandying French terms around. They were like shiny new toys, and, more and more, without even thinking about it, I spoke French – or Italian – with Martine and Philip, and often with James too.

Martine stretched – arms straight up and wrists crossed – and performed a little pirouette. "Yes, my dear Gwendoline, but this is a very chic, retro crowd, a lot of gray and white and bald pates – and lots and lots of money, probably billions of euros if you add them all together. They get their thrills from re-enacting the past, you know, the wild and perverse 1960s and 1970s, or even the imagined 1920s, playful and harmless forms of transgression, nudity, sex on stage, painted bodies, sequins, all that sort of thing. It's the Sexual Revolution Revisited – the nostalgic oldies' tour."

"The past is not dead," I said, "It's not even past."

"Precisely, Gwendoline. You are a font of ..."

"Clichés," I said.

"Oh, pooh, pooh! Dear sweet Gwendoline, I would never have said such a thing. I was going to say erudition, since if I'm not mistaken, you were quoting William Faulkner." She pirouetted again and bowed. She was having fun, delighted with her brilliant idea – getting us here, to this point of depravity – and clearly feeling titillated and frisky. In the rising humidity, and in the bright lights of the room and in the late afternoon light coming in from the full-length French doors, her long black silk T-shirt, clinging to her as if it were wet-look latex, had become semitransparent, sculpting her curves in silvery dark shadows and bright highlights. She was excited like a little girl.

James and Philip, who had gone to see about our dinner reservations, came in and looked at the work in progress.

"I hope, Master, you will be pleased," I said.

"He'd better be pleased," said Martine, pirouetting and sketching a little bow; I had never seen her so playfully skittish; I think the whole thing was going – in the nicest possible way – to her head. Little girls do like to show off.

"Now, gentlemen, you must leave," said a young makeup woman who strode up to us like a sergeant major about to humiliate some terrified young recruits.

"Really?" James raised an eyebrow. He looked adorable, I thought, in his penguin outfit. I wanted him around. On the other hand, it would be fun to present him with a surprise package, the finished product – me, transformed into an owl.

"You mean we cannot stay?" Philip was shocked; on set, he was boss; in fact, as Martine had explained to me, he was an absolute – if benign – dictator. Everyone snapped to attention and obeyed him. "On the set," she said, "dear, dear Philip is God."

"No, gentlemen, absolutely – out you go! Shoo, shoo!"

James quickly kissed me and said, "Good luck, Gwen. I'll see you when you are an owl."

"Yes." I kissed him fiercely. The moment, I felt, was poetic, possessed, potentially, of great pathos. It was his last glimpse of me as a human being. I was about to be transmogrified, metamorphosed, like one of those hapless unlucky mortals punished by a vengeful god or goddess in Ovid and the ancient myths, girls turned into moo-cows, or laurel bushes, or tree trunks or losing their voices and becoming, as did poor Echo, a mere echo – a pale reflection of her master's voice.

James and Philip disappeared, out the entrance, heading towards the park.

"Now, let us start." The young makeup woman was slender and about two inches shorter than I. A stiff vertical tuft of purple hair ran down the crown of her head from her forehead to the nape of her neck; bright abstract tattoos glowed on both sides of the razor-like skull tuft; four large round brass earrings hung from each ear; a full nose ring hung from her septum. Tinted rimless glasses were perched on her nose, which gave her thin pale face what would have been a rather pinched and scholarly look, except for the nose ring. She was wearing a light black leather vest which was open and revealed tattoos and a navel ring; when she turned around, and the vest swung open, I glimpsed pierced nipples adorned with nipple rings. She was wearing black leather short shorts, and one of her legs was brightly tattooed with what looked like a green-and-scarlet serpent or dragon. The patterns were bright, strong, and intriguing. Well, well, I thought, she is a more interesting spectacle than I will be.

She stood contemplating me. "Take off your clothes," she said.

All I was wearing, of course, was the T-shirt. I lifted it off. In an instant, I was naked, except for the phosphorescent scarlet flip-flops.

The pre-preparations early the day before in a studio in Paris had involved me being waxed again, totally. I looked down at myself. I was sure my Bermuda Triangle, my cozy furry little Heart of Darkness, was feeling totally humiliated by all of this – and furious. But I would make it up to her, somehow, someday. She would grow and grow and luxuriate and be coddled and worshipped and adored!

"My name is Lou-Lou." The young woman raised a pierced eyebrow and considered me – my body, her canvas, her blank page.

"I'm Gwendoline."

"Yes, the owl."

"Gwendoline, the owl," I said, reasserting my human presence, my human name; I wanted to cling to at least a vestige of my humanity.

"Gwendoline, Gwendoline," she repeated as she walked around me, giving me a critical up-and-down, head-to-toe, once-over – I was the raw material out of which she was to create an owl.

"Can you do false tattoos?" I asked. Contemplating Lou-Lou,

her strange, defiant, self-made, electric beauty, I suddenly had the idea I would like to be, briefly, a tattooed woman like her, almost a circus freak. I wondered – would James and Martine approve?

"Of course, Gwendoline! I can do anything." She stared at me with her pale blue eyes, almost watery blue, framed by the rimless glasses; there was a steely cool look about her, which I found perversely attractive. Her skin, where it was not tattooed, was chalk-white.

"Yes, Gwendoline, I could tattoo you from the crown of your head – which I would shave – to the tips of your painted toes, and not leave a millimeter of skin untouched." She gave me a knowing smile.

Some people have X-ray vision for other people's perversities and darkest, most secret and twisted fantasies: she was one of those. I smiled back at her and blinked. At that moment, a sort of bond was sealed between us, a pact, which, sometime in the mysterious, unknowable future, might turn out useful.

"The first thing, we must prepare you for the owl mask," she said.

"Okay. You're the boss."

"I'll watch," said Martine.

"Yes, you watch," I said.

"But don't talk, Mademoiselle Aubin. You'll break my concentration." Lou-Lou favored Martine with a dominant glare.

"Okay. I promise." Martine grinned. "Cross my heart!"

"Here, sit down on this stool, Gwendoline. Now, let me begin. This will feel heavy and sticky at first. She took out a tube of thick clear liquid and smoothed my hair down with it and combed my hair into place – saturated with the thick gel – and she let the gel set, so my hair was tightly plastered to my skull, pressing down close, like a close-fitting metal helmet. "Your lips will be free, under the owl mask, so the lipstick must be very bright. You will be wearing a collar."

She painted my lips a scarlet red. Then she lowered the owl mask over my head and fitted it tightly. It covered my entire head and my ears and went down to the nape of my neck. Only my mouth was left free. I could see out through the openings – which had plastic owl eyes for lenses – but my field of vision was suddenly narrowed. And my own eyes were now invisible. I was an owl.

Lou-Lou locked a thick leather collar around my neck.

I touched the collar. It was thick, heavy, black leather and steel.

"It has a device where, if you move your chin, just like this," she demonstrated, "it makes an owl call, quite loud."

I tried it, and I found my new owl voice: "To-wit, to-whoo! To-wit, to-whoo!" I was pleased. Now I could do an owlish Shakespearean "To-wit, to-whoo, To-wit, to-whoo."

"And, dear Gwendoline, when I switch this little switch, the collar electronically paralyzes your vocal cords."

"What?"

"You won't be able to speak, not human speech. It will automatically replace your human voice with your voice as an owl."

"How can I ...?"

"It's easy."

"But I don't want to ..." I began to say. She switched the switch. My voice faded. It became: "To-wit, to-whoo, to-wit, to-whoo."

Damn, I thought, but it was a thrilling too! I was transformed – this was metamorphous as the Ancients dreamed of it – Naughty, Rebellious Girl into Owl.

"To-wit, to-whoo, to-wit, to-whoo."

"Now, put your arms behind your back."

"To-wit, to-woo?"

"Arms behind your back, I say! Obey, Owl, obey!"

Owl obeyed.

Lou-Lou held my arms, stroked them for a moment with the points of her sharp fingernails, giving me a delicious little tingling frisson that rippled up to the nape of my neck; then she bound my wrists together with a leather thong, and then my upper arms, so tight that my shoulders were twisted back.

"Ouch," I wanted to say, but it came out: "To-wit, to-whoo, To-wit, to-whoo!"

Martine, still in her T-shirt, was watching this. I stuck out my tongue. She stuck out her tongue and grinned. She was delighting in this – the minx! I was being magically transmogrified into an object, as per her plan, and she was still human, gazing on me, her plaything. It was a deliciously alienating and objectifying experience.

The two painted guys in their G-strings and the two naked painted silver and gold girls had stopped whatever they were doing and were watching. I wanted to wave or bow, but of course, pinioned as I was, I couldn't.

Lou-Lou worked with leather thongs, winding them around and around, until my arms were pinioned tightly behind my back, by what felt like a crisscrossing net of leather straps; she then attached this rigid thong net to the back of the collar.

"Now we will give you wings," Lou-Lou stepped back and contemplated her work. "But of course, they are folded and locked wings."

"To-wit, to-whoo, To-wit, to-whoo?"

"No, Owl, you won't be able to fly."

"To-wit, to-whoo, To-wit, to-whoo!"

She attached a cascade of feathers to the thongs and to the collar; apparently, all this was designed to make my pinioned arms look like wings folded behind my back.

When this was done, she ran her finger up my naked

shoulder to the thick collar that was attached to the skin-tight owl hood.

There was a definite connection, I felt, between Lou-Lou and me. I was beginning to feel disloyal to Martine and a trifle naughty.

Then, though my feathered, round, thick-lensed owl eyes, I saw Martine. She stepped into my field of vision. She winked and stuck out her tongue. She had, as usual, read my thoughts, registered my desires, and seen clear through my lust. I had a giddy frisson – it was clear I was utterly transparent. Everybody saw right through me.

Martine mouthed, in French, "I love you!"

My scarlet lips mouthed the same message, which set off my Owl Voice

"To-wit, to-whoo, To-wit, to-whoo!"

Finally, I was allowed to look at myself in a mirror. It was a full-length mirror. Whew, I thought, whew. The Owl spoke: "To-wit, to-whoo, To-wit, to-whoo!"

"Let us add one of the finer touches." Lou-Lou knelt before me and set about placing the labia ring. I felt a bit nervous about this.

"To-wit, to-whoo, To-wit, to-whoo!"

"On, don't fuss, Owl. This won't hurt." She glued the ring on with a little transparent bandage-like patch, which felt cool and wet at first, then warm and solid, as if it had been welded to my flesh. She had placed it just next to my labia; the ring was light plastic, but it looked like silver or steel, and it looked like it pierced my flesh, but it didn't. It was as light as a feather.

Lou-Lou stood up, stepped back, picked up a brush and artist's palette, squinted at my breasts, and began to rouge and lacquer my nipples and areolae bright scarlet.

Now, came the scarlet high-heeled shoes, into which, obviously, I was locked.

Now I was finished and ready, it seemed.

I looked at myself in the mirror. I was naked, with an owl head, and with no arms, a hybrid creature – a human-owl. Viewed from straight on, my arms were tied so tight behind my back, they were invisible; I had no arms.

Martine clapped.

The two naked men – well, almost naked – clapped, and one of them shouted, "Bravissima!"

"To-wit, to-whoo, To-wit, to-whoo!" I turned to Martine. She was still in her long black T-shirt and flip-flops, waiting for her costume and makeup.

Lou-Lou held out a chain and turned to Martine. "Would you do me the favor, Mademoiselle Aubin, of attaching the chain to the Owl, please?"

"With pleasure!" Martine took the chain and knelt in front of me. She balanced the chain between her hands – testing its weight. "Now, Owl, you belong to me!" She attached the chain – which looked like steel but was light plastic – to the labial ring.

"To-wit, to-whoo," I couldn't look down, the collar and owl mask were too rigid, "To-wit, to-whoo."

Martine stood up and grinned – a truly wicked grin. How happy she was! "To-wit, to-woo," she mocked, "To-wit, to-whoo."

"To-wit, to-whoo!" That was all I could say. My paralyzed vocal cords tickled.

Martine tugged, gently, on my leash. "Come, Owl, come and see your future subjects, come and appreciate your kingdom."

She led me by the chain to one of the ceiling-high French doors. We peered out from behind the curtain, which was thick brocade.

Outside, a huge crowd had gathered. Tables and chairs had been set up in a vast space. There must have been thousands of people. The women were in evening gowns and cocktail dresses, the men in tuxedos. This thing was much bigger than any performance I had ever participated in – and much bigger than I had imagined.

A trickle of sweat snaked down my spine, under my folded, pinioned wings. The immense, clamorous crowd was terrifying.

The light began to fade. Night was coming on. Men in gilded scarlet court costumes were lighting giant, free-standing torches. The yellow-gold flames leaped up. People turned and watched. They seemed awe-struck by the setting and the solemnity.

Beyond the lawns and gardens, and over the edge of the forest, the sky was menacingly dark. I detected the distant rumble of thunder. I wanted to see more, but with my arms pinioned behind my back under my owl wings, I couldn't push the heavy curtain aside. My helplessness gave me a thrill, a mystical feeling – abnegation and abasement, the exaltation of abandonment. As if in becoming totally helpless, in disappearing, I had become all-powerful, I had dissolved into nothing and everything, I was everything and everywhere, and I was nothing and nowhere. I was thrilled, too, that Martine was my mistress, that she would lead me out onto the runway, between the columns of flame and between the rows of banquet tables. This would certainly be an adventure. The guests were beginning to sit down. They were all very important. And there were thousands of them. As they talked and gossiped and laughed, it created an immense low sound, the threatening murmur of an incoming ocean tide.

Lou-Lou came up behind us. "Turn around, Owl," she said. I did. She knelt and tugged at the ring and chain to make sure they wouldn't loosen. They didn't. She checked the collar. "Try to speak, Owl."

"To-wit, to-whoo, to-wit, to-whoo!"

"Oh, this is delicious!" Martine proclaimed. "Behold our owl!"

She turned to the two guys in their sparkling G-strings. "Is she not beautiful?"

"Magnificent!" they said, in chorus. Their lean, painted bodies and G-strings glimmered and gleamed.

"To-wit, to-whoo!" This was excellent, I thought – I am an idol and an icon.

"Perfect." Lou-Lou had been observing my every move. She was obviously pleased with her creation. She turned to Martine. "I think, Mademoiselle, we shall now begin your preparations."

"Of course." Martine bowed her head – an obedient actress or schoolgirl.

"I think for you I shall apply a bright chalk-white foundation, and some rather bold patterned makeup; your lips should glow scarlet, to match the Owl's."

"To-wit, to-whoo, to-wit, to-whoo!" Ah, ah, now the tables would be turned: I wanted to see Martine morphed into something rich and strange. I was lonely, being the only monster.

"Of course," Martine frowned. I could see she was doubtful. The bright lights of the makeup space went right through her T-shirt. Her body, I sighed, was so utterly exquisite, and it was a body I knew so well. Nostalgia and yearning surged up. I wanted to touch her – but of course, pinioned as I was, I couldn't move a muscle – she was just out of reach, and thus even more exciting.

"Mademoiselle Martine, take off your T-shirt," said Lou-Lou.

Martine obeyed.

Now she was naked. For some reason, this greatly pleased my pinioned blinkered owlish mind.

"Sit here, Mademoiselle," said Lou-Lou.

Martine glanced at me, and then she sat down on the high wooden stool. Lou-Lou began to apply the foundation, working quickly, efficiently, until Martine's face was a polished white

Geisha-like or clown-like mask. Lou-Lou nodded towards me and said, "Like you, your friend, the Owl has magnificent skin, it is so pure, and in her case so white, a perfect blank canvas. I would be delighted to tattoo her, give her a different look."

"That is a marvelous idea," said Martine through half-closed lips, as Lou-Lou applied paint to her cheeks.

"To-wit, to-whoo, to-wit, to-whoo."

Lou-Lou glanced at me and favored me with a knowing, thin-lipped, thrillingly cruel smile – I could see that she was contemplating transforming me into a fetish masterpiece, a deliciously shivery prospect. This Lou-Lou person was a most promising talent. I would add her to my collection. She began to concentrate, applying the lipstick to Martine's lips. She gave Martine the most scarlet lips imaginable. "Perhaps we need an extra touch of mascara," she said. And, with gusto, she began to apply it.

I could see that Martine enjoyed being putty in the hands of this exquisitely sadistic artist, but at the same time, she was nervous about the final result; and I could see, too, from her glances that Lou-Lou was envisaging another cruel transformation for me. The liquid rose in my loins. I was wet in anticipation. I hoped the chain wouldn't fall off.

"No fear of that," said Lou-Lou, glancing at me, and as if reading my thought. "It will need a special solution for the patch to be detached from your skin."

"To-wit, to-whoo?"

"Don't worry, Owl, I'll give the dissolvent to your master, Monsieur James. He will, when he chooses, release you from this witch's magic spell."

"To-wit, to-whoo."

Martine's eyes were now sculpted by silken black mascara that curved wickedly upwards towards her temples. She was a crazy – hyperbolic – version of that cartoon superheroine Harley Quinn.

At the corners of Martine's mouth, Lou-Lou added upward curved wings of pure scarlet – a turning Martine's deliciously delicate mouth into a clown's cartoonish smile. And she shadowed in bright scarlet spots on the cheekbones, a clownish parody of the virginal blush.

Lou-Lou helped Martine into a short latex tunic and sandals.

Martine looked as if she were a slave boy or slave girl. Lou-Lou examined the ensemble. She circled Martine like a bird of prey closing in on its victim. "I think, Mademoiselle Aubin, you would be better as a jester or clown. This slave girl outfit is not original. It is banal. It is tame. It does not match your mask. Please remove this costume."

"What?" Martine's clown face formed itself into a pout.

"Yes. I think we can paint a jester's costume on your body. It will be even more titillating, more fitting, I think."

"Oh." Martine looked at Lou-Lou and then at me.

"To-wit, to-whoo." My round yellow owl eyes stared.

With a smirk and a shrug, Martine yielded. "Yes, Mistress Lou-Lou. You're the boss. I surrender." And, slowly, with delicately prolonged lascivious gestures, and miming the flirtatious over-the-shoulder glances of a gifted stripper, Martine gradually, bit by bit, inch by inch, slipped out of her latex slave tunic, and then, with one brave toss, she threw it to a chair where it landed, neatly, and hung, neatly folded, over the back. My clownish lover was once again like me – naked.

Lou-Lou pulled a paint kit out of her large suitcase of supplies and set to work with theatrical gusto. One leg she sprayed scarlet, the other she sprayed coal-black and she painted on a false corset, complete with titillating details. Within minutes Martine was painted and transformed into a jester. Lou-Lou fitted her with stiletto-heeled shoes with floppy points and jingle bells that jangled with each step she took.

"To-wit, to-whoo," I liked that touch. I sketched a little dance step. "To-wit, to-whoo!"

Martine shot me an evil clownish glance.

"Now, dear Clown," Lou-Lou said, "let us add a nice floppy fool's cap, or even better a jester's cap equipped with floppy horns and bells – to match your shoes."

"A fool's cap, me? Hmm." Martine crossed her arms and tapped her foot. The clown face took on an adorably cross expression, particularly with the mouth twisted up in a clown smile; I could see the wheels turning; she was tempted to revolt; but she had set this whole monstrous Owl-and-Jester enterprise in motion, so she didn't resist – she would accept the full consequences of her folly.

Lou-Lou rummaged in her basket of supplies, made a choice, held it up, contemplated it, and placed the tight elastic cobalt blue jester's cap – perfectly equipped with two bright floppy rubber horns topped by swaying bells – on Martine's head. Lou-Lou fastened it securely. Martine's hair and ears disappeared. The cap went down to her neck and snapped into place. Lou-Lou anchored it by adding a thick collar – with a ring a leash – and locking it into place. Martine's horns swayed in protest. Her fool's bells jingled. Her foot, when she tapped it, sang out – tinkle, tinkle.

Our two masters, James and Philip, suddenly appeared, looking handsome, debonair, and tuxedoed – like two heroes out of a James Bond film. Philip's eyes went wide. "My God, what has she done to my Martine?"

"You can see very well what she has done to me," Jester said;. The bright, painted grin struggled to turn into a frown. One silver tear appeared at the edge of Jester's eye. Her clownish fool's mask was perfect – exquisitely grotesque and framed in cobalt blue. Her horns swayed and jingled. With each shift of light and flicker of a muscle, with the slightest gesture, her painted body glowed and shimmered, an iridescent, perfectly buff, particolored, motley exemplar of naked sculptural perfection. The wild colors made her look like a painting by Kandinsky.

"Well, this is a wonderful creation," said Philip. He came close and inspected Jester-Martine. Turning to Lou-Lou, he said, "You are a genius."

"I try," Lou-Lou bowed.

"I'd like your card, if I may."

"Yes, absolutely." Lou-Lou handed him a card. She winked at me. "Owl, do you want one too?"

"To-wit, to-whoo!"

Lou-Lou attached a little tag with her card to my collar. "There," she said, and patted me on the bum.

"To-wit, to-whoo!" I almost blushed, realizing yet again that my secret desires were so transparent. From behind my round yellow owl eyes, I was watching James. I trembled in anticipation of his reaction. He was looking at me with an expression that was somewhere between awe-struck and bemused.

Philip was mesmerized by this new apparition – his lover and his protégée. "I think, Martine, that we will do a film with you as a clown or jester – a 19th Century circus or vaudeville setting, something like that 1940s masterpiece *Les Enfants du Paradis*. You will be a waif – forced to play the clown and beg in the streets for your crumbs of bread. And then, driven to cynicism by the cruelty of the world, you become a clown-jester thief and assassin, a girl clown serial killer, stalking the rooftops and sewers of Paris in search of prey. Fabulous!" He circled Jester, not daring to touch her. She had become a delicate work of art, a figurine.

Jester waggled her horns, stamped her foot, and jingled her bells. "Damnation! I was afraid something like this would happen – that this ungodly outfit would give Philip ideas!" It was cute. She was furious! Well, not really. It was clear that she was amused and certainly tempted by Philip's idea. She was playing at being annoyed. She knew how to wiggle her bells – and her ass – and put the fear of God into a man. Creating uncertainty in your lover is a savvy strategy.

"May I touch her, and kiss her?" Philip glanced at Lou-Lou. "She's your work of art. I don't want to disturb anything."

"Go ahead," said Lou-Lou, "Absolutely. It won't smear, it won't stain your shirt or tuxedo, and it definitely won't wash off."

"What?" Jester turned to Lou-Lou. The painted fists curled. It looked like Jester was going to leap on the makeup artist. "It won't wash off??"

"Not without the special soap."

"Bloody hell!"

Philip put his arms around her, swept her up, and kissed her. Her cap bells and toe bells jingled; her high heels kicked in the air.

"I'll give you gentlemen all the supplies you need to free Jester and Owl from their enchanted spells and turn them back into princesses." Lou-Lou handed two neatly wrapped little kits to James. He took them absent-mindedly. He thanked her absent-mindedly.

So far, James hadn't said a word. He had been standing there, apparently in shock, just staring at me, his mouth open, his eyes wide. Finally, he spoke. "My little Owl," he said, "my delicious, beautiful superb little Owl. My little Owl in chains!"

"To-wit, to-whoo, to-wit, to-whoo!"

"She can't talk. She can only hoot." Jester, still lolling in Philip's arms, turned towards us, her turquoise and kohl-ringed eyes blinking "Something to do with the collar."

"Yes, the collar has a speech inhibitor," said Lou-Lou, "Try to speak, Owl."

"To-wit, to-whoo, to-wit, to-whoo!"

"You see."

"Utterly charming," said James, "You have muted Gwendoline!" He clapped. "Transformed her into Owl. How wonderful!"

"To-wit, to-whoo, to-wit, to-whoo!"

Philip put Jester down, and all three of them – Jester, James, and Philip – examined me. "Owl is most interesting," said Philip. He leaned closer. "These feathers are magnificent. And this is perhaps the brightest lipstick I have ever seen. It positively glows."

"How do you feel, my little bird?" Jester's face was close to mine; Jester's breath was warm and sweet; she put her painted palm flat on my backside, and left it there; she caressed me slowly, working her way around my hip.

"Now, now, Jester, we don't want Owl to get too excited, do we?" James touched my breasts, just a feathery fingertip caress; he curved his hand under my left breast and lightly pinched the nipple. The nipple, already painted and lacquered, was, of course, erect, straining at the bit – the shameless thing!

Under assault from my two lovers, I shivered, overcome by an ecstasy of sensuality, of self-consciousness shame, and delicious, warm humiliation. My breasts swayed, feeling fuller and fuller, bigger and bigger, warmly cupped by James' strong, comforting hands. The feathers of my wings brushed back and forth, tickling my backside. James' gaze reflected bright burning flames of desire; he stared into my round plastic feather-framed owl eyes. He smiled his wicked pirate-of-the-bounding-main smile. I was his slave, his pet, his bird, his Owl. His teeth gleamed, a carnivorous jungle hunter.

Oh, but he was handsome in his tuxedo, the bright white of the shirt setting off his dark tan, and the five o'clock shadow that seemed always to be there. I dreamed of the two of us, all alone, in paradise. We would go sailing, really sailing, somewhere far away, on a blue, blue sea, under a cloudless sky. Or, wearing just a leopard skin loincloth, he would pursue me, through some jungle, and catch me, on a pristine beach, and possess me right there, and we'd dance a wild tango, by a blazing bonfire, under the waving palms and coconuts.

James put his arm around me. "We should go dancing," he said, "Some wild dancing – tango, that sort of thing." I rustled my feathers and nuzzled him with my owl's beak and my human lips. Even when I was a mute owl, his mind was truly in tune with mine.

"Don't touch, eh? Do as I say, but not as I do," Jester gave James a dark jester's smile. The bright scarlet corners of her mouth, turned absurdly upwards, gave to her smile a diabolic clownish edge, doubly intense because of the bright white ceramic-like foundation cream, turquoise mascara and eye shadow. The contrast between the classic beauty of her features and the clownish Jester's mask was poignant: Parody glows brightest in the shadow of original perfection. Jester was stubborn, and, in her light-hearted, ironic way, possessive; she had not taken her hand off my hip, and James insisted on caressing the excited damp undercurve of my right breast.

"Precisely," James smiled, "But, my dear Jester, perhaps a little heightening of the tension in Owl is useful, before the great performance."

"Certainly," said Jester.

"To-wit, to-whoo? To-wit, to-whoo?" What, I wondered, were they going to do now?

"That sounds like an interesting idea," said Philip, who was standing back, studying the tableau: A man in a tuxedo and a naked Jester were busy caressing a naked woman with the head and wings of an owl. I sometimes had the impression that Philip looked at all of us through a camera lens; that we were all acting

329

in a little drama for him alone. "What exactly do you have in mind, James?"

"Ah, ah," said Jester, her clown bells jingling, "Something wicked, I am sure – I think I know what he is thinking."

"Come on, guys," I felt like saying, "Let's calm down." But I didn't say a word. I couldn't say a word. I only spoke owl. I was no longer me. I was Owl.

"To-wit, to-whoo, to-wit, to-whoo."

"Charming," said James.

"To-wit, to-whoo, to-wit, to-whoo."

"More and more charming," said James. "Well, ladies and gentlemen, and Owl, my idea is this." James took a tube of liquid gel that he had stashed away with his supplies and carefully inserted the slender pointed plastic nozzle between my already wet labia.

"To-wit, to-whoo, to-wit, to-whoo?" I had to go on stage in a few minutes! What the hell was he going to do?

"Be careful! Don't let the gel touch the ring," Lou-Lou looked up from a schedule she'd been examining, and peered over her glasses, "It might weaken the glue."

"I'll be careful. We certainly don't want the chain falling off," James squeezed the tube – hard. A hot spicy spurt shot inwards. Suddenly I was liquid, dripping, a warm wave of excitement, partly physical, partly psychological, swept over me. Spicy heat spread up my belly, and rippled down my thighs; it tingled, burning, tickling, titillating. Oh, oh, oh! I was at the mercy of two of my most favorite people, James and Jester, and I was the object of their desires, and I was helpless, and there were other witnesses, Lou-Lou the punk sadist, Philip, the brilliant film director, framing the scene as if he were on a film set, and the other makeup and costume people who were passing by, all stopping to gaze at my helplessness: they could do with me whatever they might wish to do. It was sublime – in a purely perverse way, of course. I trembled with a transcendent sense of submission and abnegation. Also, the whole thing, I must admit, was totally ridiculous, utterly absurd – and hilarious. But my inner laughter came out in owl speak, so …

"To-wit, to-whoo, to-wit, to-whoo." I said brightly. I was not at my most articulate; I wanted to say, "Master James, you and Jester, and Master Philip are overdoing it! Owl wants to leap on all of you."

But, as I have said, my human self was gone, invisible, banished. I was no longer a subject; I was, as they say, an object. I could only hoot. "To-wit, to-whoo, to-wit, to-whoo." Saliva rose, and my excitement meter soared. I licked my lips. My sex was hot, aroused, eager, slick with liquid its lips glowing, dripping lasciviously. My thighs trembled, my hips were eager to capture and enclose something. I was hot and horny as hell. Unpinioned, I would have jumped on James, torn his clothes off, and had sex, right there, right then, in front of the whole crew. I would do it – I could do it – right here in the vast change room in this immense château. "To-wit, to-whoo! To-wit, to-whoo!"

Luckily for public opinion, I was pinioned. A dreadfully scandalous scene – which would have certainly made the papers – was narrowly averted.

We drifted close one of the tall French doors that gave onto the château's park. The heavy brocade curtains hung, portentous and still; white muslin curtains drifted in, billowing, pushed by sudden gusts of hot damp air; a breeze, hesitant and sporadic, was rising. Outside, in the garden of the château, among the fountains, and along the main garden alleyway, was an immense esplanade, where a low, stage-like runway had been set up. The people were already at their tables on the huge lawn. The crowd was vast – it numbered in the thousands. Darkness had come.

The electric lights were turned down. In the giant torches, flames flared upwards, towering yellow spirals lighting up the trees and the sky. It was as if we were in some vast ancient temple – out on the vast esplanade, a pagan rite of blood sacrifice was about to begin. It was almost time.

There was a distant roll of thunder.

"Was that thunder?" Philip peered at the sky.

"To-wit, to-whoo!" I blinked. A distant blue-white flash flickered, lighting up a great reef and shoal of steel-blue clouds, racks of black, and streaks of yellow light. Yes, it must be thunder.

"This will be spectacular," said Philip.

"It certainly will," said James, "as long as the weather holds." He frowned and glanced at the sky. The weather had turned heavy and moody; the weather radar – which we'd checked before driving down to the Loire – showed a warm front, with lines of thundershowers, dense clusters of heavy rain, to the west of Paris, marching east, and, perhaps, sweeping south, towards the Loire.

"Oh, oh," said Jester.

"To-wit, to-whoo!" said Owl.

"Hopefully, the storm won't get here until the event is over." James straightened his tie, stretched his neck. It was indeed humid.

"Gentlemen, the show is about to begin. You'd better go to your seats." Lou-Lou motioned to James and Philips.

"Of course, of course. But, darlings, we will not be far away," James turned to us. He kissed me on the lips and gave my waist a warm sweeping caress, his fingers leaving my skin slowly, with regret. Then he and Philip headed for the exit. Their table – our table – was just off the esplanade, quite close to the stage and runway. If we got into trouble, our two gallant knights could leap to our rescue.

There was a roll of drums, a fanfare, and the spectacle began.

A girl dressed in acrobat tights – they looked very sleek and alluring – pirouetted out from behind the stage curtains, danced a few steps on the runway, and then announced, though the loudspeakers, that the spectacle was about to begin.

The orchestra tuned up for about thirty seconds, a chaotic, cacophony and painful jumble of sound, and, then, suddenly, without warning, it switched into formal, highly-structured mode, playing some exquisite, grandiose, 17th Century French music, very elaborate and baroque, beginning with a piece by Jean-Baptiste Lully, the overture to his *Ballet de la Nuit*.

There were several scenes before ours. The first was a long scene, in which people dressed in costumes from the court of Louis XIV pranced around – kicking their legs very high – in some mime show the import of which I didn't at all understand. The public, though, seemed to adore it, and laughed at what must have been all the right places. They must have seen allusions and references that I missed. I knew that Louis XIV had good legs and that he liked to show them off – in scarlet tights no less – and that he adored dancing, but other than that, I didn't know much about the inner workings of the court of the Sun King. And hidden as we were, and blinkered as I was, I could only catch indirect glimpses of what was happening.

Then there was an acrobatic act by two almost naked Russians, a man and a woman, swinging from a trapeze, and leaping over each other, and hanging upside down over buckets of flame. From what I, an owl peering owlishly, could see, it was truly spectacular.

Next – the two young men, naked except for those glittery transparent G-strings, dancing and twirling around with the two girls wearing nothing but transparent G-strings, pranced out on to the stage and began to do some sort of allegorical or symbolic dance. I didn't understand the allegory, but their bodies were slick with paint, and it was luscious in a sexual, tantalizing way; they mimed intercourse in a rapid-fire kaleidoscope twirl of poses that would have made the authors of the Kama Sutra blush with jealousy. This excited Owl. Owl shifted her weight, first one leg, then the other. Owl was wet with desire, with that, powerful mentholated warming lubricant James had injected her with. Owl tapped one stiletto heel impatiently. Yes, Owl decided that, definitely, Owl and James should go dancing – should do the tango, alone, on some beach, or in some exotic club; Owl would be dressed in a minuscule elastic G-string. My owl-mind drifted. I was always daydreaming of things James and I might do together – and quite a few of them we did do together.

Out on the runway, one scene followed another. Some of the scenes were exquisitely and perversely erotic. There were static tableaux, with the characters just standing still, representing 18th and 19th Century classical paintings, works by Fragonard or Ingres or Delacroix, or famous impressionist paintings. And the performers were painted, so it did look like images in a painting, and not real people.

I suddenly discovered that Martine and I were to be the climax of the show. This was doubly intimidating! The slender girl in tights, who was acting as the Mistress of Ceremonies, stepped forward, alone, into the spotlight. Thousands of eyes gazed upon her. There was silence, a frightening silence, with just a few coughs here and there, and a sound in the distance, of church bells. Lit up by the crisscrossing brilliant beams of light, the young woman began to read, in French, a summary of the *Story of O*. Then she read excerpts from the scene that leads up to O's appearance as Owl at the elegant soirée in the château gardens. The tension among the huge crowd, the thousands and thousands of people in evening gowns and tuxedos, seemed to rise, palpably rise, as the girl, in her thin, clear, beautiful voice, amplified immensely, read the text which outlined, in graphic detail, the stages in O's absolute degradation, which was *my* absolute degradation. As I have explained, Owl, in the novel, was a successful Parisian photographer, snobbish, impeccably elegant, very chic, part of the cream of Parisian society; but, for love, she, or, rather, I – I had put myself entirely in the hands of my unscrupulous lover, René, and I had allowed myself to be exploited – penetrated, pierced, depilated, blindfolded, chained down, held prisoner, sodomized, branded, violated in every possible way, by a multiplicity of men and women, until I was no longer me, no longer a successful woman of the world, no longer a Parisian woman, no longer a woman or a person at all – no ...

I was nothing.

I was a pure object.

I was zero; I was a blank canvas.

I was an empty space, where anyone could project their most obscene and violent fantasies and desires.

I was O.

I was Owl, a Zero, a Cipher, an empty page upon which anything could be written; I was the naked, depersonalized, dehumanized female body, exalted and degraded and gazed upon and objectified – idolized and fetishized and disdained and feared – by all and sundry, all of which, well, I blush to admit it, all of which was rather exhilarating, as a mental and theatrical experiment, and experience, and a blush of excitement and endorphins, like after running a marathon or playing soccer, flooded through me.

The girl finished reading. She bowed. She was a slender, boyish figure.

In immense space, there was a hushed silence. Then the music rose and thinned to a single clarinet, a sinuous sensual tragically melancholy melody, a single melodic line, the incarnation of glory and, of, sublime abjection and solitude, rising, and hanging, all alone, in the murmuring night air.

The girl in tights came to the place where Martine and I – Jester and Owl – were standing hidden behind a panel, and then, together with two naked girls who were to bow to the public as if they were presenting us, Jester and Owl walked out from behind the panel, and advanced into the bright floodlit space. We were totally exposed – to thousands of people, at least three – maybe four – thousand.

We were projected, in close-up and medium shots, on giant high definition screens placed around the park.

Martine walked just in front of me, leading me by the chain. Her particolored brightly painted body appeared translucent, almost transparent, as if it were a body of glass, a living, moving statue, caught in the flickering incandescent light of the flames and spotlights. Every feature and detail of her body was visible; every detail was carved in light; every detail flickered and swayed, in suggestive relief, shadow and light; every lineament of desire shone forth, incarnate, in a slender, voluptuous, living anatomical sketch, as the floodlights shifted their angles and as the tall flames of the giant torches wavered in the evening breeze; my body too must have seemed as if it were wrapped in flame and shadow.

The girl's voice began again; with sweet, delicate, almost childlike sensuality, she narrated the apotheosis of humiliation, the scene of O's – of Owl's – exposure to the elegant and snobbish multitude.

Martine glanced back at me. Her eyes, trapped in the hieratic bright smiling Jester's face, seemed enormous, even bigger than usual.

She was frightened, I suddenly realized, perhaps terrified. She was startled, I think, shocked by her own nudity and exposure. I don't think she had imagined, not until this instant, how naked and exposed we would be. Her bold and playful idea of revenge on me – her brilliant conceit of – an homage to O – was now real. And she had a sudden intimation that it might end badly. This was not a self-contained film set. This was not an intimate fashion shoot. This was not an art gallery or a restaurant. This was not cavorting and making love on the rug in front of the fireplace. This was too big, too open, too exposed. Visibly steeling herself, she turned away from me, straightened her shoulders, tugging gently on my chain, she bravely led me forward, out onto the runway – up on the esplanade – further into the abyss. I turned my rigid Owl head to look at the public and out of my round yellow Owl eyes, I could see, framed by my feathers and beak and flickering in the half-darkness, an ocean of eager, carnivorous faces, row upon row upon row of white faces, hardly a black or Asian face among them, ovals of white, as if they were whitecaps on waves marching inexorably towards the shore. The public was huge – yes, at least three thousand people, all in formal dress, tuxedos and ball gowns.

The girl's voice faded.

As Martine and I walked forward – accompanied now only by very formal 17th Century baroque music – there was at first a hush, as if in awe; then people began to clap, and people clapped more and more and, as we advanced, perhaps twenty meters down the runway. The applause rose like thunder. People began standing up to get a better view. People pushed forward to get closer: the famous Martine Aubin and her notorious lesbian lover, Gwendoline the Freak, were there, in the flesh, naked and exposed, to be touched, to be fondled, to be photographed! One man leaped up onto the esplanade runway. He was clapping. This worked like a signal. People left their tables, they raced and stampeded towards us; tumbling over each other, people over-turned the tables, they climbed, leaped, jumped, onto the run-way; people were crawling, bounding, hurdling towards us; they rushed in, crowding, pressing around us; behind all the shouting, crying, whooping, the music continued solemn, majestic, as if this were a religious ceremony, a ceremony of sacrifice.

And the sacrifice might be us! We could be crushed, trampled to death, torn to pieces.

My neck was held tightly by the collar, and the mask with its feathers blocked my vision, already restricted by the narrow round yellow plastic owl eyes; I could only see straight ahead, maybe thirty degrees to each side. I moved my chin, activating my owl voice.

"To-wit, to-whoo, to-wit, to-whoo, to-wit, to-whoo!"

The owl call fell in a moment of silence in the music; it echoed in the immense space. There must have been a microphone close by. It picked up the owl cry and made it enormous, a pagan cry thundering from the skies.

The stampede hesitated; the crowd looked up, a sea of startled faces. There was a moment of awe and doubt – faced with the im-mense inhuman cry that seemed to come from my lips.

"To-wit, to-whoo! To-wit, to-whoo!" It echoed from the woods, from the walls of the château; it flooded the whole space. "To-wit, to-whoo! To-wit, to-whoo!"

I, the notorious Jezebel, Gwendoline the Wicked, had ceased to be human. I had gone beyond and outside myself. My abjec-tion was total. I was an icon; I was no longer human; I was a sac-rifice, a statue, merely an image. I was a voice, the giant voice of Owl.

The owl voice triggered a paroxysm of excitement.

Voices rose around us: a cacophonic Greek chorus, the clamor of a rising tide of judgment, aggression, and hysteria: "Look at that!" "How could she do such a thing?" "See, totally naked!" "See, she's waxed, totally waxed." "See, the labia are pierced and locked by that ring." "See, look at the chain." "See the bright lips – the owl's beak – what a monstrosity." "How frightening!" "Is this real?" "Is the chain real?" "Touch it, tug it!" "Let's find out!"

The murmur was thunderous; the crowd pressed closer, we were surrounded; people were only kept back, a few feet away, by some residual sense of decorum or morals of those in the front row; but mobs, usually, don't have morals: mobs, in the blink of an eye, turn vicious; the heat of all those voracious hungry lascivious eyes was heavy upon us; their hands reached out. "Touch her!" "Touch her!" "Touch her!" "Touch her!" "Seize them!" "Seize them!" "Take them!" "Take them!"

Two women stepped forward and pinched my breasts and slapped and punched my belly. A large fat man, wearing the pin of the Legion of Honor, his eyes bulging and his face crimson, crowded in close; he stared as if he were terrified of what he saw; his color rose; he licked his fat red lips; the people around him crowded close, bolder and bolder. The fat man tried to elbow them back. A thin woman in an off-the-shoulder semitransparent black silk evening gown, ran her finger down to my labia and probed, her face close to mine, then she brought her fingers to her lips and licked, staring at my eyes all the time. I could feel her breath against my lips. She reached out, ran her finger down the slope of my breast, and pinched my nipple. "You are delicious," she whispered, "I want to eat you." I was the only one who heard her.

The clamor rose. I might be separated from Martine. And the chain! It might get ripped off. Ouch! That could do a lot of damage!

A tall thin man wearing a monocle leaned close, put his hand under my right breast, tickled it, and whispered, "Very fetching, my dear. My taxidermist could do wonderful things with you! Just imagine it, you, stuffed and mounted, perhaps on a little pedestal, next to my fireplace."

Through the narrow slits of the owl eyes, I had the impression of a throng of people, closing in like a lynch mob, but a lynch mob dressed in tuxedoes and long formal gowns, more and more of them, closer and closer: a woman with a long narrow face and yellow eyes; a girl with russet freckles and blushing cheeks and very red lips; an older woman with a pince-nez, a distinguished narrow face, and carefully coiffed silver-gray hair, who touched my breasts with her fan, tickling my nipples. I was afraid the crowd would get out of control and tear us into little bits, out of curiosity or lust, but up until now at least – with a few exceptions – they were quite polite about it. I was just a body, hieratic, impersonal. My self, whatever that was, if there was such a thing, was invisible behind the owl mask; it was all designed, on purpose, so that I would be revealed in body only; to ensure that I would be rigid, absolutely without any human personality. "Both of them have the most beautiful bodies," one of the women said. I caught glimpses of Martine, barely, though she was close, and still holding my vaginal leash.

The stares converged. Martine and I were empty spaces, screens upon which any movie could be projected. I could feel, I could almost see, people projecting their desires and reveries onto Owl – some wanted to *be* Owl; some wanted to possess Owl; some wanted to be Jester, leading Owl on her leash; some wanted to be my mistress, some wanted to possess my mistress: She was Clown Waif, and she was Evil Jester, and she was a star, Martine Aubin, a cluster of archetypes. Some were in awe of Owl, almost religiously, as if an ancient totem had come back to life; some, of course, were revolted, and fearful – as if I had broken – which I had – which we had – ancient taboos.

The temperature rose. Mass hysteria fluttered. People ogled, pressed closer, they poked at us, they pushed in and held up phones to take videos and pictures, selfies. Lights flashed. In the brilliance of the floodlights, they were hardly needed. It was garish and dazzling, all of it.

One man grabbed Martine, squeezed her, and shouted, "Say Cheese!" He held out his arm and took a selfie. Others joined him.

I was being hugged. Selfies were being taken, with the naked, chained Owl, and with the naked Jester-Clown.

How delightful!

It was in danger of becoming a riot. My Owl mask was so rigid I couldn't see who was hugging me. Clammy hands and bodies and sequined dresses and crisp tuxedos pressed my flesh, my breasts, my belly. Luckily the chain had not yet been torn off. Martine came close, squeezing next to me. A guy grabbed her, and shouted, "This way, Martine!" She turned. And he took a photograph.

I caught glimpses of James and Philip struggling to get to us. One woman, fighting to grab Martine, was seized by someone behind her who tore half the woman's pearl-and-gold dress off, leaving the deeply tanned, skinny, nut-brown woman naked down to the waist. The woman didn't care. But she changed her target. She pushed her way to me and pinched one of my breasts and swung around, and held out her phone – one more selfie. As the camera flashed, she put out her hand and pinched my nipple, "Thanks, Owl," she laughed, her face very close to mine; she slapped me on the buttock and disappeared.

James was beside me. "Are you okay?"

"To-wit, to-whoo." I nodded.

"We'd better get to our table," said James. "This is getting out of control."

"To-wit, to-whoo!"

"I'm fine, but I'm hungry," Martine said, sheltering in Philip's arms, right next to me.

It was impossible to move. An ocean of people jostled us from every side, pressing closer, and closer. My Owl face was only a few inches from Jester. I could feel her breath, see the grains of gold in her bright sapphire eyes. "How are you doing, Owl?"

"To-wit, to-whoo!"

At that moment, ominously, there was a rustling sound, a hushed whispering sound, as if of an oncoming wall of water – the rain was on its way. Jester made a clownish grimace. Her chalk-white nostrils flared, her deeply mascaraed eyes narrowed. "Oh, Owl, I fear we shall be drenched. The heavens are about to open. The gods are angry! They disapprove of our cavorting!"

"To-wit, to-whoo!"

The rain came, in one instant, a pure wall of water moving through the trees and across the lawns and past the tables and giant torches like a giant misty veil; then, it was upon us, a tsunami from the skies. Within seconds, people were soaked, blinded by water. They panicked. Tuxedos wilted; dresses shriveled into glassy transparency. People ran every which way, they galloped, leaped, trotted – the men in tuxedos, the women in long gowns which they had to hold up. In masses, they stumbled over each other. By the dozen, they tumbled, flat on their faces. Fistfights broke out. People toppled and rolled over each other. The fat red-faced man with the Legion of Honor fell flat on his enormous belly, then turned on his side like a giant fetus; people trampled and clambered over him, he tried to crawl away, he was kicked and trampled on; he rolled over and over, and fell off the esplanade runway onto the gravel below. I caught a glimpse of him as he tried to get up; he was pushed down again, disappearing.

James' arm was tight around my shoulders. He had taken the chain from Martine. Through my soaked feathers and owl eyes, I caught blurry glimpses, snapshots of chaos. The half-naked women – who had pinched and slapped me and whose pearl-and-gold dress had been torn off by the crowed – got tangled up in the shreds of the dress; kicking herself free, she tossed away what was left of the dress – emerging almost naked from its ruins, just sequined G-string panties. The fat man with the red face who had tumbled off the runway was lying face down in the gravel. He looked dead. People fought, climbed, crawled their way over each other, fists flew, nails scratched, thumbs gouged, ears were pulled, wigs and toupees torn off, jackets shredded, dresses exploded, trousers fell down, belts snapped; chairs and tables were flipped over, batted out of the way, bottles of champagne flew through the air. Canapés rocketed skywards. More and more people were being crushed.

Then, suddenly, the runway was empty. The only person left was the tanned woman, now naked except for those sparkly G-string panties and very high-heeled scarlet shoes; she managed to get to her feet. She was holding a small rectangular pearl-white purse with a gold clasp and handle. The rain slashed down; water cascaded over her; it looked like she was standing in a waterfall. She looked around and shrugged. She bent over, pulled down her panties, stepped out of them, and tossed them away. She glanced back at me, grimaced, grinned, waved, and stuck out her tongue: sisters in nakedness. Still in her high heels, she climbed off the platform, went to one table which hadn't been overturned, picked up a bottle, sat down, and started to drink from it.

Lou-Lou appeared beside us. "Are you all right?" She glistened with rain. Her scarlet crest and tattoos shone brightly.

"Yes, we are," said James.

"To-wit, to-whoo! "To-wit, to-whoo!"

"Hunky-dory," said Martine.

"Fine as fine can be," said Philip.

"The crowd is getting wilder." Lou-Lou nodded. "See them out there! They are attacking the gendarmes and overturning cars. I don't know what has got into them. Maybe the champagne was spiked. The only safe way out of here," Lou-Lou pointed, "is to go in the opposite direction, into the woods, or into the château." As the rain poured over her, her tattoos and piercing rings shone as if they had been covered in fresh varnish. She looked delicious. She shone like a candy-apple in a country fair. I was tempted to bite. She glanced at me. "Owl?"

"To-wit, to-whoo!"

She winked and rubbed her eyes to clear away the rain. She had read my thoughts. "We will meet again, Owl!"

"To-wit, to-whoo!"

"Into the woods, we go." James rubbed his hands; he was soaked, steaming with water, and excited, like a child.

"Yes, that's a splendid idea, much more interesting than the château," said Philip, holding Jester close.

"It is time, Owl, for a real adventure," said Jester, her bright particolored face, her sweet clownish lips, pressing close to my lips.

"Well, I'll see you again," I hope, shouted Lou-Lou, raising her voice to be heard over the thunderous downpour.

"Absolutely," said Philip, wiping the water from his eyes. "I want you to create the new Martine look for our next production."

"To-wit, to-whoo!" said I. "To-wit, to-whoo!"

Lou-Lou waved, blew us a kiss, and disappeared into the shadowy entry to the château.

Immersed in the wave of warm water, I shivered in voluptuous delight. Water hammered on my shoulders; it streamed from my feathers and dripped from my beak. Miraculously, my owl eyes had not fogged up, but I only had a narrow slit of vision between the heavily drenched feathers. It seemed, if possible, to be raining even harder. James put his jacket over my shoulders. My pinioned winged feathery arms didn't make this easy.

Philip suddenly produced a leash and attached it to Jester's collar.

"What the hell?" Jester looked startled. Rain poured over her clown face; silver drops shone at the end of her lashes; her varnished, brightly painted body – scarlet and coal-black legs – was beaded in sparkles and streaming with rivulets of rain. She reached up and kissed Philip and put her arms around him. "Oh, my Master," she said, "My Maestro, my Creator, my Pygmalion!"

"Mademoiselle Jester, I am merely your humble lover," said Philip, "your servant and your slave. I cannot begin to tell you how much I love you and how much I owe you." He knelt and kissed her tummy. She gazed down at him, the water streaming from his thick black hair, his broad shoulders bright with splashing rain; she glanced at me, her blue eyes bright, burning crystals in the clown mask.

James, gallantly, kneeling before me, detached the leash from my labial ring and attached it to my collar, which was certainly a welcome change from having it attached down below.

"Time for a stroll in the woods, oh, Owl." He embraced me and kissed my lips.

"To-wit, to-whoo." A stroll in the woods sounded extremely perilous and temptingly yummy, though, truly, I would prefer that my pinioned wings were released. If we were attacked in the woods by a mob or a gang or by a big bad wolf, I'd be helpless. My arms, lashed with tight crisscrossed leather thongs behind my back, were numb; I feared they might wither and fall off; I would become the Venus de Milo, Aphrodite, an armless wonder. On the other hand, helplessness has its own rewards: the rain was warm, a steamy all-over sauna and shower all in one, and bound as I was, and exposed, I was aroused; the night was young; I was eager for adventure.

At that moment, a second, even thicker wave of rain, a veritable solid wall of water, hit us. But, undaunted, James and Philip led us off the stage, across the gravel paths, and through the garden, past the tables – many of which were turned over. The naked nut-brown lady was sitting alone, taking swigs from a bottle. She gave us a friendly wave – Jester and James and Philip waved back – and on we went, into the forest. It was a truly formal forest, not a forest at all in the English or natural sense of the word, but lines of trees and bushes ranged in formation as if they were ranks in an army, being inspected by a general; but such, as I have learned, is the French way: They are Cartesians, addicted to logic and method; they cannot leave nature alone, but must impose a plan and give it orders and turn unruly overweening irrational beauty into a disciplined model of geometric perfection; their attitude to sex is a bit like that too; it occurred to me, that the French approach to sex was a geometry of power. It was an extension of military tactics and strategy to the dinner table, the alcove, the boudoir, and the bedroom, and very refreshing, I found, in its frankness, like the games Martine and I played, it gave a channel to passion and lust and allowed us to talk of anything, however dastardly, however obscene, without hypocrisy, and made it easy to reveal any part of ourselves we might want to reveal; the amorous battlefield laid bare is a fine and lovely place. The 18th Century novel *Dangerous Liaisons* was typical of this approach: a man sets out methodically to conquer and debauch a virtuous and unconquered beauty, just as if he were setting up a siege, with cannons and catapults, and sappers, and feints and maneuvers, stratagems and tactics and spies, to capture a fortified town. The author, if I remembered correctly, was Pierre Choderlos de Laclos, an army officer, a specialist in artillery. No wonder the Marquis de Sade – that master of geometric sadistic cruelty – was a Frenchman. My mathematical mind delighted in some ways, in this Cartesian mania for imposing order on everything. But part of my soul yearned for wild romantic disorder, the maze-like unpredictability of a true forest, a true jungle, the Amazon, or a rain forest, or perhaps some wild archaic English garden caprice, with grottos, and cupids, and twisted perverse mysterious and overgrown winding paths. One of the delightful things about Martine, I thought, was that she combined both aspects admirably – pure unbridled unpredictable passion, and a very French ironic clarity about herself, and her motives and feelings – and about me too. Oh, yes, yes, yes, I did love her!

I could hardly see out of my owl's mask; my wings, pinioned behind my back, were soaked; water streamed down my body – I was a statue under a hot, steamy Niagara Falls, which was all shivery keen, lusciously smooth, and warm, like being caressed all over.

Philip and Martine walked ahead. Streams of rain shrouded the lamps that lined the walkway. Philip took off his jacket, slinging it over his shoulder. Martine's arm was tight around Philip's waist. Rivulets of water coursed down her body; silver drops sprayed from the ends of her floppy jester's horns. The jester's paint, as Lou-Lou had promised, was resistant to rain; my delicious Clown-Jester glowed, her brilliant, particolored Jester's body glistened, voluptuous in the lamplight; she walked with that swaying, sensuously servile gait which stilettos can impose, particularly on a gravel walkway. Her perfect perky buttocks, lit brightly by the lamps, swung with casual nonchalance, brightly painted, one buttock glossy coal-black, the other buttock bright scarlet. I blinked. Lightning flashed.

A tremendous, deafening clap of thunder reverberated through the trees – the gravel shook, the lampposts vibrated, we trembled. James tightened his grip on my waist. "Steady, Owl," he whispered. I nuzzled him with my feathers and my beak; he patted me on my backside, sliding his hand over the curve of my buttock. "To-wit, to-woo, To-wit, to-woo!"

And so, in the pouring rain, we continued walking on the gravel path, not entirely easy in scarlet stiletto heels and with one's arms pinioned behind one's back. I feared I would stumble, but James held me up, his arm strong and tight around my waist under my pinioned feathery wings, steadying me and holding me close.

Suddenly, a white gazebo surged up. It was in front of us, like something out of a dream, impeccable and sparking, freshly painted, glowing with rain, an image of old-fashioned perfection. With tall thin metal columns and an ornate roof – replete with bright, dripping metal curlicues – and an open wooden stage, it must, once, have been the setting for summer band concerts. I could almost hear the music and see ghostly dancers whirling around in a waltz.

We were alone in the forest, or so it seemed. The rain, dense and steamy, continued, tropical and warm – made just for us. We were wading through a sauna. We climbed up the bright wooden steps into the shelter of the gazebo.

As we came out of the rain, all the sounds of the forest were suddenly clearer, more distinct, and magnified: rain drummed on the wooden roof of the gazebo, it rattled on the gravel of the path; it pattered, with a hushed whisper, on the leaves of the neatly ranged trees. Another blinding flash lit up the alleyway, dazzled our eyes with light. The thunder echoed. It shook the pillars and roof of the gazebo.

James pulled me close and kissed me.

"To-wit, to-whoo," I kissed him back. "To-wit, to-woo!"

Peering out from my owl mask and owl eyes, I could just see his face: water streamed down his cheeks; sparkling drops glittered in his eyelashes; his lips glowed then, with a swift intake of breath, I felt his lips on my lips; and his breath mingled with my breath, and his body pressed against my body.

He stepped back and lifted his jacket off my shoulders and hung it on the gazebo railing. He hooked my leash to an elaborate metal curlicue in the gazebo's iron railing.

"To-wit, to-whoo." I licked my lips. Attached to the metal railing of the gazebo, I wondered if I was a candidate for electrocution.

James unbuckled his cummerbund, opened his shirt, slipped out of his braces, unzipped, and opened his trousers, and took them off. He swiveled his cummerbund around so he could get at its hooks. It had a black-and-red plaid pattern. He unhooked it, liberated himself and hung the cummerbund, with his braces, over the gazebo railing, then he was quickly out of his shirt, and his stockings, his stocking suspenders, his underpants, and a cute undershirt that was decorated with a large smiley face: Ah, I thought, how much it takes to hold up a man, and to keep him together! Almost like corsets!

Naked like this, we were, of course, courting the risk of being arrested if a pair of gendarmes happened to casually stroll by – not a very high risk in this thunderstorm and downpour. Besides, I imagined the gendarmes had their hands full trying to stop the elite mob from tearing itself apart and from wrecking the château. But the possibility of arrest and public humiliation – however faint – only added spice to the delight of being here, naked, with my man. And then there was this: James was once again risking himself to pleasure me. There he was – the very man himself, the very thing, poor bare, forked animal out in the storm, out on the heath, like poor Tom when he was glimpsed by mad King Lear; but, however pathetic we humans when naked may truly be, to me, my master, still glowing and wet from the rain, was sublime, muscular and dark, a tense pillar of energy, he was my very own man, my jungle madman, my Tarzan, naked in the forest; he had hunted me down, and now he held me captive by a leash of love and servitude and adoration. Philip, I saw, had followed James' example, and had stripped down to the naked man. He and Jester were locked in a fierce embrace, her bright particolored body interlocked with his dark, tanned body. The two horns of her blue jester's cap jiggled, and the bells jingled.

For some reason, I found the fact that our two men were naked, while Jester and I were, in a way, clothed, particularly exciting. Jester was adorned in paint, and I had my feathered pinioned wings and my owl mask. I was a totem, my man was transparent and naked; he was my servant and my slave, and he was that pure thing – a naked male animal, and, tonight, he was mine.

"To-wit, to-whoo," I invited my servant with my owl call.

He kissed me; the kiss was fierce and unending, or so it seemed, an eternal kiss, a kiss that would carry us into infinity, his arms around me, grasping me, clasping me under my pinioned arms; his lips explored mine; our lips merged in one; my eyes were closed; it was pure sensation: the pouring rain, my dripping feathers, my pinioned arms pressed together, my shoulders pulled back tight, my breasts tensed and straining forward; his chest, hard and smooth and muscular against my breasts; his hands on me; his lips meeting my lips; his tongue mingling with my tongue. I breathed him in. Inwardly, I sighed, "Oh, Master!" But it came out as a quizzical "To-wit, to-whoo?" He whispered, "Oh, Goddess, oh, beautiful Owl." He held me so tight it was as if he wanted to consume me, merge my body in his, to absorb me totally.

Finally, he stepped back, unhooked the owl mask-and-hood from the collar, and lifted it off, and placed it carefully on an iron bench, which was the only furniture in the gazebo. My face, now, was naked.

And then, standing in the rain, we made love, me with my arms still pinioned behind me, totally at his mercy, thrilling at my helplessness, and entrusting myself totally to his love, his amorous skill, and his generosity.

He knelt before me. His kisses explored my belly; his tongue entered my labia, my eager lips; he stroked and sucked and caressed my clitoris.

"To-wit, to-whoo, to-wit-to-whoo, to-wit, to-whoo!"

He stood up; his lips were on my lips, his tongue merging with my tongue, and, as he entered me, I was being lifted up, cleaved in two, totally possessed; every nerve echoed, resonated, exploded. I cried out:

"To-wit, to-whoo, to-wit, to-whoo, to-wit, to-whoo!"

Pinioned as I was, I leaned back, against the railing, my heart beating fast and faster; thunder roared; lightning flashed; rain poured down. At that moment, somehow, part of my mind noticed that Philip was performing the same service for Jester; she was leaning against the railing, her head tossed back, her bright floppy horns wagging, light glancing off her cobalt blue skull, her bells jingling, each muscle of her glossily colored body, sculpted in flashing light, tense, wrapped in ecstasy. This redoubled my excitement. And, as I wondered at her pleasure and enslavement and Philip's, I was swept away in my own maelstrom of passion.

≈

Then, later – much later – the storm abated; the rain ceased; it was deepest night, a soft, dark night. Water dripped from the trees, the air was warm and still. We left the magic gazebo, and walked towards the riverside. When we reached the river ...

When we reached the river, James stopped, looked at me, and

said, "Look, this is almost dry!" He held up the owl hood. He contemplated it. "Yes, it's dry." Then, holding it in front of him, he came towards me with an evil mischievous gleam in his eye.

Oh, oh, I thought. "To-wit, to-whoo, to-wit, to-whoo?"

He kissed me. "Oh, Owl," he said, "Oh, divine Owl!" He lowered the hood-mask over my head, tightened it, and locked it to the collar. I had ceased, once again, to be me. I was Owl, merely Owl. To what further degrees of servitude would James take me? "To-wit, to-whoo?"

We walked along the river, past groups of poplars, past a miniature château. We met two or three revelers, stragglers, who were wandering under the trees, ties undone, jackets askew, evening dresses torn and soaked. They looked dazed, one of them was holding a champagne bottle by the neck. He called out, "Want a drink? Want a drink? We've got more in our car!"

"Thank you, but no! Thank you!" James called back.

Everyone we met stared, of course, at the Clown-Jester and Owl. One woman, in a long, ragged silver dress, circled around us, staring at Martine, and I thought she was going to abandon her man and follow us, but he pulled her back, and I heard him say, in French, "Clara, don't make a fool of yourself!"

Finally, with James leading me by my leash, we went up a narrow lane from the river to the parking lot for the château. Our car was there. It was one of the few left. We climbed up the steep path and got to the car.

"May I have her?" Jester asked, eyeing me.

"Why, of course, Jester," James handed my leash to Jester. She pulled me close and kissed me on the lips. She pressed her glistening, wet, warm, painted body against mine. She leaned back and smiled. "Why don't we go to that club you mentioned, Philip? The all-night dancing and fetish bar; you told me it's not far from here."

"Yes, but Owl will need some covering," said Philip, "Owl is naked, wonderfully naked. But the place does have rules. Minimal rules, but rules."

"To-wit, to-whoo?"

"Well, yes, we may have just the right thing." James produced a minuscule transparent net thong or G-string and two scarlet pasties with bells dangling.

"To-wit, to-whoo?"

"And me?" said Martine, "What about me?"

"Yes, I forgot," said Philip, "You, Jester, with your face exposed, are even more naked than Owl."

"I think we have just the thing for Jester." James produced an identical set – a transparent net thong and two scarlet pasties, with bells dangling.

"Damn," the bright Jester face pouted, "A girl is left with no dignity."

"In a sense, you are already dressed." said Philip.

And it was true. The paint on her body was as bright as when it was first sprayed on. Lou-Lou had promised that the paint was sweat- and rain-proof, and so it was: Martine was still locked in her role as Jester. This was amusing. "To-wit, to-whoo!"

Jester looked down at herself. "Am I ever going to get rid of this stuff?"

"I have the formula," said Philip, "it's in the kits Lou-Lou gave James and me. If you are a very, very good, totally obedient Jester, then a special soap, and a long hot cruel shower and sadistic rubdown should do the job."

"It had better." Jester turned her jingling floppy horns and wicked clown smile to me and winked a dark turquoise and anthracite wink. Surrounded by silky black, her blue eyes glowed like orphaned sapphires.

"Now, Owl, let us free you from your chains." James turned

to me. He began to untie the leather thongs that held my arms in thrall; it was complicated, but he managed it; he lifted the feathery wings from my arms, and finally, I was free, albeit still a collared Owl with the voice of an Owl. I flexed my arms. Whew! There were thong marks from my shoulders to my wrists. They began to fade. James leaned over my arm. "Here, Owl, I'll kiss it and make it better." He began to kiss his way up my arm, first one arm, then the other. It tickled. I wanted to giggle.

"To-wit, to-whoo, to-wit, to-whoo!

Standing next to the car in the steamy air, with thunder and lightning echoing in the distance, Martine and I helped each other put on the scarlet pasties and minuscule thongs. With these bits of fabric, we were effectively naked. Our men stood back in patriarchal splendor, observed our work and decreed that it was good.

When we got into the car, James lowered the top, and we drove down little winding side roads; the moon came out and kept us company; it was a blurred, steamy, pale moon that ducked behind ribbons of cloud and flirtatiously shrouded itself in low semitransparent veils of mist. As we sped along beside a river, the moon sailed with us, in silver ripples on the water, and poplars and weeping willows and other shadowy moonlit trees swept by, darkly lining the shimmering silver.

The ride was stimulating. The leather car seat was stickily possessive under my backside; the steamy night air licked with a thousand eager lascivious little tongues my thighs and breasts and tickled my shoulders and my collarbone.

We came to a small village, narrow streets of white stone houses; no lights were on; there were no people in the narrow, cobblestoned, sloping streets. I could see from behind my owl mask that a clock tower said it was one o'clock in the morning. How had time passed so quickly? James pulled over and parked in a small square. "We get out here."

"To-wit, to-whoo?"

We got out of the car. I suddenly wondered if James, who could be a trickster on occasion, intended to disembark Jester – with her glittering particolored body and her clown's face and still in her Jester's cap with its horns and bells – and me with my owl hood – nude, except for pasties and G-strings, as we were – and then drive off to have some drinks with Philip, leaving we two next-to-naked waifs to fend for ourselves. It might be fun in a high school prank sort of way, but surely, he would not play such a dirty trick. Besides, it might be dangerous.

"No, I certainly would not play such a dirty trick," James said, "And besides, it might be dangerous." He grinned and laid his hand on my thigh. He had, as so often, read my thoughts. Our two souls did seem to dance to the same tune.

I turned my owl face to him. "To-wit, to-whoo?"

"Yes, Owl, I do sometimes think I understand your every thought." He kissed me, on my scarlet lips, right under my beak, and his tongue probed my tongue. Our tongues danced their little liquid dance, becoming one fluid entwined silken creature. I wanted to bite him, to suck him into me, to consume him; I yearned to cry out in delight. His hand snaked up my thigh, and his fingers pried open and snuck under the G-string, drawing it as tight as a violin string. He whispered into my owl ear, "I knew you were thinking that Philip and I might disembark you two beautiful demoiselles here, virtually naked as you are, Owl and Jester, and then spin off and leave you, helpless and exposed, cast away and desperate, but of course, we would never do any such thing! We would not even think of it!" His warm, strong hand explored my silk smooth pubis, giving it a gentle massage, which escalated quickly and quickly went deeper. I was wet in anticipation. I must have a trigger-happy clitoris, is all I can say. It's like a super-sensitive joystick. A flick of the finger and I skitter all over the map. Inwardly, I sighed: Oh, oh, oh! The rubber and steel collar, holding my neck erect, and locking the owl mask in place, was tight like a loving strangler's grip; it raised my blood pressure to perilous heights. I squirmed. Yes, I was definitely getting excited – yet again.

How long ago had I had my last orgasm? Half an hour? I should cut down on the vitamins. My nipples, always ready for a tussle, were pushing hard under the pasties, aching with yearning. I wanted James' hand to caress and soothe my breasts, to cup and weigh them, to lick and massage them, to suckle and suck them. The Earth Mother rose up in my loins, shimmied her way into my breasts, to the very nipples, and licked at my lips. I wanted to be milked. I should say "moo" instead of "to-wit, to-whoo!" Indulging in these mammary and ruminant musings, I shivered from exquisitely painful pleasure – earthquakes and seismic tremors rippled up my belly, inward and outward, and down my thighs, a true riptide of explosive seismic activity, with the epicenter remaining precisely where it was supposed to be. I blurted out a non-cow but ecstatic moonlit owlish, "To-wit, to-whoo!" It was, indeed, a strange way to broadcast an orgasm. I wondered if any of the villagers and farmers were eavesdropping from behind their closed shutters.

≈

So, there we were, standing on the cobblestones, Jester and I teetering in our high heels. Jester sidled over and ran her hand down my side. She twanged the string of my G-string. "You look fabulous, Owl," she said.

I wanted to say, "And you look fabulous too, Jester," but, being Owl, I remained silent. I did stroke her tummy.

The old-fashioned gas lamps caught every curve of her body and made the particolored black, turquoise, and scarlet glow with a thousand little fires.

James put up the roof of the car and locked it.

"Where now, gentlemen?" said Jester. Her voice startled me; hypnotized by her appearance, I had for a moment forgotten that, unlike me, she could speak.

"The club is just around the corner," Philip pointed, his tuxedo jacket slung over his shoulder. He looked every inch the perfect French film director, thick long tousled black hair, an open shirt, and big dark eyes that seemed so sincere, so deep, that you wanted to leap into them and drown yourself in his all-encompassing, all-understanding soul. I could see why Martine – Jester – was so taken. If I hadn't had James, I too would have been tempted.

"To-wit, to-whoo!"

"Yes, Philip is pretty, isn't he?" James half-closed his eyes and gave me a lazy look.

"To-wit, to-whoo!"

James laughed. He put his hands on my shoulders, "Ah, Owl," he said, "Ah, divine, sublime Owl!" He kissed me, another long, lingering kiss. He took my hand – his grasp was dry and firm and strong. We walked down the little cobbled street, my heels and Jester's heels making that nice pony clip-clop echoing wobbly sound that exaggerated stilettoes are excellent at producing. We went around a corner into a short, narrow, dead-end cobblestoned lane, with rough-hewn walls of stone on both sides, and found ourselves facing a high, ivy-covered, barbed-wire-topped wall of stone, with a small green door in the middle of it. There was a brass buzzer beside the door but no markings or signage of any kind. Above the door, I noticed, was a camera, half-hidden by the ivy. Its little sensor light blinked red. It was staring down at us. It moved back and forth, and up and down, giving us the once-over.

James glanced at Philip and pushed the buzzer.

A voice said, in French, "Good evening. What can I do for you?"

Philip spoke a few mysterious words in French, "The Dark Prince has emerged into the double moonlight." It was a code, I imagine, an open sesame, and in fact –

The door swung inwards. We entered a small formal garden and walked to the other side where there was a door in another wall; it opened as we approached and led to a small circular classic stone vestibule; here, an arched stone staircase spiraled downward. We clip-clopped down the staircase and came to a low-ceilinged crypt; it was utterly silent – the silence of the tomb. And in fact, I felt like we were heading downwards into a tomb-like world, an underworld kingdom of the dead.

Suddenly an invisible door slid open, and we entered a vast space with strobe lights and with thunderous music and with a long modern-looking stainless-steel bar. People were dancing. Many were in sadomasochistic gear, black leather, and latex, and chains. Several people, two women, and a man, wearing only loin-cloths, were chained spread-eagled suspended to the stone walls; it didn't look comfortable. There were tables around the edge of the dance floor. We were ushered to a table by a tall young woman in a black-and-red frilly burlesque type latex corset and black stockings and stilettos. As soon as we sat down, a waitress in tights served us drinks.

We danced. James held me tight, still imprisoned in my owl mask. Finally, he unhooked the mask from the collar and lifted it off; he switched the collar's speech inhibitor to "off." I could speak. So now I was a human being, for a change. But, for some reason, I was content to remain, for the moment, silent.

I danced with James. I danced with Philip. Then, while James and Philip watched, Martine and I danced together. The music slowed to a soft low romantic beat; the strobe lights ceased, the lights dimmed, and shifted colors in a regular rhythm. The other dancers left the floor, and Martine and I continued to dance, a slow dance, embracing each other, the shifting light flowing softly over us.

"We're crazy," Martine said, leaning in close to me, and rubbing her body against mine.

"Yes," I whispered, nibbling at her ear, as we danced close to a wall where a gentleman wearing a black leather jockstrap was suspended spread-eagled shackled on a giant black steel wheel that rotated slowly as if the gentleman were being roasted slow motion on a spit.

"And we're show-offs," said Martine, swinging me out and away from her, right to the end of her outstretched arm, and, slowly, gracefully, pulling me back.

"Absolutely, we are exhibitionists." I moved my hands down to her waist so she could bend herself backward, in a tango dancing pose, I was her caballero, she was my femme.

"Shameless." She grinned, swinging back up to me, and putting one hand on my waist, and another on my shoulder, and swinging us off, her now leading me, as the music segued into a waltz.

"Yes, shameless," I breathed. We spun around, our heels clicking; it seemed effortless. As they say – we were dancing on air. Philip and James were leaning towards each other, their heads together, still deep in some intense discussion, and only glancing up, once in a while, at us.

"It doesn't take a genius to see that we are utterly, hopelessly debauched." Martine swung close, looking me straight in the eye; she kissed me on the lips, then swung away, eyes half-closed, dreamily.

"Do you feel strange?" I pulled her back. We danced around a wall where three people, two girls, and a man, naked except for G-strings and a jockstrap, were gagged and blindfolded and suspended, spread-eagled, like the man on the turning wheel, except they were suspended directly on the wall, not on a wheel, and they were pinioned into frieze-like immobility, not rotating in celestial motion.

"What do you mean, strange?" Martine sidled past me, sliding her brightly painted body smoothly against mine, rubbing close. She looked into my eyes and raised a clownish, spectacularly painted eyebrow.

"Strange, doing this?"

"No, not at all. Lots of others are strange like us, or stranger, much stranger; pleasure and ecstasy come from strange places. At least, I think so. Just look around!" She nodded towards a platform on which a woman, lying on a bed-like table, was vacuum sealed in black plastic; she looked like a semi-realist sculpture, partially realized, rising out of liquid black marble.

"I see what you mean," I said.

"*Voilà!*" Martine smiled, slapped me on the backside.

I glanced at James and Philip. They were both looking at us now, smiling. "Our men are voyeurs," I said. They waved. I waved back.

Martine followed my wave and turned, and staged a flashy, exaggerated little bow-curtsy, a Jester's homage, towards our two gentlemen; then, with a dramatic tango-like move, she put her hands on my hips, seizing me, a formidable grip, and swinging me away. "Yes," she laughed, "but they are engaged voyeurs; they usually make themselves part of the show."

"More screen-writers and directors, I think ..." We twirled and twirled around – I was dizzy with everything whirling past in a blur, the walls, the lights, the suspended people on the wall, the turning wheel.

"Yes," Martine slowed us down. "Sometimes they orchestrate and direct us, but I think I direct Philip more than he directs me, except on stage and in the movies of course."

"James directs me." The music slowed to a soft feathery syncopated beat.

"Yes," Martine brushed her lips against my ear, "Sometimes, but he has a sense of what you want. Above all, I think he wants to give you pleasure and earn your love."

"I think so, yes, definitely yes."

"And, darling, tell me, do you still want me?"

"Yes, definitely, yes. I love you, Martine. You know I am *in* love with you."

"Isn't it awful? I'm *in* love with you too! You are the very flame of my desire. Oh, Gwendoline – remember that rug, that wonderful rug!"

"I do. I do remember."

And, so, we kissed, and, so, we danced. And, as we drifted around the dance floor, all alone, the only ones dancing, I wondered at the man suspended upside down, at the two girls and one man spread-eagled on the wall, at the girl sealed in the vacuum bed, at the man rotating spread-eagled on the giant slowly turning wheel.

Philip and James were watching us closely. Then I could see Philip explaining something, in very animated fashion, to James and James was nodding, and smiling "Those two are cooking up some mischief," said Martine, brushing her cheek against mine, touching her lips to my ear, sweet, sweet breath, and pressing her body, slender and precise, close against mine. "Yes, I'm sure they are," I whispered, "And so am I." I ran my hands down her backside and grasped the two cheeks of her sweet ass. I was tempted to rip her G-string off, but I didn't.

"You thrill me, Gwen, whatever you do – and don't do." She looked into my eyes; her lips brushed mine, and then she kissed me, fiercely. "I love you, Gwen," she breathed. Her bells jingled, and her clown face was utterly adorable. "I can't say how much I love you!"

"Not more than I love you." I kissed her on the end of the nose, then our lips locked in the fiercest of kisses, and we danced, and danced and danced.

≈

When we got back to Paris, the sky was milky white with little traces of yellow and rose. Dawn was breaking. James and I left Philip and Martine in front of Martine's apartment. Martine was still Jester, the brightly painted naked clown, caught in the dawn's early light. She and Philip waved and then disappeared inside the big door of the building.

James put the Porsche in the reserved spot in the indoor parking lot, which was only a few blocks along Boulevard Saint Germain from our flat. James, always the perfect planner, had brought along a silk sheet to cover me during our urban excursion. As we stood beside the car in the concrete parking garage, breathing in the smell of oil and gasoline and fresh paint that was all around us, and bathing in the garish bluish-pale light that makes everybody look like they have pimples, he put the sheet over my shoulders but left it open so it wafted around me like an old-fashioned nobleman's cape. I clasped it in front of me to cover my nakedness, clothed as I was in just the brightly colored pasties and sparkly tinsel G-string.

Hand in hand, we walked past the large stone buildings, the storefronts, the newspaper kiosks. The air was wonderfully fresh. Humidity glowed on the cobblestones, on the mottled bark and broad flat leaves of the plane trees. My heels clicked in the morning stillness. There were very few people on the boulevard. One man went by on a bicycle and gave me a double-take, and then doffed his cap in salutation. Feeling like royalty, I gave him a regal nod, and a slight, courtly bow.

A handsome young couple, both tall, and both blond, with

rucksacks, came out of a side street looking confused. They asked us if we could point out the way to the Saint Germain subway station. It turned out they were Germans, from Hamburg. We pointed the station out to them, and as I was pointing, the sheet opened and fell partway off my shoulders, which had a nice effect on the young Germans. The girl said, "A party – you were at a party?"

"Yes, we were," I said, "in the country."

"And it was a fine party too," said James.

"But we never did get to eat," I said, suddenly realizing I was starving. The rain had come, and the crowd had stampeded, before we were able to dig in and consume the wonderful feast which had been promised. I pulled the sheet back around me, lightly, and let it waft open freely – since otherwise, I'd have to clutch it desperately to me, which would have seemed excessively, ostentatiously, modest.

"It must have been a great party," said the girl, whose name, she told us was Angelica.

"It was," I said, "So great I forgot all my clothes."

They both laughed and thanked us for the directions and headed off towards the metro station Saint-Germain-des-Prés.

"Goodbye!" We waved at the two young Germans as they walked down the boulevard. They turned around and grinned and waved.

I was wet and eager but exhausted when we got home. I declared I wanted to make love, and I wanted to eat an omelet.

"You will burn me out and quickly turn me into an old man," James said. He was fully dressed; with a smile, he pried off the pasties and lifted off the G-string.

I sat, naked, my legs crossed, on the rug, by the unlit fireplace, and watched as James undressed slowly. He stared at me as he undid all his buttons and liberated himself from all his formal black-tie contraptions. I stood up slowly, timidly, and he pulled me to him and held me against him, and we just let our bodies feel each other, just let our minds and sensibilities dissolve into each other.

We made love, slowly, gently, in front of the empty fireplace, and then my stomach growled. James laughed and laid his head on my belly so he could listen to its ravenous rumblings.

Deciding I was too famished to take time to make an omelet, I ran to the kitchen and got some ham and brie sandwiches out of the fridge, and two glasses of wine, hurried back, carrying my treasures.

We ate, sitting there, as if we were camping, naked, on the rug in front of the fireplace.

Then we showered. He shampooed me, and soaped me all over; he used the special shampoo – and a vigorous massage to get rid of the guck Lou-Lou had put in my hair, and he used the special astringent soap to remove the ring next to my labia; Once that was done, and I was sparkling clean, I shampooed my master, and I soaped him all over, everywhere, in great detail.

We stepped out of the shower, and, wandering around the flat, we toweled each other down.

"You are a very brave girl." He was vigorously massaging my scalp, drying my hair.

"I am crazy as hell. I'm a total idiot."

"I wouldn't say that." He set to work, gently toweling my back and between my legs, "You're an explorer, that's what you are."

I dabbed with the towel at his chest, glowing muscles, tanned skin, black hair. "James, tell me: Am I still dangerous? You used to say I was dangerous."

"You are more dangerous than ever." He kissed me.

Finally, as Paris was just beginning to awaken, we slid into bed, and I immediately fell asleep.

And I woke up, feeling totally refreshed but vaguely aware that

I had had a nightmare. I tried to remember what it was about, but it was gone; it had faded into wispy nothingness, leaving not a rack behind. James was gone, his side of the bed empty. My heart did a flipflop of fear.

I got out of bed and tiptoed to the kitchen.

Sunlight streamed in. I made coffee and warmed up some croissants, and I turned and saw James standing there, framed in the kitchen door, holing a bag of croissants, smiling. "Well, my little pet, how are we this morning?"

I rushed into his arms and begged him to hold me, to hold me tight; I wouldn't let go, and I didn't want him to let go, and so, even as we drank our coffees and ate our croissants, he held me in an embrace of steel. "Never, never let me go," I whispered, kissing his cheek. This was dangerous. I was revealing my needs, my weakness, my dependency, my underlying hysteria.

"I will never let you go, little one, you are mine, and I am yours." James kissed me, patted me on the bum, and said, very cheerily, "What about going for a long Parisian walk – and then we can lunch in some friendly little bistro?"

And so we did – we went for a long walk – almost four hours, and we found a small bistro, and we ate on the terrace under the chestnut trees, letting time drift by, letting the delicate shifting shadows of the leaves lull us into a sense of security and happiness. Nothing bad can happen to you, when you are sitting on a sidewalk terrace in a Parisian café, can it?

That evening there was a note from Kate. The situation was beyond desperate: The jihadists had attacked three hospitals and massacred the patients and the medical staff – raping all the women and castrating and mutilating and finally executing all the men. The plague, too, was spreading, and it was mutating even faster than they had feared. "I think we may lose this battle," Kate wrote.

And there was a note from Claudia. "I see from some wonderful photographs you are an Owl now, reliving *The Story of O*. This is admirable – and quite spectacular. You do take the libertine philosophy to its farthest and most delightful extremes, my darling. Just make sure, though, that you don't leave yourself vulnerable. Underneath your sunny, optimistic, devil-may-care attitude, Gwendoline, you are actually – I can see this with my long experience and old woman's eyes – very sensitive and vulnerable. I hope you don't mind my saying this, but you are too precious to me. I love you. I care for you. I do not want to see you hurt."

I replied to both. I warned Kate to be careful – not that such a warning would have any effect. Kate would do what she felt she had to do.

I decided I'd try to help her – in any way I could, and even if I had to go behind her back. I checked with all my contacts in the World Health Organization. They asked me to help them update some of the statistics and to use my epidemiological model – which I had designed to help track and predict the spread of diseases, ideas, terrorist and criminal networks – to try to make some predictions, with probabilities attached about the future spread, the future vectors as they put it, of the disease, the possible venues and avenues, and carriers by which it could spread.

I asked James if he had contacts in the area. Yes, he certainly did. He knew the President of Senegal and the leaders of two of the neighboring countries. He said he would get ready to activate his contacts. "They may have to mount a rescue operation for the medical personnel. I suspect the French and the Senegalese are preparing for just that eventuality."

"Maybe we could hitch a ride," I said.

"Hmm, Gwen, that would be dangerous – and possibly illegal."

"So?" I shrugged.

"I see your point."

I spent the next few days hacking into intelligence sites – I also had legitimate access to some of their material because of my past services and because I had pals in the intelligence services and because they deemed me useful. I shared what I knew with James. He and I began to lay out a plan to get us to Africa quickly, if the need should arise.

Meantime, life continued. I published two more papers on epidemiology and terrorism and ideological contagion in the era of the Internet. I gave two talks in Paris, and one quick one in London, and James and I spent more and more time together.

The Owl-and-Jester Caper, as it was called, became famous – articles all over the place, in dozens of languages; it made Martine into even more of a star, and I was her sidekick, an icon of kink. In the public's mind, Martine and I were more and more closely linked – we were "weirdly polymorphous lovers" as one paper put it.

Late one afternoon – almost dusk in fact – I was climbing the stairs to the flat after giving a seminar in the morning and after spending the late afternoon working, on a café terrace, near Place de la Sorbonne. Outside, it was raining hard, one of those sudden super violent thunderstorms that can hit Paris in summer, waves of water slashing against the windowpanes. By pure chance, James came home behind me so that he got to the landing just as I was putting the key in the lock. We were both soaked. He had neglected to take an umbrella, and my umbrella had collapsed just as I came out of the subway.

"Look at you!" I said, "You're soaked!"

"Look at you! You're soaked!" He put down his briefcase and pulled me to him. We squelched together like two amorous sponges.

"Kiss me," he ordered. I kissed him. Our kiss was wet, cool with rain, savory with our tastes; water ran through our hair, down our faces, into our clothes.

I managed, breathless, to disengage. "Oh, you, James! You, you, you!" I opened the door, and we entered.

As soon as the door closed, we stripped. I grabbed two towels, and we began to towel each other down. "I took the liberty of ordering Indian," James said, "It will arrive any minute."

When the food arrived, we sat down, cross-legged, on the rug in front of the fire, with a tray of delicious food, steaming in front of us, and we ate. I had pulled on a long semitransparent and clingy silk T-shirt, and James was wearing tight boxer shorts. A cold bottle of Chablis completed the feast.

"Yummy!"

James told me that he thought he had the Czech deal "in the bag," as he put it, and he asked if I could do some more "due diligence," that is some high-tech hacking and snooping, on a particular private Swiss company that seemed to be involved in some back-up finance for one of the Czech company's deals. "Yes, Master, I would be pleased to snoop."

I told James about the seminar I'd given just before noon – it came with a delicious luncheon – at the Institute of Political Science, and about my afternoon doodling and writing at a café table on a terrace in the Place de la Sorbonne, and about the latest developments in the consultancies I'd developed with Interpol and with the FBI. The French had asked me to give a talk at the Military Academy too – next week – and I had agreed.

"Hmm," James grinned, "Owl is becoming famous."

"Darling, Owl, as Owl, is already too famous, or, rather, infamous. I crawled over to him, on all fours, and gave him a hot spicy peck on the cheek. My mouth was full, cheeks bulging. I was chewing on a delicious, scrumptious, steamy, spicy piece of chicken vindaloo. I crawled back and settled down in my own little space and washed the vindaloo down with a full glass of Chablis, so chill, such a perfect match for the hot, spicy, richly aromatic chicken.

We finished the meal. I carried the tray to the kitchen to put the leftovers, carefully wrapped, in the fridge, and to put the dishes and cutlery in the sink to soak.

The windowpane, close to the sink, was rattling, slashed with thick bubbly, bouncing streaks of rain. I glanced up. A bolt of lightning lit up rooftops; in the distance, on the hilltop of Montmartre, it lit up the ghostly white silhouette of the Church of Sacré Coeur, a strangely gloomy and oppressive building. The thunder rolled in, shaking the windowpanes.

James, carrying the last of the dishes and the empty bottle of wine, came up behind me, and, having disposed of the dishes and the bottle, he put his hands on my thighs and lifted the long slithery T-shirt up over my shoulders and, as I stretched my arms above my head, he slipped it off me, leaving me naked. He tossed it onto one of the kitchen chairs. I turned to him and realized he had taken off his boxer shorts and was deliciously naked and ready for action. I seized his erection in one hand, and, going up on tiptoes, I kissed him, and I said, "Oh, I almost forgot –"

He closed my mouth with the violence of his kiss, delicious sweet violence. And I kissed him back, and, kissing, we waltzed our way back to the living room and to the rug in front of the fire. He lowered me down on my back; he kissed me again, and, seizing my wrists, he stretched my arms above my head and pinned me down under him.

We were about to give battle.

"What did you almost forget, my darling?" He stared down at me. I bent my face and shoulders up and kissed him, not so easy with my wrists still pinned tightly down on the rug. He looked deliciously sexy. The reflections of the fireplace flames rippled over his burnished tanned body. Our lips just touched.

"What did I almost forget?" I gasped.

He kissed me, again, a hard, imperial kiss.

I sighed. "What did I almost forget?"

His erection was enormous; it grazed my belly; it was hot, hot, hot; I licked his lips; I wanted to free my hands and touch him, but he was in a deliciously cruel mood; he held me down, tighter and tighter, determined to delay our mutual satisfaction and to play out the agony of our wrestling game to the very last ounce of sensual and orgasmic suspense – cruel, cruel man!

"I think I've forgotten what I almost forgot," I whispered.

"Well, it will come to you, I am sure."

He released my wrists. We rolled onto our sides. I kissed him, and with one hand, I took possession of the glorious erection – the old Phallic God raising its delicious head. It was rock hard; I caressed it softly, timidly, reverentially, and then I kissed him on the lips.

"Now, I remember what I forgot." I tightened my hold on his cock. I was not going to let it escape. "A fashion magazine wants me to model for them – you know the new, expensive, slightly daring one, intellectual, avant-garde, it's a bit like *Vogue Italia*."

His hand was on my pubis, and his fingers, slick with saliva, were opening me, exploring, delicately, teasingly, my labia and my ever-eager clitoris.

"Have you got time to do it?" His eyes gazed into mine.

My eyes, I felt, were going bleary. I was wet; I was trembling; I was panting. "It'll take half a day," I breathed. I swallowed hard; my heart hammered away, making a racket in my ears. "Maybe a day," I managed to whisper, "Maybe more."

He stroked my hair, he traced the outer edge of my ear, and his fingers danced down the nape of my neck. I shivered in pleasure. He smiled. "Then, you have time. It will make you legitimate."

"Legitimate. Hmm ..." I freed myself, and I slid down his body; we were both lying on our sides, facing each other. I took the luscious erect cock into my mouth, and I licked and sucked it carefully; then I looked up at him. "You mean my kinkiness and nudity will have one more seal of approval, after that article in *The International New York Times* and the piece in *Le Monde* and the long essays in *Slate, el País*, and *Die Zeit*, and *The New Yorker*."

He tousled my hair. "Yes, and it probably means more fame and money – not that you need more fame or money."

I nodded. I took his cock in my mouth again, thoughtfully this time, pensively. It was warm and full, and bursting with energy. It filled my mouth to overflowing. I licked and sucked and sucked and licked, creating the greatest suction I could. Then I withdrew, drew back, and contemplated my work; I licked the very tip of it, and I looked up at him. "I'm going to check with Martine. Usually, she and I do these things together."

"That's true." He said, lying down on his back.

I crawled onto him, sat up astraddle his midriff, and lowered myself down, guiding him into me. As I bent down, he leaned up and kissed me. He was deep inside me now; the tension was unbearable.

Amused, he gazed into my eyes. "Yes, Martine is wise and savvy. It's a good idea to consult her. She knows the journalistic world, and you two should always be on the same page."

"Yes," I said, "I won't do it if Martine doesn't want me to."

"Oh, Goddess," he sighed.

I rode him, up and down, I tensed and loosened my thighs; his hands were now pressed tight and strong in the small of my back, forcing my body into an arc, then his hands were on my breasts, then on my hips, then on my breasts again – caressing, touching, squeezing, and twisting the nipples, this way, then that, with little surprise moves, pizzicato, toccata, crescendo, diminuendo ...

"Oh, oh, oh, oh God, oh, oh!" In a great shuddering shameless gush, I came, and came, and came. It went on, and on, and

on, and it was so delightful, so ecstatic, it was exquisitely painful. Like a wounded little animal, I found myself trembling and
whimpering from pleasure; and so it was that my Master kissed
me and comforted me; he stroked my hair and whispered sweet
nothings, a lullaby-like murmur; all the while, he remained deep
within me, large, monstrous even, but moving slowly now, gently
now, melting and merging into me, dissolving me, as if I were a
warm, dripping, tidal flow of melted butter.

Gently, he turned us both over, moving as one body, so he was
on top of me, and I was under him; he kissed me, a deep penetrating, very serious, very literal kiss, a kiss that meant what it
said. His body – with all its tense, straining, smooth muscles,
pressed down on me, on my whole body and I welcomed him as
he thrust still deeper into me; I gazed at him when as he lifted
himself away, ever so slightly, tightening the angle between our
bodies; and, then, I sighed as he slowly lowered himself, kissing
me lightly, a teasing kiss, his lips just touching mine, a feathery
licking breathing light playful caress.

He whispered against my lips. "Who is the photographer? And
what are you going to wear – or not wear?"

I swallowed. Still trembling, I managed to whisper, my breath
mingling with his, "They will tell me."

"Ah, I see." He was sliding slowly in and out of me, teasing, tantalizing, cruel. I cantilevered my hips, levering them upwards,
tightening my thighs, my vagina. His lips touched mine. I gazed
into his eyes. "You," I whispered, "You, you, you!"

"You," he echoed. He plunged deeper, far deeper this time –
how was this possible? It must be an illusion!

I must resist! I would submit no more! My fingers were
clenched in his hair, holding on desperately. His hands were
everywhere; his fingers were everywhere; he was inside me, outside me, everywhere touching me. I was his skin; he was my skin.

I was his body; he was my body. It was a mad struggle – a sweaty, slick, slippery, wet, desperate battle to the finish – I fought desperately to avoid coming, to fend off orgasm. I was going to force him to come – and with me: he had to come with me! Equality! All at once and at the same time! So we wrestled for dominance, for pure raw power, our bodies locked in battle, lit by the flickering flames of the fireplace, tumbling, squirming, wrestling, fighting on that deep soft tickly rug, with its tiny fingers of probing fabric – an added complication – caressing each millimeter of skin, setting each tingling nerve on fire. The battle raged. "Oh, oh, oh, you," I cried, "damn you!"

"Come on," he whispered, "come on, little filly, come on, surrender, little filly!"

"Surrender?" I flashed, "Never!"

"Ah, ah, ah!" he grinned, "Oh, yes, you will!"

While we tussled, thunder and lightning raged over Paris: the storm entered the room – like a soundtrack symphony – as blue and orange flashes lit up the French doors, so I could see, when my head was turned sideways, vivid instantaneous flashes, luminous momentary silhouettes, of stubby geranium pots, trellises, tall narrow chimneys, and the looming dome of the Pantheon.

I clung wildly to him, squeezed my thighs, and willed my vagina, a truly acrobatic Amazon warrior, to capture him, crush him and hold him prisoner, to force him, squeeze him, stroke him, bring him to the very brink of ecstasy – to make him pay homage, to make him surrender. It was a valiant slippery tug-of-war.

The battle swayed to-and-fro.

Sneaky and Machiavellian and muscular he was, and he resorted to every trick, every subtle, artful device, to give me so much pleasure that I would be driven to immediate surrender, so that I would dissolve, explode, give up my empire, collapse whimpering and howling into a mad animal frenzy, scratching, licking, thrashing, screaming, sucking, drooling, swearing, while he would, of course, retain full cool masculine patriarchal mastery, lofty Apollo lording it over my wallowing Dionysian Banshee, demonstrating total self-control and maintaining an imperious unyielding lofty erection.

The battle continued. And then, in one surprising, shuddering, unexpected moment, the climax of the conflict was suddenly upon us, in one huge whoosh of a rush, like a hurricane. We teetered, just for an instant, on the edge, together, resisting, fighting it, yes, suddenly allies, resisting together, fighting that damned tsunami, that damned earthquake, that damned volcano!

But it was all in vain: it was curtains! Kaput! K.O. Knocked out!

Thus, verily it came to pass: It happened like an explosion of fireworks, a showering of Roman candles, a burst of unbearable pleasure, of instantaneous nothingness: the world went black, stars blossomed in my eyes, and we whirled suspended there, in the instant. I clung, and I clung, and I clung.

Yes, so it was: we came; both of us, in the same instant, and it lasted, and lasted, a true earthquake with many, many aftershocks. A true study in complex many-layered seismology: Many, many shock waves echoed one another, traveling at diverse speeds, radiating out to the furthest limits of the universe – of my universe.

Whew!

We lay, exhausted, he on his back, me sprawled on his chest, my fingers playing in his hair, his fingers wandering down my back – tracing the spine, the two dimples below my waist, the curves of my hips – wandering onward to my bum; there he lingered; he seemed never to tire of exploring my buttocks, and, then back upwards he went, on the return journey, tracing with his fingers, the crack of my ass, up the base of my spine, into the small of my back, and then up my backbone, each touch setting alight muscles, tendons, vertebrae, each touch spreading a tingling thrill through me like an electrical storm drifting over the lazy torrid exhausted earthy summer landscape that was me. Even dazed and half-conscious as I was, this brought me, again and again, to the very razor's edge of orgasm; then, delicately, with a veteran savvy sadistic torturer's sure touch, my master lured me back, lulled me, pacified me, and held me there, in limbo, suspended, in unbearable stasis, putty in his hands, alight with desire, and deeply in love.

≈

To get permission to do the photoshoot and the magazine interview, I called Martine – who was in Venice shooting with Philip – their new erotic cloak-and-dagger adventure story. Marine thought it was a super idea. I should do the photoshoot and the interview; she gave me her permission to talk about our relationship – including the sex. And if the interviewer wanted to check anything with Martine, she would make herself available.

I checked with Claudia, and she agreed with James that it would make my eccentricities even more legitimate than they had already become; I would be more of a "cultural object," not just "an oddball fetishist bisexual masochist addicted to exhibitionism and bondage," so said grandmother Claudia. It would be art, she said, and would put me, very modestly of course, in the company of Madonna or Lady Gaga or Beyoncé or Kim Kardashian or Miley Cyrus – whom I really liked – or other heroes of the Pop art scene – who specialized in kinky, occasionally subversive iconography, and teasing semi-nudity – I would, Claudia said, be in the company of, say, Jeff Koons – the multi-millionaire pop artist – and his former muse the Italian porn star and politician,

Cicciolina. "Okay," I said, "It sounds cool! Soon I'll be in a museum!" "Don't laugh," said Claudia, "It could happen."

≈

The photoshoot involved Agnes Sinclair; she was the French journalist-editor who had commissioned the photoshoot and who was going to write the article which would wrap around the photographs, and there was the photographer, a blond German woman, and her assistant, and some makeup and costume and lighting people. It turned out to be a much bigger deal than I had expected. The shoot took place mostly in an old industrial park near the Seine, the sort of location fashion photographers love: a few gigantic rusting abandoned metal hangers with lots of old steel or iron beams and corrugated iron, lots of oil and grease, lots giant rusty old machinery, gears, and pistons, and cables, and levers, and cranes, heaps of rubble and scrap, lots of complex grainy tactile, visual texture – flaky rust, bubbly oil, gas-streaked stucco, grease-stained gears, pitted gravely surfaces, smeared and broken panes of cracked glass – giving contrast and paradox and edgy suggestiveness: virile, macho images you can feel under your fingertips.

Merely glancing at the machinery evokes the – macho – violence and exploitation of the early industrial era, muscle, and sweat, and conflict. Just looking at that stuff makes you think about the class struggle, and coal and oil and steam and gas and Karl Marx, and Friedrich Engels, and the Dark Satanic Mills.

It was a dark, cloudy, hot, moody day, very photogenic and atmospheric, suggestive of an old black-and-white 1940s film noir. The heat was building up under the low brooding utterly immobile stratus clouds. Sweat pearled from every inch of my body. I had to drink two extra espressos to keep from dozing off from heat and boredom. Several times I was about to fall flat on my face. Photographic sessions, like work on movie sets, consists of lots of waiting around while everything is prepared, then shifted, changed, prepared, changed again, and prepared again. I was photographed wearing shorts, old-fashioned skin-tight hot pants, with a skin-tight T-shirt, and I was photographed dressed as a scholarly looking schoolgirl wearing oversized glasses and sucking a lollipop Lolita-fashion which nostalgic retro concept – with its echoes of Vladimir Nabokov, did seem to me mildly transgressive with its possible pedophile allure and implications. But fantasy is not reality and people – if they are going to survive – must learn, I think, to make the distinction between fantasy and reality; and those who have such forbidden fantasies must learn to sublimate them and keep them within bounds, and never, never act them out in their primitive literal form; Mistress Nicole's work, as she had explained to me, was, in part, to provide a safety valve for such dangerous impulses, and a safe place where they could be worked out and acted out without endangering anyone. To know that such feelings exist, and to recognize them, are, I think, already a step forward – towards prevention and sublimation – displacement from harmful to harmless forms of expression. I was photographed as a femme fatale in a long sheer gown, which gown suggested quite clearly that I was wearing nothing underneath, but without precisely revealing anything in particular, which is very artful and requires a whole science when you think about it; and I was shot, too, as a stripper, in a G-string, doing a pole dance, and I was shot, prowling outside on a pile of rubble next to the Seine, naked and painted all over in black and white stripes, like a zebra, naked that is except for a minuscule black-and-white G-string; and, then, still in zebra mode, I was shot on the edge of the Seine, with a tugboat and barge in the background, and then I was photographed on the barge itself with two sailors watching me, and then in the tugboat cabin, at the wheel, with the skipper looking over my shoulder, instructing me how to wield the wheel, all with me still as a zebra-girl; and I was shot in a café on the Seine, in a miniskirt, and also, in the old catsuit and hood, prowling around, cat-like, on one of those tea room barges or houseboats that are anchored on the Seine just under Notre Dame. It took three whole days and involved lots of makeup and costume changes. At the end of it all, I was exhausted. I went home and whimpered; James put me to bed and fed me lemon tea and biscuits. I don't know how models do it!

≈

A week after the shoot, Agnes Sinclair wanted to interview me for the article, which would go with the pictures. When I arrived at our rendezvous, at the fashionable bohemian Left Bank rendezvous point, Café de Flore – just a few steps from Saint-Germain-des-Prés – I spotted Agnes sitting on one of the tables outside, on the sidewalk of rue Saint-Benoît. I hurried to her. I shook her hand and sat down. I was a bit breathless. "I'm sorry I'm late."

"You actually aren't late. We were to meet at 11:30."

"Oh, well, then I'm almost on time." I glanced at my watch, "Actually, I guess I am precisely on time. How strange! In any case, I'm delighted to see you again." Now that we were sitting down, face to face, I had time to examine Agnes. During the photoshoot, she hid her face behind oversized sunglasses, had worn an outsized leather jacket, and strode around like a Wehrmacht general giving orders.

She was a thin-faced, attractive-looking young French woman, probably about my age, with rimless glasses. Her curly auburn hair tumbled down around her face, a sprinkling of russet freckles highlighted her pale skin and marched neatly across the bridge of her nose; she had wide, eager, gray eyes and a nice mouth with just a suggestion of overbite – and an adorable tiny gap between her two front teeth. Also, she had very precisely delineated kissable schoolmarm lips. "I think I'll have tea," I said, "and perhaps the tuna sandwich with a salad."

"Wise choice," she said; then, "What does it feel like?"

"What does what feel like?"

"Being famous."

"More like infamous," I said, "It doesn't feel very different from before; I'm actually, aside from the exhibitionism and the public performances, a very private person."

"Really?"

"Yes, I spend most of my time at home working, and then sometimes I give a lecture or two, and I may be teaching at Cambridge next year – just seminars with one or two lectures." I had been instructed to play down my security work. It wasn't secret, exactly – which would have been impossible – but it wasn't for general public knowledge either. It was deemed best that I be considered flippant, frivolous, and superficial, a sort of crazy geek-freak.

The waiter arrived and took our orders. He knew me and always called me "Mademoiselle Clermont." He was back almost immediately with our tea.

Agnes opened her iPad and turned it towards me. There was a rather nice black-and-white photograph of me, naked, in the owl mask, being led on a leash by Martine. "This performance has received huge coverage and has turned you into a minor icon. But isn't this degrading?" she asked, with a cute sly little smile that was not entirely hostile.

"I don't think so."

"Why not?"

"Degradation is in the eye of the beholder. In these cases, where it is all make-believe, it's not so much a physical condition – being naked or not is meaningless – as a state of mind.

People do have the weirdest fantasies. This is a classic fantasy of enslavement. And we were just acting it out, putting on a show, making it public. I think it's good to let the light in, on these fantasies, these desires, subject them to irony and fun."

"Hmm," she looked skeptical.

"Look!" I took a sip of tea and glanced at some girls in school uniforms who were passing, laughing and shouting, down rue Saint-Benoît, heading away from Boulevard Saint Germain. "Games are just games. They are not reality. Fantasy is fantasy, not reality. Playing at being a slave is not the same thing as being a slave. It's the opposite, actually, because it implies trust and partnership – equality, in fact. You must absolutely trust and be equal to the one you have designated as your master. There's a fair bit of humor and parody and irony in almost all eroticism, I think."

Our sandwiches arrived and salads. The waiter set them down with a theatrical flourish, as if he were performing on stage. He knew me as a semi-regular who, in off-hours, sometimes sat here with an iPad or a laptop and a notebook. He and I sometimes exchanged remarks about the weather, or about politics and world events. "Mademoiselle Clermont," he said and gave me a gallant little wink before he headed off to look after a tourist couple who had just sat down.

"Humor in eroticism?" Agnes tapped her pencil, skeptically, against her lips. "Really?"

"Yes, really. I mean, dressing up as a naked owl! That's about as silly and ridiculous as you can get. And being led by a naked clown-jester whose bells were making a racket! Martine and I were being positively goofy! A Jester is a clown and a trickster, after all. And I am not really an owl. Nakedness and eroticism are a bit like paradise – a return to innocence, to the Garden of Eden. Humor helps open the gates of innocence."

"Really?" She paused, looked down at her iPad. "Do you believe in paradise – and original sin?" She passed the tip of her tongue along her upper lip. Her gray eyes narrowed, looking inquisitorial and skeptical; her eyes were fascinating, I thought, and I wondered what really went on inside that pretty head of hers.

"No, I don't believe in paradise, not in a literal sense. But I think everybody believes these things at some symbolic level – that we have lost paradise somehow, and that we deserved to lose it; that it's our fault we don't continually live in a heavenly state of bliss. It is a myth, of course, but a pretty universal myth. Unfortunately, it's a myth that is exploited by a great many ignorant and evil people – the instigators of terrorism, for instance. Maybe the womb was paradise, or an ideal childhood, or a mother's love. Maybe adult love – the unity and partnership – is a surrogate for paradise."

"Let's talk about all these naked images. You've been shown in various fetish outfits, or chained up, blindfolded, or hooded, or handcuffed, or in various revealing outfits, or offering yourself to your lovers – James and Martine. Are you a victim? Are you being exploited?"

"Well, some people might think so. It depends on what you mean by exploitation. If being photographed naked – or in chains or whatever – means I'm being exploited; then, I'm being exploited. But, no, I decide what I do and what I don't do. I want to explore different sides of myself and my partners, different fantasies, and relationships; at least for me, that's the way it is. Nakedness and exposure are part of that. Being seen to be enslaved is part of that – and of course, these images are often parts of art performances and fashion shoots."

"Isn't aesthetic pleasure just a euphemism for sexual pleasure, for a sexual come-on?"

"A sexual come-on! That sounds like fun." I put my hand on her arm. She didn't withdraw it. She licked her lips and stared at me.

Her skin was warm and smooth like silk. "Agnes, I don't think the two things – sex and aesthetics – are incompatible. But that is a complex subject!"

"It certainly is, a complex subject," she said. Her gray eyes were unblinking and gazing straight into mine; it was as if we were in a silent competition, who would be first to blink or look away. I slowly withdrew my hand from her arm. She smiled and blinked.

"Yes," I said, "it is complicated. Is a gothic cathedral sexual in some way? Is it a sublimation of desire? If a mystic nun dedicates herself to Christ or if a priest declares that he is 'wedded to Christ,' I think, almost certainly there is an element of eros involved, of yearning, of desire, of hankering after unity with another; but this doesn't, I think, diminish the sublime nature of the nun's or priest's vocation or feelings. It's liberating to confront the sexuality that might be present in all aspects of life – there's nothing shameful about desire. There'd be no life without desire, not human life, at least."

"Liberating – that's an interesting word."

"We need to be liberated from fear. I think that much of society has become so fearful of sexual abuse, so fearful of anything that might be 'inappropriate,' so politically correct and sissified, it has become hysterical about nudity, about physical contact, about glancing at somebody, about complimenting somebody, about touching somebody, even lightly, about desiring anybody. Even playing at sexual enslavement can be liberating."

"Really? Can you give me an example?"

"Yep. Once I was totally blocked, unable to finish an article I had to write. The deadline loomed. So, James suggested he would chain me to my computer and not release me until I had finished the damned thing. I agreed. It was very effective. I was excited, of course, a buzz with an undertow of fantasy. It was totally silly and it turned finishing the paper into a game."

"So, Gwendoline, you're saying being perverse can make you more empathetic and a better person?"

"I'd never thought of that. Hmm. Maybe, Agnes, maybe. Of course, some very wicked people are perverse – serial killers, for example. So, I wouldn't say kink is the answer to the world's problems. But some forms of kink involve playing roles, acting, and that can help develop empathy; you put yourself in another skin, as it were. Kink is like acting – it's a form of imaginative projection, getting out of your own skin and into another skin, either a physical skin – like a restraint or a catsuit – or a psychological skin, like in erotic fantasy."

The light was falling in a very delicate way on Agnes's bare shoulders; and the chairs and tables of the café, lined up on the sidewalk of rue Saint-Benoît, caught in sunlight and shadow, looked like they were in a painting by one of the impressionists, dappled with light; and sprinkles of golden light were caught in Agnes' hair, a sparkling diadem. Two men, outlined by the light, were discussing something on the sidewalk. A woman, a few tables away, was feeding her child ice cream, a spoon of vanilla at a time, lit up by the sun. The warm breeze moved the leaves and speckled the glimmering light. I sighed. Beauty is everywhere.

Agnes had unbuttoned the top buttons of her blouse. I noticed she was not wearing a bra. She consulted her notes. "What about the theme of *transgression* – it used to be fashionable, particularly in France – to say that perversity was a sort of revolution, a way of overthrowing social mores and the rules of the social order."

"That's what the fans of the Marquis de Sade used to claim. Civilization is a charade, and underneath the charade are primal bestial perverse homicidal desires. So, practicing sexual cruelty and perversion are ways of stripping off the illusions and revealing, dramatizing, the brutal raw truth about the human condition. That's the idea, I think. But, as for me, I don't think kink is revolutionary; it can be a protest, of course, but it can be the reverse, a way of letting off steam and not changing anything at all; kink is childish in a way; but what's wrong with being a child, a perverse child?"

"Polymorphous perverse?"

"Sometimes."

She consulted her notes and licked her lips, and then looked up at me, and caught me appreciating her. She managed a thin smile. "So, Gwendoline, let's talk about original sin and the need for redemption. Is that what you are looking for in your 'games' – redemption?"

I kept my appreciative gaze focused on her. I liked the way the changing light emphasized her freckles; I loved the delicacy of her collarbone. I cleared my throat. "Maybe, in a way. Love and desire are like forgiveness. You desire me – so my life has meaning. It's redeemed. I desire you – so my life has meaning. It's redeemed. It works both ways, desiring and loving, or being desired and being loved, gazing at someone, and being gazed at."

"So, Gwendoline, you're a sort of mystic – of sex and perversion."

I raised an eyebrow. "I wouldn't say that, not quite ..."

She tapped her pencil next to her teacup. "I mean you have a philosophy about it – and you find deep emotions, or so you say, and feelings, when, say, you are being an owl, and led by a chain held by your girlfriend."

"Yes, it can be pretty exciting, even exalting."

"And what about your relationship with Martine Aubin? As we all know, she led you by the chain in the Owl Performance, and she was naked, painted as a jester or joker. It is said that you are her lover."

"I am her lover. Or she's mine. She'll tell you so herself."

≈

A few weeks after the interview, the magazine produced the glossy photo essay which led with a photograph of Agnes and me at the Café Flore, looking very respectable, with my friend the waiter hovering in the background.

Then, on the following pages, there were photographs of me, as a zebra, a schoolgirl, a Goth vampire type, and so on. And on the pages opposite the photographs, the whole interview word for word, embedded in the descriptions Agnes wrote of us sitting there, chatting, on the side terrace, at Café Flore. I sent her an email saying how pleased I was.

"Wasn't so painful, was it?" said James. "Her description of you – 'an elegant, delicate and false ingénue, who speaks like Plato and Aristotle' is perfectly accurate. Soon you will be teaching philosophy and the libertine way of life at Oxford and Stanford."

"Hmm," I was serving us a big plate of penne all'arrabbiata. "I'd better lie low and clam up for a while."

"Afraid fame will go to your head?" He uncorked the bottle of Beaujolais.

"It might. I'm getting carried away with own importance. My head is swelling by the moment. You'll grow to hate me."

"Never!"

"We'll see about that."

"Darling, you should never doubt me." He kissed me, and, of course, it was a luscious slow-motion eloquently reassuring kiss.

After eating, we settled down on the divan, side by side, and I checked my email. There was a long breathless note from Kate:

Dearest darling, I am jealous. You are in Paris and pretending to be a naked owl – Yes, I've seen the photos and videos too – and drinking champagne and Chablis and having fabulous sex with your lovers – limited for the moment to James and Martine, if I understand correctly – while I am here in a horribly hot place with utter chaos all around us and no lover whatsoever.

We went inland from Senegal – where the plague has not yet reached. And we are now in a country where the plague is spreading out of control from village to village and with the jihadists – a band of Islamist religious fanatics that have come south from the Sahel – raiding villages and preaching at gunpoint that all medicine is a western plot, that quarantine is also a western plot to force everyone in each village to die, that any blood we take as samples are designed to capture the souls of the poor locals and cast some sort of voodoo spell on them, and that any injections we give are just guaranteed to sterilize the poor locals so they will no longer be able to have children and thus this will leave we Europeans, and African Christian and animist tribes from the south, free to continue to govern the world which we Europeans have done, it seems, since the Mongols destroyed Baghdad – I think in 1258 but correct me if I'm wrong – and since Ferdinand and Isabella tossed the Moors out of Granada in 1492 or since the Ottomans failed to capture Vienna in 1529 and again in 1683. These chaps seem to celebrate their failures, and they seem to have forgotten their success – not really an exercise in positive thinking, I think. No wonder they hate everybody – and, I suspect, above all, themselves.

The jihadists – or murderous raping terrorists because that is what they are – use cellphones and video cameras and the Internet and Twitter and YouTube and SUVs and Automatic weapons – but they mix up all this modern western technology with the most incredible hodgepodge of eschatological and messianic religion and medieval superstition and nonsense – that some evil imams in some oil-financed Saudi-financed madrassas and mosques have undoubtedly taught them – and of course with a total contempt for the societies and science that produced all the goodies they use as weapons and delight in as consumers – they take selfies while cutting people's heads off or kidnapping and raping women and reducing girls to slavery. All of which is quite ironic when you think that Muslim societies in their days of splendor were leaders in science and incredibly curious about the world and, compared to Europe, incredibly open and tolerant.

Excuse my language, but they drive me mad: They are a dreadful and unsavory lot of sadists and false visionaries some of whom, apparently, speak good French and even eloquent American or British English with lots of cute and clever colloquialisms, words you and I use – damn them! Then, with all this superficial linguistic sophistication, they go ahead and torture and massacre everybody, Muslims, Christians, Animists, Secularists, Jews, anybody they can lay their hands on. One despairs of human nature. Of course, they are, in part reacting to a lot of Western abuse and greed and arrogance and evil and misguided Western policies that have led to hundreds of thousands and even, with the slave trade and colonialism, to millions of deaths. I won't argue with that.

But their response is criminal, exists in a sort of time-warp, and, in the end, I am sure, will be utterly counter-productive. Fanaticism wins in the short run, but often, in the end, the good people unite and finally save the day, or the fanatics turn on each other and destroy their own revolution. Or so I hope at least.

These clever fools are so eager for the apocalypse they might just bring it about. And in Europe, as we all know, they make converts left right and center – with idealistic naïve girls – ready to murder and torture for their very own Jihadist lad – girls from the privileged West flocking to join these 'warriors of the desert.'

Well enough of that!

It gets me all worked up, the useless, cruel, wasteful idiocy of it all.

Now, dear Gwendoline, we have been plotting the patterns of the spread of the disease using your algorithms and models, but I could certainly use more of your mathematical savvy and brilliance in deciphering some of the data. And, of course, as you know better than anyone, the difficulty is that the plain facts, the basic data are often lacking; these are small villages in jungle and forest, and are some out on the edges of the savannah and desert; they often don't report in – partially because they are terrified and intimidated, partly because there aren't enough trained personnel to do the front line reporting.

Some of us, dreadful outsiders, me and two Chinese doctors, one man, one woman, both very pleasant, and one Japanese specialist, and one savvy and desert-wise Algerian who knows by heart a lot of poetry in half a dozen languages, and a couple of French doctors, six Senegalese doctors, and eleven nurses, all of whom I pal around with, we are all going to head for what is called the 'front line' to see what can be done to improve things on the ground.

Picture this, darling: Right now I am sitting in my underwear – panties and a chemise – soaked to the point of utter transparency – in a sort of temporary setup, really a tent, and I am absolutely glowing with sweat, rivulets running everywhere, and my face is as red as a beet! I hope you appreciate the picture.

Totally erotic, is it not?

Writing to you, I feel absolutely sexy! I can certainly picture you! Making frantic love with James and cavorting with Martine – just the very idea makes me dreadfully jealous! Do you think your luscious Martine would be in the mood for a cool female threesome if I ever get out of this neglected front-line hellhole?

Well, I mustn't complain; really, I am one of the privileged ones. The local doctors and nurses and the scientists here are marvelous – generous, super-intelligent, on top of all the latest science and techniques, and as brave as lions. They are facing odds few of us can even imagine. And, unfortunately, their pay levels and living conditions are often abysmal. The local government has been scandalously neglectful in developing sufficient trained 'cadres' to look after its own people, and international aid has been absolutely insufficient The local people, too – the civilians – are models of courage and determination; they are resolved to fight back and survive – whatever the odds. It is a huge privilege to work with them and have some of them as friends.

Well, I shouldn't drag you into my struggles here – full of delights and horrors as you can imagine!

Let us speak of more interesting things! As for our shared perversities, and your wonderful shameless performances! You wicked girl! I'm not sure whether I would have preferred being Owl being led, or Jester leading Owl by a leash.

In any case, you have, my darling, far surpassed my own feeble attempts at libertinage. The Innocent Pupil has soared beyond the Fetish French Schoolmarm I once was.

I adored the photographs of you as Catwoman and as Owl. I shall need a refresher course in naughtiness when I get back. I loved the skin-tight catsuit episode, with you as a faceless spider woman, slinking through the Roman night, and terrifying the natives. I have thought about it often and used it in my dreams and daydreams.

And the episode where you and Martine, both dressed in nakedness as it were, chatted up the Professor and his wife at that restaurant in Rome has had me in stitches, and also quite excited several times, late at night, or under the shower when, really, I had nothing else inspiring to think of.

Did you ever look up that interesting antique dealer you mentioned who has her shop on via Coronari in Rome? I should so like to see her collection. I have a weakness for Second Empire and Victorian excess.

And the little transvestite and transgender club – where everyone confessed their sins to you – it sounded lovely! James, by the way, I think, is truly in love with you – who is not? He seems to me to be a keeper, hold on to him!

But, my darling, tread softly and lightly, for that, in my experience, is the way to hold on to a man. Make sure he doesn't think you are desperate to hold on to him. To keep what one wants, one must not show too clearly that one wants it. Flirtation and seduction – flatter without terrifying the poor chap.

Men want to be desired but not owned.

All men I think are afraid of being prisoners, something to do with their mothers and diapers, cribs and toilet training, I'm sure.

But, then, you darling, know better than anyone that freedom is a necessity and that mothers can cause problems!

Always blame the woman, I say! Whoopee!

Must sign off now, darling! I need some sleep before we head deeper into the 'heart of darkness' (not your Heart of Darkness, darling, but a quite different 'heart of darkness' – a heart of darkness of fanaticism, terrorism, and disease that is ravaging this beautiful country and its wonderful people).

Love you as always,

Kate.

I read the letter to James. He listened; he smiled, and he laughed at all the right places. But he frowned. He was worried. "That is, at this precise moment, one of the worst places in the world to be, if not the absolute worst. And Kate is headed straight into it."

As we undressed, I told him how I'd tracked the advance of the

Jihadists and of the plague; they both seemed to be headed towards the same place. And that was where Kate and her friends were headed now.

James was just about to step into the shower. "Join me?" he said.

"Yes, Master." I slipped out of my panties, folded them neatly, and followed him.

James sponged me down, all the while looking very serious. "As you know, I have friends down there – in Senegal, at least. And I have friends in the local government. And I'll see what I can find out too from my friends at the World Health Organization. As you suggested, Princess, we may have to launch a rescue operation."

The news in the next few days got worse and worse.

And a week later, a news flash said that the so-called jihadist rebels had surrounded a large refugee camp. The aid workers and scientists were isolated. Briefly, the local hospital had been over-run. Many patients and doctors and medical personnel had been killed. The jihadist terrorist group had the unpleasant habit of raping and sexually enslaving the women they captured – when they didn't just rape and kill them – and beheading the men.

"Kate cannot be dead," I said.

"We will certainly act as if she is not," James said.

James and I conferred over a large foldout map.

"Kate is there," I said, pointing at the map.

"Well, I do know the President of the country," James said, "And, as I said, I know the President of Senegal, and several of the French and Senegalese officers, who are stationed, with troops, just across the border. There's a French base, here, outside Senegal, just outside this town."

"Yes," I said. "But there is a diplomatic stalemate. Nobody is going to try to defend them or rescue the villagers and the medical personnel. The French have been ordered not to move."

"I know." James rubbed his chin. "We might have to bypass legal and diplomatic channels."

"You mean, just do it ourselves?"

"Yes."

I poured over maps; I called my contacts – in the US, in France, and Italy and Switzerland, and Africa. I put together as full a picture as I could. "There may be one route which is close by – and it may provide a way into and out of what is left of the camp," I told James. "And here are several of those French military units you mentioned in that very neighborhood, but, as I said, they have not been given permission to go across the border."

James frowned, glanced up from the map, and gave me his beautiful decisive, strong-jawed, I-am-in-control look. "Okay, let's go."

"You are crazy," I said. But I was thrilled.

"You're a terrorism expert, Princess, or have you forgotten?"

I just stared at him.

"We'll be welcome there, I'm sure." He smiled.

The next few days were a blur, a kaleidoscope of impressions, a tumbling series of flashes, and then periods of darkness when, briefly, we slept.

We flew to Dakar. It was my first time in Africa. Everything was noisy and colorful and much brighter than I was used to. The people were gracious and friendly. We stayed one night in La Demeure Hotel in Dakar. Then we went inland, using a private plane, and then, seemingly by magic, we were in a French military base, across several borders, in an inland country, where James knew some of the French officers; in fact, he seemed to be an old buddy of the commander of the base, and the commander showed us the situation on the map, and we talked to some of the scouts they had sent out, both French and local, and to the drone operators, who were doing reconnaissance; and we were allowed to look at drone footage – and to watch some of the drone feeds in real time. The road I had located from satellite photographs had been cut two weeks ago by jihadist groups, but it was now – just possibly – open, briefly open, since the jihadists had switched their attentions to a village farther to the east.

Apparently, the jihadists were busy killing all the men and raping and kidnapping all the women and the girls. The boys, mostly, they raped first, and then they killed. I had read everything I could find on the terrorist group, on the terrain, on their financial links, on their tactics. I pulled out my laptop and put it next to the map. I talked to the French intelligence guy, André De Valle. He and I had been introduced at a conference in London and exchanged a few jokes. He was not the sort of guy to fight over turf or to refuse the insights of a woman. He and I sat down with his Senegalese intelligence officer colleague a very knowledgeable and ironic guy who spoke five languages – Mansour Niang – and using pen and paper, and a couple of laptops the three of us did as thorough an analysis as we could of the choices the terrorist group faced: which way would they move? What routes would they follow? What would they do next? What was the timeline on all of this? "These people are not necessarily rational, not in the sense we have of rationality at least," said Mansour, "they like to kill for killing's sake, they believe the end of time and of the world is near, the Day of Judgement is about to come, the Mahdi is about to return, and many of them are on drugs."

The French commander, General Jean Marseille, traced with his finger, on the map, some of the hypotheses resulting from our analysis. "Yes, that is a reasonable guess," he said, "but they may swing further south, since the drought has made this river – here on the map – easy to cross where it wasn't just two weeks ago. Water's down to about fifty centimeters at one point, I imagine. So, if they are going to attack the village and camp, I would guess they would begin from here."

"Ah, yes," I said.

"Gwen and Mansour and I agree on that," said André.

"So, that would mean, if we are going in to save the people in the camp, we probably have only a few days to do it," Mansour glanced at the general, "And we won't be able to save everybody."

The garrison was eager to get into action. Many of the men – both the French and the locals – had friends across the border. In particular, many of the African troops had relatives in the threatened area since the tribal boundaries did not coincide with the political boundaries. Finally, permission came through from Paris and from the local capital to send a limited force across the old border and enter the contested area, a "limited humanitarian incursion to save lives and protect the innocent and then to get out of there – fast."

"This is a contradictory mission, of course," General Marseille stared at the message. "If we go in and leave right away, we'll be leaving lots of people behind – we won't be able to protect the innocent, thousands and thousands of them."

"Yes, but –" André glanced at me.

"Some are better than none," said Mansour.

"That's true," said Marseille, "We'll do it; we must do it, but I don't like it."

≈

So there we were, in a column of armored cars and SUVs and armored motorcycles, with a mix of African and French troops, heading along the single narrow open route leading to the village and the first aid station; it was a rutted, dusty road through bush and then out into what was almost desert and then again into forest, and then into a valley, with heavier vegetation and dangerously higher ground on both sides of us. Two helicopters flew above, watching for danger from the higher plateaus on both sides of the road. Small drones were deployed closer in to detect enemy forces, or, if possible, mines and explosives.

We safely got to what was left the refugee camp, which was really a long straggly village; it had been attacked once, and about half of the buildings had been burned. Their generators had all been destroyed; they had no electricity, and they had been cut off now for more than two weeks – the news only leaked out to the outside world after a long delay. Many of the villagers and refugees had been killed in the first jihadist incursion. The road that I thought was open had been closed until two days ago. The villagers and staff didn't have vehicles to escape. But the jihadists had not taken the village completely, and then there had been a respite. For ten days now, the jihadists had been busy with other massacres; but they were probably about to close in again, this time for the final killing. We had slipped in, in the brief moment, between two blockades, and we were probably just days – before the final assault.

In their first incursion, the jihadists had wreaked chaos and murder. Many of the houses were smoking carbonized shells and the ancient monuments – a library of sacred Islamic texts and a temple – had been dynamited and bulldozed and smashed beyond recognition. The people who greeted us were half-starved shadows of themselves, often dressed only in rags. They moved sleepily, awkwardly, stumbling like zombies. Bodies were lying everywhere. Flies buzzed over the cadavers. One blond Scandinavian-looking woman was lying on her back, her face, half obliterated, was a mass of iridescent buzzing flies. She was naked, her breasts had been hacked off, and her vagina cut out. Her body was bloated and pulsing with maggots. Next to her, lay a young African woman; her handsome face strangely peaceful and untouched; her uterus and her intestines had been ripped out, buzzing coils of black-and-red meat in the dust. We began to gather the survivors. I looked everywhere for Kate. Nobody seemed to know anything.

One of the African doctors wiped his forehead, stared at me through his half-smashed glasses. He was so tired he could hardly speak, but he said I might look in at a small hut down a side street at the far end of the village. "An epidemiologist? Was she a member of the specialist group that came from Senegal? A white woman with red hair?"

"Yes," I said.

"One of the women mentioned someone like that. I think your friend may be there. She might even be alive."

James was busy conferring with the military: an attack was expected at any minute. So, with a local nurse, Antonia Faye, who was carrying an AK-47 slung over her shoulder, I walked down the dusty path to the hut, which was about 100 meters away. "These people are beasts," Antonia said in French, "I'm a nurse. My job is to save lives, to help people. But if I have to kill some of them, I will. It makes me crazy when I see the things they do. And they talk of God!" She spat into the dust. We passed two burnt-out cars and an overturned truck; a half-carbonized body hung out of the truck's cabin. When we got close to the hut, I saw that the building was a mud hut. There were two female bodies – African nurses – lying in the dust in front of the hut. They were very young. We stopped. I swallowed fighting back a temptation to be sick. "I knew them," said Antonia. "One is my cousin. A very funny girl, she was always playing pranks. You should have seen her smile. I can't tell you the rage this fills me with, absolute rage." She took the AK off her shoulder, cradled it, and looked around, narrowing her eyes as if searching for somebody or something to shoot. The flies made shifting colorful clouds over the two girls' faces, an interminable deafening buzzing sound. The stench was unbearable.

Antonia shrugged. "I must go tend to others. I will send somebody if I can." We shook hands, in a strangely formal way. "Good luck," I said, "*Bonne chance.*"

"You too," she said in French. "I will send somebody, if I can find somebody, to bury the bodies."

I faced the hut, my heart beating. I had no idea what I would find inside. There was no door, just a hole-in-the-wall, with strings of colored beads hanging down, rattling slightly as the air moved, just a dark hole, opening into the interior. Outside the light blazed, but inside, I sensed, was smoky, pungent darkness. Cautiously, I pulled the beads apart and peered inside. As my eyes adjusted, I saw a pile of books on a little metal shelf in one corner, and a computer and an iPad on a fold-up table. Two metal chairs of the fold-up kind one finds in auditoriums. A map pinned up on a sheet of plywood that was leaning against a wall. Narrow small barred windows and flies everywhere. I brushed the curtain of beads aside and entered.

Kate was lying behind a thin white muslin curtain in one corner on a camp bed. I knelt beside her. She was in soiled panties and a filthy sweat-soaked T-shirt. She looked emaciated – cheekbones showing more than usual – and was almost certainly dehydrated. She was unconscious; it was clear she had had diarrhea and had not been washed. A young black girl was sitting on the dirt floor next to her, half-naked and unconscious, just leaning against the wall, with one arm resting limply on the edge of Kate's camp bed. A plastic glass lay on its side on the dirt floor. It looked like the girl had been trying to give Kate something to drink and had collapsed. The girl opened her eyes, looked terrified for a minute, then with a big smile, said, very softly, "*Bonjour, Je suis Sara, Sara Diallo*," and closed her eyes.

I had three bottles of water with me and some chocolate-and-peanut-butter power bars. I made Sara drink, and I gave her a bite of chocolate. She perked up a bit. Her French was cosmopolitan French – the kind you would hear in a café near the Sorbonne. "I'm okay, just exhausted, I think. Try to do something for Kate. She had a bad fever," Sara said. She took the power bar from me and began, slowly, carefully, to eat.

I tried to make Kate drink some water. Her eyes were still closed, but she accepted the water. Her hand even went up to help hold the bottle.

Sara and I eased Kate out of the soiled panties and the filthy T-shirt. We rolled her sideways and managed to put a towel under her. I began to sponge Kate down while Sara looked for clothes in Kate's wardrobe – a bit of metal scaffolding – a fresh T-shirt, panties, shorts.

Kate was slathered in thick gooey sweat, and her temperature seemed high, though, without a thermometer, it was difficult to tell, particularly since the air was so hot and so humid. I laid my hand on her forehead. Her eyes fluttered open. "Gwen, darling, what are you doing here? I must be hallucinating."

"No, I'm real. James is here too. We came with soldiers. We came to get you and your friends out of here."

In spite of her protests, I insisted Sara rest. I would look after her. Sara was still weak. I spent the day and night feeding and nursing her and Kate and washing them both with water I was able to carry from our supplies – the Jihadists had poisoned the wells by throwing in cadavers. While I was in the midst of this, the jihadists attacked the far end of the village; at one point we could hear the battle raging up and down the streets not far from us.

Sara was certainly less ill than Kate. As she said, it was just exhaustion. On the second day, she felt well enough to go back to work and headed out to help the other wounded – the new wounded. Also, the troops were busy burying and burning bodies.

I stayed with Kate. She was semi-delirious. "How sweet of you to come! I need a bath. Giorgio needs a bath too. Giorgio was my friend. I think he's dead, you know, but I'm sure he needs a bath. You know, thirst is a horrible thing. Dehydration can lead to madness, you know. I do believe I am absolutely bonkers right now, Gwen. Do you think I am bonkers, Gwen, darling? Am I entirely out of my skull? How is Sara? Is she better? I worship her. She is so bright and brave and beautiful. I heard you two talking. Or did I imagine it? You look so beautiful, Gwen. And James is such a perverse dear, handsome and perverse and rich and brave, which is just what you deserve, darling. I was very jealous when I read about you and Martine and when you told me about being an Owl and about dancing and wrestling in paint with the famous beautiful Jo. Oh, dear, I'm delirious, aren't I, darling."

At one point, bullets were whizzing around in front of our hut; a few huts away from ours, a jihadist SUV Toyota was blown up by what must have been a bazooka. The jihadists retreated, but two of the local soldiers who had come in with us had been captured. A little later, we learned that one had been killed outright – just shot in the back of the head and left behind. The other was tortured, then killed. When the soldiers found his body, his head had been hacked off, and his hands. And his legs. His eyes had been poked out. And his penis and testicles had been cut off, probably while he was still alive. The soldiers were furious and vowed revenge; the villagers were terrified that the jihadists would return.

The helicopters flew in circles, to see if they could locate the jihadists. This was dangerous because the jihadists almost certainly had surface-to-air missiles.

"They are retreating there – to this point," one of the officers said. "I think these ones have to be hunted down. I'm going to do it. To hell with orders."

"What about the wounded?"

"We'll leave them here, in the village, for the time being."

So, I stayed with Kate. Things got pretty hairy. Fighting raged. Wounded were coming in. Our route out of the village had been cut off, so they said. We were stuck. Days passed, and then a week passed. Politicians in Paris and New York and Dakar and in the local capitals were arguing whether an effort should be made to get us out – or not. "Politicians talk and talk," said James, when he dropped in to see us, "And we hold on and on!" He smiled. His smile was extra bright, almost feverish, and his face rimed with dirt.

Kate was weak, but she was soon strong enough to help, and she and Sara – who was Kate's special friend and who was from a neighboring village where everyone had been killed – and I began to help a doctor in one of the nearby medical tents. It was chaos. We could hear gunfire rippling at the edge of the camp and village. One column of jihadists again headed straight for the camp, storming towards us, full speed. They were driving a hodgepodge column of SUV Toyotas, and pickups and they were armed with automatics and bazookas and light portable mortars and grenades. It was not clear that the soldiers could keep them back. We were truly in a war zone.

"I never thought we'd die together – not like this," I put my hand on Kate's shoulder.

Kate glanced at me. "No, me neither."

"We're not going to die," said Sara. She gave us her bright shy smile. "I won't allow it."

I was holding up a drip for a soldier who had lost both legs; his black skin was turning gray. Sara and the doctor were trying to cauterize the stumps. The soldier was naked except for soiled underpants. He kept looking at me, desperate bloodshot eyes. How he remained conscious, I don't know. There were flecks of saliva at the corner of his mouth. He said something. "How old are you, Mademoiselle?" he asked in French.

"Twenty-three" I said, "almost twenty-four."

"My sister was nineteen. They raped her and cut off her breasts and killed her," he said. His eyes closed. I put my hand on his forehead. The doctor, who was Senegalese, was swearing. "Hold this," he said, to Sara. It was a tourniquet. Sara had her hands full. "Kate, you do it," she said, nodding to Kate. "Yes, you do it," said the doctor. Kate, her face dark with sweat and dust, took the tourniquet from the doctor and turned it as the doctor ordered and held it tight. I could see the strain on her face. She smiled and winked at me. I smiled back. "That's good," said the doctor, "that's good." Sara had blood up to her elbows, and splashes of it on her face. The heat in the tent would have been unbearable if we'd had time to think about it. Sweat ran down my face, and down my back. The explosions and firing were again getting closer.

James came into the tent. He was filthy, his jacket torn, and blood down one side of his face. "It's not my blood," he said. "We still seem to be cut off," he added, looking around. "In which case ..."

"In which case, we can die together, James."

He kissed me, squeezed my shoulder, and went out of the tent.

He and I had discussed this possibility on the flight from Paris to Dakar. If we fell into the hands of the rebels, James would shoot me and then himself. Kate had joined our suicide pact. I had a Beretta in my backpack, just in case. But the plan was that James would shoot both of us, and that would be the end of it: eternal darkness, certainly better than falling into the hands of these fanatics. Sara and the doctor had made a similar pact.

Religion can inspire people to build cathedrals, raise children, help their neighbors, create great civilizations, be kind to strangers, and help the poor, the weak, the distressed, but it can also inspire people to commit the greatest crimes imaginable, mingling their own sadism with belief in some idiotic divine mission. It is so stupid it would be comical if it were not so arrogant, presumptuous, and horrible and cruel.

The soldier opened his eyes again. "Nobody should see such things," he said.

I wiped his forehead. "Yes," I said, "You're right. Nobody should see such things." I paused. "You are very brave," I said.

"What choice is there, but to be brave," he said. "You are not a nurse," he added, "Why are you here?"

"I came to save a friend." I nodded toward Kate, who was straining to keep him from bleeding to death. The doctor and Sara were cauterizing the wounds. Sara glanced at me; she even managed to smile. There was a sizzling smell of burning flesh. The soldier said, "Your friend, and the man who came, he is also your friend."

"Yes, he is my friend."

"You are lucky," he said, his eyes closing, "you have good friends."

"Yes, I am lucky," I said. I wiped away more sweat, and the sweat was getting in his eyes, so I cleaned the sweat from his eyes, as best I could, while holding the drip.

"You are a good person, I think," he said, his eyes briefly opening.

"I am not entirely good. I am perhaps a bit naughty."

He bared his bright, blood-rimmed teeth in a smile. He was just a boy, I realized. His broad, creased lips were gray, his teeth shone. Lines of bright blood framed each tooth. "A girl like you must be naughty. How can you learn if you are not sometimes naughty?"

"You are a philosopher."

"I was a runner. The fastest boy in the village."

404

"Ah," I said.

"Now, if I live, I shall study art. I shall show the world what I have seen – I shall use my hands and my eyes. I shall go to Paris; I shall go to New York and Beijing. I shall tell them. How can people not know these things?"

He stopped. His eyes for a moment were brighter, then closed, then opened and stared, then he coughed up a gob of blood, a bright crimson splash. His body convulsed, jerked upward,

"Oh, God!" Sara covered her mouth.

Kate said, "I think ..."

"He's having a heart attack." The doctor glanced up, "I have to continue here; I can't stop."

"Pound his chest?" Sara's eyes were very wide

"No, too much internal damage." The doctor concentrated. "Just hope. Just pray, if you believe."

"Hold my hand," the boy coughed.

I took hold of his hand. He squeezed my hand. He coughed up more blood, splashing on my arm and chest.

"Stay," I said, "don't go. Don't go. You have to tell the story ... Tell the story ..."

His eyes were brighter; he squeezed my hand. His eyes went still, still as glass, his lips trembled, they spurted blood, and his grip relaxed, and he was gone. I glanced at the doctor. He shrugged. "It's over."

Sara sighed. She took the tourniquet from Kate and said, "I'm needed in another tent." She dropped the tourniquet in the rubbish bin and nodded at us and left.

Kate bit her lip and looked at me. She was flushed and covered in dust and sweat. "It makes me want to kill people," she said, "It makes me want to kill people."

"Yes," said the doctor. He wiped his forehead, took off his glasses, wiped them, put them back on. He looked away, to some invisible distance. "Yes, it does make you want to kill people."

"Yes." I stood back. I was still holding the boy's hand. I let go.

His hand fell away from my hand. No one else seemed to think to do it, so I closed the his eyes. All the patients in the tent were

dead, except one young man sitting on a small wooden chair in the corner whose eyes were covered in a bloody bandage that wrapped around his head. Mortars were going *pom, pom, pom.* The sound seemed closer and closer.

"We are finished here," the doctor tried to wipe his hands, but he realized he was just spreading the blood around. "Can you guide that young man?" The doctor glanced at Kate and me.

We nodded. "Yes, we can."

"He speaks good French. Help him if you can. Perhaps with the trucks and the helicopters, we can get out of here." The doctor had turned his back to us; he was packing a few things.

I went over to the young man. "Can you come with us? I think we are leaving."

He was sleeping – or unconscious. I put my hand on his shoulder and shook him gently.

He stirred and seemed to wake up.

"We are leaving," I said in French, "Will you come with us?"

"Where are you leaving to?"

"We don't know, not yet, anyway," said Kate. She knelt beside him and took his arm, and he then took her arm so she could guide him, and she stood up, and he followed. "What about Omar?" he asked.

"Omar?"

"My friend – Omar Sarr – the boy who was wounded in the legs, the fastest runner."

"He ... he died ..." I said. "He died just now."

His mouth went rigid, and his body stiffened as if hit by an electric jolt, then he said, "Ah, perhaps it is better that he is dead. He will have gone to God or to paradise, perhaps. He will not live to see more of this."

We were out of the tent now, the doctor, Kate and I, with the blind young man. He was holding onto Kate's arm. There were dead all over the place. "It's extraordinary the plague has not yet caught us," said Kate. "It is so close. I felt I was breathing it sometimes."

"Yes, it is close," said the young man, "The people in the village next to mine. It is said they all died of it, every single one."

The tents were flapping in the wind. Dust swirled everywhere. At the far end of the village, French and local soldiers were loading a column of trucks; the whole village – all the survivors – were scrambling aboard. The armored vehicles were lined up, engines running. I heard firing.

James came through the swirl of dust. He had an assault rifle; I think an AK, slung over his shoulder, and a pistol in his hand. "We've called in air support. I'm not sure they'll get here in time. And if the jihadists get into the village, well, then air support is problematic."

"Can we retreat out of the village?" I put my hand on his arm.

"We'll try. It's difficult." Narrowing his eyes against the dust, James looked around. "We don't know exactly where the jihadists are. The drones are out of action. And one of the helicopters is damaged."

Two open-topped French Army armored cars came racing up the street, spurting up a huge cloud of dust. They skidded to a halt. "Pile in, come on, quick! *Allez, vite, vite.*"

"Well, here's our ride," James grinned. There were sharp creases of tension around his mouth and eyes, reamed with dust and oil.

Sara and the doctor and Kate and I, leading the blind young man, followed James through the swirling dust to the vehicles.

James helped hoist us aboard, with the blind young man.

"This will be tight," said one of the French paratroopers. "Keep your heads down as much as you can." Next to him, an African officer was manning a heavy machine gun.

The car spurted ahead, skidded to a stop. James reached down and pulled up two children, a boy, and a girl. They huddled down next to me. I put my arm around them. They were probably eight or nine years old, half-naked, covered in dust and splashes of blood.

Again the cars raced ahead, in front of them, two motorbikes with machine guns mounted on sidecars, and in front of that the column of trucks and armored vehicles; suddenly shells were falling around us making great plums of yellow dust, and the cars zigzagged to the right, to the left, the machine guns were roaring, the motors were screaming, gears were grinding and changing. The air was dense with dust, gun powder, gasoline, diesel fuel. The noise was deafening. Showers of dirt and sand fell around us, and on us. The two children, hot, dusty little bodies, squeezed against me. The blind boy asked Kate what was happening. I could just hear him. She had put her arm around his shoulders so he knew she was there. We were crowded into a tiny space.

"We're making a run for it," Kate shouted, "in three armored cars, a convoy of trucks, and some motorcycles. We have French paratroops with us and local army units, or what is left of them, and the jihadists are shooting at us, mortars I think, and maybe bazookas."

"Oh," he said, "I pray to God that we make it, but if we do not, we are in His hands."

"I reckon you are right about that," said Kate, who was most definitely a non-believer.

"Yes," I whispered, holding the children tighter.

It was a roaring swirling dusty chaos. A helicopter, whirring, and rumbling appeared above the column and then swerved off to the side. It tilted downwards and fired off rockets; great whooshes of fire went up on both sides of the road in front of us. A spiraling trail of smoke went up towards the helicopter.

James was standing beside the French paratrooper; both of them were firing into the woods on either side of the road. The soldier on the machine gun kept swinging it around, firing in great bursts. The helicopter veered away, and the spiraling trail of smoke swirled around after it, the helicopter went higher, and then the spiraling trail of smoke exploded like a Roman candle, and the helicopter was still there. It came zooming down again, at a steep angle, as if in revenge, letting loose another roar of rockets. Both sides of the road lit up with huge explosions, and there was a wave of dust in my eyes – and a whiz-whiz whistling sound and I felt a stinging sensation just above my forehead – for a moment I couldn't see anything, just feel the two children, hot, smooth, sweaty, dusty little bodies, pressing next to me, little hands clinging to my back and shoulder; I blinked, but still couldn't see anything, just darkness, and flashes of light; I felt my face, it was wet; I licked the wetness, and I thought, "Oh, blood, probably my blood, maybe that's why I can't see. What if I'm blind?" For a moment, there was a cold chill in my chest, emptiness in my belly. I thought, "Oh, what the fuck!" I held the two children even closer, hugging them. I wouldn't say anything; everybody's too busy. I don't want to be a distraction. I heard Kate's voice, shouting through the chaos, "I think you're bleeding, darling, are you okay?"

"It's nothing," I shouted back, "I'm okay." I blinked, and I saw light, a huge explosion, yellow, with streamers shooting up against and above the trees; then everything was dark again, velvety darkness, deeper and deeper, like spiraling downward, then it was dark with red blotches, and yellow streamers, and then

I saw the African soldier manning the machine gun – he was standing next to James – the soldier turned glanced at me, a question in his eyes. I blinked against the blood that was getting into my eyes. "I'm fine," I shouted. I grinned. The soldier gave me a thumbs-up, and he turned back, and started firing – thump, thump, thump ... James glanced at me, concern written on his face. He was filthy with oil and dust and sweat. He dropped down and crawled over to me.

"Gwen, you are you okay?" His face was close.

"I'm fine. It was just a shock. I'm fine." Half my face, I learned later, was covered in blood. But my vision had returned to 20/20. I saw James clearly, the pores of his skin, the stubble, the tan, the streaks of grease and dirt and gunpowder, the glow of the sweat. It was all ultra-real, high definition. Adrenaline, I guess. His hand went to my face. "There's a wound, just above the hairline, and lots of blood. I think you were hit by a piece of shrapnel."

"I'm fine." I leaned forward and kissed him. "I love you – Oh, you foolish wonderful perverse brave man."

"And I love you, Gwen." Then he was gone, up beside the soldier, who was pointing at something. He and James began to fire.

We were out in the open now, scrub instead of woods, and a jet aircraft came screaming over, quite low, and there was a huge mushroom of fire behind us. Then we were racing along a road that was tarmac in places and bumpy.

The helicopter was moving alongside, slightly in front of us. The road was mined – so it was dangerous, but I guess we were weighing a certain death and torture against a chance at life. Any chance was a good chance. It was a bit quieter now.

Then one of the trucks, just ahead of us, went up in a whoosh of smoke and careened off the road, and exploded, flipping into the air and turning over. Our armored car and the other trucks swerved off the path and went around the burning carcass. The caravan kept going. An African officer was suddenly beside us, standing up on a motorbike, shouting, "*Allez, allez, vite, vite!*"

No one said anything, not for a long time. James glanced at me and shook his head; the commander of the convoy had made the right choice. Nobody, well, almost certainly nobody, would have survived the explosion, and if we had stopped, we would have been, as the old expression goes, sitting ducks.

We were now moving through flat savannah. Dust rose around the column. I asked the children their names. They spoke a little French, and they told me; he was Amadou, and she was Awa.

Five hours later, we were at an airbase. We went in through the barriers, the barbed wire, the cement, the zigzag barriers, and the guard posts, and then we stopped. Soldiers – French and local – and doctors and nurses were waiting for us.

Kate helped the blind young man down from the armored car. I had Amadou and Awa. What was I to do with them? "Keep them close for the moment," one of the soldiers said. Sara suddenly appeared. She hugged me and said she had some people she had to look for. I hugged her back. She disappeared around a corner – and was gone.

Kate and I and the blind young man and the two kids stuck together. We were given a tent with other people. A doctor saw to my head wound. It was superficial but I had had a shock, probably concussion. That would explain the temporary blindness. "So, you must be careful. If you feel dizzy or sleepy, tell us immediately."

There was a pavilion with showers. I took the two children to the showers. "We shall clean you up," I said. They looked at everything with wide eyes. They didn't ask questions. I think they were in shock.

"I can translate for them," the blind young man said. So, we asked a few questions.

"I knew their parents," the blind young man said. "They are all dead. They have no one now."

I undressed the two children and put them under the shower and still wearing my jeans and my T-shirt – and a plastic shower cap to keep my wound dry – I scrubbed and soaped them; then I toweled them down, and I asked one of the soldiers standing guard next to us if there were clean clothes for the children. He said he would see.

I was soaked now and still filthy dirty.

"I think we'd better shower, too, darling. We stink, and we look like hell," said Kate.

"Yes, okay. You are absolutely right."

The soldier came back with clean clothes for Amadou and Awa. I helped them dress, and Kate and I left the children with James and the blind young man. And we showered. It was a steamy little shower, at one end of the pavilion, canvas partitions, and a big empty room full of equipment.

"This would be very exciting, darling, if we were back in Paris or Boston," said Kate.

"Well, perhaps we will get back there," I said. "You are recovering your equilibrium, I see."

"Thanks to you and Sara and James. I would have died if you had not come. Sara might have died, too – she was totally exhausted. She sacrificed herself to save me. By the way, now that you have experienced the front line, what do you think?"

"Well, I can see how difficult it is to get the right statistics and information in these conditions," I said, in English, in my most owlish academic manner, with a hint of an Oxbridge accent. "It does make precise analysis awfully difficult, my dear, most frustrating indeed."

"Oh, Gwen, you are an absolute idiot – I do love you so," she said, and she kissed me, the same beautiful Kate as always, freckles, red hair, lively eyes – I was transported back in time, almost three years ago.

Somewhere someone had found fresh jeans and T-shirts, so Kate and I were soon back to a semblance of our usual selves.

James hadn't bothered to shower; he was still filthy, busy working with the soldiers to sort out the refugees and find supplies for them. We found some villagers – distant relatives – who could look after the blind young man and the children. Amadou and Awa did not want to let go of me. Kate borrowed a phone and took a picture of us. I wrote down their names. The blind young man said he would look after them – he would find people who could look after them.

Sara and the doctor and Antonia came to say goodbye. I knew little about them, but I felt that we were all brothers and sisters, and if we were tossed up again in some future tragedy, we would help each other to the very end. There were lots of bright smiles, and tears, and underneath it, was a sense of emotional and physical exhaustion and shock and lots of mourning that would probably go on for a long, long time. Underneath everything, we were all numb. It was as simple as that.

A helicopter landed. It took us to a border post, just over the Senegal border. Then James and Kate and I were taken to Dakar in a military convoy. We spent one night in a luxury hotel by the seafront, and James was finally able to shower.

The three of us had dinner that night in a very fine French restaurant.

The transition from massacre and danger to comfort and what passes for civilization – and I quite like traditional civilization – actually I worship it – was abrupt and dizzying.

I wasn't suffering any dizziness or headaches. I was feeling chipper except my heart ached for the people who had died, my friend the philosopher boy, Omar, the runner, the fastest boy in the village, and his friend, Seydou, who had been blinded, and for the two children, Amadou and Awa, whom I wanted, in part of my heart, to adopt and take to Rome and Paris, and look after them and coddle them and spoil them and see them grow up in a peaceful, happy land – where they would be able to realize whatever dreams they had if they had any dreams, and it occurred to me that probably they had never had time for dreams, except little personal dreams, or maybe they had, maybe their dreams were just as vast as the whole wide world, and I had just not had time to learn about them.

"So finally, we meet," said James, to Kate.

"Yes, we did meet out there in the village, but it was hardly a relaxing way in which to meet," Kate smiled. "I am rather jealous of you and Gwen, you know, and I must warn you: I am very protective of Gwen."

"So am I, Kate," James put his hand on her hand.

"You are truly a beautiful specimen, James," Kate said, "I think you are very lucky to have found each other."

I could see that Kate, though she was smiling and happy, was still weak. She'd been operating on nervous energy these last days.

And shortly afterwards, we were on a flight to Paris. Kate fell into a deep sleep and didn't wake until we were landing at Charles de Gaulle airport, and then she was dizzy and disoriented.

"I think I'm out of it, rather," she murmured. James and I got her through customs, and we drove into Paris, and we decided we'd better take Kate straight to a clinic, just in case. And so, we did. James knew the owner of the clinic. And the owner was very much aware of Kate's father's reputation as one of Britain's leading and most influential surgeons: so, Kate was assured of the best of care.

"Get me out of here, quick, Gwen," Kate whispered. "I rather feel it's like being locked up in a loony bin. You know those old horror flicks where the young rookie reporter gets locked in a crazy house, and can never get out, and of course, then she becomes crazier than even the craziest of the inmates."

"Like being buried alive," I said.

"Precisely, darling, that's it precisely."

"You will be out sooner than you can blink," I said, "In any case, your father and mother are on their way from London – they will liberate you, and you will return to us."

James and I headed back to the flat – my flat as he insisted on calling it – and we showered and we went out to the corner bistro for steak-and-frites and a bottle of wine, and we staggered back to the flat, and we fell into bed and slept in each other's arms like two drowned sailors. One of my arms lay across his chest, and I lay face down, feeling I was so tired I would never move again.

≈

I woke up. Sunlight was streaming in from the balcony. I stretched, voluptuous feeling like a cat might feel, the white silk nightgown was strewn across the foot of the bed, I turned to kiss James and saw he was not there – for a moment my heart plummeted.

Oh, God! He has left me! How insecure I am! What a fool I am! Then the doorbell rang. My heart trembled again. Who could it be? I swiveled around and sat on the edge of the bed, then stood up and reached for the nightgown.

And then he appeared, in jeans and an open shirt, from the balcony. "Ah, you are awake," he said.

I rubbed my eyes. "Yes," I said, shaking my head as if getting rid of a bad dream.

The doorbell rang again.

"Coming!" James shouted towards the door.

I grabbed James and tilting my face up to his I kissed him. He ran his hands down my sides and smiled, "Shall I get it, or you?"

"I'll do it," I said, and I wrapped the nightgown around me, tied the belt, and opened the door. It was the concierge with a big smile and with breakfast from the café down the street – croissants and jam and café au lait. "Welcome back, Mademoiselle," he said.

I almost swooned with pleasure.

CHAPTER 16 – TWILIGHT

A week later, I was back in Rome to speak at – of all places – the Pontifical Institute for Culture – the Catholic Church is in some ways very catholic. My sexual antics had not lost me any of my mathematical and scientific Jesuit friends – indeed, I think they thought I was a fascinating phenomenon that should be studied, and that I needed extra special tender loving spiritual care.

I was alone in the big flat just off the Tiber and close to Piazza Farnese, and I managed to do lots of work, either crouched over my computer in the flat, or out at a café table in Campo de' Fiori or on Piazza Navona.

I wandered the streets, just thinking. Walking is a great way to generate new thoughts, just let the mind go loose, let suggestions come, let down one's inner guard, let the casual sights seen trigger new associations, quirky oblique indirect thoughts.

And I did some more consulting – a bit of work for Interpol and a quick half-hour telephone discussion with the Italian Interior Ministry.

The talk at the Pontifical Institute – it was about child-trafficking and mathematical analysis of smuggling routes – went very well. I had lunch with some of my acute and interesting Jesuit friends – brilliant, passionate, idealistic men.

James was in South Africa for a week, and Martine was in New York. I had a long WhatsApp conversation with Claudia, who said she would like to come to Rome; she wanted to meet my man, this infamous and brilliant James Hewitt Spenser. No, she wouldn't stay with us; she'd stay at a small hotel nearby, which she knew very well, and which was just off the Ponte Sisto, named after Pope Sixtus IV, the little pedestrian bridge built in the 1470s and that crossed the Tiber, and joined old historic Imperial Rome, on the right bank, with the tangled little neighborhoods on the left bank, in Trastevere, or "Across the Tiber," as that part of the city is known. She would be right next door, she said, but she didn't want to interfere with our work and our routine. I was sure she and James would adore each other.

≈

James got back from South Africa early one morning, and I thought he would want to go directly to bed, but it was a glorious, warm day, and he said, "If you have time, let's go to the beach!"

"Yes, Master, your princess does have time. Besides, summer is ending; we must take advantage of these last golden days."

"Precisely!"

So, we drove in a warm breeze and under a cloudless sky to the beach south of Ostia, the nudist beach, and we parked the Porsche on the road of old broken asphalt, in the smell of sage, and tar, and dust.

I took off my clothes, and walked naked, with James in his bathing suit and carrying our supplies in a backpack slung over his shoulder, through the scrub and the dunes. When we came to the top of the last dune, there was the beach, stretching away, north and south, and there was the little hot dog and ice cream stand, its colorful little flags bravely fluttering. And there, magnificent and spreading out towards infinity, was the sea, bright silver and gold under the sun.

We walked down to the very edge of the water, and then we spread our towels, and we lay down and not far away were several couples, some of them naked and some of them dressed, and some little kids, not wearing any clothes, playing in the gentle surf or building little sandcastles; people were swimming too, farther out, leaping and splashing like dolphins; a group of adolescents, some with bathing suits some naked were kicking a ball back and forth.

"Your soccer team," said James.

"Yes, it looks like them."

James lay on his stomach, and I sat astride him, and massaged his back with suntan oil, and then he did the same for me, both sides, and I put on a very large straw hat, and we sat there, and lay there, talking and then just watching the immensity of the sea – and it does seem like infinity, an infinity which you can touch, an infinity which is intimate and close, an infinity into which you can plunge, but still, as it stretches away and joins with the sky and the sun, it is truly infinity.

I went to the stand to buy hotdogs, and the young girl remembered me from before, "*Ciaò, Signorina, non ci siamo visti da molto tempo* – Hi, Miss, I haven't seen you for a long time."

I put lots of mustard on the hotdogs and carried them back safely so we could eat them with that delicious chilled white wine that tastes vaguely of the earth, and the sulfurous depths of the south – earth, sea, and sky.

"And the sun god too," James said, "which is fire."

"The four elements," I said. "Earth, water, air, and fire."

"Exactly, the four elements: Aristotle would be proud of you, my darling," James said.

≈

Late that night, James and I made love. We were on the terrace lying on a mattress that I had placed under the blue striped awning. The night above us was warm and clear, all the stars and constellations on display.

James caressed me, and touched me, and it seemed as if his touch was everywhere. I rode him, and then I was under him. I sighed in ecstasy. I closed my eyes; he was in me, and I wondered – as I always did – why it seemed so unique each time, an explosion of pleasure and trembling as if the world was being born, and the whole universe.

I grasped his shoulders, and I kissed him, and, then, suddenly, without warning, I came in a galloping orgasm, a rippling outward tsunami of pleasure that seemed to tear me apart. I cried out, "Oh, oh, oh," and he was still in me, still thrusting, still possessing me and, then, gently, slowly, he turned us over so that I was on top of him and his cock was still in me, more and more powerful; his fingers, curving down over my bum, entered, me, and Oh, sodomy I thought, Oh, oh, oh, and his tongue was in my mouth, Oh, oh, oh, and I was filled, from every direction and every way; I was abolished into thunderous stormy non-existence; the pleasure so great now it was painful, Oh, oh, oh!

It went on and on. I was in darkness, blinded; his tongue and my tongue, our lips locked in struggle; his fingers opening me up, deep inside me; his cock deeper and deeper and touching the most sensitive points. I heard and felt myself scream, cry out, and shudder, and at the same time, in the utter darkness, I was suddenly transported out of my body, I was suddenly soaring above us; I saw myself, splayed open, a shipwrecked waif sprawled on my lover's body; I felt him open me again, and I felt his chest against my aching breasts; I soared up, higher and higher, until I was above the terrace, looking down on the striped blue-and-white awning, fluttering in the breeze, I was looking down on us, down on the mattress and the deckchairs and the flower pots with the geraniums and stone benches and the terrace balustrade; then, still sweeping upwards, I looked up at the stars, at Polaris, at the constellations, at Cassiopeia, at Arcturus, at Sagittarius, and Scorpius, I glimpsed wheeling galaxies. I soared above the top of our building, I looked down on the slanted roof tiles, the little chimneys sticking up, and the moon bright on the tiles, and then on the street below us, and the Ponte Sisto, and the Tiber, running between its tall embankment walls, and the Lungotevere, with traffic, and Piazza Trilussa with its memorial to the poet Trilussa, and the little crooked cobblestoned streets of Trastevere, and the narrow, winding, lamplit alleyways leading from our building to Piazza Farnese and to Campo de' Fiori and I looked down on people strolling in the Campo, and people sitting in the little cafés at the side of the Campo, and on the statue of Giordano Bruno, and children playing around the fountains, splashing in the water, even at this late hour, and I saw people out on a terrace having dinner by candle light on Piazza Farnese, and the little street winding its way to the little piazza where Alfredo's terrace was crowded with the glamorous evening crowd, the awnings and umbrellas fluttering lazily, and then I was above the whole city, sprawled around the winding Tiber, seeing the seaside, at the seaside beach town Fregene and Ostia with the ruins of the ancient port of Rome, Ostia Antica, and I saw the nudist beach where we had spent the day, where, in the past, I had walked naked along the coast with James by my side, where I had played soccer, naked, with those teenagers, where I had eaten ice cream under the sun and where James and I had made love in the water, and inland I could see the Apennine mountains, the great jagged backbone of folded up shattered rock that stretches down the whole Italian peninsula, and to the south and north I could see the dead volcanoes, with their lakes in their ancient caldera, the collapsed mouths of the volcanoes, Lake Bolsena, Lake Bracciano, the Alban hills, lake Albano, and I could see the Vatican too, and Saint Peter's and Saint Peter's square, and colorful specks under the street lamps which were tourists in bright clothes or tourist buses with Chinese and Japanese writing, and fluttering flags.

And suddenly I was in myself again, squirming, biting licking, touching, caressing, kissing, slippery with cum and sweat, and James was still in me, deeper, deeper, the tip of his sword – oh, those wonderful martial images – the tip of his sword touching, just now, some magic place, and I bent upwards, and his body arched towards mine, and I came again, and again, and again, and finally I subsided, and lay on James, and his breath was smooth while mine was ragged and I said, "You must come, James, my Master, you are cruel, you make me feel all alone, delicious and delirious, but alone."

He smiled and kissed me and turned me over so I was lying under him and he withdrew from me, almost entirely, but not quite, and then slowly, he entered me again, sword-like, and I felt myself, slippery, smooth as butter, wet sloppy clay to be molded by him, my artificer, my demiurge! He plunged deep into me, like an angry god, like a sword of fire, as if he were going to cleave me in two; then his lips were on my lips, soft, then hard, tentative, then hungry, and he whispered, "oh Gwen, oh darling, oh Goddess." He was kissing me so violently; his tongue was so deep, I felt he was going to devour me, break me, and consume me in a pyre of flesh and virtual flame. Deep inside me, a solar nova burst, a brilliant light, as if the universe were being born; it radiated everywhere. I teetered on the edge of Oh God knows what, and then I felt a shudder enter his body, I felt his legs, entwined around mine, tremble and tense, and I felt the wave come, like a tidal wave, a tsunami, and it hit me, with a shock that almost lifted my body out of itself.

I trembled, and I felt myself come, and he came, and together we cried out, choked, intermingled, our flesh and our bodies as one, in a spasm, and trembling, and aching arching delicious tender violent explosive rush of joy and pain and oblivion and awakening.

And so it echoed and continued, and it was like an earthquake that showed no signs of tapering off and then finally, yes, it did, and yes, yes, we began to come back to earth and I was aware suddenly of the sweat on my body, of James' lips on my lips, of my belly, sticky with sweat and cum, pressed against his belly, and of his arms holding my arms down and stretched above my head, as if he were crucifying me, and I was aware of the stubble of his cheeks, and the strong muscles of his legs, and of his hair, tangled and long and gleaming with sweat, and I was aware of the awning, flapping gently and slowly in the breeze, and I was aware too of the breeze and of my own hair slick with sweat and my pubis pressed against him, and of his cock, still in me, but less strong now, tenderly there, a presence, like a memory, like an echo, and he remained on me, the delicious crushing weight of him, and he began to stroke my sides and finally, slowly, he withdrew from me and he rolled off me and he pulled me with him so now I was splayed out on him, and my eyes were looking into his. He kissed me and smiled and said, "You are a dangerous girl, Gwen."

"Hmm," I murmured. I kissed him, and my finger outlined his eyebrows, his nose, his forehead, his hairline, and I tugged at one of his earlobes, and I kissed the end of his nose, and then I moved my lips along his lips, barely touching, barely breathing, and then I kissed him. "I am yours, Master," I breathed.

I lay there, my fingers moving in his hair. I listened to his breathing, and to the rhythm and music of all the sounds around us. My eyes were half-open, my wet eyelashes reducing everything to a muted nighttime haze and whir of sensation.

I stretched. "Shall I make us a snack, Master?" I asked, touching his lips with my lips.

"Yes, darling," he said, "I'd love a snack."

CHAPTER 17 – BETRAYAL

It was autumn. James and I were back in the flat in Paris. I had been to Cambridge and had come back the night before. James was about to leave for Istanbul.

He was packing and he was already dressed in his traveling clothes, a classic business suit. I was in a black turtleneck and black jeans and black running shoes and I had been in the room I used as an office, banging away on the computer keyboard, churning out a rather long report on the statistical analysis of terrorist networks: "Logistics, Information, and Murder" was the inspiring provisional title.

It was a clear, crisp day outside, with a deep blue Parisian sky, and the autumn leaves tumbling down on Boulevard Saint Germain and already some of the smells of autumn and winter in the air – roasting chestnuts in little stalls, and the perfume of savory, sugary crêpes, and somehow the smell of coffee sharper than in summer. "Do you mind if I leave some of my things in the flat?" He glanced at his suitcase, and at some of the clothes piled on the bed.

"Mi casa es tu casa," I said.

"Ah, thank you, darling."

"After all, James, this really is your flat, not mine."

"No, it's yours."

I felt like a gauche teenager, circling around a boyfriend who was about to go away, or like a nervous mother who was about see her son leave on a perilous journey. I wanted to touch him, to smooth down his lapel, to stroke his tie, to caress his hair, to touch his lips. I was standing by the bed. "James, do you mind if I ask you something?"

"Not at all, ask away!" He looked up from his suitcase and smiled.

"Don't be upset."

"Whatever you ask, Gwen, I won't be upset."

"James, since we met ..."

"Yes?"

"Since we met have you been with other women, I mean, have you had sex with other women or another woman? I'm not going to be jealous. I promise. I'm not going to make a scene. You can be truthful."

"No, there have been no other women since I first laid eyes on you." He came to me and put his arms around me and pulled me to him and kissed me.

"I want you to be free, James," I said, and I kissed him, and I looked into his eyes, and it was true, with my mind I wanted him to be free, I wanted us to be free, and of course I was free with Martine. But I had no desire whatsoever for any other man but James. In my heart, I didn't want him to be free: selfishly, and violating my own principles, I wanted him to be mine, my man, my love, my soul ...

"I don't want to be free, Gwen. I want to belong to you."

"And me to you," I said. I was still gazing into his eyes, looking up at him, and I fear my gaze was just a little bit worshipful, just a little bit frightened.

His eyes crinkled in that delightfully understanding smile he had. He stroked my hair. "When I'm with you, Gwen, sometimes I feel I'm the child, and you're the adult: that you are the elder, and I am the junior; you accept everything and anything. You play all the games, the games we share, and yet you never lose your sense of yourself, you never lose your dignity. And we can talk about everything and anything. You are very generous to me, and with your friends, particularly with Martine and Kate. And that makes me adore you – even if I dare say it, worship you."

I kissed him. "You are too kind, James, too generous. You have opened doors for me, and I have gone places with you and because of you, I would never have gone, places in my mind, in my soul, and of course, places in my body, and in the world."

He kissed me again and held me. And then he finished packing. I helped him. "Are you going to be sad?" he glanced at me as he shut the suitcase.

"No, I'll try not to be. I have lots of work. And tonight, Martine may come over; we'll cook and maybe watch a movie – Philip is in Los Angeles for the week."

"And so, you and Martine may get into some mischief." He kissed me, and held me, his hands firm on my backside.

"We might." I almost blushed.

"You know, Gwen, it may seem strange to people, to other people, but you know I approve; you and Martine are perfect for each other; it's good that you have each other. It's good for you not to be my prisoner."

"You are a sublime idiot, my love," I said. I kissed him. He was standing at the door. He usually traveled tourist class on ordinary airlines, and he usually took the bus and train to the airport – and to get there, he walked to the subway station. For a man who was so rich, his personal habits were almost austere.

After one last kiss, I stood in the doorway. He went to the elevator, pushed the button, it came. I watched him. I ran to him and gave him one more last kiss and helped him stow the suitcase in the elevator.

Then he was in the elevator, separated from me by the little folding wooden and glass door, and the elevator creaked its way down to the ground floor. I stood there for a moment, and then I walked back into the flat and went to the French doors, then out onto the balcony. I saw James about to turn a corner, down on the sidewalk, right beside the patisserie shop. He turned, saw me, and waved, and blew a kiss. And then he was gone.

He'd promised he'd phone me as soon as he got to his hotel in Istanbul.

He never did.

WORKS BY
GILBERT REID

SHORT STORIES
So This is Love: Lollipop and Other Stories
Lava and Other stories

GRAZIA SERIES
Son of Two Fathers (with Jacqueline Park)

ADVENTURES OF V
Vampire vs Vatican
Vampire Clone
Pandemic Book 1: Party Balloons
Pandemic Book 2: The Gateway
Extinction Book 1: Girl with the Golden Eyes
Extinction Book 2: Revolt of the Angels
Extinction Book 3: Elysium

GWENDOLINE SERIES
By Gwendoline
The Shaming of Gwendoline C
Gwendoline Goes to School
Gwendoline Goes Underground

To receive a free book or novella
And to get notes on writing and other topics:

Sign up at

https://gilbertreid.com

Please write a short review!
Just two or three lines.
Post it to Goodreads or Amazon
or any other book group you may belong to.

And send it to Gwendoline:
gwendolineclermont305@gmail.com
or to: **gilbert@gilbertreid.com**

GILBERT REID is the author of two short story collections: *So This is Love: Lollipop and Other Stories* (2004, 2019) and *Lava and Other Stories* (2019). He also co-authored, with Jacqueline Park, the historical novel *Son of Two Fathers* (2019). He has written extensively for television and radio. Most notably he researched, wrote, and narrated two five-hour radio series: *Gilbert Reid's Italy* and *Gilbert Reid's France* for CBC's flagship radio program IDEAS. His many television series include *Paths of the Gods, For King and Empire, For King and Country,* and *Sir Peter Ustinov in Burma: Road to Mandalay*. After thirty years in Europe working as an economist, university lecturer, diplomat, script doctor, journalist, and adventure travel guide, Gilbert now lives in Toronto.

https://gilbertreid.com/

www.ingramcontent.com/pod-product-compliance
Lightning Source LLC
Chambersburg PA
CBHW020250030726
47499CB00001B/135